THE TRUTH
ABOUT
UNSPEAKABLE
THINGS

Cover Design by Michelle Fairbanks

Interior Formatting by Amanda Reid for Melissa Williams Design

Paperback ISBN 978-1-948604-96-3
eBook ISBN 978-1-948604-97-0

Library of Congress Control Number: 2021900810

www.emilyamyers.com

THE TRUTH ABOUT UNSPEAKABLE THINGS

EMILY A. MYERS

This book is dedicated to the dreamers, young and old.
Daring to dream is half the battle.

*The truth about unspeakable things
cannot sit quietly in our minds.*

---

*Our pain must be acknowledged.
The unspeakable must be spoken.*

CHAPTER 1

The salty New Orleans air fills my lungs as I stumble over uneven concrete walkways. Each time I return home, I believe something will be different—a new storefront, a new neighbor, a new aroma that doesn't include the special ingredient of sewer. Instead, I find everything as I left it. History, culture, modern conveniences, and unshakable emotion meshed together in a not-so-perfect, colorful medley. On most days, I wouldn't trade this city for the world, but tonight is different. Tonight is the night I have to see him. Tonight is the night I end my engagement.

My suitcase drags behind me as if it shares in my reluctance to return home. The sound of the French Quarter trumpet players lets me know I'm close and the conversation I've been avoiding for a month is all too near. I will hurt him. No, I will hurt his pride. To hurt him requires him to have loved me more than his own selfish desire for carnal pleasure.

Beauregard Thomas and I met shortly after I graduated college. He's a bit older, classically handsome, and he caught my eye with his not-so-accurate description of a work of mid-century art to one of his clients at a local art festival. I was covering the event for the online publication I still work for and was forced to step in and save him from himself. He then offered to thank me over dinner, and we've been together ever since. Well, until I walked in on him with one of his female clients.

I shake my head. Even though I've been away for a month, the memories of that night are still vivid in my mind. Most vividly, I remember the picture of us that sat on his bedside table. It was taken the night he proposed. And there it was, a reminder of our happiest moment together, just inches from his sweat-laden body and the naked brunette that straddled him.

I thought I could get past it. I thought my time away would provide me with a renewed sense of love and commitment, maybe even understanding. I tried to find ways to justify his actions. I wanted to blame myself, because it would be easier to do so than admit the truth. But what *is* the truth?

I've wracked my brain as to how he could do this. Was I not fulfilling him? Am I no longer attractive to him? But the more I tried to reason away his unreasonable actions, the angrier I became. How long has he been seeing her? Are there multiple hers? Was our relationship ever real to him? And with the anger came reality, the obvious truth—I don't trust him anymore. And without trust, I can't be with him. I can't marry him.

My last few days abroad, I spent my downtime googling how to end an engagement, how to break it to your parents and friends, how to cope with the loss. Because that's what it is. It's a loss. I spent three years of my life with this man. I envisioned a life with him. No. *We* envisioned a life *together*, which only makes this more confusing. How could he make plans with me if he didn't plan on following through? How could he . . .?

Home in sight, I pull out my phone and text Beaux, telling him I've landed and will be by soon. I think I do it as insurance that I won't chicken out. Despite my knowing that our relationship is over, there's still a small part of me that wants to make it work. Why? I can't explain. Perhaps it's because that's what I've always seen as right.

Take my parents. I can't remember the last time I've seen them truly happy with each other. Of course, the world wouldn't know that based on the performances they give, but they've managed to make their marriage work for over twenty-five years out of sheer obligation and determination. I admire that about them, despite disagreeing with pretty much everything else they stand for. So, why can't I do that with Beaux? Why can't I get past this?

I reach home and swing the iron gate open, trotting up the stairs, dragging my suitcase along. In no mood to search for my keys, I pound on the door until Kat, my roommate and best friend of seven years, yanks it open with enough force to send both our hair flying.

"It's about time!" Kat says, pulling me inside by the hem of my t-shirt.

"What?" I ask.

I stumble inside to see our French cottage completely transformed into a New Orleans night. French lanterns illuminate the small space. Fake ferns fill every corner. Vines along with rows of string lights drape from the ceiling and make the living room feel like an enchanted garden. Beyond it is the kitchen and dining room, where beignets are stacked high and strangers dressed in white chef outfits move about as if in a fit as they prepare a meal—I bet more delicious than anything I've ever tasted. And yet, in all the perfection, in all the beauty, is an underlying feeling of dread.

"Welcome home!" everyone cheers, and by everyone, I do mean *everyone*. Kat, our friends, my boss, coworkers I never speak to, my parents *(Oh God!)*, and, of course, my fiancé, Beaux Thomas, stands in the middle of them all.

He's dressed in a gray suit, per usual, with a wide grin spread across his face. *That*, that is why I can't get past this. I can't forgive him, because I don't believe he's sorry. He stands here now, the orchestrator of this grand gesture, with an air of confidence about him. If he thinks some pretty decorations, pressure from my family, and a delicious meal are enough to make me forget his infidelity ever happened, then he is sadly mistaken. He may be a master negotiator and one of New Orleans's top corporate attorneys, but that won't get him out of this one.

My insides twist as Beaux moves toward me with quick pace. I feel myself go pale. I move my hand to my stomach to help ease the pain.

I can't do this now, here, in front of everyone I know. If I had to guess, it's probably why he took the initiative to plan such an extravagant party the night of my return. He wants to prolong the inevitable in a last-ditch effort to get me to change my mind. He knows he messed up. He just doesn't know how to admit it.

I release my suitcase from my grasp and shove my hands in

the pockets of my sweatpants as Beaux embraces me. My legs grow heavy as he pulls me into his arms. His touch is fire to ice. And where our bodies used to fit together seamlessly, there are now holes and gaps left in the wake of his actions.

"Welcome home," he whispers, nuzzling his nose into my long blonde hair.

Beaux kisses me as the crowd cheers. His lips move against mine like the many times before. But I don't give in to him. As if strapped to the table of a psychotic doctor, sedated yet conscious, I stand still and allow Beaux to put on a performance for the both of us that rivals my parents' very best. Any remaining ember of our connection is snuffed out by the memories of us being replaced by the memories I have of him and the woman who is not me.

As our kiss ends and Beaux pulls away from me, I find a glimmer of confusion in his crystal-blue eyes. The red excitement in his cheeks fades. His lips droop. He knows our relationship is over. With this shared realization, my chest aches.

Three years—I gave three years of my life to this man. I confided in him, relied on him. He met my love for adventure and expanded it in so many ways. He served as a pallbearer in my grandfather's funeral. He spent holiday after holiday with my family. I trusted him. I trusted him to protect me, to never hurt me. I imagined a life with him where I would stand next to him through his success and failure and he would do the same for me. Was it perfect? No. But it was the life I chose for myself, and he was the man. Now, it's ruined. And I'm left heartbroken and questioning our entire relationship.

I turn to face our guests and take a deep breath as I prepare an excuse to cut the party short. Beaux and I need to . . .

Before I get a chance to speak, Beaux turns to our guests. "Thank you all for coming tonight and helping me celebrate my fiancé's return," he says. "As many of you know, being apart this past month while Emma worked abroad has been uncomfortably difficult for us both."

I cross my arms over my chest and bite my lip to keep my composure. This isn't how I want to do this. I thought he and I would talk first, one-on-one, at least have a respectful goodbye considering the time we've spent together. But perhaps it's better this way—abrupt and raw, just like his infidelity.

"But now, she's back and hopefully not running off again anytime soon," he says.

His words send electricity through my bones. I look to meet his gaze. Blood rushes to my brain as his lips spread into a smile once more. I manage a small one of my own so as not to cause a scene. Though, my cheeks burn as Beaux's motives become all too clear. If he can't convince me to stay with him, he'll make our breakup appear to be my fault.

Everyone laughs as Beaux continues his doting, yet manipulative speech.

"So, in honor of our upcoming nuptials and Emma's return, tonight we will enjoy the incredible food of Chef Jean Black, who will also cater our reception," Beaux informs us all.

My flesh ignites as Beaux rubs salt in the wound he created. Chef Jean Black was one of two components of our dream wedding that evaded us. He's world-renowned and expensive, even for Beaux, not to mention booked until kingdom come. And yet, by some miracle, he's here and it doesn't matter because Beaux cheated.

Maybe I should be grateful that he's trying to make it up to me with a party and Chef Jean Black. Maybe this is his way of saying he's sorry. *But* . . . I hesitate.

Everyone cheers, praising the Chef, and Beaux prompts me to do the same by nudging me in the back. Not wanting to cause a scene, I oblige and join in with everyone's applause as Chef walks us through the grazing station. Crab dip, bruschetta, stuffed mushrooms, and homemade focaccia. It all looks delicious. And like Beaux's presence, it weighs heavy on me as I take this final hour to mentally prepare for the conversation I must soon have—the conversation that will close the door on Beaux forever and open one to a world of the unknown.

* * *

"Emma!"

I'm pulled from my zombie-like state by Kat, who is unwittingly co-hosting the Welcome Home party from Hell.

"Kat," I say through a mouthful of mushroom.

"Let's get you changed," she says, eyeing my sweat-pant ensemble.

"Oh, I don't think it really . . ."

"Come on," she says, half dragging me from the kitchen to my bedroom. Something tells me my clothes aren't what she wants to talk about.

Kat closes my bedroom door behind us. As she does, the tall wooden plank lowers my mom's giggle and Beaux's shoptalk with my father to a hum.

I move into the pale gray room, past the bathroom the two of us share. The stench of unclean clothes mixes with the work of Chef Jean Black, and I nearly vomit.

"Are those my Roxie Jeans?" I ask. "The ones I wore right before I left?"

"Yep," Kat says, guiding me to the bed.

I roll my eyes. God only knows what else is in there, or, worse, what's underneath it all. Once, Kat and I didn't make it to the bottom of the laundry pile for three weeks. When we finally did, a mouse had made it his new home.

"Now, how was Greece?" Kat asks as we sit on the edge of my bed.

Feathers escape my down duvet underneath our weight. They float in the air around us before falling amongst the pounds of blankets and pillows that are pretty to look at but the New Orleans heat never allows me to use. I don't answer her, because I know she didn't drag me in here to talk about Greece. Instead, I take in the rest of the familiar space and take solace in my last moment of the life I've come to know.

My room, like everything else, is just as I left it. Books and shoes clutter my floor. My dresser stands in the corner between my floor-length mirror and bookshelves. Bracelets, necklaces, and other mementoes from my travels clutter the top. Half-opened drawers stuffed full of neutral-colored clothes jut out. I suppose that's one good thing about being home. I'll finally have something to wear other than the same four outfits I've worn repeatedly for a month.

Ash covers the cement flooring of my brick fireplace to my left. To think it's older than I am, than my parents are, still surprises me. I like it though. It makes me feel small, insignificant even. And despite the negative connotation of the word, it relieves my tension. If this structure still stands, after all it's been through, lived through, then so can I.

I exhale and move my eyes to my hands clasped tightly in my lap. Kat sits quietly beside me, which is a dead giveaway she knows something is wrong. Otherwise, she'd be blabbing my ear off about everything I've missed since I left.

"Emma," she whispers then. I close my eyes in response.

Okay. No more stalling. No more performance. No more staying quiet for other people's comfort.

I turn to Kat and find comfort in her presence. Through so much, she's stood by my side—college and all its trials, graduation, the feud between me and my parents when I decided to stay in New Orleans instead of moving home, meeting Beaux, becoming a freelance writer for Conde Nast Traveler, getting engaged, wedding dress shopping, and now she is the first person to learn the truth. We're not the fairytale couple everyone thinks we are. And Beaux is not a prince, no matter how many parties he throws or expensive gestures he offers.

I take a deep breath and . . .

* * *

Kat sits next to me, mouth open, as she processes all that I've told her. I managed to make it through the recount of events without crying. Though, it was a struggle to keep my frustration in check. The more I talk about it, the more I think about it, the more I crave for this performance, this lie, this part of my life to be over. I've wasted enough time. He's *stolen* enough of my time, my love.

"I can't believe I never saw it," Kat says then.

"No one saw it Kat. I sure didn't, anyway."

My cheeks blaze red as I shift a portion of my anger from

Beaux to myself. It's not that I was oblivious to Beaux's flaws, I just never thought they were worthy of concern—his late-night phone calls, the canceled dates, how he never wanted me to move in with him, how he hated sleeping at my place because it wasn't fancy enough for him, and how his work always took precedence over us. I let everything slide, because I admired his ambition and determination to make his dreams come true and I never had a reason not to trust him. He had—*has* goals, and he encouraged me in my own professional pursuits. At a time when I desperately needed encouragement, he gave it to me. So, I justified his behavior so that he never had to.

He never had to apologize or explain himself, because I didn't make him. And now, he's trying to make up for his actions in the only way he knows how—with extravagance and spontaneity. But it's too late. There's too much damage, too much pain to overcome.

"Yes, but I should've known," Kat says. She has always prided herself on being a good judge of people. "And this party . . ." she says, running her fingers through her strawberry curls.

"It's okay," I tell her.

"No!" she exclaims. "If I would've known all this was happening between you guys, I never would've agreed to host it. He . . . he manipulated me," she says, realization dawning on her. "And for you to come home to this, to him . . ." She groans. "I'm so sorry, Emma."

"It's not your fault, Kat," I say. "I . . . I should've told you everything before I left, but . . . I just . . . I didn't want it to be true."

Kat nods. We both lie back against the covers and stare at the ceiling. I wince as the sounds of the party grow louder. It's as if Beaux wants to remind me that he's still here, that they all are.

"You know, when he announced Chef Jean Black as the caterer, I felt guilty. Angry, but guilty."

"*Why?*" Kat asks.

"Because he's trying, at least, that's what I'm supposed to think," I say. "It's what I want to believe."

"But you don't believe it," Kat says. "You don't believe he's being genuine?"

"No. Maybe it isn't fair of me to think this, but . . . I think he wants me to forgive him, but I don't think he's sorry," I tell her. "And if Chef Jean Black doesn't save the fragments of our relationship, then Beaux at least wants to use him to save his reputation. If the truth came out about what he did, not just that he cheated, but that he cheated with a client, everything he's worked for will be lost," I say. "But if everyone we know witnesses him offering this expensive, romantic gesture to me upon my return, no one would believe an accusation against him. No matter what happens between us, tonight was his way of saving face."

"So, what now?" she asks.

I close my eyes and listen to find Beaux's voice amongst the crowd. He's talking about his most recent conquest at work, a female CEO whose board of directors wants her out on the basis she spends too much time with her kids. I wonder if he'll have sex with her. Maybe he already has.

I open my eyes then, finally ready to answer Kat's question.

"I can't do this anymore," I whisper. "I can't be in a relationship where there is no trust and he . . . he destroyed my trust in him. So, I need it to be over. I need these people gone. I need time to process," I say. "I just . . . I can't prolong it anymore."

Kat nods and shoots up to a sitting position. "Consider it done."

CHAPTER 2

I give Kat a small smile as she leaves the room to send everyone home. I hear her tell them, despite their protests, that I have a jetlag-induced migraine. Thanking God that that is *not* the case, I stand and find myself in front of my mirror.

I look tired. My long blonde hair drapes down my chest, limp and lifeless. The pale skin beneath my green eyes is sunken in exhaustion. My cheeks are hollow, and my natural curves depleted from the lack of grease-laden food in, no pun intended, Greece.

I exhale and move to my dresser to grab a ponytail. Not finding one on top, I open drawer after drawer in search of where they hide. As I do, my fingers trip over something heavy. I close my eyes, recognizing the soft touch of the burgundy velvet ring box Beaux proposed to me with. Inside it rests a stunning, two point five-carat diamond, emerald cut on a solid gold band. I suspect it costs more than mine and Kat's rent for a year, which is exactly what I thought when Beaux gave it to me. Well, that and *damn*, it's heavy, and do I really get to wear this for the rest of my life?

I slip the emerald cut diamond onto my finger one last time. The gold band is cool against my skin. Yet, it no longer feels heavy. Perhaps because the weight of the ring was never measured in metal. It was measured in promises, vows. Promises that are now broken, and vows we never had a chance to make.

My thoughts are interrupted by a sharp *ding* that makes me jump. I pull out my phone to find three missed calls from my mother, two angry texts, and one voicemail from my father. I listen to the voicemail first.

Hey, Sweetie! Just checking in on you. Kat said you weren't feeling well. I guess maybe it was too much excitement after twenty hours of travel. Feel better. Call us if you need anything. Love you!

That's my dad for you—short and to the point, but always there when you really need him. My mom, on the other hand . . .

Emma Louise Marshall—how selfish of you to send guests home without entertaining them, without even a goodbye. Your father and I drove over five hours to be here. Not to mention all your other guests, including your boss, who took time out of their schedules to show their support for you. I thought I raised you better than that. And Beaux—you embarrassed him. And, based on the look on his face, I'd expect to hear about it. What have I always told you, Emma? Men like him don't come around often. Look at your father and me. We've been married for twenty-five years and have two beautiful children. Don't you want that? Well, it doesn't come without sacrifice and humility. You messed up, my dear. Now, apologize and make it up to Beaux. He went through a lot of effort to organize this. Call me tomorrow to let me know how it goes and we can talk about your hair for your wedding. I was thinking with your face being so, well, wide, you may want to leave your hair down. Having it up would just accentuate things you don't need to accentuate.

I roll my eyes, turn my phone off, and place my engagement ring back into its velvet box.

Before I introduced my parents to Beaux, my parents and I hadn't spoken in six months. They were heartbroken when I chose to stay in New Orleans after graduating college. Perhaps, even more so, my mother was ashamed of me, ashamed she had a daughter so strong-willed—or disobedient, as she views it. For six months, the only communication I received from her were texts on Sunday that read, *"I'm praying for you."*

Maybe I'm being ridiculous, but if you knew my mother, you'd know how condescending she is. Anything that doesn't go according to her plan is a sin. I was destined for Hell the second I left home in her book. *Until* I introduced her to Beaux. Beaux was—*is* handsome, wealthy, and comes from a well-to-do family. He rivals my dad in career success. He hunts game with the best of them. He has a charisma and humor that allows him to control any room he walks into. And, perhaps most important of all, he looks good on the family Christmas card. He's been on three of ours to be exact.

Beaux represents an answered prayer for my mother. Now, instead of being ashamed to mention her daughter who flew the nest to Louisiana's most dangerous and sin-filled city, she can brag about her daughter, the travel writer, and her hunky, rich fiancé.

I won't lie. It was nice. It was nice to be back in her good graces, to feel like I had a mom again. Even though I chose to leave Presley and stay in New Orleans despite her and my father's protests, I wasn't prepared for the emptiness I felt without them in my life.

When I told her about Beaux, she was proud of me and excited for me. Maybe she even felt like she could relate to me a little more. After all, she met my father at about the same age, and he was older than her by several years, like Beaux is for me. But my dad has never cheated on my mom. He's never made her feel like she couldn't trust him. Despite their other issues, they have a foundation of trust, a foundation I no longer have with Beaux. And if her text is any inclination, without Beaux and our upcoming wedding, there isn't much else tying us together.

It's sad, but, I think part of me hoped I could find a way to forgive Beaux, not for the sake of our relationship, but for the sake of my relationship with my mother. Beaux brought us together in a way we'd never been before. With him out of the picture, I'm afraid of what my relationship with my mother will turn into. That is, if a relationship will exist at all.

The house is quiet now except for the sounds of Chef Jean Black and his team clearing the food and packing up their catering truck. Beaux will be in to see me soon. And, if my mom's text is worth the time she spent typing it, this conversation is going to be even harder than I thought.

As I wait, my heartbeat quickens. My palms sweat. I'm not sure what to expect of Beaux. Will he fight for us? Will he yell and throw things? He hates nothing more than being embarrassed in public. And, if my mom is right, that's exactly what I did. I embarrassed him. Yet, in this moment, I'm not sure which version of him I'd prefer. I've seen Beaux angry, though his anger has never been directed at me. But when Beaux wants something, his persistence is unmatched and unwavering. It's one of the things I've always loved about him. He doesn't give up. But, this time, he doesn't have a choice, and I'm not sure how he's going to take it.

Beaux swings the door open. His face is beet-red. His jacket is off, and his top button is undone. Slivers of blonde hair have worked their way out of the massive amounts of gel he uses to suffocate them.

I guess I'll find out.

* * *

Beaux sits next to me on the bed. He doesn't speak. Neither do I. I wrap my arms around myself as my forehead throbs. I contemplate what to say, and just when I think I've got it figured out, my tongue swells in my mouth. In all the time we've been together, we've never been this quiet. It's strange, strange to just be with him. And soon it becomes too much for me to stomach. As Beaux's breathing slows, I work up the courage to face him, turning on my bottom so I cannot easily turn away from him.

"Beaux," I say.

"Don't do this," he whispers, cutting me off.

I bite my lip and drop my eyes to my clasped hands. My cheeks feel tight as emotion swells behind them.

"Beaux, I . . ."

"I love you," he says, turning to face me. His blue eyes plead with me, the same blue eyes I found myself captivated by when we first met. In them I see a piece of him I've only ever seen once before—*desperation*.

He confuses me. How can he seem so confident before, arrogant even, and play the crowd as if everything is fine, and then turn around and beg for me to forgive him? None of this makes sense. When I don't respond, he continues.

"Emma, I'm sorry. I know I messed up. I know I hurt you, but . . ."

But. I close my eyes as that word radiates through me. Nothing good ever comes after *but*.

"It was meaningless. It was only one time. It was a mistake I will never make again," he tells me.

I want to believe him. For the sake of three years, for the sake of my heart, for the sake of my mother, I want to believe him. *But* . . .

Opening my eyes, I ask, "But how can I believe that? How can I believe you when you say it was only one time and it will never happen again? I . . ." I pause to compose myself. "I trusted you."

I exhale as my swelling emotion leaves me. Clarity replaces it.

"I trusted you and you broke that trust," I say. "And I don't even understand why you cheated in the first place. You didn't act like you were unhappy. There were no signs that I'm aware of, so how can I believe that it would never happen again, if I never even thought it would happen the first time?"

"Emma," Beaux breathes. He leans forward and buries his face in his hands. "I know I broke your trust," he mumbles into his palms. "But . . ."

"Stop saying *but*," I say, cutting him off. "*But* is an excuse, a way for you to justify what you did, and there is no justifying it. And I'm not going to justify it for you. You should be taking responsibility," I say, throwing my hands up in frustration. Now, my clarity is fading into anger.

"So, let me take responsibility," he begs. "Let me make it right," he says, turning to face me. "Let me have a lifetime to make it right."

He places his hand on my thigh as if the simple gesture will change my mind, will make me remember the good times, the intimate times. But all it does is make me angrier.

We had something. *We . . .* And in all his explanation, he hasn't once told me why he did it, why he felt the need to be with someone else.

"Why?" I ask. My voice cracks as I speak.

"What?" he responds. His face contorts in confusion.

"Why do you want to make it up to me?" I ask. "Why did you throw this party tonight? Why are you pretending you care?" I ask, moving his hand from my thigh.

Rage bubbles inside me as I speak. I can't hold it in any longer.

"I . . . *I do.* How can you not realize that?" He attempts to move closer to me once more, but I stop him with my words.

"Because you cheated," I say. Verbalizing it is powerful. Calling him out to his face is powerful. He blushes and stutters as he attempts to deny it, to justify it, to explain it. Again, I stop him.

"You slept with someone else, a client no less," I tell him. "And now, you expect me to believe you care about me, that you love me, that you want to be with me?"

"*Yes*, that's what I'm trying to tell you," he says, raising his voice.

"*No!*" I yell. "You can't love me *and* cheat on me. You can't rebuild the trust that's been broken. You can't make this up to me, like all the times you canceled dates because something came up at work," I say. "Was that even the truth? Was it really work all those times, or was it someone else?"

"Emma," he says. I hear his patience waning, but still, I press on as salty tears drip down my face into my mouth.

"That night," I say. "That night you chose someone over me. You chose a one-night stand—or maybe it was two, maybe it was three—regardless of how many times, you chose someone over the woman you promised to live the rest of your life with. And you can never take that back," I tell him. "So, don't pretend to care for me and love me now when you don't."

My chest burns with a fire that is unquenchable. I want him

out of here, out of my sight, and out of my life. Any hope for a respectful end is gone.

"Emma," he says once more. *That tone!* That annoying, condescending tone. It's like I'm a child that needs scolding. "You . . . you're overreacting," he says. "I had sex with her, yes, as you saw. And . . . I'm sorry you had to see us," he rambles.

"*Us,*" I scoff. "Shouldn't you be sorrier you gave me something to see?"

"Yeah," he says, exhaling. "And . . . I am, but . . ."

"*But,*" I repeat, shaking my head. Just as I thought, he's not sorry he did it. He's just sorry he got caught.

The flames of rage burn out inside me, leaving me charred, raw, and exhausted. I can't do this anymore. I can't stomach this fight.

I stand from my place on the bed and walk to my dresser. My fingers find the ring box in the top drawer, and for a second I consider not giving it back to him. After all the pain he's caused, I should keep it for severance pay. But I can't. Keeping it would allow me to hang on to the better parts of him when I need to forget they ever existed. It'll be easier this way.

I pull the ring box out of the dresser and take one step towards him. That's when he stands, towering over me.

"Think carefully before you say another word, Emma," he warns me. "I don't take kindly to those who back out on a deal," he says. "You should know that by now."

Anger consumes him. His face turns a deeper shade of red. His fists clench. It's a side of him I've only ever seen a few times and never directed toward me. I take a moment to compose myself.

With resolve, I say, "Beaux, I don't pretend to be perfect. I . . . I don't know why you cheated, but I realize now that I made it easy for you to. I didn't hold you accountable or pressure you to put me first. I made it easy for you to do whatever you wanted behind my back, because I trusted you not to. Maybe I even let my mother convince me that you were better than me and that I'd never have better than you. But what I know now is that I do deserve better. And one day, I'll have it," I tell him.

I am surprisingly calm as I speak. As if our relationship is a door cracked open, I take one final opportunity to close it.

"What I know is that we're done," I say.

My hand is heavy as I offer him the ring box. Enclosed inside the velvet-clad box is more than a ring. It's all the plans we made together, the house we envisioned living in, the children we hoped to have. It's the family holidays, the dates, the dreams we both hoped to achieve with the other by our side. It's our life together enclosed in fabric the color of blood.

Beaux stares at me for a long while, then shifts his eyes to the wall. He once made love to me as he pressed me against it. At least I thought it was love. It was rough and exciting. But, as time has shown, that can only last so long.

I exhale, roll my eyes and . . .

Beaux knocks the box to the floor and slaps me hard across the face. I scream and stumble backwards, but he yanks me to him before I fall. He pushes me on the bed, locking the entrances before he gets on top of me. He yells in frustration. Salvia drips from his mouth and tears fall from his eyes. I do not hear what he says. My eyes are too terrified by what I see to allow my ears to listen.

"Beaux," I choke.

He shakes me, throwing my body repeatedly into the cushions of the bed. I try to fight him off, but my arms are paralyzed in fear. I think I begin to cry. I can't tell if the wetness on my face is of my making or his. He hits me again and again, and I scream. Blood pools in my mouth to the point I feel I may drown in it. There is a reprieve in his assault. I gasp and spit the blood on my white duvet.

My adrenaline slows, and the pain of my wounds overcomes me, but he isn't done.

Beaux moves his hands from my shoulders to my throat. He squeezes and with more and more pressure, my mind goes numb and my insides burn. I flounder and try to push him off, but my efforts are in vain.

The room around me fades. Blurred edges inch closer and

closer to his face, yet I still see him, over me, choking me. Until I see nothing at all.

With darkness my eye's reward, my ears betray me, and I am now aware of the hell surrounding me. Beaux screams and grunts as he uses more force against me. The pain should be greater than it is, but my body shuts down with each passing second there is no fresh air in my lungs. Kat pounds on the door, crying and cursing. She yells into her cellphone for the police to hurry. I try to move my lips to tell her to run, but I'm unable to. My body is heavy, weak, and numb as it jolts back and forth under Beaux's pressure.

In my last moment of consciousness, I feel Beaux press hard against me with all his weight. Sirens echo in the background. Hot against my neck, he whispers, "Now, we're done."

CHAPTER 3

I sit on the edge of my mattress and watch as the rising sun invades my room. It illuminates my pale walls as the light shines through the windowpane. To my left, remnants of last night's fire crack within the confines of my fireplace. On each side, shelves lined with my favorite books glisten in the morning light, as do the dust particles floating in the air. In front of me is my mirror and dresser with travel polaroids displayed on top.

Yet, the space feels foreign after months of sleeping on the couch. I had to repaint and clean and get rid of things that reminded me of him, of that night. Still, I sit nine months later, and I still feel him in this room, watching me, touching me, hurting me.

I wrap my arms around myself and tug my comforter up higher over my chest. Despite it being new, in the right light, I sometimes think I see the remnants of splattered blood staining the white surface.

My reflection stares back at me in the mirror. She looks . . . tired, sad, maybe even older. *Geez.* I roll my eyes, looking to the shoes and clothes, some clean and some not, scattered across my bedroom floor. Perhaps I didn't do enough cleaning.

When it happened, I thought it would be easier to forget all the good memories and make more room for the bad ones. I thought I could get over him quicker; and I guess you can say it worked. I have no romantic feelings for him whatsoever. But what I do have is far more damaging.

I fear him and the reality that the man I gave my heart to could hurt me the way he did. I'm scared of *my* judgement, because *I* picked him. I allowed him into my world. And I'm scared to pick another, scared he'll be just the same. Most of all, I'm scared . . . scared this fear will never go away.

"Emma!" Kat calls.

Beep. Beep. Beep. My alarm goes off and I hit snooze without a second thought.

"Emma?"

"I'm coming. Ten minutes!"

"I'm clocking you," Kat says from outside my room.

I groan and force myself out of bed. It's Sunday, and on Sunday, we brunch. Bessy's is our place, always has been since we first moved to the Marigny. It's small, casual, and the walls are the color of sunflowers. It's also a hub for local artists. Every third Sunday, one will come and show off their interpretation of Blue Dog. The painting is then added to the house collection, and once a year there's a viewing for profit, all of which is donated back to the city's Creative Concepts fund. Bessy's is one of the only places *he* didn't take from me. He never had the desire to join us.

I wash my face, brush my teeth, drench my pits in deodorant because the humidity is real, and sniff-check last night's shorts before grabbing a white t-shirt from my to-be-folded pile. I slip on some sandals and grab a few bracelets and necklaces from atop my dresser. A little Chapstick and my fedora and I'm ready to go.

"*Really?*" Kat asks, hands on hips.

"What?" I ask, glancing down at my outfit.

Two weeks ago, she shaded my messy bun and leggings into oblivion. Since then, I've tried to feign effort. I realize she's just worried.

"Ten minutes and you look like that," she exhales. "You're never allowed to be a slob again. It's too easy for you not to," she says. She turns on her heels and her strawberry bob bounces as she walks.

"Yeah, okay," I say, following behind her. "Because *you're* such a slouch."

"Comparison has nothing to do with it, darling," she says in her oh-so-Kat way. "You're a babe. It's time you remember it."

"Well, I'll add it to my to-do list," I tell her in my oh-so-Emma way, despite my urge to smile.

Kat smirks. We toss our purses over our shoulders, grab our keys from the hook, and are ready to go.

We open the front door to bright light and blazing temperatures, and I instantly regret not bringing a ponytail.

"Cheers to Mother Nature," I say.

"Oh," Kat says, her tone perky. "Looks like they found someone to take Mr. Turnip's old house. And by someone, I mean a *fine* someone. You should go introduce yourself," she nudges.

"Um, *yeah*. I'll get right on that," I say, turning to lock up.

"*Come on!*" she begs. "The fact that the guy now lives in Mr. Turnip's old house, it's like his spirit is blessing the union." I roll my eyes in response. "Fine," she concedes. "But if Mr. Turnip were here, he'd make it a point to introduce himself, just like he did with you and me. Besides, what hope does our neighborly relationship have if we walk right by while he sweats in the southern heat unpacking that U-Haul all by himself?" Kat asks.

Her ginger brows raise as if daring me to disagree, and she has a point. Helping the guy out would be the neighborly thing to do, and Mr. Turnip wouldn't have it any other way. But something tells me that's not her motivation for the kind gesture.

I shove my keys in my pocket and turn, following her line of sight.

The nameless guy looks to be about twenty-six, maybe twenty-seven. He has black, tousled hair, which is too perfect to be natural, tattoos that cover his tanned arms, and icy eyes that stare into mine. *Wait!* Stare . . . into . . . he's staring . . . I'm staring. *Shit!*

I turn, awkwardly, and face our front door like I forgot something. Which, clearly, I have—*my mind*. Our cat, Grey, pokes her head through the curtain and watches me with inquisitive emerald eyes. She knows it too.

"Well, that was just great," I mutter, giving Kat the side-eye.

"Oh, stop," she whispers to me. "Hey, there!" she calls over to him, her voice rising in pitch. *You've got to be kidding me.*

"Uh, hey!" he says back. His voice is deep and raspy, but not like a smoker raspy, more like a . . . a soulful raspy. "I'm Julian," he says. *Hmm.* He's definitely not southern. He must not be from around here.

"Nice to meet you, Julian," Kat says with all her charms. "I'm Katherine, but everyone calls me Kat, and this is . . ." She looks at me with blue bulging eyes and pokes at my stomach until I face him. Finally, I do, shrinking away from her aggressive tactics. "And this is Emma. She's single."

I feel like a prize on *The Price Is Right*, but I can't say I expected anything less.

"Say something, Emma," Kat says, leaning into me.

"Um, hi," I stutter, giving him a small smile and an awkward wave.

"Put your hand down. Put it down," she scolds me.

"Hi," Julian says back. His wide lips draw into a smile. Clearly, we amuse him, and I can't say I blame him.

"We were just on our way out, but you seem like you could use some help," Kat says, returning her attention to the black-haired boy, *man.* My insides twist. "How about we give you a hand and then you can join us for Sunday brunch," she offers.

"*Really?*" I ask, turning to face her. I don't want to seem rude, but . . .

"It's the neighborly thing to do," she says to me.

"Or the slutty thing," I say back. My face scrunches in protest.

Julian, sensing my hesitance, doesn't accept Kat's offer. "Oh, um, thanks, but it's really okay. You girls have plans. I don't want to interfere." *Thank God.*

"Nonsense," Kat says. "What are neighbors for? I just need to grab something from inside, but Emma will be right down," she assures him.

Realizing Kat is not one to take no for an answer, he gives in. "Cool," he says, grabbing another box from the truck. I give him one last smile as he makes his way inside his new home, then . . .

"*Are you insane?*" I screech.

"Oh, come on, Emma," Kat begins, but I cut her off.

"No, *you* come on," I tell her. "How could you do that? How could you just volunteer us for manual labor and then brunch with a complete stranger? He could be a serial killer or one of those perverts who become obsessed with anyone who shows them the slightest kindness," I say, looking over my shoulder to ensure he didn't hear.

"Not to mention," I turn back to her, my voice low. "You made me seem like a desperate crazy person by broadcasting my relationship status. *God!* I knew you would do this," I say, moving past her to the porch swing.

There's a noticeable silence between us.

"I'm . . . I'm sorry," she finally says. Her sun-kissed cheeks flush in embarrassment. I obviously caught her off guard with my outburst.

Kat and I met at Tulane, in a communications course, actually. How ironic? And ever since I've known her, she's been the over-bearing, pushy friend that keeps everyone on their toes, and I love her despite it because she's also the friend you can count on, the one who understands, the one who doesn't judge. But God, on days like today, it takes great effort to remind myself of her redeeming qualities.

"I know," I say, plopping down on the swing. "And I forgive you."

I drop my eyes to my wrist and move my bracelets back and forth. I don't like it when we fight. I don't like to fight with anyone, but sometimes it's necessary.

"It's just . . ." she begins, but stops herself.

"Go ahead," I tell her. "You can say it."

Kat breathes heavily and takes a seat next to me.

"We don't talk about it," Kat says quietly. Her fingers fidget back and forth in her lap.

"No," I say coldly. "We don't." My skin begins to itch with the reference of *it*.

"When you decided to clean out your room and start sleeping in there again, I thought . . . I thought you were better," Kat says. "I thought you were ready to start being yourself again, to do fun things, normal things," she rambles on. I wince as she says *normal*. "And the nightmares," she starts.

"Kat," I beg.

"They've only gotten worse," she says, ignoring my plea.

"Kat."

"You've been so . . . so isolated for months now, even from me."

"Yes," I snap. "I have been isolated. It's because I don't want to have conversations like this," I say, throwing my hands against my thighs.

"Okay," Kat says, swallowing her tongue. I realize she means well, but . . . "Well, if you don't want to talk about it, then maybe you could erase it—or him, rather. Replace the bad memories with new good ones. Julian seems nice and he's certainly attractive," Kat rambles on. "Maybe you can finally get over B—"

"Don't," I say, pointing my finger at her. "Don't say his name."

Kat snaps her lips shut.

"I'm sorry, Emma," she whispers. "I'm sorry."

I close my eyes and rest my head in my hands.

"I know," I whisper back.

Kat moves her hand to my back and brushes through my long, blonde hair with her fingers. Her touch is soothing, but it took months for me to accept her touch, to accept any touch from another person.

She is the only person, aside from me, who knows the truth of what happened between me and Beaux—well, the *complete truth*. My friends saw the bruises on my face and neck. They didn't see the ones on my abdomen and thighs. It took weeks for all the traces of his fingers to leave my skin. My forehead crinkles as I remember back. It's impossible to think about without feeling like I'm suffocating, drowning in my own blood. Every time I looked at myself in the mirror, I felt him. My skin burned and ached where he had once been. That's when the nightmares started. Still, I didn't press charges. I couldn't. I couldn't bring myself to accept . . . Well, I suppose I still can't. By the time I visited my parents, all remnants of the encounter had faded, and I let them believe their own conclusions as to why the relationship failed. Not surprisingly, my mother blamed me.

Sometimes I wonder why I didn't press charges. He would've

been ruined, and he never could've hurt me or anyone else again. But I guess I knew that wasn't exactly true. Even if I had my day in court and managed to win against one of the city's top corporate attorneys, the scars he left me with are more than just physical.

I've made progress, but . . . I will never be *normal* again, as Kat puts it. I will never again be *me*.

Kat pulls her hand away and I hear her suck in air. I sit up to pull her in for a hug.

"Come here," I say. We swing back and forth. "I *am* over Beaux. I have been since the second he laid a hand on me." She winces. "But I can't just erase the bad memories, Kat," I say. "I can't just repaint my room, put on a little makeup, get a new boyfriend and be fine."

She pulls away from me then.

"Is that how it came off?" she asks. "Oh, Emma, I didn't mean . . ."

"I know," I say.

"It's just, I worry."

"*I know.*"

My eyes move to Julian as he emerges from his house. I bite my lip. Maybe it wasn't fair of me to ask Kat to keep my secret. It's clearly taking a toll on her, it's just that it's hard enough to convince people I'm fine as is. If everyone knew, it would be impossible.

"Even if I was ready for someone new, which I'm not," I tell her. "But if I was, it certainly would not be with him."

"Why?" Kat says, perking up. "He's hot!"

"Yeah," *Oh, crap!* If you give Kat an inch, she'll take a mile. "But he's our neighbor," I say, before Kat jumps out of her seat.

"*So?*" Kat asks. "What does that have to do with anything?"

"If you think leaving him to unpack his U-Haul by himself isn't very neighborly, then what about when we don't work out? Did you think about how uncomfortable it would be to see him every day after being . . . *intimate*?" I ask.

"I guess not," she admits with a half-hearted smile.

"You see?"

"Yeah, I just . . . I want you to be okay," she says, her blue eyes peering into mine. "I want to know he didn't break you."

Her words are like a gut punch. My cheeks tighten as I hold back tears. My throat burns as I fight to not stutter.

"He didn't," I finally say, much to her relief. "So, come on." I stand. "Let's help this guy with the last of his things, brunch it up at Bessy's, and then have a normal Sunday evening, just the two of us, watching *Gilmore Girls* reruns."

"Sounds like a plan," she says, pushing herself up from the swing. "But, um, I actually did forget something. So, um, you can go on down," she tells me. And, once more, she is unable to conceal her happy thoughts of me in the arms of Julian. I'll have to get his last name for the background check I plan on running.

"Of course, you did."

"Love you!" she squeals, running back inside. I exhale.

CHAPTER 4

Julian's U-Haul sits between our house and his. It's small. He either doesn't have many things or doesn't plan to stay here long. I push our wrought-iron gate open and walk as slowly as possible until I round the corner of the truck. My stomach tightens. My palms sweat.

"Oh, thank God," I say aloud. He isn't there.

I fan my face with my hand and mentally scold myself for being so uneasy. There are only a few boxes left, a rug, a guitar case, and a painting. *Hmm.*

I hop inside the U-Haul and walk to the back where a large hand-painted canvas rests. On a white background, there are faint, charcoal lines that make out the shape of a woman's face. Long hair cascades down her left shoulder and pools at the bottom of the canvas. In her hair there are words: *good, innocent, hopeful, faithful, trusting,* and so on. On the right side of her body, more words are etched into the lines that make out her face, shoulder and chest: *damaged, hurt, second-guessing, scared, liar, thief, evil.*

"It's interesting, isn't it?"

I jump and twist to see Julian standing at the edge of the truck. Up close, his hair is even more perfect, his eyes icy green. He's wearing ripped blue jeans and a black t-shirt that drapes over his long torso, hanging almost to his knees. The contrast of the darkness of his shirt and the bright colors in his tattoos makes for a vibrant appearance.

"Um, I . . ." I catch myself staring. "I'm sorry, I—I shouldn't have invaded your personal space. I was just curious. I've never seen a painting like this before," I say, turning back to it. "I'm still not sure I understand it."

"Sure, you do," he says, jumping up into the cargo hold. I sense him moving closer. My heartbeat quickens. "It's just hard to admit to ourselves."

He stands beside me now, towering over me by at least a foot. In such proximity, the smell of mint and rain floods my nostrils. If I weren't so tense, I'd inhale it.

"I . . . um," I stutter. "I see . . ." I focus on the painting once more, allowing my nerves to dissipate. "I see a girl," I say. "But I don't think she's what's important."

He turns towards me. Surprise washes over his features. I glance between him and the painting, taking a deep breath.

"In the lines of her hair, face, and body, I see words, contrasting in good and evil," I say, pointing to the painting. He still hasn't taken his eyes off me.

I drop my hand to my side and take a step back to assess the painting once more, moving out of his line of sight.

"You're right," I say. "It *is* hard to admit, but I think it's telling us we all have both good and evil inside. And . . . and the expression on her face, though not fully drawn, depicts a struggle, like the one we all face each day we choose to be happy versus sad, to trust instead of not, to be good instead of evil."

Wow. The painting is interesting, aesthetically, but moving emotionally. It makes me think of my own struggle with trust and effort. For weeks after the encounter, my bones felt heavy. I could barely move to wake up in the morning, to eat, to talk. Everything felt raw. My throat feels scratchy just thinking about it. While my effort has improved, my trust hasn't. I'm not sure it ever will. Therein lies the struggle Julian's painting depicts. We're always one choice, one day away from a completely different life. And when it all comes crumbling down, well . . . I blame him for . . . for everything, but I also blame myself.

I move my eyes to his back. He stands in front of me now and nods his head in validation of my response. Up close, I see his tattoos more vividly. Well, some of them. On his left forearm he has a guitar with lines drawn through it. On the lines are musical notes. To what, I'm not sure. Peeking out from underneath his shirtsleeve is the bottom of a cross on his shoulder.

From it, rose petals fall down his bicep. Each one grows more dried and crumbled as it reaches his elbow.

He turns suddenly. I pull my eyes from his body and finally am forced to face him. My lips part as I take him in. At first, he doesn't speak. His eyes move back and forth across my face as if searching for some answer to a question, some truth to a lie. I want to turn away from him. The twisting of my stomach tells me so, but I can't. My eyes won't leave his.

"Um, I'm sorry. Was that not it?" I ask, breaking his search. He blushes, and his lips draw up into a smile.

"No, um," he says, taken aback. "That was actually spot on, which is why I'm speechless," he admits. "I painted that two years ago, and no one has ever understood it. Some people don't even notice the words, but you, you saw them, and you understood the message," he says, turning back to face it.

"You painted it?" I ask, moving to stand beside him once more.

He nods. I watch his face as he examines his work. There's a pain in his eyes I recognize all too well. I wonder . . .

"Hey, guys," Kat says from behind us. Again, I jump. "Whatcha looking at?"

"Geez, Kat, way to give someone a heart attack," I scold her.

"Oh, nothing," Julian says, turning to face her. "Just this painting I found Emma scoping out," he says, winking at me. "After you," he says, motioning for me to walk ahead of him.

"Oh, Emma *loves* art," Kat says. I roll my eyes at her exaggeration of *loves*. "She's actually a writer for the New Orleans events, culture, and lifestyle magazine The Hub. She practically reviews art for a living among other culturally important things," she explains.

"Oh, give it a rest, Kat," I say, jumping from the trailer to the street. "He doesn't need to hear my life story."

"Oh, I agree," Kat says, playing innocent. "But obviously you two have a common interest of art and *oh*, look at that," Kat says. My body tenses. "A guitar case," Kat notes. "Do you like music, Julian?"

"Oh! It's practically my life," he says, hopping down from the U-Haul.

"*Really?*" Kat asks, giving me a knowing look. "Emma loves music too. In college she was actually in a few musicals," Kat says, yanking me by my shirt to move closer to her and Julian. My cheeks burn bright. Still, I oblige, crossing my arms over my chest.

"*Really?*" Julian asks. His eyes light up, and I can't tell if it's because he sees how uncomfortable Kat is making me or because he's actually interested in my musical history.

"Yeah, um, a few, but that's not really important right now," I say, turning to Kat. "Why don't we do what we came to do and grab a few boxes?" I ask her. She ignores me.

"Julian," Kat says.

Here we go.

"Did you know Emma is a genius?" she asks.

"Okay, Kat, stop."

I move past her and Julian and grab the closest cardboard box I can find. It's heavy as hell. I contemplate putting it back down, but that would just prolong the torture.

"You want this inside?" I ask Julian. "Yeah, inside is good," I say before he can answer. He chuckles.

I leave them on the street and struggle up the porch steps to his open front door. In the background, Kat rambles on. There's no telling what story she's concocting. Probably that I'm a virgin astronaut and CIA spy all in one. My job for The Hub is just a cover. *God.* I can't imagine.

I make it through the front door and cool air welcomes me in along with a sense of calm. The two of them are exhausting. Well, Julian himself isn't exactly exhausting, but being around him is. Every part of my body is in knots that tingle with each inch closer we get. And it's not his fault, but . . . it just is.

I shake my head in frustration and drop the box in the first open space I find. I exhale and shake my arms out. They're like noodles.

Cardboard boxes surround me, along with furniture still in plastic-wrap. Julian's house is set up much like mine and Kat's.

You enter into the living room, which spans the entire width of the shotgun-style house. Separated by nothing more than an exposed brick fireplace, the kitchen and dining room flows off the living room.

I make my way from my place in the living room to where Mr. Turnip's dining room table used to sit. Now there is nothing. Nothing but a stream of light flowing in from the large floor-to-ceiling windows that stare plainly at the side of the next house over.

Mr. Turnip loved this neighborhood, loved New Orleans. But he hated, and I do mean *hated*, the view from this window. He always complained about how the windows were too beautiful to not have something equally as beautiful to look at. Not to mention, the next house over wasn't fond of landscaping. My lips draw into a pained smile as I remember him.

I can practically smell his famous spaghetti. He'd make it every Wednesday night with extra garlic. I remember, he'd sing as he cooked and answer my tedious questions about trigonometry. We'd play checkers afterwards and watch Jeopardy. He was like a father to me. Well, a grandfather due to his age.

I wrap my arms around myself and approach the window. The sun streams in, warming my skin. I close my eyes and relish in its touch. I imagine Mr. Turnip wrapping me in his arms like he did the night my mother cursed me in the street and swore to never speak to me again. It was the night of my college graduation, and I'd just finished telling her that I wasn't moving home. She stormed out of the house. Mr. Turnip just so happened to be sitting on his front porch having a nightcap. He saw the whole thing.

My parents drove away and like so many times before, Mr. Turnip embraced me and made me realize I wasn't alone. As if Beaux and the aftermath of our demise hasn't been difficult enough, Mr. Turnip passed away five months ago. And I have never felt more alone.

"Thinking about Turnip?" Kat asks from behind me.

"Huh?" I turn. "Oh, yeah," I say, moving my eyes back to the window. "You know he hated this thing. Well, not the window, the view. He'd always say, 'If only those damn people would plant a rose bush,'" I say with a laugh. "He was a character." I drop my eyes to the floor.

"He was," she agrees.

"Um, Turnip?" Julian asks. I'd nearly forgotten he was here.

"Yeah, um," Kat begins. "An old man named Mr. Turnip used to live here. When Emma and I moved in next door, he helped make us feel at home. And um, over the years, he was kind to us."

"So, what happened to him?" Julian asks.

Out of the corner of my eye, I see Kat turn to me. I purse my lips and turn to face them.

"He died," I say, not making eye contact. "Apparently, he fell and broke . . . something. It was sudden."

"Damn," Julian curses. "I'm sorry to hear that." When he speaks, I detect a sense of sincerity that surprises me. He must not be a stranger to loss.

"Thanks. Um, I'll grab a few more things from the truck," I say, moving past him.

"She's taken it harder than I expected her to," Kat mumbles as I reach the front door. I slow my pace to listen to what she says next. "She's had a rough few months."

No!

"Kat!" I say, louder than I intended. "You coming?" I ask, spinning in her direction.

"Yeah, um," she says. "Right behind you."

We finish unloading Julian's things in a matter of minutes. The talk of Mr. Turnip's untimely departure killed the mood—and Kat's incessant talk of me and my lack of significant other. By the time we've finished, I've decided to skip brunch at Bessy's, but the emptiness of my stomach and our fridge overrides my decision.

"All done," Kat says, washing her hands in Julian's sink. "Are we ready to head to Bessy's?"

My eyes move to Julian, who wipes sweat from his forehead with the back of his hand. Our eyes lock, and as if sensing my hesitancy, he rejects Kat's proposal.

"You know, I hate to back out after you girls helped me with the truck, but I should really start unpacking. Besides, you two have done more than enough to welcome me to the neighborhood. Mr. Turnip would be proud," he says, causing my chest to tighten.

At that, I pull my eyes away from him and give the house one last glance. Now that Mr. Turnip is gone, I doubt I'll be back.

"Emma? *Emma?*" Kat says.

"Huh?" I ask. "Oh, um. It's no problem," I say to Julian. "Welcome to the neighborhood."

At that, I turn on my heel and walk towards the door. Kat follows behind me, surprisingly without protest.

"Oh, Julian," I say, turning suddenly. His name sounds strange crossing my lips.

"Yeah?" he asks, taking a step toward me.

"When Mr. Turnip passed, Kat, and I helped pack up his things for auction. He didn't have any family, at least none that cared to visit the house," I explain. "But we never could find his checkerboard. If you happen to find it, would you mind letting us know? It's kind of sentimental."

"Of course," Julian says. A warm smile spreads across his face, one I can't help but return.

"Thanks," I say. With that, I close the door behind me, and Kat and I head to Bessy's.

CHAPTER 5

Snuggled in a pile of warm blankets, I sit on my mattress and type while mindlessly eating Oreos. This is how I spend most Sunday nights, finishing up work from the past week and preparing for my new assignments. Tonight, I find myself raving about a new restaurant in the Quarter. I can still taste the eggplant parm. *Okay, that's gross.*

On the opposite side of the bathroom we share, Kat and her boyfriend Demetri attempt to keep quiet as they ravage each other. It's on nights like this I realize just how thin these old walls really are. I roll my eyes and return to my . . .

Buzz, buzz.

That's weird. Who would call this time of night? My eyes flit to the clock on my dresser. It's after 8:00. I hop off the bed and shuffle through the blankets in search of my phone, tossing each one frantically to the floor. My insides clench as I see my sister's name and photo flash across my screen. I take a deep breath and pray this isn't what I think it is.

"*Okay. Okay,*" I whisper to myself as I pace the room. No need to overreact until there's a reason to overreact. I answer just before my phone sends her to voicemail.

"Hello? Eva? Is everything all right?" I ask. I try not to sound too concerned but fail in doing so.

Eva squeals through the phone, just high-pitched enough that I can't tell if she's in pain or pure joy.

"Eva!" I yell. My palms sweat. Okay, now I sound desperate.

"I'm engaged!" she yells back. I don't respond. "Did you hear? I'm engaged!"

I drop my phone to my hip and exhale. *Engaged?*

"Emma? Are you there?" her voice vibrates against my thigh.

"Yes!" I finally say back. "Yes, I'm here. I heard. You're—you're engaged! Congratulations!" I say, despite the utter confusion and exhaustion taking over me.

I drop to the floor and rest my back against the edge of my mattress, tugging a blanket over my exposed legs.

"You don't sound too excited."

I can feel her disappointment through the phone. Eva is three years younger than me, and the epitome of a southern debutante. She's smart, but not too smart, perky, put-together, a God-fearing woman, and an amazing baker. Any man would be lucky to have her, but . . .

"No," I say. "It's not that. It's just . . . you caught me off guard." In more ways than one. "When you called so late, I thought something might be wrong. I'm just . . . readjusting and . . . yes, I'm very excited for you," I exhale.

"Well, you better be," she says. "Because you're my maid of honor!" she squeals again. I cringe at the sound.

"I would love nothing more," I tell her. "How *is* Bill?"

"Oh he's . . ." she begins what will undoubtedly be fifteen minutes of non-stop praise for her soon-to-be husband.

Bill is, well, I guess I can't say much about him. I've only met him once. After Beaux and I broke up, I spent a weekend in Presley, my hometown. At that time, he and Eva had just started dating, and my impression of him was perhaps jaded by my recent experience.

He's tall with blonde hair, dresses well, is a small-time kid from a neighboring town turned successful investment banker, and is six years older than Eva. Which, given the age difference between me and Beaux, may be the underlying cause for my lack of enthusiasm for the relationship. There are too many similarities for my comfort.

"He proposed in Natchitoches on the riverbank. Isn't that so romantic?"

"Yeah, yes," I say, tuning back in. "And that's where you two met, isn't it? He was a guest speaker in your Econ class?"

"Yes, he was," she says. Another five-minute rant sparked.

Am I wrong for approaching Bill and Eva's relationship with caution? Is it fair of me to question their engagement? I don't know Bill, so I shouldn't judge him, but it's because I don't know him that I worry. Besides, Eva is young and naïve, and even the people you *do* know can surprise you. A lesson I, unfortunately, had to learn the hard way.

"Eva," I say. Her name slips before I realize what I'm doing.

"Yeah?" I hear the caution in her voice. I'm sure the thought has come to her that I might not be the most supportive member of our family, considering my relatively recent breakup. And I want to prove her wrong, but . . . this is *so* fast and . . .

"Emma? Is that you? Isn't your sister's news just so exciting? They make the most gorgeous couple. And her ring! It's the size of a small blueberry," my mother exclaims.

Anne Marshall speaks into the phone without giving me room to answer. I see what she's doing and more importantly, what she's asking me not to do. *Don't ruin this, Emma, like you ruin everything else. Don't rob your sister of her happiness just because you robbed yourself of your own.* In so many words, that's exactly what's she saying. How do I know this? Because when I *did* spend that weekend in Presley and explained that Beaux and I had called off the wedding, she blamed me.

To her, Beaux was the most perfect, gorgeous man that she'd ever seen. Now, she speaks of Bill in the same way. She was so happy for me, proud of me, because nothing else in my life was worth her pride, and I threw it all away. And that's why I didn't tell her the truth about what happened between me and Beaux. I didn't even tell her the PG version, which was that he cheated. Who can say if she would've even believed me if I had? Or worse, what if she blamed me for that too?

I knew she would take our breakup hard, but I could barely get it out of my mouth before she was jumping down my throat. We haven't talked since.

"Hi, Mom," I say, forcing civility. I don't answer any of her prompts.

"Eva," my mom says. "Why don't you give me and your

sister a moment. She sounds tired, anyway. You and I can look through the wedding magazines when I hang up."

"Okay!" Eva says.

I imagine the smile on my sister's face, and the image tugs at my heart. Not because it makes me sad, but because I know the happiness she feels now won't last, and I don't want to see her broken the way I was, the way I still am.

"Goodnight, Emma," she says. "And keep your phone close by. Bill and I want a quick engagement, so the wedding planning will happen fast. I need you available for input."

"I will do that," I say. "Goodnight, Eva."

Eva hands the phone back to my mother and I bite my lip in restraint.

"So, how have you been?" my mom asks. "It's been a while." I sense the disappointment in her voice, perhaps even a bit of sadness. I close my eyes as I speak.

"Nine months. And I'm . . . I'm good," I lie. "I'm working a lot and—"

"Well, isn't that nice?" she says, cutting me off.

"Yeah, um," I stutter. "Yeah, I guess."

There's a moment of silence between us. Neither one of us knows what to say. In all honesty, I miss my mom. I missed her long before Beaux and I ever even met. It just so happened to be that my being with Beaux is what gave us common ground. Now that he's gone, her judgement is more present than ever—or it would be if we were talking to each other.

A relationship between a mother and daughter shouldn't be built on the shoulders of a man, be it Beaux, or be it my father. My father has always encouraged me to have a better relationship with her, to end all of this conflict. But even he can't fix this problem.

"Well . . ." my mother says, breaking our silence. "How are you otherwise?"

My lips lift into a small smile. Is this a genuine inquiry as to my mental state?

"I'm . . . well, I'm not really sure what I am," I say. "This last year has been hard. It's been strange learning how to be alone again, single, among other things."

"Well, maybe if you're still feeling sad about everything with Beaux, then it's a sign you should reach out to him. I mean, maybe you just got cold feet and you're fighting that reality," she says. "You know, I didn't tell you, but we didn't cancel the deposit at the venue."

"*What?*" Sharp pains shoot up my neck to my temple. My head throbs.

"We moved the date," she reveals. "If you reconcile now, you'll still have plenty of time to prepare for an October wedding. Oh, the weather in New Orleans would be beautiful then. Not too humid and . . ."

"Mom, stop."

"Excuse me?"

"I said, stop," I tell her. "Is that what you've been telling everyone up there? That we postponed the wedding?"

She doesn't answer, which is all the answer I need.

"Mom, when will you accept that Beaux and I are over?"

My throat feels tight just saying his name. But for some reason, it's unavoidable when it comes to my mother, which is a huge reason why I've refrained from talking to her.

"Oh, Emma," she says. "You two were so perfect. And Beaux was just fascinated with you. I'm sure if you wanted . . ."

"But I don't want it, Mother," I say, cutting her off. "I don't want him. I don't want anything to do with him. And, quite frankly, I never want to hear his name cross your lips again."

There's a brief pause before my mother responds.

"*Fine.* Just . . . just promise me one thing," she begs.

"I won't ruin Eva's wedding," I tell her. "I won't be a Negative-Nancy or a Debbie-Downer. I won't express to her I think she's too young and they haven't been together long enough. I won't explain to her that the older you get the more you know what you want, and the longer you're with someone the less perfect they appear."

My mom breathes heavy in the phone and I imagine she drops it to her side just as I did earlier.

"I'm sorry," I say. "I realize none of that is helpful," I admit.

"No, it's not," my mom says. "And yes, if you could keep your thoughts to yourself, I would much appreciate it. Your sister is happy, and Bill is a nice guy."

"Yeah," I scoff. "I thought Beaux was too." *Oh no!* I cover my mouth with my hand. Thankfully, my mom doesn't engage my slip-up.

"Look," my mom says. "I don't know what happened between you and Beaux, but things are simpler in these parts. There's no hustle and bustle, no long hours, long distance—"

"No time to second guess the most important decision of your life," I say, cutting her off.

Again, my mother exhales.

"Sometimes all time does is allow the Devil to creep into your mind and distort what you know in your heart," my mother says.

It's a nice thought, but is it really true?

"Eva knows she loves Bill, and she doesn't want to waste any time in a state of limbo. After all, we saw how a long engagement treated you and Beaux," my mother says. I roll my eyes at her remark and fight the urge to disconnect the line.

"Eva and Bill are getting married the last weekend in May," she reveals.

"The last weekend in May?" I yell. "That's like two months away. How . . .? How can you even plan a wedding in two months? When is she even supposed to get a dress?"

"Well, that's what she and I will figure out tonight," my mother says. "Eva and I will share more details with you as we figure them out."

"O . . . kay." My shock is undeniable. Both because my sister, the southern belle she is, is going to put together a wedding in *two* months, *and* because my mother, the Mistress of Wedding Planning herself, is allowing it to happen.

"This is a good thing, Emma," she assures me. "Remember that. Goodnight, dear."

"Goodnight, Mom."

The line goes dead and I'm left in koala pajamas on my

bedroom floor, stunned, listening to the sounds of Kat and Demetri making love in the shower we share.

* * *

In need of fresh air and a distraction from what is apparently my life, I head to Mimi's, another one of mine and Kat's favorite spots. It's about a fifteen-minute walk from our place and is home to the best live music and tacos in New Orleans.

Inside, exposed brick walls lined with large, black framed windows surround me. On the lower level, bodies move back and forth to the tunes of an acoustic guitar. I recognize the musician as one of Kat's favorites.

"Upper or lower?" the hostess asks.

"Upper," I tell her. She grabs a table menu and leads me up the metal staircase to the upper lounge, where the food is served and the views of the stage are the best.

"Will anyone be joining you?" she asks as I take a seat at a highboy table overlooking the stage.

"No," I say. "It's just me."

She smiles and takes away the empty water glass and extra napkin opposite me. The simple action sends a sharp pain through my chest.

On the night of my little sister's engagement, I'm alone at a bar. And if that isn't painful enough, I don't trust myself to uphold the promise I made to my mother. I don't trust myself to keep my opinions to myself. And that breaks my heart, because if Beaux had never . . . if he had never cheated, if he had never hit me, if he had never broken me, I wouldn't be so jaded. I . . . I would still believe in love, in the concept of honorable men, and I . . . I could be the maid of honor—the *sister* Eva deserves.

Tears fill my eyes, blurring my vision. I'm not sad. *I'm not.* I'm angry, angry that among everything else, Beaux gets away with this too. I wipe the wetness from my eyes with the inside of my black t-shirt and wave the waiter down as he passes.

"Hey, can I get a margarita on the rocks with salt and the chicken tacos," I ask.

"Sure thing," he says.

I adjust my chair, yank my jeans up to make sure my behind doesn't show, and put my cellphone on silent in my purse.

"All right, this next performer is new to our stage. All the way from Los Angeles, California, please welcome Julian Cole on the violin."

I turn at the announcer's remarks and watch as Julian, dressed in the same black t-shirt and ripped jeans as earlier, takes a seat underneath the spotlight and begins to play.

CHAPTER 6

I am entranced by Julian. Well, his music. It's soft, tortured, and tangible. As he moves his bow back and forth across the strings of his instrument, triceps clenched, jaw sharp, the music moves around me. It caresses me and forms a warmth in my chest and a swelling of tense emotion in my cheeks. I want to cry, like *really* cry.

He doesn't make eye contact with the audience. Instead, his eyes are closed, and he moves his head back and forth with the movements of his bow. The bodies on the dance floor beneath me mimic his movements. In an eloquent symphony, they dance.

The waiter comes and places my drink in front of me. I grab it and sip at it mindlessly without removing my eyes from Julian. He's a musician, a true musician, the kind who moves people without a word.

"Hey! Is this seat taken?" I turn at the unexpected, husky voice. Across from me stands a red-faced man with bulging drunken eyes.

"Yes," I tell him. I move my gaze back to Julian.

"Oh, really?" he says, pulling the stool out. I cringe, closing my eyes. "Because it doesn't seem like it," he slurs.

I fight through the pit in my stomach and turn to face him once more, placing my drink on the table between us. "Well, it is," I say, attempting to add more bass to my voice. "Please leave."

"Oh, now you don't mean that," he says, plopping down. He smells, and not just like alcohol. My head throbs and my fingers tingle as he moves closer to me.

"I assure you, I do," I say, but it's no use. He's firmly planted on the stool across from me and doesn't look like he plans to move anytime soon. If he takes another sip of the half-empty glass of beer he's holding, he won't be able to stand even if his manners return to him.

I groan and reach for my purse, which sits in the middle of the table. He places a heavy hand over mine. It's wet with sweat and sends electricity racing through me—*not* the good kind.

"Now, where do you think you're going?" His words twist my insides into knots and draw the sweat from my pores. My cheeks flush.

"Away from you," I scold him. I snatch my hand from underneath his and grab my purse. I didn't even get my tacos.

I get up and make my way toward the staircase, checking my peripheral to make sure he doesn't follow me. Perhaps his level of intoxication will work in my favor.

Reaching the staircase, I give Julian one last glance. He's just finished his third and final song of the night. Finally looking up to the crowd, everyone cheers and gives him a standing ovation. He smiles, and it is a gorgeous smile. It reaches his icy eyes, creating small lines. And with one swift movement, those eyes lock with mine and unlike earlier, I don't look away. Neither does he.

* * *

Outside Mimi's, I walk quickly in the direction of home, fumbling for my cellphone in my purse. Kat and I have a rule that if either of us is out at night alone, we call each other. Attackers are less likely to act if the person is on the line with someone who could call for help. Finally, I find it, but am disappointed to see I only have ten percent battery remaining. *Really, Emma?*

"Hey, sexy! Wait up!" I turn to see the red-faced guy from the bar along with two equally intoxicated friends following behind me. They have sickening grins on their flushed faces that only tell me one thing. *Run!*

I walk quickly and hook a right, scanning the street for neon *Open* signs.

"Public place. Public place," I say to myself. *Nothing.* Everything is closed. My throat begins to close as panic takes over. I gasp, lifting my hand to my throat as if it will allow me to get more air. It doesn't.

I look behind me and see the three of them round the corner. *No!* I turn forward and, pushing through the panic, take off running through the scarce puddles of light. The few drunken pedestrians wobbling along turn and watch me. Unfortunately, even if they wanted to help, they couldn't.

As I run, I remember back to last week. I read about this girl, a few years younger than me, who'd left a bar alone. Her body was found discarded in a dumpster, beaten and mutilated. She'd been . . .

Beaux straddles me, forcing me into the bed with all his weight. My blood turns to ice as his eyes go dark. He looks at me with a ferocious lust that is foreign, angry, and . . . evil. I barely have enough air left in my lungs to breathe, let alone scream, as . . .

"No, no, no!" I scream. I lift my hands to my head as if to zap the memory from my mind. My vision starts to fade. My ears begin to ring. All I hear are the three men's heavy footsteps, their sadistic laughter, and my labored breaths.

I gasp for air as my legs grow heavy. Blood rushes to my brain as my endurance wanes. For obese drunkards, they move quickly. I hook another right and . . .

"Woah!" he says.

"Ah!" I scream, tumbling into the warm body of a stranger. I shove him with the little energy I have left to create distance and ready my fists for . . . *Julian?*

"*Emma?* You okay?" he asks, reaching out to steady me.

"I . . ." I begin but can't force out the words. *Oh no.* I stumble toward the brick wall of the nearest storefront for balance.

"Emma?" Julian moves with me, placing his hand on my back for support. "Emma, what's happening?"

"Run," I choke.

Once more, our eyes lock. Though my vision starts to blur, I see a ferocity in him that both surprises me and extends a level of comfort I haven't felt before. His forehead crinkles. His bright eyes blaze. And suddenly, he moves from my side, leaving his violin case at my feet.

My stomach twists in stabbing agony as Julian leaves me. I force myself to turn in his direction, hands on my knees.

He stands with his arms crossed and the same steel in his eyes he just shared with me as he stares down my approaching stalkers. I want to tell him to run and that it's not worth it. There are three of them and two of us. And considering I can't even stand straight, I can't imagine being much help if it comes to a fight.

What is he thinking?

"Gentleman," he says as they inch closer. Their clumpy footsteps grow louder as they approach. I can't see them, but I see their shadows, quite large shadows. I gulp down the salvia pooling in my mouth and try to force myself to a standing position.

"Hi, uh," one begins. "Have you seen our friend? Blonde headed girl, black t-shirt, nice ass?" They chuckle.

My chest tightens as they speak, and I manage to take a step back.

"Yeah, you're no friends to her," Julian says. "Now, I suggest you head back the way you came. We don't want any trouble, do we?" he asks, letting his arms drop from his chest to his sides.

His fists ball and clench, putting the muscles of his forearms and biceps on full display. The simple movement reveals his tattoos in a way I didn't notice before. There are more of them—a lot of them. The flickering flame of the gas lantern above him illuminates the images on his arms in a way that's mysterious and . . . intimidating. The question is, will they take the warning or are they too wasted to care?

I hear mumbles that I can't make out and finally, the shadows turn and disappear. I realize then I've been holding the little breath I have and give in to the exhaustion of my muscles.

I exhale and drop to the aged concrete beneath me, resting my head against the cool brick of the building behind me. If I had the energy, I'd hate myself for leaving the house, for putting myself, *and Julian,* in this position. But as it is, I don't have energy for anything other than regulating my lung's exertion and ignoring the smell of dirty seawater and sewer that invades my being.

Beaux opens my bedroom door. Light pours into the room, illuminating his frame as he exits. He walks tall, calm, and disconnected. Kat screams and throws a lamp at him. It shatters into a million pieces as it hits the hardwood floor. Beaux pays her no mind, nor the small cut she managed to give him. As his frame disappears from view, I close my eyes, giving into the numbness. He pays the brokenness no mind, not of the lamp or of me. And he has no idea what he's done.

Tears flood my face as my exhaustion disables my defenses. All these memories I'd locked deep inside me . . . I shake my head in an attempt to forget them once more.

Julian, eyes focused on the backs of the three men, doesn't move from his watchdog position until he's certain they won't return. I wonder what I would have done had he not been here to intervene. Would I have fought them off, or at least tried to? Would I have given in in the hopes they'd spare my life? As it stands, I'm not sure I have much of a life left to take.

My eyes close and behind them images of the dead girl's body flicker like the gas flame along with the face of a boy with black hair and icy green eyes.

"They're gone," Julian breathes, dropping to his knees beside me. "You're safe now," he says.

I roll my head to face him. His eyes scan my tear-drenched face as if looking for signs of damage. He wants to help me. But he doesn't know the signs to look for or the enemy I truly face.

"I will never be safe," I tell him then.

His forehead crinkles and his eyes narrow. I look away from him then.

Regaining control of my body, I finally say, "And you're crazy."

"What? What do you mean?" he asks. As he speaks, the crinkle returns to his forehead while the intensity leaves him.

"You were outnumbered, *heavily* outnumbered," I say,

emphasizing that a single one of them could have crushed him. "Why did you risk getting hurt for . . .?" I stop myself before finishing my question. What he did was stupid, not heroic, and I won't allow my choice of words to say otherwise.

"*For you?*" he interjects.

I turn to him then. His lips draw up into a playful grin, and his cheeks allow the slightest hint of pink. Like his music, his grin is intoxicating.

"Yeah, I mean, in general," I say. My attempt to ease the tension between us doesn't work as his grin transforms into an all-out, teeth-bearing smile.

"Well, it was simple. Either I get hurt or you do," he says, moving his eyes from mine. "It was the neighborly thing to do." At that, we both laugh, and I imagine what Kat would do if she could see me now, rather see *us*. It's then that I realize how close our bodies are and . . .

"On that note, I think I've overstayed my welcome at the Concrete Inn. I'd better get going," I say, pushing myself to a standing position.

"*Seriously?*" Julian asks, standing to tower over me.

"What?" I ask. Taking a step back, I cross my arms over my chest.

"You really think I'm letting you walk home alone?" he asks.

His eyebrows raise as he speaks, and I find it strange how normal the small movement makes me feel. I guess because Kat and I often share quizzical looks with one another. Mostly so when we think the other one is doing something incredibly stupid. And I guess he's right—just because I escaped one set of prowlers doesn't mean there aren't more lurking. Home is still ten minutes away.

"Fine. I guess the smart thing to do *would* be to walk together. We are going to practically the same place, so, let's walk," I say, turning on my heels. I don't wait around for more banter. I'm queasy as it is. But I'd be lying if I said Julian's presence doesn't give me at least a little bit of comfort.

Julian grabs his violin case from the sidewalk, slings it over his shoulder, and moves in stride with me.

* * *

The air around us is thick with humidity and the silence between us. It makes my hair stick to my exposed neck, and my fingers swell as blood rushes to them. It seems so long ago that I watched Julian play his violin, even longer that my sister told me she was engaged, and my mother begged me not to ruin it for her.

"God," I say aloud, lifting my eyes to the starry sky.

"What's wrong?" Julian asks. He turns his head to face me.

"Nothing," I breathe. "Just . . . thinking," I tell him, which isn't a lie.

"Just thinking is code for 'my mind is about to explode but I have no idea how to begin telling this total stranger about my life-and-death dilemma,'" Julian says.

I turn to him and this time, I'm the one with a brow raised. *Who is this guy?*

"Close?" Julian asks, mimicking my motion.

"Okay," I say, forcing my eyes ahead. "First of all, don't act like you know me. Second, it's not life and death. Though, I guess it depends on who you ask." Like my mother and Eva. "And finally, I wouldn't be walking home with you if you were a *total* stranger."

"Even though we live next door to one another?" he asks.

"Yes," I nod. "Even though we live next to door to one another. But you're right," I tell him. "I . . . I don't know where to begin or if I even should. I just . . . I have a lot going on right now and tonight didn't help any of it. I didn't even get my tacos," I mumble.

"Tacos?" Julian asks.

"Yeah, Mimi's has the best tacos and I like to eat them when . . . when I have a lot on my mind," I exhale. "Guess that drunk asshole was a sign from God I need to cut the carbs or at least, stop trying to escape every major problem I have," I reveal before I can stop myself. "Um," I stop walking. "Can you pretend I didn't just say that?"

"If that's what you want," Julian says, taking one step in front of me. "But for the record," he says, turning to face me. "I don't think God sends signs in the form of drunk assholes, and I certainly don't think you need to cut the carbs."

I bite the inside of my mouth to keep from smiling, but it's no use. "It *is* what I want, thank you," I say, moving past him. He smirks and follows beside me.

"On the bright side, I did get to hear you play," I tell him, glancing between him and the sidewalk ahead.

"That's a bright side?"

"Your modesty is cu . . . nice," I tell him. "But yes, it was. I was honestly impressed." He returns my compliment with a coy expression. "*As a journalist* who covers the culture scene of a city known for its music, I was impressed," I clarify. "Though, I will admit, surprised."

"How so?" he asks, dropping his head.

"Well, I—I hope this doesn't come off as ignorant, but I'm surprised someone from LA plays that well and . . . with that much pain," I say. My voice grows soft. Did I just cross a line?

He smiles a small smile, more to himself than to me, and the flutter in my stomach subsides.

"Well, I guess you're not the only one whose mind is plagued by the unspeakable," he whispers.

"I guess not."

Porch lights welcome us home. The TV in the living room illuminates Kat and my cottage. I better keep this quick before she sees me with Julian.

"Well, um, thank you—"

"Listen, Emma," Julian cuts me off.

"Yeah?"

"I was just going to say, um . . ." Julian fidgets, shoving his hands in his jean pockets. "I know tonight was crazy and probably not how you planned on spending it, but maybe one good thing came of it," he says.

"And what's that?" I ask, watching him closely.

"I know you don't want to talk about it now and I get that. Trust me, I do," he says. "But . . . if that changes, and for some reason Kat isn't cutting it, well, at least you know you have another friend close by."

His words shake me. I can't tell if he's trying to assert himself into my life after knowing me for less than twenty-four hours or if he's placing himself permanently in the friend zone? And I'm not sure which one pisses me off more. Even more so, I'm not sure I'm comfortable with caring.

"Emma? Did you hear me?"

"Yeah, um," I take a step back. "The thing is, we're not friends," I tell him. "You—you played beautiful music and I complimented you on it. And when I was at risk of being attacked, you stepped in, like any decent human being would. And we walked home together, because we live next door to one another. So, we're not friends. We're neighbors. *Neighbors*," I tell him, as I push the gate open.

"Is this you running away from another problem?" he asks. His lips draw into the playful smile I've come to love.

"*You* are *not* a problem," I assure him. "You're my neighbor, *a* neighbor," I tell him, removing any sense of possession from my verbiage.

"All right, Emma," he says, taking the few steps necessary to reach his property. "Well, goodnight—*neighbor.*" He laughs.

I roll my eyes, fumble for my keys, and leave him to himself, slamming the door behind me.

CHAPTER 7

"*Crap!* Is there any coffee left?" I ask, stumbling out of my bedroom as I slip into my black, strappy heels.

"Woah! It's been a while since I've seen the stripper heels," Kat says as she slurps down her cereal. "What's the occasion?" she asks, nodding her head toward the half-full coffee pot.

"Oh! Thank God!" I groan, stomping across the kitchen to my only hope for survival. "I woke up late, *again*," I say, grabbing a thermos. "And I barely had time to review my notes for today's interview. Not that it matters," I mumble under my breath. I move to the fridge, grabbing the milk.

"Fran was adamant that this is meant to be a fluff piece, a welcome-to-the-neighborhood, ooey gooey sap story no matter the fact that we've had enough big business come in and take all the charm out of our Mom and Pop shops!" I find myself raising my voice and force myself to take a pause as I search for the sugar.

"Oh yeah!" Kat exclaims. "Today's your big interview with that music exec who bought Lucid."

"Yeah," I exhale, tossing way too much sweetener into the warm liquid. "And I wouldn't call it big as much as I would cheap." I turn to face her, leaning against the kitchen countertop.

Ever since Beaux and I broke up, I haven't felt safe traveling alone. I've been taking less and less assignments with Conde Nast and more here in the city. Which only amplifies my rage when a story like this is given to me. I went from traveling the world, immersing myself in different cultures, and telling the truth through an undiluted lens to being concerned with local politics and big business.

"You know, I love Fran, I do," I say. "But New Orleans is known for its rich musical history, and Lucid Records has been a privately-owned staple in our community for over a hundred years. It's not right for such an iconic legacy to be snuffed out by increased rent prices," I tell her. "*That's* the story I should be telling," I say, loud enough for Fran herself to hear.

I sip my coffee in the hopes it will calm me down. No such luck.

"I know," Kat says. Her blue eyes soften as she lets her spoon slip into the milk before her. "And I also know that Lucid was the first job you had when you moved to the city," she says with pause. "*And* that Mr. Turnip helped you get it."

I nod and exhale.

Kat and I met freshman year at Tulane, but it wasn't until sophomore year that she moved in with me. Freshman year was tough. I was alone in an incredible yet dangerous city. I had no friends. I barely had enough money to survive. My parents didn't approve of me attending college so far from home, so they didn't help much. But Mr. Turnip knew I was struggling, and he put in a good word for me with the owner at Lucid. That was the first time since leaving home that anyone showed me kindness. And Lucid quickly became my cornerstone. Without it, I'm not sure New Orleans ever would have felt like home. Well, it, *and* Mr. Turnip.

"I miss him," I tell her. My eyes move from the drink in my hand to my feet. My toes are like sausages about to split open under pressure. Red and achy, I already feel blisters forming.

"I know," Kat says once more. "But that's why this interview *is* big and why you're the best person to do it. You love Lucid and you appreciate its past. If you can't include it in your article, then maybe you could share it with the new owner," Kat suggests.

My lips lift into a small smile. Her words ease the pounding in my head, at least a little bit, and I take a moment to inhale the rich scent from my thermos. This is my favorite part of the day. Pure silence, caffeine, and warmth. It's a shame it doesn't last longer.

"And who knows? Maybe he won't be so bad," she says. And, like clockwork, moment over.

"*Yeah*," I scoff. "I'll carry that token in my back pocket, but the truth is, they're all the same. Men like . . ." I stop myself by biting my lip. I barely allow his name in my thoughts, let alone in the words I speak. I shake my head. "Anyway," I say, my forehead scrunching. "Men, powerful men, all they care about is money, because the money allows them to keep their power, their status. This guy will be no different," I tell her, taking another sip of my coffee.

"Well, I guess that explains the all-white power suit," she says, looking me up and down. "You only wear that when you have something to prove, and prove you will," she says, yanking open the fridge in search of more sustenance.

"Thanks, Kat," I mumble, remembering back to the last time I wore this suit. It was the day I first brought Beaux to my hometown to meet my parents and in that moment, I *did* have something to prove. Not that Beaux was a great guy or worthy of their approval, but that I was. I knew they'd love him. *Hell*, we've been broken up for nearly a year and my mom still prays we'll reconcile. But me? I was the one who left town to escape their proverbial watchful eye, who had the courage to do things her way, who gave up the security of family money, and who chose not to return after graduation. I'd gone my own way, and I was determined to prove to them that I was right and I hadn't made a mistake in doing so.

In hindsight, I think that's why I looked past so many of Beaux's red flags. I wanted it to work, but maybe not for all the right reasons. I wanted to make them proud, even if it meant giving up a piece of myself to the accomplishment of marrying a powerful man and the life that would come with him. I loved him, don't get me wrong, but . . . I didn't require him to love me, not in the way I deserved at least. I thank God for revealing Beaux in all his horror, before it was too late. Still, I guess that's up for debate.

"You know, I think I'm going to change," I tell her. "I don't have anything I need to prove."

* * *

I swapped my heels for black flats and my white pant suit for black jeans and a navy blouse that's slippery on my skin. My feet thank me as I stroll down uneven sidewalks lined with mid-morning musicians and street art. Soft moans of the trumpet fill the thick air. I'm tempted to pile my hair on top of my head but decide against it for the sake of professionalism.

I see the music studio up ahead. With its bright blue exterior, it's impossible to miss. I can practically smell the old paper sleeves of the records and the dust piling up in the corner. Oh, and of course, the damp brick walls shrouding it all in salty darkness, with the exception of the hanging fluorescent lights.

The words that came out of my mother's mouth the day she discovered where I worked *almost* rival the words she spoke the day she found out I wasn't returning home after graduation. I can't say I was surprised. While college in the Crescent City intrigued me, I never planned on living here.

I wanted to come to New Orleans to expose myself to cultures untouched in my hometown of Presley. I wanted to meet new people, learn new things, become my own person and have my own life rather than the one my parents were ready to push me into. And I guess you could say I did what I set out to, a little too well, because when the time came to pack my bags and move back upstate, I didn't. I couldn't.

I found a family here in Kat and Mr. Turnip and the few others in our tight-knit circle. A family that didn't judge, without predetermined plans for me or expectations for how my life would turn out. I let go of everything that had been drilled into me since birth. And yet, somehow, I ended up with Beaux. The fact that my parents loved him should've been enough to send me running in the opposite direction. But after years of being a disappointment, it was nice to make them proud, nice to fit into their plans for once.

The night I broke things off with Beaux should've been the night my home felt like home again, but with Mr. Turnip's passing, Kat's new relationship with Demetri, and now the selling of Lucid, New Orleans has been anything but home since the night of my broken engagement.

I take a deep breath and push the swinging door open to splotchy, dull light. My eyes adjust as my ears find a familiar tune playing softly on the record player. The cracks and pops on the track take me back to early morning shipments. Lucid is a small shop, so there was only ever one worker at a time, maybe two during high tourist seasons. Half asleep, I'd lug in cardboard boxes filled with records and t-shirts. Pupils dilated, legs heavy, the only thing that kept me awake was the sizzle of the record dancing through the darkness.

A small smile lifts my lips and . . .

"Oh, Emma! Long time no see!" Mr. Edgar's raspy voice brings me from my memory. My eyes search the space for him.

"Mr. E!" I say, finally finding him. He stands next to the checkout bar wearing jeans, a white t-shirt, and a fedora as old as me.

"Oh, sweet child," he says as I cross the room and pull him in for a hug. "What have you been up to? Seems it's been forever, but you haven't changed a bit."

"Oh, well, don't let the makeup fool you. Wish I could say the same for you, though. I see a few more greys peeking out from underneath that cap since the last time I saw you," I tell him as I pull away.

"Oh now, don't you lie to an old man," he tells me. "You'll go straight to Hell." He wiggles his finger at me and we both laugh.

"So, what can I do you for?" he asks. "You know it's fitting you came in today. You'll be one of my last sales."

"*Last sales?*" I ask. My forehead wrinkles. "I thought . . . I thought you were staying on as manager even though . . ." I stop myself, unwilling to verbalize his wound.

"Even though I had to sell, yes," he mumbles, dropping his eyes to the concrete floor beneath us. "Yes, well, I was. But it's just too painful, too many memories," he admits. I nod. I know the feeling all too well.

"Anyway, the, uh, the new owner seems nice. *Well* . . ." He pauses. "Nice enough for someone who now owns your family's legacy. I just—I couldn't sit back and see this place torn to shreds like all the other local shops. Just couldn't stomach it."

I shake my head in frustration. My cheeks flush, red and hot.

"It's not fair," I say.

"Oh, sweet child," Mr. E says, placing his withered hand on my shoulder. "Don't you know by now that life isn't fair? If not, you will soon."

With that he moves past me and drags his fingers over a row of dust-topped albums. The dust fills the air, illuminated by the light hanging above it, and we both cover our mouths and noses.

It's an unspoken custom at Lucid. When the dust flies, don't complain—just cover your mouth and keep on working. It's perhaps the only thing this place and my hometown have in common and as such, I've been living by the ill-thought-out philosophy my entire life. It's exhausting and I'm this close to . . .

Mr. E's eyes shift to look behind me, and I'm suddenly aware of the footsteps drowning out the record player. My eyes squint. I purse my lips. To hell with professionalism. I spin on my heels, moving my hand to my hip. My mouth opens and— "Julian?"

CHAPTER 8

"Emma?"

Julian mimics my surprise as he makes his way from the storage loft to Mr. Edgar and me. "Is everything okay?" he asks, looking me up and down. My cheeks blush and I fail to answer out of pure shock. Is *he* the new owner? *There's no way!*

Julian's eyes and parted lips shift from surprise to concern in a matter of seconds, and I'm pulled from my confused state and reminded of our encounter last night—or rather, the encounter he rescued me from.

"Oh, *yes*," I finally say, waving off his concern. "I—I was just um . . ." I move my eyes to my shoes in an effort to regroup but am hardly given the chance before Mr. Edgar interjects.

"Wait," Mr. Edgar says. "You two know each other?"

Mr. Edgar looks between Julian and me with eyes yellowed from age. His cheeks, speckled with coarse gray hairs, light from within and before I can explain, he bursts into a fit of laughter.

"Mr. Edgar?" I ask, as the old man hunches over, eyes watering. Mr. Edgar waves his hand out to me as the laughter takes up much of his oxygen. Julian closes the distance between us and helps me get Mr. Edgar up right again.

"I'm fine, child, I'm fine," Mr. Edgar says, gasping. His hand shakes in mine, yet the light in his face still glows. "It's just . . . maybe there's hope after all," he says. My lips part in confusion, and I search his eyes for answers. What does he mean, hope after all? And what does my knowing Julian have to do with it?

Mr. Edgar gives me one last look and a nod of the head that tells me *thank you*. I know he's not one for emotions, and saying goodbye would be just too hard. I return the gesture with a nod and a slight squeeze of his hand. Tears blur my vision, but I fight through them. I won't make this moment any harder for Mr. Edgar than it already is.

He lets go of my hand and shifts his gaze to Julian. His lips fall into a flat line.

"Take care of my family's legacy, young one," he says to Julian. "Approach every day with a love for music and a respect for creativity."

He turns and gives the room one last look. Rows of records stand before us. Walls filled with memories surround us.

He turns back to us then. "And take care of the ones you love. Without family, without someone to share the fruits of your labor with, the job is just a job. And this place, this city, and those who step through that door, deserve better than that, you hear me?" Mr. Edgar asks Julian.

"Yes, sir," Julian responds and like yesterday, I hear a sincerity in his voice that surprises me. "I'll take care of her."

Julian's words ignite my body, and the hairs on my arms rise beneath the slippery fabric of my blouse. *Why?* I can't explain.

"Yes." Mr. Edgar nods. "I sure hope so." And, with that, he turns on his heels and slowly makes his way toward the exit. As the door swings shut behind him, the light in a room full of darkness, and a feeling of warmth leaves with him. He was right. It was never the place that was special. It was the people. It was him. It was Mr. Turnip. It was everything my life used to be that made this city home. With each person that leaves me, the more darkness surrounds me.

"Emma. *Emma?*"

Julian waves his hand in front of my eyes to pull me back to reality. He stands before me—hair high and tousled, wearing dark skinny jeans and a gray t-shirt so thin I can see the contour of his abs perfectly. He looks nothing like the big businessman I thought I'd find. Yet, he is. He's the new owner of Lucid, and *I* have to interview him.

I wipe the remaining wetness from my eyes on the inside of my shirt, clear my throat, and stand tall.

"Hi, I'm Emma Marshall," I say, extending my hand. "I'll be

interviewing you today on behalf of The Hub, New Orleans. Do you mind if I record this?"

Julian's cheeks flush, and a coy smile spreads across his lips. "Not at all," he says, his voice slightly deeper than usual. "I'm Julian Cole, co-owner of Cole Creative, Director of A&R for the label, and now owner/manager of the infamous Lucid Records here in New Orleans. Welcome to my world," he says, taking my hand in his.

* * *

Julian walks me through the small retail space, pointing out the areas he'd like to upgrade.

"The space is already small, and the fluorescent lights only make it appear smaller," he explains. "I'd like to remove them, do some recessed lighting, bust out a wall and add some windows for natural light. A fresh coat of paint wouldn't hurt either," he mumbles to himself. "And I'm sure you've noticed the cleanliness isn't really up to code, so I'll be initiating some new policies to ensure customers have a clean and organized shopping experience," he says, turning to face me.

He's very professional with his hands behind his back, perfect posture, and clear speaking voice. Yet, I can't help but feel a disconnect between the Julian I see now and the Julian I came to know yesterday. Frustrated, I pause my recorder and shove it in my back pocket.

"Something wrong, Ms. Marshall?" Julian asks, yet unlike before his face shows no sign of true concern. Rather, he's only asking out of obligation to appease the woman interviewing him. I exhale and move past him, creating more distance between us.

"No," I finally say. "It's just, I was wrong to think you'd be different. So was Mr. Edgar," I say with a nod. "I think I've got enough. Thank you for your ti—"

"Emma, wait," Julian says, blocking the exit. He exhales and shakes his head before moving his eyes to mine.

"So, it's Emma now?" I ask. "No more 'Ms. Marshall'?" I taunt, crossing my arms over my chest.

"You started it," he says, his voice low. I bite my lip. "Look,

I like Emma. I can talk to Emma. But Ms. Marshall?" He shrugs his shoulders. "Well, she brings out Mr. Cole, and Mr. Cole isn't exactly someone I like being. I mean, why do you think I volunteered to leave LA for some renovation mission any number of people could've handled?"

As he speaks, his mind drifts. His eyes glass over as he remembers back. The plumpness of life leaves his cheeks hollow.

"Well, why don't you tell me?" I ask. "And while you're at it, why don't you tell me what you love about this place, not just the things you want to change," I tell him, eyebrow raised.

Julian nods and meets my gaze with a smile. And just like that, the cold, matter-of-fact Mr. Cole is gone, and back is the soulful, compassionate violin player who just might have what it takes to run this place with honor.

"Well, the place has good bones, and the location is great," he tells me. "Paired with the musical history of New Orleans, the property is a unique asset for our record label. And even though it could use a few upgrades, I love the soul of this place."

His words catch my interest.

"Lucid has been the primary record shop in New Orleans for over one hundred years and, what many people may not know is that, in the twenties, it was home to a hidden speakeasy," Julian continues.

"What?" I ask, choking on dust. "I mean, I guess it's possible," I breathe, fanning the air in front of me. "But how would I not know that?"

"Well, it's not public record, nor common knowledge," Julian says, leaning against the checkout bar. "The family didn't include it in their records for fear of evidence that could be used against them. Mr. Edgar only recently discovered the hidden space when he had it inspected for listing."

I nod. "So . . . where is it?" I ask, looking around.

"Follow me," Julian says.

Julian leads me behind the checkout bar, down the hall toward the bathrooms. The lights above us flicker and, for some reason, the corridor feels smaller than when I worked here. Maybe it's just my proximity to Julian that makes it feel like the walls are closing in, pushing us closer together.

We reach the bathrooms, but instead of entering, Julian flips a light switch, which works as a doorknob to a secret staircase.

"Woah."

The wall separating the men's and women's restrooms shifts, and Julian pulls it open to reveal a staircase leading to straight darkness. "Are we . . . going down there?" I ask, half-wishing he says *no*.

"Of course we are. But you'll need to use your phone for light. There're no windows, and the electricity isn't up to code," he says, pulling his out.

"Okay," I say, feigning bravery.

It's not that I'm scared of the dark, it's just . . . a secret room that no one knows about and probably hasn't been inhabited in a hundred years. What if there're rats or dead people's bones or worse? What if Julian really is a serial killer? Sure, I meant it as a joke yesterday—well, sort of, but I never did run that background check. *Damn you, Emma!* If I live to see the outside of this record shop, that's the first thing I'm doing.

Julian leads the way and the old, wooden steps creak under his weight. I grab my phone from my back pocket, thankful that I charged it overnight, and shine the light at my feet.

"*Oh, God!* What is that smell?" I ask, covering my nose with my free hand.

"It's decades of mildew and water damage," Julian says. "We're having it cleaned as soon as we can, but because no one knew it was down here, hurricane water stood without being pumped out. We could've requested Mr. Edgar handle the cost before the sale was finalized, but God only knows how much it'll be. I didn't want him spending his retirement on this just so I could turn around and make money off it," he explains.

My eyes shift from the steps to the back of his head. My chest tightens.

"Thank you," I say.

Julian reaches the landing and turns to help me with the last few steps.

"For what?"

The small amount of light between us glistens against his icy green eyes so beautifully it's hard to look away.

"I, um . . ." I miss the last step and Julian is quick to catch me. His arms are tight around my waist, as are mine around his shoulders as I hang on for dear life. My head briefly rests on his chest, and I hear his heartbeat. It quickens as the distance between us closes. I pull away before the lines of professionalism and neighbordom are crossed.

"Um, thank you," I say, adjusting myself, "for that and, uh, for not taking Mr. Edgar to the cleaners."

I inhale, though the horrid smell surrounding us makes me regret it.

"*God, it's terrible!*" I say. Julian laughs. "I uh," I close my eyes as the odor sears them. "I know this place is a dump," I admit. "I mean I love it and so do the people of this city, but it does need work, and you definitely could've asked Mr. Edgar to take responsibility for it, or at least pay him less for the property, but um, you didn't. And I . . . I thank you for that," I tell him.

"Of course," Julian says. Though his forehead crinkles as if there's something else on his mind.

"What?" I ask, my voice muffled by my hand.

"It's just," Julian begins. "I'm just curious why you care so much, about this place, about Mr. Edgar?" he asks. "I mean it's obvious you two have history and that his last remarks were just as much about you as they were this place."

What? No. If he thinks that then that means he . . . He promised Mr. Edgar he'd take care of me. But that doesn't make . . . "Oh, no," I tell him, taking a step back. "I don't think so. He was just—this place meant everything to him, and he just wanted it left in good hands," I assure him.

Julian raises his eyebrow as if to say *yeah, right,* and I cave. Removing my hand from my nose, I brave the smell and—

"I used to work here," I reveal.

"What? *Really?*" Julian asks.

"Yeah," I exhale, letting my phone drop to my hip. "All

throughout college, even when I interned at The Hub," I tell him. "The guy who used to live in your house," I begin.

"Mr. Turnip," Julian interjects.

"Yes, um . . ." I'm pleased he remembered. "He helped me get the job. He and Mr. Edgar were good friends. And uh, they both looked out for me when—when I didn't really have anyone else," I admit, dropping my eyes to my feet.

"Emma—" Julian begins.

"What is that?" I ask. Big mistake. *Huge.* The light from my cellphone illuminates the soggy floor beneath us and the giant, and I do mean *giant*, rats surrounding us.

"Ah!" I scream.

I turn and race up the stairs, leaving Julian to fend for himself. I trip and crawl the last few steps to the open door.

Reaching the main level, I stand and shake my body to make sure nothing latched onto me.

"*Ew, ew,*" I say as I shiver.

My entire body feels wet, and the air conditioner of the main floor turns the moisture on my skin to ice.

Laughter precedes Julian as he makes his way up the creaky steps much slower than I did.

"Why are you laughing?" I yell into the darkness. "That was creepy!" I tell him as he comes into view.

"*That* was funny."

"Oh, yeah? Well, then this must be hilarious," I say as I slam the door shut, leaving him in rat-infested darkness.

"Oh, come on," Julian pleads. "Let me make it up to you."

I bite my lip to hold back laughter. "And *how* do you plan on doing that?" I ask, hands on hips.

"Let me take you to Mimi's. You never did get your tacos," he says. My smile falters, and I pull my arms up over my chest. Is he asking me . . .? "For the interview, of course," he says, his voice echoing from the other side of the wall.

My stomach grumbles, and my mouth waters for chicken tacos. And even though I'd never admit this out loud, I don't mind Julian's company.

"*Emma?*"

Realizing I haven't responded, I flip the light switch and pull open the secret door. Julian comes into view. His t-shirt and forehead are slightly damp from the moisture downstairs. Our eyes lock and I say, "For the interview."

CHAPTER 9

Mimi's is less crowded during the day than at night, and Julian and I quickly get a table overlooking the stage.

"I'll have a sweet tea and the chicken tacos," I say to the waiter. He nods and turns to Julian for his order.

"And I'll have the chicken tacos and a glass of red wine," he says, handing over his menu. The waiter leaves us and as if my expression demands an explanation, Julian replies, "*You're* on the clock, not me."

I laugh. "No, it's fine. Just know I'm not responsible for what you say while intoxicated and therefore, what ends up in my article," I tell him, tossing a napkin over my lap.

"Fair enough," he says, leaning into the table. The simple movement draws attention to his wrists and the bracelets that cover them. My lips part and I drop my eyes to my hands clasped beneath the table. My wrists too are shrouded in bracelets.

"So, um," I start racking my brain for article-related questions. "Sorry, I . . . I lost my train of thought."

He smiles and his eyes pierce mine through hooded dark lashes. "It's okay, Emma. I won't tell if we take a break from article talk. I mean, a girl has got to eat."

"I guess," I say, moving my eyes from him to the stage beneath us.

"So, what made you decide to work in a record store, if you don't mind me asking?" he says, drawing my attention back to him.

"Oh, um. Well, to be honest, it was more out of necessity than desire," I admit. "When I first moved to New Orleans for college, I didn't know anyone, and I didn't have much help from my parents. I couldn't afford to live on campus, and I honestly couldn't afford to live in the Marigny either, but it was safer than most areas I could afford," I explain. "But it wasn't long until I was drowning," I say, moving my eyes from him to my clasped hands.

"My choices were to either suck up my pride and give in to my parents, which meant moving back home and never thinking of doing anything for myself again, or find a way to make ends meet. That's when Mr. Turnip spoke to Mr. Edgar, and that was that. I'm sure in the short amount of time you spent with Mr. Edgar you can see how inspirational he is, how he's one with the music," I say with a smile. "He and Mr. Turnip allowed me to be one with myself and with that came a respect and appreciation for this city and the arts, an even greater one than I already had," I say with a nod.

"So, basically, before Mr. Turnip and Mr. Edgar, you were uncultured," Julian says in all seriousness.

"*What?* No!" I say, my voice rising in pitch. His flat lips break into a smile at my outburst. "No, I was—I was sheltered, at times I'd even use the word trapped. I used to think I'd never amount to anything but someone's daughter and then someone's wife and that scared me," I reveal. "So, I ran. But I don't know. I feel like I've been running for so long, I don't even know what I'm running towards anymore," I admit.

"Hmm," Julian muses. "And here I thought you had it all figured out."

"No one has it all figured out. Some people are just better at making it seem that way," I admit.

He nods and thanks the waiter as our drinks are delivered. I sip at my sweet tea and he at his wine. The small distraction gives me a moment to contemplate why I'm revealing so much of myself to him—another question I don't have an answer to.

He opens his mouth to ask me another question, but I beat him to the punch. I've got to get things back on track.

"You mentioned earlier that you volunteered to come to New Orleans and that you aren't fond of being *Mr.* Cole," I say. "Does that mean the Lucid project is just a distraction for you, or do you think you'll be here long term?" I ask. "Helping manage the store, after the renovations are done," I clarify.

Julian smiles. "Is this for you or your article?"

"Just answer the question."

He takes another sip of his wine and . . .

"I hope to be in the wonderful city of New Orleans for as long as possible, working hand-in-hand with my employees, and ensuring total customer satisfaction," he says in his "Mr. Cole" voice. "But, off the record," he says. My interest is peaked.

"I like the change of pace and scenery," he admits. "Maybe I *am* finding myself distracted in New Orleans, but that doesn't necessarily mean I'm going to rush back to LA when the honeymoon is over."

His words light my insides on fire, and I can't tell if it feels good or not.

"That's an interesting way of putting it," I say.

"How so?" he asks, leaning closer.

"Two orders of chicken tacos," the waiter says, placing two warm plates between us.

"Thanks," we both say.

Once again, we're left alone, but this time I don't feel the need to control the conversation. I do, however, feel the need to stuff my face.

"Look, no offense, but I've been dying for these since last night, so it may be ten minutes before I'm the respectable Emma you've briefly come to know," I say, mixing the Pico into my rice.

"Ha," he laughs. "Well, I look forward to getting to know the not-so-respectable Emma and seeing what these tacos are about."

"They're best dipped in sour cream and a pop of jalapeño in each bite," I tell him as I suck down my first bite.

"Oh, I'm lactose intolerant," he says. I raise an eyebrow and watch as he discards the cheese and sour cream from his plate. "*What?*" he asks, noticing me staring.

"You poor soul," I tell him, before taking another bite.

Julian swaps the dairy products for Pico, peppers, and

guacamole and moans in agreement that these are in fact the best tacos he's ever had.

"I told you," I say.

For the first time in what feels like forever, I feel at ease. Maybe it's the tacos. Maybe it's the adrenaline from almost being eaten alive by giant rats. Maybe it's just Julian? He doesn't know about my past. He doesn't know about Beaux or what happened the night we broke up, and I like that. But I still don't know enough about him to let my—

As if sensing my moment of reprieve, the Devil strolls through the doors of Mimi's hand-in-hand with the woman at the center of our demise.

"*Emma?*" Julian asks, noticing the change in my body. "Are you okay?"

I turn, searching for an exit or hiding place. There's nowhere to escape to. I can't . . . I can't do this. I can't see him. I haven't seen him since . . . My hands begin to shake, and I drop my taco to my plate. My cheeks turn pale. My lips quiver.

"I—I . . ." I start, but I am unable to form a complete sentence.

My eyes find Beaux once more and as if paralyzed, I'm unable to look away. He walks, hand-in-hand with a brunette woman wearing a red dress. It's the same dress I found on the floor of Beaux's apartment right before opening his bedroom door to reveal her naked body on top of his. His blonde hair is slicked back. He wears a gray suit with a white button-down shirt. It makes his deep blue eyes even bluer.

"*Emma?*" Julian says again, following my line of sight as I watch Beaux and his new girlfriend walk up the stairs.

My heart pounds in my chest as my blood rushes to my head. I lift my hands to my head as it begins to pound.

"Emma? Is there a problem? Is that guy . . .?" Julian begins, but I cut him off.

"Shhh," I say, managing to lift a shaky finger to my lips. It's then that I notice my face is wet, wet with tears that won't stop.

The room grows quiet. All I hear is my rapidly beating heart and the sound of Beaux's Gucci loafers pounding against the metal of the staircase. *What am I going to do? He can't see me. I can't see him! I can't . . . I can't do this!*

Before I realize what's happening, Julian stands before me. He moves his hand to my cheek and wipes a falling tear. His eyes search mine for the truth, for clarity, for permission. And just as Beaux reaches the platform, Julian's lips crash into mine, blocking me from his sight.

Our lips move effortlessly together, soft, gentle, and yet completely intoxicating. I consider pulling away. After all, this doesn't make sense. I'm not ready for this at all. But . . . I don't. I let Julian kiss me. I let him tilt my chin up so he can slip his tongue into my mouth. I let him move his hands up and down my back. I let him shield me from Beaux, who makes his way to his table none the wiser.

When Julian pulls away, my body begs for more, but my mind knows not to ask for it. Somewhere in the middle of our moment, my tears dried, and no new ones fell. My heart rate steadies, as does my shaking body. And for a brief moment, I forget about Beaux and the woman in the red dress.

"What do you say we get out of here?" Julian asks, breathless. Unable to speak, I nod and allow Julian to help me down the stairs.

* * *

I push through the wrought-iron gate and take the steps two at a time until I reach the front door. I fumble for my keys. My body is weak after sprinting the whole way home.

I told Julian I'd wait outside for him to pay, but I couldn't. After the adrenaline of our kiss wore off, I couldn't stay one more second within fifty yards of Beaux. And not to mention, *what the hell was that?*

I fall through the front door, scaring Grey as she lounges on the couch. "Sorry, sweets," I say through labored breaths. I slam the door shut behind me, locking it, and drop to my knees.

It won't be long until Julian shows up at my door and I have no idea what to say. *What can I?* He can't know about Beaux, about our engagement, my . . . He just can't know. Everything will change and I was just starting to feel comfortable with him, with myself. But he's not stupid. He saw what happened when Beaux came in, how I reacted. He kissed me to save me, but . . . what if it was more than that? Part of me wants it to be. Unfortunately, I confiscated my body's right to make decisions for me a long time ago. And my mind knows this isn't right, not right now at least.

Knock, knock, knock. "Emma! Are you there?" Julian calls through the door.

I gasp at the sound of his voice, covering my mouth with my hand. Grey watches me from across the room and hisses at the door. She thinks she's a guard cat.

"Emma, look, if you can hear me, I didn't mean to overstep. I just . . . I saw you were upset, and that guy obviously had something to do with why. I just wanted to help. I . . . I hope this doesn't ruin anything between us. I know we're just neighbors," he concedes. "Of course, after today, maybe we could change that to just friends?"

I hear him sigh through the door. I take a deep breath to calm myself. He's just as confused as I am.

Gathering my strength, I push myself up from the floor and work up the courage to face him.

Julian turns, surprise washing over him as he sees me.

"Emma . . ." he starts, but I stop him.

"Julian," I say, raising my hand. "We *are* neighbors." He nods, though I can't ignore the disappointment in his features. "*And* friends," I admit. At that, his eyes meet mine with a renewed hope that I wish I had more of. "It's because of both that we can't talk about what happened today, at Mimi's, ever again."

He nods.

"We had excellent tacos after a professional interview. No one worth mentioning showed up, nor did anything of an intimate nature occur," I clarify.

Again, he nods. I exhale. And just when I think I'm in the clear, he says, "If that's what you want."

CHAPTER 10

"I'm not going," I grumble into my pillow.

"*Yes, you are!*" Kat says, struggling to pull me out of bed by my legs.

It's been a week since I last saw Julian. Well, a week since I last saw anyone. After Mimi's, I did my best to avoid him and anyone who might ask too many questions, namely Kat. *Why?* Because I have no idea what to say. The kiss was unexpected at best and incredible at worst. I *can't* have feelings for Julian—not yet, maybe not ever. The scars from my last relationship take precedence over any desires I may have for a new one. And if Kat caught the slightest whiff of something between me and Julian, it would inevitably lead to the fact that Beaux is the reason we shared a kiss. And that can of worms is even more complicated than the first.

"Uh!" I groan. I move the covers off me and push myself to a standing position. I knew my shot at getting out of Friday night drinks was slim.

"Fine," I tell her, "but don't act funny when I have nothing to say."

"Oh, you'll have something to say," she tells me. Her tone makes me feel like a child again. My mother used a similar one when forcing me to go to pageants and social dinners I couldn't have cared less about.

"You've been quiet and scarce all week," she says, ripping through my dresser. "You know what that tells me?"

"Nope," I say, adjusting my bun.

Kat turns to face me. Her coral lips droop in disappointment. "You're hiding something and from *me* of all people," she says.

Her blue eyes look even bluer when she's upset. She drops her head and returns to my dresser in search of something way too revealing.

"And I don't like secrets, Emma. And I don't want you to feel like you have to go through life alone. That's why we started Friday nights at Brocatos in the first place," she tells me, as if I need reminding.

"I know," I tell her, exhausted.

"So, put on your big-girl pants and get ready to drink up and tell all," she says, tossing a pair of ripped, black skinny jeans at my face. I slip them on while she searches for a shirt.

"*Oooh*, how long have you had this?" she asks, holding a silk silver tank top. It's backless and barely has enough chest coverage for a fourteen-year-old.

"High school," I tell her, snatching it away. "And no, I'm not wearing it. I don't even know why I still have it. I bought it sophomore year to get back at my mom for pimping me out to the senator's son. I told her if she wanted to treat me like a slut, I might as well dress like one too. She nearly fainted when I came down the stairs in it."

"Well, Mama Marshall may not have approved, but I sure do. You should wear it," she says, plopping down on the edge of the bed. "I mean it's not like anyone here is going to scold you, and you should take pride in your body, in your sexy woman-ness," she tells me.

I nod, moving the thin fabric between my fingers. "Maybe next week," I tell her.

Kat approves of my more conservative, all-black look as long as I let my hair down. Apparently, it looks sexier that way. I oblige and we head to Brocatos, our Friday night spot since senior year of college.

* * *

Brocatos is dark, the only light coming from ancient glass chandeliers and the row of windows looking out on the water. Unlike Mimi's, there's no live music and no clusters of humans swaying to the beat. Soft tunes play from the speakers overhead. Booths line the exterior wall overlooking the gulf with small bar tables filling up the rest of the space. I inhale as the chef prepares my favorite crawfish dip.

"Emma! Kat!" Ethan and Kris wave to us from our regular booth.

"Hey!" Kat squeals. "And they already have the apps and first round," she whispers to me.

"Gotta love their punctuality," I whisper back.

I met the blonde haired, brown-eyed Ethan sophomore year when I started helping out in the theater department. He's charming, sarcastic, completely in love with his boyfriend, Marcus, and an amazing actor. He was just cast in the off-Broadway production of *My Fair Lady* here in New Orleans. The three of us met Kris junior year when she harassed us at the cafeteria to sign a petition against racial segregation in on-campus Greek communities. Her name starting with a K sealed the deal for Kat, and the four of us have been best friends and weekly drinking buddies ever since.

"Nice of you to show up," Kris says as Kat and I take our seats.

"Emma and I had a disagreement on attire this evening. Not to mention she wanted to bail altogether," Kat reveals.

"*What?*" Ethan and Kris say in unison.

"It's fine. *I'm* fine," I assure them. "Let's just talk about something else," I say, downing the purple shot in front of me.

The three of them watch as the purple liquid sets my throat ablaze. I open my mouth to suck in air, but it only makes it hurt worse.

"Oh, God! What the hell was that?" I ask, finally catching my breath.

Ethan and Kris look at each other.

"It's called Purple Death, honey," Ethan says. "We were waiting to see which one of you would be stupid enough to try it first. Looks like we both lost."

"Hey!" Kat yells, and the three of them laugh. If it weren't for the instant buzz, I'd be angry. Nevertheless, I join them in their fun, fully aware that I'm not making it out of this bar without saying something I'll regret.

Three drinks later, I can barely feel my toes or sit up straight in my seat. It's not like me to drink this much. Maybe my subconscious believes Kat will be forced to bring me home early if I get too intoxicated. Or, at a minimum, anything I say can't be taken as truth if I can't even remember saying it. Either way, I win. At least until the hangover hits tomorrow morning.

"Uh," I moan. Just the thought of my head hanging over the toilet makes me wish my head was over a toilet.

"What's wrong, sweetie?" Kat asks, moving her arm around me to help hold me up.

"I just . . . I don't feel good," I say. My vision blurs and I force my eyes closed to help with the dizziness.

"She needs food. Waitress?" Ethan calls. "Can you take these away and bring us a Ginger Ale, Gatorade, and a generous helping of the macaroni and cheese?"

"Yeah, sure thing," the waitress says. Though my eyes are closed, I can feel hers on me. "I'll bring some bread too."

"Thank you," Kris says.

"It's okay, Emma," Kat says. "Just lean into me. We'll get you feeling better real quick." I lean into her and inhale the strawberry scent of her skin.

"You smell nice," I mumble with a smile. "You know who else smells nice? Julian." I laugh.

"Who's Julian?" Kris whispers to Kat.

"Our new neighbor," Kat whispers back.

"Must be a fine neighbor to grab Emma's attention," Ethan says. "She's barely looked at a man, let alone had drunken fantasies about one since . . ." He stops himself, yet the sheer implied mention of one Beauregard Thomas triggers me.

"*Don't*," I say, shooting up straight. "Don't say his name."

"I . . . I wasn't, Emma. I promise," Ethan says. "I was just saying that this Julian must be really special."

"Alright, Gatorade, Ginger Ale, bread, and Mac and Cheese," the waitress says, placing the hangover remedy in front of me. "Anything else?"

The three of them look at me and wait for my response.

"It looks like brains," I say, and before I can stop myself vomit spews from me onto the waitress's shoes.

"Okay, let's get her home," Kat says.

Kris apologizes to the waitress and leaves an extra-large tip. Ethan agrees with Kat. And the second the vomiting stops, I am moved from the booth to the backseat of a cab.

"Are you sure you don't need our help?" Kris asks as Kat slips in next to me.

"No, it's okay," Kat says. "I'll text you when we make it home." I rest my head in her lap.

"See you next week," Ethan says. "Emma, if you can hear me, I'm sorry. Call me when you feel better," he tells me, though I'm unable to respond.

* * *

"Alright, home at last," I hear the cab driver say. "Can I help you ladies inside?" he asks, a bit *too* eager.

"No," Kat tells him. "We've got it."

My head falls against the seat as Kat slips out of the vehicle.

"Ow," I groan, moving my hand to my head. It's throbbing.

"Come on, Emma," Kat says. I open my eyes and see her reaching out to me. "It's time to go home." I nod and attempt to force myself to a sitting position. I'm too weak. My throat fills with bile.

"Look, sweetie, I really don't mind helping," the driver says. "Here—"

"Don't touch her," Kat yells. Her voice sends shock waves down my spine and I suddenly find the strength to lift myself upright.

"*What?* What's happening?" I ask.

"I was just trying to—" the cab driver starts.

"No need," a familiar voice says, "I've got it from here."

I turn to see the fuzzy outline of a boy with black hair and tanned skin. As the figure moves closer, I smell the faintest hint of fresh rain and sweet mint. As he moves his arms around me and helps me from the cab, I know I am safe. I know I'm with . . .

"Julian," I say, allowing my body to move with his. And as if through sheer force of will, my vision clears just long enough to take him in. His eyes are hooded with intensity. His forehead wears wrinkles of concern. This is the third time he's rescued me and without request, without promise for something in return. He cares about me, and I—I can't help but . . .

"You *are* special," I say, in response to Ethan's question. "Thank you for always saving me."

Julian stops. His eyes peer into mine. His lips, soft and wide, are so close I think they may touch mine. Instead, he smiles and scoops me into his arms, carrying me up the stairs.

* * *

"Why should we date one another?" Lorelai asks Max.

"Because we're clearly attracted to one another," Max replies.

"Well I'm attracted to pie. It doesn't mean I feel the need to date pie," Lorelai responds.

* * *

I wake up on the couch with a smile despite the heavy tension pulsing from one side of my head to the other. The episode of *Gilmore Girls* continues as I pull myself from the grogginess of sleep.

I find my phone on the floor next to a wastebasket, a bottle of water and three Advil with a note that says, *"Take Me."* I oblige and discover via my glaringly bright cellphone that it's 4:00 a.m. and I'm not alone. Julian sleeps on the opposite end of the sectional in a t-shirt and sweatpants. If I weren't battling a migraine and mild nausea, I'd be more startled by his presence. It seems even my shock signals are dulled by the alcohol I consumed.

It's then that I notice the handwriting on the note. It isn't Kat's, so it must be his. *But why . . .?* Choppy visions of Purple Death, the waitress's face when I threw up on her shoes, and Julian as he carried me inside flood my already achy mind. *Classy, Emma.*

I force myself from the couch and gently place my blanket over Julian's resting body.

"Stay," I tell him as if he can hear me.

I walk to the kitchen and brew myself a cup of black coffee— God's gift to the inebriated—shower and then settle back into the couch with my laptop. My headache has started to ease, as has my stomach. And since Julian has somehow made it a habit of being in my life, it's high time I get to know him better. And what better way than a deep dive into his digital past?

I go to Facebook and have to try a few different search options before finding him under the name J. Lorenzo Cole. His profile isn't set to private, but it isn't exactly easy to find. That tells me he's a private person, though I wouldn't have guessed it from his photos. Julian has over five thousand photos spanning less than ten years. Most of them are of him at parties, probably for his music label.

He wears a lot of suits and expensive watches and drinks a lot of expensive alcohol. I can tell by the glass it's served in and the hue of the brown liquid—Macallan 25. Beaux used to drink the same thing and dress the same way and surround himself with the same types of people. As does my father. Suddenly, my nausea returns.

Before learning that Julian was the new owner of Lucid, I told Kat all big businessmen are the same. And in these photos, Julian looks just like the type. Yet, he doesn't look like himself, at least not the Julian I know.

Julian hasn't posted a picture with a girl, a musical instrument, or even a selfie in two years. *What was that he said?* The painting in the U-Haul, he said he'd painted it two years ago.

"What happened to you?" I ask aloud.

Julian adjusts himself on the couch, and for a moment I think I've woken him. A few grunts and heavy breaths, and he's back to a state of sleepy bliss. With Julian settled, I continue my search through his past. The photos of Julian start to change two years prior. No more t-shirts *or* smiles. He became Mr. Cole, the person he doesn't like. I soon realize I won't find the answer as to why on his Facebook. It doesn't even look like his.

Next, I search for an Instagram. If he's been painting, he probably has pictures of his work there and maybe some other facets of the real him. Sure enough, I find two Instagram accounts linked to him—one for Mr. Cole, the facade presented as Julian on Facebook and one with his first name only—*Julian*. It's a private account.

I contemplate sending him a follow request but realize that may come off as stalkerish. Still, my hope is restored in knowing he is more than the person his life demands him to be.

In my final search for answers, I google *Cole Creative*, the name of his record label. *Wow.* He represents a lot of artists. Well, his company does. *But wait* . . . If it's *Cole* Creative, then who's the other Cole? If Julian is the Director of A and R, then who's the president?

I find the *About* page in hopes of learning more about Cole Creative's Founders. Unfortunately, I find my answers and the source of Julian's pain.

Two years ago, Cole Creative founders John and Alyssa Cole were killed in a single-vehicular crash. Their sons Mason and Julian continue their legacy and love of music as the President and Director of A and R for Cole Creative.

I look to Julian as tears fill my eyes. He lost them and in them, he lost himself.

I wipe my eyes, sip my coffee, and pull up my article for The Hub where I left off. It seems I have a few more things to add.

CHAPTER 11

I clasp my hands at my knees to hide their shaking. "Mom. Dad? I . . . um," I begin. "Unfortunately, Beaux and I have decided not to get married," I say, a bit too quickly. "We're no longer together."

I hardly recognize my voice as I speak. Perhaps it's reality that doesn't seem real. I never imagined Beaux and I wouldn't get married. Even after finding him in bed with another woman, I gave myself a month to think things over before ending it. I thought I was doing the right thing, the sensible, honorable thing. Turns out, all I did was give him hope, or rather feed into his ego.

He's a powerful man because people think he is. People give him power by being in awe of him, even afraid of him. Even when I thought I was different, when I thought I was standing up for myself and taking away his power to hurt me . . . he hurt me in ways I never imagined being hurt. He showed me his true strength when I thought I'd beaten him. I was a fool and for once, my mother will be right about me. I ruin things. But not my relationship with Beaux. No, that was . . . that was already dead. Instead, I ruined myself by allowing myself to believe I could defeat Beauregard Thomas, that I could stand strong in his presence. Now, I'm not sure I'll ever stand strong again.

I work overtime to avoid my mother's sharp gaze as she

and my father process the news. She is a woman with many talents, most of which I'm ashamed to know, yet her ability to spot a liar is beyond reproach or criticism. And though it's true Beaux and I are no longer together, my answer to my parents' follow-up question won't be. It can't be. I can barely stand to be in my own skin, my bruised, beaten, tainted flesh. To speak the truth—the sheer thought riddles my body with needle-like anxiety.

My father leans forward in his seat, moving the brown liquid in his crystal glass back and forth. The sunshine beaming in through the antebellum windows of my childhood home in Presley strike his dark hair and illuminate strands of silver gray. He looks older now, older than a mere fifty years.

My mother, beautiful as ever, looks to him from her seat across the room. I know that look. It's the one she points at him as if to ask, "Are you going to say anything?" My dad, per usual, ignores her and the look and processes the information over another glass of scotch.

I take a deep breath, close my eyes, and brace my trembling body for what happens next. My mother and I have come to many blows, agreeing to disagree on most things. But . . . just as I was unprepared for my broken engagement and what transpired afterwards, so shall be my mother. And without her knowing the full story . . . how will she ever accept this—accept me again?

"I would ask what happened, but . . ." my mother says, throwing her hands up in the air. "I think I already know."

She stands from her seat and stomps in her heels over to the bar cart to pour herself a more-than-stiff drink. Cue one of her lesser qualities. Once my mother's mind is made up, there's no changing it. All the years that I tried, I was wrong to think I could. I was even more wrong to think it was healthy for her opinion of me to shift because of who I was dating.

Beaux was a band-aid in the mother-daughter relationship of Anne and Emma Marshall. And now, I don't have the energy to fight her fight anymore or please her. So, what do you think happened, Mom? What story will you tell yourself and all your friends? Whatever it is, it can't be worse than the truth. Maybe I'll tell it to myself too.

The setting of my parents' home fades from view, and I realize I've been dreaming. A brief moment of darkness is shattered by the morning sun streaming through Kat and mine's linen curtains. My head is heavy as I wipe the sleep from my eyes and squint in the sudden light.

"One, two, three . . ."

My eyes pry open so suddenly I'm not sure if they'll ever close again. The sultry voice, the sharp perfume, the sudden shift in emotional energy surrounding me—it can only mean one thing, or rather one person.

"Is this another dream?" I ask aloud, too afraid to move my eyes from their view of the ceiling.

"Not quite, darling," my mother says. "Call it an unexpected visit."

I gasp, rolling off the couch to the floor. My body aches with the sudden movement. As I stand, I take in my mother. She stands tall before me, arms crossed over her chest, red lips pursed. Her wavy blonde hair is drawn back in a low bun, though she'd never call it that. And her slender neck is adorned with pearls. She wears white skinny jeans, a silver blouse and navy blazer paired with loafers that cost almost as much as our rent for a month.

"*Mom*," I say, moving my damp hair behind my ears.

"What . . . what are you doing here?" I ask, feigning poise. What person drives nearly six hours before sunrise and doesn't even think to call or text? How the hell did she even get in? *Oh, no*. Please don't tell me . . .

Despite all internal protests, my eyes follow a trail of fresh-brewed coffee, a steaming skillet, grease-laden bacon, and clanking dishes until they find Julian setting the table for a family breakfast.

What the . . .?

"*Emma!*" Eva squeals. My sister drops the silverware on the table and runs toward me in heels nearly as tall as her. Her navy shirtdress and golden-brown hair bounce in unison as she moves.

"Oh, I missed you," she tells me, pulling me in for a hug that hurts.

"Hi, Eva. I . . . I missed you too," I say slowly. It's not that I'm not happy to see her, it's just—

"Breakfast is served," Julian says from the kitchen. His sweatpants and t-shirt are covered with Kat's *Kiss the Cook* apron. His hair is tousled. His cheeks are flushed. From the heat of the stove or embarrassment, I can't tell. No telling what stories my mother has told him—or worse, insults. His tattoos, one of my mother's pet peeves, are on full display in his pale, paper-thin shirt.

Julian joins us in the living room, handing my mother and sister each a cup of coffee before falling back to my side. He clasps his hands together behind his back and stands, jaw clenched. *Oh, no.* Mr. Cole.

"*Mmm,*" my mother moans. She sips her coffee like she would wine. Her red lipstick stains the rim of the white mug. "Needs sugar," she says, handing the glass back to Julian.

"*Mom,*" I start. "Julian is—"

"Just a friend," my mother offers up. "Yes, well, that's obvious," she says, giving him a disapproving once-over.

"*No,*" I say, drawing their attention, especially Julian's. "I mean, *no,* that isn't what I was going to say."

Julian watches me closely.

"I was going to say that Julian isn't your errand boy," I tell her, taking her coffee mug from him. "If you'd like sugar, *I* will get it for you. After all, this is *my* house that you so graciously decided to visit."

I move past Julian to the kitchen, leaving the three of them to themselves. What *the hell* are they doing here? And more importantly, what did she say to Julian to make him so uncomfortable?

"Kat," I whisper. "If only you didn't sleep like a bear in hibernation," I mumble.

"What's that, dear?" my mother asks from behind me.

"Nothing, Mom," I say, stirring in two hefty teaspoons of sugar. Composure, composure, composure. You can do this, Emma, even though you don't know what *this* is.

"Here you go, Mom," I say with a smile.

"Thanks, sweetie," my mom says, sipping at the overly sweet beverage. "Just right," she says with a little jump.

I smile once more and turn to fix myself a cup. Taking a bit longer than usual, I close my eyes and breathe deeply.

I'm accustomed to nerves when in the presence of my mother. It's a characteristic instilled in me since we had "the talk" in fifth grade. Yes, *fifth*. But this time it's different, amplified. And despite the bulk of my attention focused on the mother I haven't seen in nine months, I can't ignore Julian. Julian, who I haven't thanked for helping me last night, who has impressed me with his cooking, angered me by letting my mother in without asking or waking me, who is still here out of no obligation to me *or* my family.

I exhale and sip at the steaming, black beverage. Julian places the plates on the island between me and my mother before taking his place next to me. Once more, he embodies an unfamiliar quiet nature. I have to get rid of Eva and my mom, at least long enough to find out what all happened before I woke up.

"Oh, Emma," my mother starts. Her shrill voice forces me to cringe. Hot coffee runs down my chin. "That stuff will turn your teeth black. Add some milk, won't you?" she asks. "Besides, you could already use a little whitening before the wedding," my mother mumbles.

"Oh, Mom, stop," Eva scolds in her oh-so-innocent way. Julian hands me a paper towel and I dab the hot liquid from my chin.

"Of course, Mom," I say, turning to face her. "Why don't you and Eva have a seat in the dining room. I'll fix you both a plate and we can . . . catch up." Not that I'm looking forward to it.

My mother's eyes move to Julian as if they speak an unspoken language. They hold each other's gaze just long enough for Julian's body to grow even more tense. Finally, my mother turns on her heel and takes her place at the dining room table. Eva follows behind her.

I exhale and mentally curse my home for its lack of privacy.

"Hey, uh. If you're alright, I think I should go," Julian says, resting his back on the island. I do the same and pretend my mother's eyes aren't glued to the back of our heads.

"*What?* No," I say. My forehead wrinkles in confusion. "Why would you leave?" I ask. Well, obviously, he'll go home, eventually. What I mean is, why does he feel the need to leave right now.

"I just," Julian starts, then stops. "I've overstayed my welcome," he says, breathing heavy. "I just—I just wanted to make sure you were okay and—"

"Thank you," I say, cutting him off. He stops. His icy eyes pour into mine. "Thank you for staying, both last night and this morning," I tell him. "My mother is a piece of work, and you being here, well, let's just say, she's on her best behavior."

"*Wow!*" he mumbles, eyebrows raised. I bite my lip and contemplate my next question. Do I *really* want to know?

"Did she . . .? Did she say something to you? You're abnormally quiet this morning," I say.

Julian smiles, more to himself than to me.

"I sure am hungry," my mother comments. "I hope the food doesn't get cold while you two discuss what to poison the unexpected guests with."

I roll my eyes. "Funny, Mom."

Julian turns and starts pilling scrambled eggs and bacon on three plates.

"Come on," I say, moving my hand to steady his. "What did she say?" I ask, leaning into him to keep my mother from hearing. His eyes move to where my hand touches his. My chest tightens and I pull away. "Sorry, um—"

"Don't apologize," he says, his voice low. "And no, quite the opposite actually," he says, returning to his task of dressing plates. "They came in about half an hour ago, bladders about to burst. Once they determined I wasn't a burglar or murderer, they went to the restroom to freshen up and directed me to make myself useful. *Hints*, breakfast," he reveals with a pained grin. "Your mom has hardly spoken two words to me since."

Out of the corner of my eye, I see her watching us. She pretends to listen to my sister as she rambles on about wedding stuff. Her hazel glare nearly burns a hole in the side of my face.

"I . . . um," I begin, but am unsure what to say. "I'm sorry," I finally say, though I can't help but admit I prefer my mother be disinterested in Julian. If she quizzed him, that means she sees him as a potential suitor. And considering my mother still thinks Beaux is my soulmate, she's the last person whose approval I'll seek when and *if* I decide to date again.

"Don't apologize," he tells me once more. "Just enjoy your time with your family. Regardless of any past disagreements or tension, which you two *clearly* have, you only get one family and a limited time together."

As he speaks, I'm reminded of John and Alyssa Cole, the parents Julian lost two years ago. My heart aches for him.

While my mother may be the reason for Julian's change in character, it's not because of something she said. Rather, it's her presence altogether. Seeing my mom makes him think of his. And while the past between Anne and me is far too complicated to resolve in a single meal or even a single year, maybe I owe it to myself to try, *again*. If not for me, for Julian.

"I'm going to go," he says then. "Enjoy your time with your mom. We can talk later."

Julian says goodbye to Eva and my mom. They mumble "Nice to meet you" and fake pleasantries. I roll my eyes, and just when I think today is destined to be hellacious, Julian leans in and kisses my cheek, soft and sincere. As he pulls away, he takes my breath with him along with any ruse that we're *just friends*.

CHAPTER 12

Two hours into dress shopping and Eva is still spouting wedding details. The ceremony will take place in the Saint Allen Chapel on my great-grandfather's land where four generations of Marshall's married, including my mother and father. My mother didn't speak to me for two weeks when I told her Beaux and I would be married in New Orleans.

The day before will be spent playing couples' games with a rehearsal dinner in the Marshall House gardens to follow. That's what people call my home, Marshall House. As if the stately white mansion nestled amongst three-hundred-year-old oak trees needed any other elements of pretentious privilege.

Feeling my mother's eyes on me, I slow my roll through the row of dresses and pretend to examine one with a corset back, as if Eva would ever be so bold.

The wedding colors are blush pink and raspberry. I'm told they've narrowed down *my* dress options to two choices. They want to see them both on me before picking one the day before. *Mental gag.*

There will be a live band for the reception along with white-collar catering. And my grandmother, God bless her soul, will play the processional for the ceremony.

Let me be clear about something. I'm happy for my sister, *if* she's happy. But how could she be, or at least, how can she know it'll last? She and Bill haven't even been together a year, and now they're getting married! *Married!* They will be legally bound to one another forever. Unless, of course, they get a divorce, but if that's an option then why bother in the first place?

I exhale and shove an ivory dress with ruffles a bit too ferociously for the attendee's liking.

"Um, miss," the short blonde says. "May I offer you a glass of champagne, perhaps a seat in our private lounge? I'm sure between your mother and sister's picks, Ms. Eva's got plenty to choose from," she says with a nod.

I compose myself and agree to her offer. Though from the bug-eyed expression on my mother's face, I don't expect her remarks for me will be so cordial.

After another thirty minutes of browsing, Eva scurries through the bridal parlor with a handful of tiaras and earrings and a smile that stretches across her whole face. I smile back and wish her well. This is a big day, or at least it's supposed to be.

I never bought a wedding dress, but that doesn't mean I didn't shop for one. I tried on close to fifty and found an issue with each one. Turns out, it wasn't the dress that was the problem. Not by a long shot.

My mom enters the parlor, champagne in hand, and plops down next to me on the stiff, upright couch. I never understood the appeal of beauty over comfort. But, of course, that is the way of the world—at least, the Marshall's world.

My mother chugs the rest of her champagne and flags an attendee for her third glass. If it weren't for Julian's surprisingly delicious breakfast, she'd be too drunk to sit straight.

"I'm sorry," I finally say, breaking the silence.

My mother breathes heavily, letting her purse drop to her feet.

"Which part are you sorry for?" she asks without looking in my direction.

"I . . . um," I stammer.

"For barely speaking to your family for nearly a year? For leaving all the wedding planning to your sister and me? For practically shredding a ten-thousand-dollar gown out of spite?" she rambles on.

"Ok, Mom, stop," I tell her. "I did not shred a wedding dress and whatever I did certainly wasn't out of spite. I love Eva and she deserves to be happy," I assure her.

"*But . . .*" my mom interjects.

That word! I scolded Beaux for using it to justify his infidelity. Am I doing the same thing by being the anti-marriage maid of honor? My mother raises a perfectly plucked brow, daring me to deny my underlying resentment. My cheeks grow hot with anger. Goosebumps tingle on top of my skin at the sheer thought.

I don't resent my sister and I don't mean to ruin this experience for her. I just . . . It's hard to be excited for something you don't believe in. Happiness, commitment, marriage, I'd like to think it lasts, but history proves otherwise. But Eva is too young, too inexperienced to realize it. And I can't fault her for that, but . . . I can't be faulted either for seeing through the charade.

I bite my lip and slouch back in my seat, unwilling to discuss it further.

"Oh, Emma," my mother says, finally facing me. "I understand this must be hard for you." *She does?* "Your little sister is getting married and all of this shopping and talking, it reminds you of when you were engaged." She's not wrong. "But sweetie," my mom says, placing her hand on my knee. "If seeing your sister get married hurts you, then maybe it's a sign you should reach out to—"

"*Stop,*" I yell. My mother jumps in her seat. "I told you I don't want to hear another word about him."

"*Emma!*" my mother says, almost as if my name is a curse word. She looks to see if anyone is watching and then leans into me. Her breath is hot against my cheek.

"Don't you ever raise your voice at me like that again. I am *still* your mother," she tells me. As if I need reminding. No one else in my life is bold enough to insert such opinions, not even Kat.

"Now, it was just a suggestion," she says, returning to her side of the sofa.

"Well, it was an inconsiderate one," I say, my eyes locked straight ahead.

"Well, *clearly*, you still have feelings for him. If not, why get so upset at the implication of him?" she asks.

I shake my head. My skin grows hotter. When will she learn

that there is no winning with me on this topic? Beauregard Thomas is dead to me *and* this family. Why can't she understand that? Why can't she love me more than she loves the idea of me with him?

"Mom—"

"Now, if that option is off the table, then maybe it's time you find someone new," she says, finishing off her glass. "And that Julian of yours doesn't count."

"*What?*" I ask, turning in my seat. "Why even bring him up?"

"Well, he was at your home in early hours and had clearly slept over. You were still asleep for Christ's sake when he let us in. That displays a level of comfort both on his part and yours," she tells me.

"What? What does that even mean?" I ask, crossing my arms over my chest.

"Well, he felt comfortable enough answering your door, meeting your mother no less. And you felt comfortable enough to fall asleep with him in your home. You are many things, Emma Marshall, but an idiot is not one," she says.

Despite the tension between us, I take a moment to enjoy her compliment.

"With you in such a vulnerable state, he could've stolen something or done far worse things to you than provide you with a throw-up basket and Advil. *Yes, I saw,*" she tells me. Her tone alerts me I'll hear more on that topic later.

"Okay," I concede. "Well, if you noticed that and the level of comfort between us, and you can't deny his breakfast was delicious, then why would you disregard him as a possible suitor?" I ask. "Not that we're even remotely dating, because we're not, but—"

"*Emma,*" my mother breathes. "Don't lie to me. You have feelings for this boy or else you wouldn't be so hellbent on defending him. And he *clearly* has feelings for you."

As she speaks, I feel his lips on my cheek. My insides tingle.

"But feelings aren't enough," she reveals, practically.

My forehead crinkles in confusion. "I don't understand."

"Of course, you don't," she says, signaling for another glass of champagne. "You live in the fairytale world of women empowerment. You think you can do it all without anyone's help. You think imperfection is a waste of time. You think marriage and compromise are outdated."

"That's not true," I say.

"*Isn't it?*" she asks. "You had a man that was prepared to take care of you," she says. "Beaux had a good job and more money than the two of you would have ever needed. He came from a good family, a family with connections. You could've stayed home and focused on your interests like writing and traveling. You could've had an easy life, Emma," she tells me. "And you threw it all away over what? Over a few lonely nights or a couple of broken promises?

"Men aren't perfect, Emma, and neither is marriage, but it *is* necessary. And Beaux?" she says, shaking her head. "You'll be hard pressed to find another man like him."

Her words hit me like hot rocks. Is this *really* what she thinks of me? Screw what she said about Beaux! I've heard that speech before. But thinking that *my* life is a fairytale, that I don't care about anyone else or their opinion, that I can't accept imperfection, is an insult in the greatest form. And to rag on Julian, to imply that he isn't or wouldn't be enough for me . . . Well, regardless of where we stand, he is a far better man than Beauregard Thomas. That much I know, and she would too if she took the chance to get to know him rather than judge him by his tattoos.

I clasp my hands together, digging my nails into my palms.

"*Mom*," I say, with more respect than she deserves. "I don't want to disrespect you nor cause a scene, but you don't know Beaux the way you think you do, and you don't know me. My life is anything but a fairytale, but maybe you're right. Maybe a relationship *is* more than just feelings," I admit. "Maybe it's respect, maybe it's communication, maybe it's safety, maybe it's even more. I wouldn't know because I've never experienced nor witnessed a healthy relationship," I tell her, fully aware of the implication towards her and my father.

My mother watches me with surprise.

"But what I can tell you is that it is much more than the clothes you wear, the money in your bank account, and the family you come from. It's more than secrets and trust issues. It's more than wondering whose bed your fiancé is in tonight, or rather who's in his," I reveal. "It's more than fear," I say. Tears distort my vision. "It's more than *necessary*," I finally tell her.

I look away from her, wiping my eyes with my sleeve. An attendant brings us both a glass of champagne while we sit in silence. *God!* How long does it take to put on a wedding dress, Eva?

"I chose to end my engagement, and I had more than enough reasons to do so," I finally say. "But maybe I *am* bitter," I admit. "Maybe I *do* cringe at the sight of wedding dresses, roll my eyes as Eva talks seating charts, and gag at the mention of Bill and all the sweet things he's promised to do after they get married." Tears continue to fall. "But that does not mean for a single second that I still have feelings for the man who . . ." I stop myself.

I wipe the rest of my tears and sip my champagne.

"Who what?" my mom asks. She watches me with wide eyes and parted lips. Every muscle in her small body seems to clench as she waits for my response.

I appreciate her listening, but I can't tell her the truth. I can't have her know . . . I shake my head.

"Nothing, Mom," I say. "Let's just never have this conversation again, okay?"

She hesitates but agrees.

I know I'm not being fair to her. If she knew, maybe . . . maybe things would be different. Maybe she would respect me more or at least understand that her talking about him hurts me. Because it does remind me, all of this reminds me, not so much of being engaged. Rather, it reminds me of what happened the night our engagement ended. The walls I've built around the truth are starting to shatter, and I'm not sure how much longer I can keep my secrets in.

"Alright! Who's ready for dress number one?" Eva squeals.

CHAPTER 13

Dinner with my mom and Eva is better than I would've guessed based on the morning's events. I guess something I said finally resonated with my mom. I hope it lasts. But despite a delicious meal, decent company, and the ambiance of one of the finer offerings of the Crescent City, my mind is more conflicted than ever.

Is it time to move on? But how do I do that if my mind is still haunted by the past? And if the two are tethered together, how do I vanquish my demons?

As I walk home, I spot the bright blue walls of Lucid. I wonder if Mr. Edgar showed Julian where the spare key is.

After Kat moved in with me sophomore year, I found myself staying late at Lucid more often. It was quiet and dark, the perfect place for me to study or think, mostly think. I thought about my mom and dad and Eva. I felt guilty for leaving them. Well, mostly Eva. She was only fourteen when I left for college. And without me there to distract my parents from her every move, she didn't stand a chance in the realm of free will. I knew this. And still, I left. Now when I look at my sister, I see my mother's reflection, only less jaded. And her marrying Bill, if it's not history repeating itself, then I don't know what is.

My mom was twenty when she married my dad. He was twenty-six. They met at college. She was a junior and a cheerleader. He was on campus for the homecoming game and after-party at his fraternity house. When your parents have been together for so long, it's easy to think they always were, that their lives have always been connected. And while this typically isn't true, it is for my mom. My mom had barely lived life before making it all about Carrington Marshall. And even though she'll never admit it, she regrets it. Which is why I can't fathom why she's so determined to see Eva marry Bill, a man six years older?

Ever since I found out she and Bill were engaged, I've asked myself, why do I care so much? Why does their happiness affect me so? It's easy to say because I have none, because my engagement failed, because my belief in commitment was shattered. But the truth is, I worry for Eva, because her story is too similar to my mom's *and* mine.

I may not have married Beaux, but he still controls me. And to be controlled by a man while you're still figuring out who you are, well, how will you ever know?

I find myself at Lucid and use my incredibly painful heels to an advantage in search for the spare key.

"Aha," I say, grasping it from atop the door frame. "Now, let's hope Julian hasn't installed some sort of security system."

Inside Lucid, I unhook my heels, tossing them to the side, and shuffle through the dusty records until I find my favorite, *Clair de Lune*. Despite my aching feet, I twirl around the dimly lit space as it plays. My long, black satin dress moves with my body in slippery elegance.

I remember the first time I heard the record. I was twelve, and it was the best thing about the pageant my mother forced me to compete in. Another girl named Sydney Mills performed a ballet routine to it, which I watched none of. After her first twirl, I closed my eyes and listened to the music as if I'd never heard music before. And in all actuality, I hadn't. Not like this.

I breathe deeply, despite the dust in the room, and lift my head to the ceiling. I twirl faster and faster, swaying back and forth to the melody. I allow the piano to drown out my thoughts and silence my demons. I allow myself to forget, and for the five minutes and thirty-eight seconds that is *Clair de Lune*, I am okay. I am free. That is, until the music ends and the deafening silence allow the voices to creep back in. Or rather, *his* voice.

I find myself in a corner, arms wrapped around my knees and my face buried between my legs. After it happened, Kat encouraged me to go to therapy, especially after I decided not to press charges. I went once, and this is what I learned, a strategy for feeling in control even when you know you're not. By making your body smaller, you train your brain to realize there's less of you that can be hurt. What they don't tell you is that it doesn't work if the pain you feel stems from inside you.

Wet tears drip from my eyes onto the shiny fabric of my dress. If my mother were here, she'd tell me how unladylike it is to sit on the floor, in a dress no less, and how even the smallest drop of water can leave a permanent stain on such fabrics as this. But she's not here. No one is. And with that realization, I let go.

Tears flood my face and dampen my dress all the way to my skin. I scream and choke as all the pain comes rushing back. Pain not only from the first time Beaux assaulted me, but the second—the time no one knows about, not even Kat. It was four months after we broke things off and . . .

"*Emma?*"

I jump at the sound of Julian's voice. I lift my head so quickly it begins to ache.

"Emma! Are you okay? What happened?" he asks.

The figure that is Julian's body rushes toward me, though I cannot see him for the tears in my eyes. "Emma, what's going on? I heard . . . I heard you screaming," he says, dropping to my side.

My lip quivers as I try to form words. I want to tell him that I'm fine, it's nothing, and that I just had a long day. I am unable to. I don't want to lie to him even though I can't tell him the truth. When I don't answer, he slings his arm around me and pulls me close to him.

His t-shirt is soft against my cheek. His arms are strong as they wrap around me. In such proximity the intoxicating aroma of mint and rain I've come to associate only with him is even stronger. I inhale it and allow it to calm my rapidly beating heart. I allow him to hold me. I allow him to be my shield, my safe place. And I allow myself to imagine what my life would be like if I'd met him first.

After a while, my daydreams are interrupted as Julian pulls me to my feet and presses me against him. His eyes search mine for permission and I don't resist him. We dance to no music at all. And for the first time, the silence isn't deafening. It's peaceful.

My tears dry and my vision clears. I look up and I'm finally able to see him. He wears worry well. Dark lashes shroud his bright eyes. A single strand of wavy black hair falls across his forehead. I move my hand from his shoulder to his face and caress his cheek. Sometimes I question if he's even real. But flesh-to-flesh, the warmth of life burns between us.

He watches me as I move my hand from his cheek to his hair. I run my fingers through it and relish in its smooth texture. His jaw clenches as if to keep in a moan. A small smile spreads across my lips as I watch him yearn for mine.

Will he kiss me again? Do I want him to?

"So," Julian breathes. "How was your day?" he asks.

I smile and move my hand from his hair to his waist. I allow him to rock me slowly.

My lips part in preparation for heavy explanation. Instead, I decide to claim the moment. The events of today and the past year don't matter, not right now.

Finally, I say, "It's better now."

Julian takes my face in his, our lips only inches apart. "Mine too," he reveals. And we continue our dance.

* * *

"Is this your plan? Fill me with alcohol and I'll spill all my secrets?" I ask him. After Lucid, Julian insisted on walking me the rest of the way home, but we found ourselves at a wine bar instead.

"Well, you did let a few endearing things slip last night," Julian says, sipping a glass of red.

"Well, *clearly* I wasn't of sound mind," I tell him, sipping my white. He laughs.

"*Obviously*," he agrees. "But then, they do say there are no more honest people than children and drunks."

I smile, wracking my brain for memories of last night. I remember him carrying me inside, but nothing else. What could I have said?

"You have no idea what you said, do you?" he asks me.

"Sorry," I admit, setting my wine to the side.

Julian laughs. "It's okay. But, um—"

"*Wait!* You're not going to tell me?" I ask.

Julian pretends to think and finally says, "No. I think I'll keep it my little secret."

"*Julian,*" I whine.

"Emma," he responds.

I smile and relax into the leather booth. This is what I like about Julian. Everything is so easy and fluid. He doesn't pry and neither do I. Well, except for the mild cyberstalking I took part in last night.

"In all seriousness, though," Julian says. "How was your day?"

I hesitate, taking another sip of my wine. Perhaps I thought too soon.

"I won't judge, or critique, or even comment if you don't want me to," he continues. "But I think there's something on your mind that you need to get out."

Finally, I nod. "Try several somethings."

Julian sets his wine to the side and leans in. "Start where you're comfortable," he tells me.

And I do. "My little sister is getting married. She's twenty-two and he's twenty-eight," I tell him. Julian nods. "That's why she and my mom came down today. My sister, Eva, wanted to go dress shopping," I say. "Which should be fun, but—"

"But your little sister is getting married and I take it you don't approve of her fiancé," Julian says.

"I thought you weren't going to say anything."

"Oh, sorry," he says. He makes the motion of locking his lips and throwing away the key. I smile.

"No, it's okay. I was just joking, *sort of,*" I tell him. "But to answer your question, yeah," I nod. "My little sister is getting married before me, and maybe I tell myself it's her age and his that makes me concerned, but maybe it's just . . . jealousy," I finally admit. "I mean honestly, I'd like to be jealous, because if I'm jealous it means I believe they're going to make it and that I want to make it with someone someday."

"What do you mean *make it?*" Julian asks.

I bite the inside of my jaw, fully aware that this ramble won't make any sense if I don't tell him the truth. I grab my wine glass and finish it off. Though, after surviving Purple Death, I'm not sure alcohol will ever have the same effect or offer the same satisfaction.

"I, um, I haven't had the best experience in relationships," I reveal. "And not just romantic relationships. I . . . I never had a real friendship until I met Kat. And the second I saw a way out of Presley, Louisiana, I took it," I say. "I got a scholarship to Tulane, because I knew I couldn't count on my parents to pay for a school they didn't want me going to. They're like that, fully unaware of how to support something they didn't choose themselves."

The waiter brings me another glass and replenishes the cheese platter between us. Despite Julian's lactose intolerance, he insisted we order it. So, I feel obligated to devour it. Not that I would've done differently had he been able to enjoy it too.

"Today was the first time I've seen my mom and sister in almost a year," I admit. "Before my sister called to let me know she's engaged, I'd only spoken to my parents twice in that time and my sister three," I tell him.

"Wow," Julian says. "Maybe that's why the energy was so tense this morning."

"No, that's just my mom," I assure him. I drop my eyes to my lap, playing thumb-war beneath the table. "Does it make me a terrible person?" I ask him.

"No," Julian says without hesitation. "Relationships are a two-way street. They could have called or come to see you. But I'm guessing there is a reason why they didn't *and* why you didn't."

I nod and sip at my wine. "Yeah," I admit. But it's not a reason I'm ready to share. "Anyway, I'd . . . I'd like to be supportive of my sister. Hell, I'd even like to be jealous of her. But I . . . I don't have much hope in relationships anymore and it makes it hard to support something that I see straight through," I say. "I mean, he's almost thirty, and she's barely twenty. He probably has their whole life mapped out for them without even asking her opinion. He'll use her," I say. "She'll be his young, beautiful wife who stays at home and raises a whole hoard of kids while he's out with his buddies drinking, golfing, and doing

God knows what else. And that will all be fine and well, *for a while*," I tell him. "But one day Eva is going to wake up and realize she's tired and lonely and her husband will be so used to getting his way, he won't know how to compromise or communicate. And they'll either get a divorce or wish they would have," I reveal. "So, if that's all you have to look forward to, then why even try in the first place?" I ask.

Julian nods and relaxes in his seat. I can tell he has a few thoughts he'd like to share but doesn't want to overstep.

"Go ahead," I tell him.

"Hmm?" Julian asks.

"You can speak," I say, finishing off my second glass of wine.

"Okay," Julian says, leaning in once more. "First, don't get mad at me. Two, I don't presume to be right. I just—I feel like you're projecting *your* feelings and past trauma onto your sister and her relationship."

"*Wow*," I say, taken aback. "Don't hold back." Not that he would.

"No, hear me out," he says. "You make good points. I mean, it's true that their age difference could pose a problem," he admits. "But it's also true that it could pose no problem at all. It's also true they could get divorced, but that's true for any married couple. And while the divorce rate is high, half of marriages still last. But it sounds like you know that. It sounds like you're more worried about her being controlled by this man and you're worried she'll be stuck in an unhealthy marriage. And I take it that worry comes from your own experience with relationships that haven't worked out or *made it*, as you say. Maybe you just need to experience the right relationship to know that there's more than hurt and resentment and miscommunication and broken promises to be had," he tells me. "And maybe, *just maybe*, your sister has found that for herself."

I absorb his words and replay them in my head. I want so desperately to believe him and I . . . I feel myself starting to.

"I take it you've never had your heart broken before?" I ask.

Julian is quiet for a moment and I mentally scold myself for being so ignorant. Of course his heart broke when his parents died. It's just a different type of brokenness.

"I take it you have," he finally says.

CHAPTER 14

Monday morning sun wakes me as it drips through the glass windowpanes above my bed. I moan and stretch, reveling in the first good sleep I've had in this room since the night of my attack. The past week blurs together behind my closed eyes. Julian kissed me, and even though I wanted to make myself believe I didn't want him to, I did. And Saturday night, as we said our goodbyes, I wanted to reach out to him, to pull him back to me and allow our lips to touch once more. But I didn't.

I open my eyes and roll to my side, enjoying the contrast of the box fan's breeze against my toasty arms. It's 9:00 a.m. and I can already tell it's going to be a scorcher.

With a small burst of energy, I force myself out of bed, brush my teeth, and search for clean leggings and a bra. I'm not sure if Demetri will be joining us for breakfast and I'd rather not find out half-dressed.

I put on my clothes and find my reflection staring back at me. Her blonde curls are messier than normal, a sign of a good night's rest. The skin beneath her eyes is brighter despite the additional makeup she was forced to wear over the weekend. And her lips are . . . pinker, plumper. They tingle as I move my hand from my thigh to touch them. I imagine Julian—

I jump as my cellphone dings from beneath my pillows. It's probably Fran alerting me of my new assignment. My article on Julian dropped today. *Oh, crap! The article!*

I tear through the feather-stuffed mounds until I find my phone. Ignoring the text from an unknown number, I go straight to my app for The Hub and scroll until I see *LA Music Mogul*

On His Plans to Save New Orleans Trademark, Lucid Records. I take a breath and click to view.

> *When LA music label, Cole Creative, purchased New Orleans trademark record shop, Lucid Records, the sounds of demolition rang in the ears of patrons everywhere. After speaking with Cole Creative Co-owner Julian Cole, I'm pleased to reveal the tune has changed.*
>
> *Cole speaks highly of the shop, noting its bones and soul could only be found in the great city of New Orleans. While there are plans to make a few modest upgrades to the store, the main goal of Cole Creative in purchasing Lucid Records is to restore the shop to its former glory.*
>
> *During the interview, Cole was kind enough to reveal a secret space hidden beneath the surface of the shop. In the 1920s, the space was used as a speakeasy, a place for drinks, dancing, and live music beneath the very streets we walk every day. Illegal at the time, no records were kept of the speakeasy's operations.*
>
> *Cole, a musician of note himself, plans to renovate both the store and the speakeasy, providing New Orleans with yet another hot spot for nightly entertainment as well as job opportunities for locals. When asked if he'll be staying in New Orleans after the renovation is complete, Cole revealed, "I hope to be in the wonderful city of New Orleans for as long as possible, working hand-in-hand with my employees, and ensuring total customer satisfaction."*
>
> *Cole admits he appreciates the change of scenery and pace of his adopted home. Cole's residency in New Orleans comes after the tragic and sudden passing of his parents, Co-founders of Cole Creative, John and Alyssa Cole.*

Since taking control of the company along with his brother, Mason Cole, there has been a noticeable shift in acquisitions at Cole Creative. More focus has been given to authentic music sources such as record shops, independent recording studios, and singer-songwriter artists. No doubt we can credit this to New Orleans's adopted son Julian Cole.

While there is no word yet on when the renovations of Lucid Records will be complete, you can find the new owner, Julian, as a violinist on regular rotation at Mimi's. Until next time, New Orleans—Emma Marshall.

"Okay," I say aloud. "Okay." It's not *so* bad. I mean . . . it's . . . it's borderline unprofessional. *What the hell was I thinking?* Oh, right, I wasn't thinking. I was half-hungover when I went in and made those changes. And referring to him as *Julian?* I mean, I get why I did it. He hates being known as Mr. Cole and I certainly didn't want to promote his persona in the city that may just be the fresh start he's been looking for. *But come on, Emma?* No first names—that's like journalism 101. And all that stuff about his parents? And did I actually include off-the-record information?!

My phone dings again and I'm reminded of the text from earlier. I roll my eyes and click out of the article. Well, if my past hadn't ruined any relationship potential with Julian, that article sure did. How am I going to explain how I knew about his parents? How could I have included that without asking him first?

"Ugh!" I yell, mentally cursing myself.

I move to my messages and see *Hey, it's Julian.* My heart sinks. How did he get my number? *Oh, God.* He's probably mad. No, make that furious. I hold my breath and click to view the rest of the message.

Hey, it's Julian. I called your office to get your number. I wanted to personally thank you for the article. I know it couldn't have been easy to admit I'm not the worst thing to happen to Lucid. Though I am a little curious about how you found out about my parents. I mean, I'm not mad, just . . . surprised. But then again, I shouldn't be. You're amazing, Emma. So, of course you're amazing at your job as well. Talk soon.

And . . . *exhale*. He's . . . he's not mad. Yet, for some reason, I can't feel my legs. I plop onto my mattress and dangle my thumb over my phone, contemplating a reply. *Thank you* seems a bit short and detached. But I'm just getting used to having Julian's number, and, for some reason, it's harder to text than speak to him in person. Perhaps it's because in-person communication always has a beginning and an end. There's an escape and decompress when we're apart. Not that I need to escape him, but sometimes it's hard to keep the truth from him, the secrets of my past. And with texting, there is a constant connection. As if Julian wasn't already on my mind enough, now I have to worry about him analyzing every word I say *and* how long it takes me to say anything.

I sit up in bed and text the first thing that comes to mind that doesn't scream desperate or psycho.

Thanks! Glad you approve.

Okay, now think Emma. Julian isn't this insecure, pathetic male that sits around all day analyzing text messages. The gesture of finding my number was . . . sweet, and it wouldn't be the first time an interviewee thanked me for a positive article.

"Knock, knock," Kat says from outside my door.

"Um, yeah, come in," I say, hiding my phone beneath the blankets.

Kat opens the door and the smell of roses wafts in with her. "I think you've got some explaining to do," she says.

Kat holds an oversized bouquet of red roses that nearly swallows half her body. They're long-stemmed and dense, probably four dozen in one vase if I had to guess. A note is attached to the center of the vase with gold ribbon that drapes to the floor. On the outside of the envelope is a single letter—*J.*

* * *

"So, what's going on between you and Julian, and don't tell me it's nothing, because *clearly*, the four-hundred-dollar bouquet of roses says otherwise," Kat says.

We sit at the dining room table, drinking coffee and eating pop tarts. This is where we have all of our serious conversations, and despite my better judgement telling me to keep quiet, I know I can't lie to Kat, not anymore.

I take one last gulp of coffee and set my cup to the side.

"Julian kissed me."

"*What!*" Kat yells. Coffee drips from her open mouth down her neck. "When? Where? *When?*" she squeals.

"Okay, okay," I say, gesturing for her to calm down. "It's not what you think. It . . . it wasn't a real kiss."

"What do you mean?" Her ginger brows crinkle in confusion as she wipes coffee from her chin.

"Well, maybe it was, it's just—" I stop.

"*Oh, no,*" Kat says, waving her finger at me. "You're not going quiet on me now. *Spill.*"

"Okay, so here's what happened." And I tell her everything.

I tell her about my interview with Julian and how we found ourselves at Mimi's. Then I have to backtrack and tell her about me seeing Julian play the night before and how he saved me from three predators. She's furious when she hears of my almost horrific encounter and makes a note to keep her relations with Demetri on the quiet side. Getting back on track, I tell her how things with Julian were easy and nice, until—

"We saw Beaux at Mimi's."

Kat's mouth drops in surprise. I think she's going to jump out of her seat and cause a scene. Instead, she sits uncharacteristically quiet, so I continue.

"He came in with his . . . *girlfriend*. And I . . . I couldn't stand the sight of him," I tell her, unwilling to go into detail on how truly disturbing the encounter was. "Julian put two and two together and he kissed me. Apparently, PDA makes people uncomfortable, because Beaux never even noticed us." I move my thumbs back and forth in my lap. My heartbeat quickens as I remember back.

"But even more shocking than seeing Beaux was how I felt after our kiss ended, how I've felt ever since," I reveal.

"And how have you felt?" Kat asks, breaking her silence.

"Like . . . like I want more," I admit.

A huge smile spreads across Kat's face and her cheeks glow pink. I imagine she's screaming *I told you so* inside her mind, but she doesn't say it, not yet at least.

"Anyway, I . . . I've tried to keep my distance ever since it happened, because I still have things to figure out," I ramble on.

"*Like what?*" Kat interrupts. Kat stands, and as if a preacher at Sunday service, says, "Emma Louise Marshall, do not run away from this. Look, I know I've joked about you needing a rebound and even about you and Julian, but . . . it's been almost a year, Emma. And you have this gorgeous, kind, thoughtful guy right in front of you and if you . . ." She pauses to think. "If you let him get away, we are no longer friends," she finally says.

"*What?*"

"You heard me," Kat says. "I mean I knew something was brewing when he insisted on staying to look after you the night of Brocatos, but hearing all of this and gauging the price of those roses—he likes you, like *really* likes you," Kat says.

Kat refills our coffee cups and sits down across from me once more.

"And you just admitted you like him to. So, what's the problem?" she asks.

I exhale and drink my coffee. This is where it gets tricky. This is where it gets uncomfortable.

"Beaux is in your past, Emma," Kat tells me. "The only one holding you back now is you."

I know she's right. I do, but—

"I know we don't talk about it," Kat begins. "And let me start by saying, I respected your decision back then and I will continue to respect any future decisions you make, aside from keeping Julian at arm's length, obviously. But . . ." She pauses, dropping her eyes to the floor. The hairs on my arms rise in response. "I know Beaux did more than hit you," she finally reveals. My lips part. My blood turns to ice. "And when you didn't press charges, you allowed him to hold a power over you that is unbreakable until you accept the truth," Kat says.

I want to tell her *"Stop! Don't say it."* but my throat tightens and I'm unable to speak, unable to breathe.

"He raped you," she says.

That word—that single word I've refused to allow in my vocabulary. My heart rate quickens, and my forehead grows hot. I feel like I'm sweating, like I'm panting.

"Emma," Kat says, taking my hands in hers. "Focus on me, just me." I do. I look into her familiar blue eyes until my rapidly beating heart forces me to close mine. I clasp her hands tighter and attempt to still my mind. It doesn't work. I see . . . I see *him*.

Blood pools in my mouth to the point where I feel I may drown in it. There is a reprieve in his assault as Beaux removes his pants. I gasp and spit the blood on my white duvet. The sight of him over me ignites my body in fear. With fear stronger than my adrenaline, the pain of my wounds overcomes me, as does the pain of him entering my body.

Beaux moves his hands from my shoulders to my throat. He squeezes and with more and more pressure, my mind goes numb and my insides burn as he moves in and out. I flounder and try to push him off, but my efforts are in vain. He is too strong.

I stare at the ceiling until the room starts to fade. "Look at me," Beaux grunts. He pulls me by my hair and forces me to look at him. As it becomes harder to remain conscious, blurred edges inch closer and closer to his face, yet I still see him, over me, choking me, violating me. Until I see nothing at all.

Despite darkness as my eye's reward, my ears continue to betray me. Beaux screams and grunts as he uses more force against me. His skin slaps into mine. The pain should be greater than it is, but my body shuts down with each passing second there is no fresh air in my lungs. Kat pounds on the door, crying and cursing. She yells into her cellphone for the police to hurry. I try to move my lips to tell her to run, but I'm unable to. My body is heavy, weak, and numb as it jolts back and forth in response to Beaux's pressure.

In my last moment of consciousness, I feel Beaux press himself hard against me. He finishes as sirens echo in the background. Hot against my neck, he whispers, "Now, we're done."

I buried this for so long. Even as it happened, as he . . . *raped me*, I didn't allow myself to call it that or even process what was happening to me, what was *really* happening to me. And I . . . I didn't press charges because I knew that meant explaining something I couldn't even understand, something I couldn't accept. I . . . I stayed quiet, and I kept this to myself. At least, I thought I did. And I guess I hoped that if I kept quiet, if I didn't allow anyone else in my world to know the truth, then maybe one day it would go away. If no one else knew, no one else would see me and treat me like a victim. I could pretend to be strong until I actually was. But . . . it didn't work. And ever since Julian and I first connected, I've had to acknowledge there is something holding me back, something keeping us apart.

I've told myself I'm not ready for a relationship, that Julian and I are just friends, and the second things got real between us, I pulled away for the sake of crossing some non-existent line. But the truth is, I was scared. I *am* scared. Because deep down I know I can't be with him until I open up about what happened to me.

"Emma? Are you with me?" Kat asks. I nod, my eyes wet with realization. Kat returns my nod and let's go of my hands. We sit in silence.

"I . . . I didn't mean to . . ." Kat finally says.

"*No*," I tell her. "Don't apologize." I pull my knees into my chest and melt into my chair. Even still, I search my mind for a way around the inevitable. Finally, I'm forced to accept the truth.

"I . . . I think I'm going to talk to someone," I say, my voice hoarse with emotion.

Kat shifts in her seat. "Like . . . like a lawyer?" she asks.

I close my eyes and pray. I pray for guidance, for wisdom, and for protection. If I do this, it won't be easy and . . . it might even be dangerous. Beaux is—well, in all honesty, I don't know what he's capable of. I never imagined he'd cheat on me, much less violate me the way he did. He hid that side of him well. And now, I'm left wondering, what other sides have I not seen? What other terror is he capable of?

"Yeah," I finally say, opening my eyes. "But . . . before I do," I tell her, sitting up straight. "You need to know the whole story."

"*What*? What part don't I know?"

I take a deep breath and one last sip of my coffee. It's cold now, just like my body.

"The other day at Mimi's wasn't the first time I've seen Beaux since the night our engagement ended," I reveal. "It was four months after, and you weren't here."

CHAPTER 15

"Kat! I need your help," I say, knocking on her closed bedroom door.

The bed creaks as I imagine Demetri finds his way off Kat. Her bare feet thud lightly against the hardwood floors as she bounces toward the door. The pit in my stomach grows as I imagine Julian and I in a similar situation.

On Monday night, he asked me over—for Friday night, that is. I struggled to answer him, partly because I was surprised at the request and partly because I didn't know what to say. I admitted to Kat that I want more with Julian, but what does more look like? Is it more kisses, more hangout sessions, full-on dates, or is it even more than that? The sounds Demetri and Kat make during their more and more frequent sleepovers makes me queasy, pale, and sweaty. Is that what Julian thinks will happen tonight?

If Kat hadn't had been home when Julian came knocking, it's likely I would've denied his request, not because I don't want to spend more time with him, but because of how I'm feeling right now—nauseous and on-edge.

Kat swings the door open, and the small breeze is pleasant against my clammy skin. I'm wearing skinny jeans and a long-sleeved black turtleneck. Need I remind you that it's eighty degrees and humid in the lovely New Orleans.

"*Yes*," Kat breathes, looking me up and down. "Yes, you do."

Kat, flushed and half-dressed, takes me by the arm and leads me back into my room.

"Okay, start stripping," she says as she moves toward my dresser.

"*What?*"

"We agree you need help and the place to start is that outfit. You'll melt before you make it down our front steps, let alone up his."

"*Fine,*" I say, yanking the turtleneck over my head. I instantly feel better, though my nerves escalate as I picture Julian brushing up against my exposed skin.

"Emma. *Emma?*" Kat asks, pulling me back to the present. I jump and realize I'm palming the discarded sweater like it's a stress ball. "Okay, I think you need to sit down," she says, helping me to the edge of my bed.

I pull a pillow over my chest and exhale.

"Emma, what's wrong? I thought you wanted this?" Kat asks, sitting next to me.

"I *do*," I nod. "But I'm not sure what *this* is and it's . . . it's scaring me," I admit. "I like spending time with Julian. I even like kissing Julian, and I . . . I'd like to get to know him better. But it's like, tonight just makes everything feel so real," I tell her. "Tonight, I'm going over to his house, *his house*, alone, and . . . it's like a real date. And I haven't been on a real date, let alone a real first date in—I can't even remember the last time."

"Okay, breathe," she says. I follow her instructions. "Julian is not Beaux or any other asshole who would push you too far too quickly. Tonight, you'll go over and have dinner. He may even play the violin, which you love," she tells me. "It will be a nice night and only what you're comfortable with will happen. If not, you'll kick his ass and then I will," she says with a laugh. I smile and nod.

"Now, take those jeans off. If you're not comfortable with dressing to impress Julian, then at least dress comfortably," she tells me.

I exhale and finish undressing. Kat shuffles through my dresser and tosses my favorite blue jean shorts at me. They're a medium wash, high waisted, with frayed edges around the thighs. I slip them on and relax into their stretch. Sticking with black, Kat finds a black muscle tank that covers my chest but exposes my arms. It's soft too.

"There," Kat says, examining her styling skills. "Now, all you need are—"

"Boots, bracelets, and my fedora," I say. I grab my black block-heel boots, brown fedora, and a few bracelets from atop my dresser. I slip them on both wrists and move to my mirror.

I look different despite wearing all of my favorite things. My lips are painted a pinky coral with one of Kat's glossy lipsticks. My eyes are shaped out with shades of brown eyeshadow and a small copper line along my lower lashes. It brings out the hazel in my emerald green eyes.

My cheeks flush as I take in my reflection. I hope I don't come off as trying too hard, but Kat insisted I raid her makeup bag. I think that's what made me opt for the more conservative outfit in the first place.

"Emma?" Kat asks, moving beside me. "Are you okay?"

"Yeah," I say, breathing through the butterflies in my stomach. "I just . . . I look different."

* * *

I lift my hand to knock on Julian's door, but stop myself. I've gone over this a thousand times. I'm safe with Julian. I like Julian. But as much as I assure myself of those things, knots continue to form inside me.

"Oh, come on, Emma," I tell myself.

Taking a step back from his door, I pace the length of his front porch. Our houses are exactly alike. At the end of the porch is a swing. Inside will be a living room, a fireplace, a kitchen and dining room. And it's not like this is the first time I've been here.

Mr. Turnip and I spent many a night playing checkers inside and many mornings sitting on the porch swing reading the paper. He'd always compliment my articles, even though he had to buy a computer to read them. The thought of him calms me, and I find myself swaying back and forth in the southern humidity on the porch swing.

I wonder what he would think of me now, what he would think of Julian. He never cared for Beaux and was keen on vocalizing his opinion on most things he had a distaste for. His was an opinion I could trust, though when I should've listened the most, I didn't.

I had blinders when it came to Beaux, at least until the end. Is that what I'm doing now, allowing myself to be blind to any and all of Julian's flaws? I sit here and I ask myself what they are. Surely, he has some. No one is perfect, but . . . I can't name them. Maybe that's why I'm so nervous. At times, Julian doesn't seem human. But is it Julian that isn't human or is it my affection for him that makes him seem so?

I jump to a standing position as Julian's front door opens. Light invades the dark shadows of the front porch, and the rich smell of chocolate finds its way to me. My stomach grumbles.

Julian steps out onto the porch, wearing his go-to ripped jeans and a black t-shirt that slinks around the contours of his abs. He holds a silver tray with two glasses of wine, red for him and white for me, and a dozen handcrafted chocolate desserts.

"I thought I'd meet you halfway, if you'll let me," Julian says.

I nod and Julian makes his way to me, setting the tray on a small table set up to the side of the swing.

"For you," he says, handing me my glass of Moscato.

"Thank you," I say. My voice is shaky.

"My mom would always make a tray of desserts to start every party she hosted. It became a family tradition," Julian says as he takes his seat next to me on the swing. "When my brother and I were younger, those desserts were the only things we'd eat the entire night. I always liked the chocolate ones."

I nod and sip my wine. He's either just as nervous as I am or is trying really hard to make me feel comfortable. Either way, his gentility eases some tension I feel inside me.

"I'd like to try one," I tell him. "If you're offering."

Julian smiles and turns to face me. Our eyes meet and I'm instantly reminded of why I find his presence so comforting. There's a sincerity in him that I've never seen or felt before.

"I'm offering," he says. With that, he hands me a rather large bite-sized chocolate cake with cream cheese frosting. I try to eat it in the most ladylike way but fail. Chocolate crumbles cover my lips and my jaw widens as I fill my mouth with the huge, utterly delicious dessert.

Julian laughs. I scold him for doing so the second I swallow.

"Don't laugh at me," I tell him, play shoving his shoulder.

"Come here," he smiles. He tilts my chin toward him and brushes off the bits of chocolate cake with a napkin.

My heartbeat quickens as his fingers brush my lips. He takes a sharp breath in as if he feels the same pull between us. His eyes flit to mine for a brief second, but instead of leaning in for a kiss, he stands.

"Now," he says. "Would you like to see what else I've prepared for us?"

My cheeks flush at my own physical urges and I fight through it with a smile.

"Yes, I would."

* * *

Inside, Julian has placed ivory candles on every table and shelf he could find. Their flames flicker and add a soft, angelic movement to the small space as well as an overwhelming aroma of vanilla. There's a navy-blue couch to my right. Above it hangs the painting Julian and I first connected over. Across the room is an entertainment center with a television and bookcases on each side with rows and rows of CDs and records. In the corner sits the record player from Lucid. Jazz plays softly from it.

"Would you like to join me in the kitchen? The food is almost ready."

I nod, noticing the large spray of food spread across the kitchen island. We walk to the kitchen together. Julian places his hand gently on my lower back as we move. I relax into him.

Once in the kitchen, I take a seat on a barstool while Julian pulls a baked chicken out of the oven. I nibble on bruschetta, baked tomato pie, and meatballs and am pleasantly surprised at the diverse spread Julian has prepared. Who knew a boy from California could cook so well, let alone know the meaning of real butter and sugar?

"So, where did you learn to cook like this?" I ask as Julian carves the chicken.

"My mom," Julian says. "She was the only daughter in a single-parent-household with four boys," Julian tells me. "My grandma's first husband, the father of my four uncles, was killed when they were all very young. And when she found out she was pregnant again, off a one-night stand with a stranger from New Orleans, of all the places, she decided she wouldn't contact the father."

I nod, finding his family history intriguing.

"So, as my mom got older, she started helping her mother out in the kitchen. Cooking for a family of six was quite a job," Julian comments. "She was seventeen when my grandma passed." His smile falters for a second. "From there, she took on the responsibility of caring for her brothers until she left Washington. And when my brother and I were born, her love for cooking only grew," he says, cutting me a small bite of chicken. "And while I am in no way her equal, I did pick up a few things."

Julian gestures for me to open my mouth and I do. He feeds me a small bite of chicken, and I have to hold in my moans of pleasure.

"That's um—that's really good."

"Thank you," he says. "Now, the plates are here. If it's alright with you, I'd like to serve your plate, but if you'd prefer—"

"No, that's okay. You can fix it."

"Okay," he says.

I make my way to the dining room, where white roses and loose sprigs of greenery fill the center of the wooden table. It's then that I notice a pop of color just outside the large windows of the dining room.

"*What?*" I ask aloud, leaving my wine at the table. "*What? How?*" I turn to Julian who approaches with two plates piled high.

"When we first met, you stood here and said Mr. Turnip always wished he had a rose bush to look out on," he tells me, leaving the plates on the table to stand beside me. "I thought it would be a nice gesture to show you that I listen, and I care about you, Emma. And I'm thankful that Mr. Turnip was there for you when no one else was. I hope to be that person now," he says, taking my hand in his.

I allow his fingers to intertwine with mine. I want to kiss him. I know that now. But I hold back, not because I'm not ready, but because I'm not sure I'll be able to stop myself once I have him in my arms.

"I think you are that person," I tell him. "At least, I think I'd like you to be."

CHAPTER 16

As we eat, Julian tells me more about his family, mostly his mother.

"She was a gentle woman from Washington," he says. "After my grandma passed, most of the money they had went into getting my mom through high school. By the time my mom was eighteen, college wasn't much of an option. So, she moved to Hollywood to pursue dancing and modeling. It was there that she met my father," Julian says with a smile.

"She always described the night they met as something out of a movie," he says. "She was dancing at a salsa club when my dad showed up with a few of his friends. They were seniors in college celebrating the end of finals and mistook the place for a Mexican restaurant," Julian says with an eye roll. I laugh. "Anyway, my dad noticed a few guys getting handsy with my mom on the dance floor. He stepped in and apparently fell in love on sight with my mom and with music. He thought it was beautiful how she moved to it. It made him hear it in a way he'd never heard it before. That's when the idea for Cole Creative was born, and so was my brother Mason about a year later," Julian tells me.

"Wow," I say. "It appears the romantic gene runs deep. This dinner is amazing, as is the décor."

"Thank you," Julian says. "But make no mistake, I am nothing like my father. Everything good in me comes from my mother."

Julian's reaction takes me by surprise. He doesn't raise his voice. He doesn't appear to be angry. Yet, his sincerity is intimidating.

"Oh," I manage to say, unsure of how else to proceed.

Julian is quiet as he sips his wine. He sets his near-empty glass to the side. His icy eyes are even colder as he takes in the blood red liquid. It's as if he's remembering something, something painful. I know because I've shared his expression far too many times.

"Julian," I say, reaching out to him.

"It's okay, Emma," he assures me. "I just . . . I haven't talked about my parents in some time. Mason, my brother, never talks about them and after a while, I guess I got used to not talking about them too. And once you stop talking, it's easier to push the memories to the side or the back, in my case," he admits. "Both the good and the bad."

"I–I'm sorry. I can't imagine—well," I stop myself. I do know the feeling of loss, but it's not something I can talk about right now. "Just know, you'll see them again," I tell him, taking his hand in mine.

Julian nods. "I'll see my mother again," he says. "But the only way I'll see my father is if I go to Hell and God-willing, I don't plan on taking that trip."

I nod, squeeze his hand, and relax back into my seat. I don't know what his father did to him, but if my own experience with my mother provides me with any inclination, it's that parents are capable of anything when it comes to their children, even despicable things done in the name of providing one with a better future.

"Well, enough about me," Julian says, adjusting in his seat. "I want to know more about you."

"Well, I've already told you about my sister and—"

"I know," Julian says. "I want to know more about *you*."

"Well, I, um . . ." I start. "I'm not sure I know where to begin?"

"What's your favorite color?" Julian asks. His face is stone cold serious. I blush.

"Pink," I admit. "But only in theory. I prefer to surround myself with neutral colors," I tell him, matching his tone.

There's a brief moment of silence after which we both burst out laughing.

"Now, that wasn't so hard was it?" Julian asks. His face lights with laughter.

"I guess not," I say, using my fork and knife to cut off another bite of chicken.

"No, in all honesty, I'd like to know more about you before New Orleans. Like why is it the second you got the chance, you left your hometown and never turned back?" he asks.

I'm caught off guard by his question and find myself shuffling remaining bits of food on my plate as I consider how to answer.

"I, um, I think we'll need more wine if we're traveling down this rabbit hole," I tell him.

* * *

"I was sixteen when I fell in love for the first time. His name was Ezra St. Germain, and he was of mixed race," I say. "He was a senior, and I was a sophomore. We dated in secret for months, because I knew my family wouldn't accept our relationship." I look down in shame as I remember back. "I grew up going to cotillions and society parties. I was a southern belle in our town's Civil War reenactments. My childhood home is a refurbished plantation for Christ's sake," I tell him. "Despite all this, I never thought of my parents as racists or even the people in my town, yet as I got older, they would tell me things like, '*Don't bring home a black boy*' and '*Your cousin Samantha got on drugs because of the black boys at her university, so stay away.*' I was immature and naïve not to see the extent of their prejudice before it was too late."

"*Too late?*" Julian asks.

I nod and take a deep breath.

"Ezra and I were at a party when someone saw us. I . . . I was careful around my parents and at places like the diner and church, because I knew my mom had eyes everywhere. Southern women could make gossiping a professional sport if they tried," I say. "But I wasn't so careful around friends, or at least, around people I thought were my friends. We were spotted and, it didn't happen instantly, but eventually people started treating me differently. The girls threatened to tell my parents. The boys looked at me differently, like I was damaged or impure in some way," I reveal.

"Ezra and I never even had sex," I tell him. "But that didn't matter to them, because it wasn't about sex. It was about the color of his skin," I say, nodding. "That's when I realized that all the things my mother had preached about—perception and reputation—were true, and I was disgusted with my hometown."

I take a few more sips of wine and blot the tears from my eyes. Like Julian with his parents, I haven't talked about this in some time, nor have I thought about it. The memories bring too much pain to be healthy.

"My parents eventually found out," I tell him. "By that point, Ezra was eighteen, and I was technically a minor."

"They didn't?" Julian asks.

I nod. "They had Ezra arrested the day of his high-school graduation. At the ceremony, they announce all the scholarship offers you've received and where you'll be attending college," I continue. "It was a moment for him to say shove it to everyone who doubted him, regardless of reason, and because of *my* parents, he missed it."

I wipe a falling tear as it drips down my cheek. My heart aches for Ezra, even after all these years.

"He and his family were denied that proud moment," I say. "And to make matters worse, my mom bribed the principal to exclude his name from the list of graduates. They made it seem like he never even existed, because if people forgot about him, then they'd forget about us and my . . . *indiscretion,* as my mother called it," I say.

"Did it work?" Julian asks.

"Yes and no," I say, taking another sip of my wine. "No one forgot. They just had enough respect for my parents that they didn't bring it up. But still, the damage had been done, and I knew then Presley was no longer my home," I tell him. "And Ezra never spoke to me again."

* * *

After dinner, I help Julian clean up. We compile the remaining food and soak the dishes in hot water. I demand a to-go plate for me and Kat. Julian laughs and obliges. Before I know it, it's past eleven and Julian is leading me to the couch.

"Now, I never did find Mr. Turnip's missing checkerboard, but I just so happen to have one of my own," Julian says. We sit on the velvet blue couch and before us, on the coffee table, is a checkerboard and score cards.

"You really do listen," I say.

"I do," Julian says. "But don't take my good manners for weakness. I'm a pretty good checker player, if I do say so myself."

"Well, I'll be the judge of that, Mr.," I respond. "But hey, can I just say, I really am sorry."

"For what?" His eyebrows crinkle in confusion.

"For . . . for putting that information about your parents in the article on Lucid," I say, crossing my legs beneath me. "I crossed a line and I shouldn't have included it without asking you first. It's just . . . when I woke up and saw you on the couch, I—I thought it would be wise to get to know the man sleeping next to me," I tell him with a shrug.

Julian grins and pulls his knees into his chest. "Look, it was no big deal. Honestly. I was just . . . surprised, I guess, that you took the initiative to research my family. But, like I said in my text, I shouldn't have been. You're great at what you do. Of course, you did your due diligence," he says. "Though, I must admit, Mason wasn't thrilled with the idea of me loving my new home," he tells me. "I believe you called me *New Orleans's adopted son*," Julian recalls. I blush.

"Yeah, um, I did," I admit, slouching into the cushions of the couch. "But, in all fairness, I was slightly hungover when I did my *due diligence* and tweaked the article," I say.

"Tell that to Mason," Julian says, moving his eyes from me to the record player. The record has ended. Static fills the space between us, only adding emphasis to the words not spoken in regard to his brother.

"Well, I mean, is he really mad?" I ask, sitting up straight.

"You would think he'd be happy to know you're adjusting so well."

"Yeah, you would think that," Julian says, standing. "But um, Mason and I weren't exactly on the best of terms when I left LA, nor did he approve of me volunteering for the transfer."

"Why?" I ask.

Julian hesitates to answer as he moves across the room to the record player. It's not like him to hold back. Perhaps I *am* crossing a line I shouldn't.

"He um . . . well, when I volunteered to come to New Orleans on behalf of Cole Creative, he didn't react well to the idea. Ever since we lost our parents, we've been sort of inseparable, sometimes to our own detriment," Julian admits. "Sometimes I can't tell if he's so overbearing because he needs me or feels like I need him. Regardless, we had a falling out and . . . my leaving has only made it worse."

I see in him now the same sadness I first recognized in him the day we met. He shuffles through his record collection in search for our next tune. If I had to guess, I'd say he knows his albums backwards and forwards. He need not see the album to know exactly which song rests underneath his fingertips. Yet, he can't take his eyes off them. Or rather, he can't bring himself to face me.

"Julian, we don't . . . we don't have to talk about this if you don't want to," I interject. I move my legs from underneath me and watch him as his lips draw into a smile.

"*That*," Julian says. He turns to me then. "That's why I like you so much, Emma. You're intuitive and smart and considerate." I blush.

"Julian," I say, dropping my eyes to the floor.

"It's true," he says.

As if by instinct, he pulls a record from his collection, barely looking, and places it on the record player. Soft jazz fills the air as Julian makes his way back to me. My heartbeat quickens as he takes his place on the couch next to me.

"I don't want to lie to you, Emma," Julian says then. "But . . .

right now, I don't know how to explain what's happening with me and my brother."

I nod.

"Of course. I get it," I assure him. Though, I'd be lying if I said I wasn't a little concerned as to the hold Julian's brother has on him. If he doesn't support Julian's decision to leave LA, the weight of his brother's disappointment may become too much for Julian to fight, not to mention the guilt Julian must feel about leaving his brother in such a delicate time. It's a pain I can relate to in regard to my own family, specifically my sister.

Julian drops his eyes to my lips then, drawing my attention from my thoughts and back to him. My skin feels warm under his gaze.

"What I can tell you," he starts. "Is that I've found a life here in New Orleans that I don't think I can part with. The music, the food, the culture," he rambles on. "*And*, there is this one girl." His lips draw up into a smile as he speaks. "She's blonde and beautiful. She's a journalist with a heart for culture and history. She knows her music almost as well as I do. And she is the reason New Orleans feels so much like home, perhaps more than LA ever did."

My insides tingle as his words caress me.

With that, Julian leans in and uses his fingers to guide my lips to his. Our lips touch, soft and gentle. He moves with care as if asking for permission before each kiss. I lean into him and bring my hand to his thick, tousled hair. It's so soft, so . . .

Before I realize what I'm doing, I press my body more firmly into his. Our kisses grow in passion. I straddle Julian as he lifts me from the couch.

My feet dangle as he holds me close and firm. I pull away for a moment, to catch my breath and allow my flushed skin to cool. A sliver of dark hair falls across his lustful eyes as he watches me. His lips are red and ripe. They quiver for more. My lips draw into a playful grin and Julian lowers me to the ground.

His breathing slows and he takes one step back as if the moment between us has ended. I shake my head and close the distance. I move my hand to his damp neck. My fingers tingle as they are met with tiny droplets of Julian's sweat. I was so worried tonight would end exactly as it is, with Julian and I naked and entangled. But now that we're together, now that I see him, feel him, crave him, there's nothing I want more than this moment with him.

I stand on my tippy-toes and bring my lips to the delicate, damp skin of his neck. Julian removes my fedora and moans as my kisses turn to nibbles.

"Come here," he whispers as he runs his fingers through my hair. Julian lifts me once more so that we see eye to eye. I wrap my arms around his neck to balance myself.

"I won't let you fall," Julian says. With that, Julian kisses my neck, and in a similar fashion to myself, nibbles my skin. I moan in pleasure and pull my shirt over my head. Thankfully, I took Kat's advice and wore my sexy bra made of navy fabric and bits of see-through lace. Julian laughs and then pulls away.

"What's wrong?" I ask through labored breaths. My exposed skin tingles under his gaze.

"Nothing, it's just . . ." Julian starts then stops. I can tell he's trying hard not to devour me. His restraint is endearing. "I don't want you to think—"

"I don't," I tell him, bringing my palm to his cheek. He's fiery hot. "But I . . . I also don't want you to stop."

Julian searches my face for any signs of hesitation. He finds none. I toy with the collar of his shirt, exposing the edge of his tattoo.

"I know it's soon, but . . . I want this," I tell him as I trace the contours of his collarbone.

"So, do I," he finally says.

Julian holds me against the doorframe as he opens the door to his bedroom. Inside, I'm curious to know what his room looks like, but I can't pull my eyes or lips from his as he carries me to the bed.

Julian supports my head as he lays me down. Feathers float in the air as we press our bodies into the down comforter. We both laugh. Julian kisses me and I kiss him as I yank his shirt over his tousled head.

"You're amazing, Emma Marshall," he whispers as he gets on top of me. "Beautiful, intelligent, just incredible." With each compliment, he kisses a different part of my body—my collarbone, my shoulder, my breast. I gasp and close my eyes as—

"Look at me," he says.

"*What?*" My body is suddenly rigid beneath his.

"I said, look at me," Julian repeats.

"*No,*" I say. Behind closed eyes, I see Beaux on top of me. Images of the attack flood my mind. My insides burn as they did the night Beaux ripped into them. My skin, wet with Julian's kisses, feels ice cold as if touched by death. "No!" I scream. Moving my hands to the covers, I squeeze and wriggle underneath invisible pressure.

"Don't touch me," I yell. Beaux smiles sadistically as he thrusts into me. "*No!*" I scream once more.

"Now, we're done," Beaux says. His ghost fades from view.

"We'll never be done," I whisper.

"Emma! Emma?" I open my eyes to a frantic Julian shaking me. "Emma, *thank God!*" Julian gasps as I come to.

Regaining my composure, I move to a sitting position, slinging my legs over the edge of his bed. The surrounding room is dark, as in painted black. Boxes of books and records fill otherwise empty corners. A beanbag sits in the middle of the room with a guitar resting close by.

I feel Julian's eyes on me as I sit quietly. Worry contorts his features, but he doesn't reach out to me. He's afraid of me, afraid he'll break me. Little does he know, I've already been broken.

I shake my head and wipe a few budding tears from my eyes. This is why I'm meeting with a lawyer. This is why I'm going to take Beaux down.

Kat was right. I allowed him to have control over me when I didn't speak up. Well, not anymore.

"That guy from Mimi's, he's the one who broke your heart," Julian says.

I bite my lip, and finally, I nod.

Julian throws his legs over the edge of the bed and stares at the wooden floor, as do I. Static fills the air as yet another record has played out.

"He did more than that, didn't he?"

I turn to him. My neck aches at the sharp movement. Despite my desire to out Beaux and take back my control, I can't bring myself to admit what he did to Julian. I . . . I can't let this disease infect any other areas of my life. Even though I'm afraid it already has.

I turn away from Julian and sit in silence until I work up the strength to apologize and say my goodbyes for the night.

CHAPTER 17

"You were quiet coming home last night," Kat tells me.

Concern and curiosity shroud her sun-kissed features as she pulls my curls into a low up-do. Tonight is the Creative Concepts Gala, and because of my well-received article on Lucid Records, I've been promoted to cover the private auction held in Jackson Square. It's a formal event, think floor-length gowns, fake eyelashes, expensive hairdos, and masques. Apparently, the paintings can go for a million dollars or more. The masques provide privacy to the large donors, but I think it's just another excuse to wear one. They are beautiful, after all. Mine is ivory with flakes of gold underneath the eyes. Embroidered gold fabric finishes out the rest with designs of roses adorned with crystals. Kat had it from one of the Mardi Gras balls she attended, along with the dress I'll be wearing.

"*Emma?*" Kat jolts me back to our rather uncomfortable conversation by tugging on my hair.

"Ow!" I yelp. In truth, she didn't hurt me, not like the memories of last night. I exhale. "I'm sorry. I just—I don't really want to talk about last night," I say.

"That bad?" she asks.

"*No,*" I admit. "In fact, it was quite beautiful and perfect."

Before me, my reflection is barely recognizable. My dark green eyes are illuminated with gold and brown shadows and false lashes. My cheeks are warm and glowing with bronzer, peachy-pink blush, and highlighter. My lips appear larger than they are due to Kat's skills with a lip liner. My mother would be proud. The real me is almost completely concealed, *almost.*

Beneath all the makeup, I see sunken skin and lips that yearn for another's. I didn't sleep last night. Once I got home, just after midnight, I sat in the shower as if the water would drown out Beaux's presence. Even more so, I wanted it to drown out the memory of me screaming and writhing in invisible horror on Julian's bed.

He was kind when I left. He did his best not to make me feel awkward or ashamed. But . . . there was something in the way he kissed me goodnight. It was so light and quick, I barely felt it. It's as if he didn't want to touch me for fear of triggering another episode. In all the beauty that was last night, that's what I can't get out of my head—our goodbye. And I can't help but think, was it *really* goodbye?

"So, why do you look like you're about to cry?" Kat asks me. I suddenly become aware of budding tears that threaten Kat's handiwork.

"I'm not," I say, tilting my head back to keep the tears from falling. "I just . . ."

Regaining my composure, I sit straight and allow Kat to finish my hair.

"I was nervous going into last night. I mean, you know. But once I got there, once I saw Julian, all my nerves went away," I say with a smile. "He cooked the most delicious meal. There were candles everywhere and white roses," I say, remembering back. "He even convinced the neighbors to let him plant a rose bush between his house and theirs. He said it was in honor of Mr. Turnip's memory and a gesture for me to show me that he listens. And he truly does."

Kat smiles as I recount the night. As do I.

"When we finally kissed," I say. I squeeze the silky fabric of my robe as I relive the moment. "I didn't want it to stop."

Kat raises her brow and I find myself blushing.

"We . . . we almost—"

"Oh my God," Kat squeals. She places the last bobby pin and scoots to sit beside me on the edge of the bed. She composes herself. "Okay, continue."

My cheeks feel hot as I feel Julian's hands on my body.

"I, um . . ." I stammer. "I wanted to have sex with him,"

I admit. "And we were going to. We were in his bed. He was kissing me and touching me, and it felt so good, unlike anything I've ever felt before. But then I closed my eyes and Julian said . . ." I hesitate. "He said something that triggered me. And from that point on, all I could see was Beaux. All I could feel was Beaux," I reveal.

"Oh my, Emma," Kat says. She pulls me in for a hug, and I rest my head on her shoulder.

"And now, I'm . . ." My chest aches with revelation. "Now I'm not sure if he even wants to try anymore." My insides burn as I hold in my tears. I'm tired of crying, even if it is over Julian.

"Emma," Kat says. "I can assure you that is not the case."

I pull away and move to my dresser in search of jewelry for the evening.

"I don't know, Kat," I mumble.

"I do," Kat says. "What did I say when Julian sent you those roses?"

They sit next to my fireplace. Half of them are dead now, but I still keep them. I still see the beauty in them.

"You said, he really likes me."

"Yes," Kat says, moving toward me. "He *really* likes you and that doesn't just go away."

"Okay." I nod. I want to believe her. It's easier to than to think of the alternative.

"Now, close your eyes for the big reveal," Kat says.

"*What?*"

"Just close them," she says, moving toward the bathroom.

"Fine," I huff. Kat always has been one for the dramatic.

I hear Kat leave the room, followed by the thud of heavy boxes hitting the floor.

"*Shit*," Kat curses. I laugh.

As Kat approaches, I hear the rustle of fabric. *It's the dress!* I hope she understands that this is a work thing and therefore, I should look understated and blend in rather than stand out. But then, perhaps, I chose the wrong person to borrow a dress from.

"Now, open!" Kat says.

My eyes grow in size and the air leaves my lungs as I am

presented with the most gorgeous, glittering gold gown. Pounds of fabric fill out the ball gown skirt, creating a cinched in waist like no other. It has a semi-sweetheart neckline held up by thin spaghetti straps. The cut is simple, yet the thousands of glittering sparkles and jewels make the gown appear fit for a queen.

"It's . . . it's," I struggle to find the right words. "It's the most beautiful dress I've ever seen," I finally say.

"I know," Kat says. "It practically lights up the room, and so will you when you wear it tonight."

My cheeks ache with how large my smile is. I can't contain myself. But . . .

"Kat, it's—it's too much for a work event," I finally say. "I'm . . . I'm a journalist, not a southern heiress."

"I was thinking something more along the lines of a southern princess, but to each their own," Kat says, tossing the dress on my bed.

It must weigh a ton!

"Regardless, you're wearing it. You can thank me when you get back," she says.

* * *

Kat was right. I look like a southern princess. Most of my makeup is covered by my masque, yet my eyes look more striking than ever. Oval shaped earnings encrusted with diamonds and pearls hang from my ears. My neck and wrists are adorned with complimentary pieces. I've never felt this beautiful.

Lights pour in through our front windows. Grey jumps from her spot on the couch in retreat. She must think someone is coming inside. She isn't a fan of company.

"That must be your cab," Kat says as she helps me into my shoes.

"Yeah," I say. I'm instantly nauseous. Work doesn't frighten me. I'm good at what I do. But this dress . . . I imagine it will attract a few wandering eyes, and the thought of people watching me, complimenting me, it makes me nervous.

"Emma," Kat says, taking my hands. "Take a deep breath. You look beautiful and you deserve to feel beautiful. Now, here's your clutch. It has your phone, notepad, and pen, and a few touch-up items," she says, handing me the small, gold bag. "Go be the kick-ass woman you are."

"Thanks, Kat," I say with a smile. "Bye, Grey," I yell, though our darling cat-child is nowhere to be found.

I open the door and nearly faint as Julian stares back at me. He stands just outside our gate, dressed in a tux. Behind him is a black town car with a driver standing by.

"*What the?*" I ask, turning toward Kat.

She stands behind me, cheeks glowing.

"Every southern princess deserves her prince," she says with a nod in Julian's direction.

Kat re-enters our home and closes the door behind her. The wrought-iron squeaks and Julian approaches. I fight through my nerves to face him.

"H-hi," I stammer.

"Hi," he says as he approaches.

He looks sexier than ever in his all-black tux. And for the first time since meeting him, he's wearing cologne. It's almost as intoxicating as his natural musk.

"What are you doing here?" I ask, making my way down the porch steps.

"Kat was concerned when you went straight to your room last night," he says. "She came over this morning and demanded to know what I'd done to upset you. I told her I didn't think *I* was the man making you so upset."

My cheeks blush in embarrassment. "I . . . I—"

"There's no need to apologize or explain," he says, reaching for my hand. "I had the most amazing night with you, Emma Marshall."

His icy eyes melt into mine.

"And I'd like to continue where we left off, if that's alright with you?" he asks.

"Well, not *right* where we left off," I say, stepping into his embrace. "But it would mean a great deal if you'd accompany me tonight."

"I would love nothing more," Julian responds.

* * *

We reach Jackson Square just as the sun sets. French lanterns illuminate the walkways. Each corner of the garden is filled with art exhibits underneath canopies of string lights.

"You know, as happy as I am to have you here," I say to Julian. "This *is* a work event for me. I'll have to interview a few people."

"Of course," Julian says, moving his hand to my low back. "You can pretend I'm not even here, as long as I'm the one who kisses you goodnight." His remark makes me smile.

"That you will," I tell him. "That you will."

Julian makes his way to the bar to get us both a glass of wine and I scope out the art scene.

Each corner of the park represents a different artistic style. There's a Contemporary corner, one for Eastern and Western art, respectively, and my favorite, the local station.

"Oh, *wow*," I mumble.

This year's centerpiece for local art is a mural of Jackson Square created entirely with beads from New Orleans's Mardi Gras parades. Every year, there are thousands of beads left in the streets. The mural represents both New Orleans culture and sends a message about the importance of recycling plastics. I open my clutch and search for my phone to take a photo.

"It's beautiful, isn't it? Though, not nearly as beautiful as you."

My skin turns to ice at the familiar voice. He places his hand on my exposed shoulder and wraps his arm around me. To my left stands Beauregard Thomas.

Everything in me begs me to run, but my body is frozen, despite his burning touch.

"Stay calm," he tells me as he examines the mural. "I'm not going to hurt you, though I won't extend the same courtesy if your little boyfriend approaches me."

Julian! No, no, no. Beaux will kill him or at least try!

"Let's talk—*in private*," Beaux whispers into my ear. His breath is hot against my delicate skin. "Mmm," he moans. "You smell good."

I gasp at his proximity. My body shakes as he leads me away from the party. I can't cause a scene. I can't drag Julian into this. Besides, he still doesn't know . . .

"Now, that's better," Beaux says. Once we've made it out of the square onto the adjacent sidewalk, he lets me out of his grasp. Regaining my strength, I take it as an opportunity to put distance between us. I never want his hands on me again.

"What are you doing here, Beaux? What do you want?" I ask. I'm surprised I'm even able to speak. This can't be real, but it is. *Too real.*

"What *I* want?" Beaux asks, taking off his mask. The string has left a crinkle in his slicked back, blonde hair. "What *I* want is to know what *you* want?" he says, adjusting his tie.

"*What?* What are you talking about?" I ask. His calm nature is scaring me. I've grown so accustomed to his dark side.

Beaux exhales and leans up against the wrought-iron fence separating us from the party, from Julian. I have half an idea to turn and run, but I don't imagine I'd get very far in this twenty-pound dress and heels. Besides, it's unlike Beaux to seek me out. He made it very clear the last time we saw each other that I was dead to him and he has long been dead to me.

"What do you expect will come of your little meeting with Clarissa James?" he finally asks.

His words take me aback. How does he know about that? I made sure to choose an attorney who has no connection to Beaux's firm. I even paid a cash retainer for fear of my credit card being hacked. He can be resourceful when he wants to be. I guess I had no idea *how* resourceful.

"Beaux," I say, backing further away from him. "That meeting is not what you think. It has nothing to do with you," I lie.

"Well, of course it doesn't," Beaux says. He pushes off the fence to close the distance between us.

"Ah!" I gasp, nearly tripping in retreat.

"Nothing happened between us, Emma," he says, towering over me. I back away, refusing to look at him. "Look at me," he says.

"*No*," I say, pushing past him.

"I said, *look at me*," Beaux yells.

He grabs me by my arm and pulls me back to him. With one arm, he controls me. My hair begins to fall around my face. My dress wraps around my ankles. I'm his to toy with and he knows it.

"*No!*" I scream, closing my eyes as I do. I brace myself for the sharp crack of his hand while praying, desperately, for someone to hear my cries.

Beaux's sharp blow doesn't come. Instead, I open my eyes just in time to see him smile. And with him he takes any sense of strength I thought I had. Because the smile of a psychotic animal such as he is more frightening than his bite.

Beaux pushes me backward, forcing my body against the rough bark of a nearby oak tree. I turn and scan the dimly lit street for passersby, anyone who may help me. There's no one, no one sober, at least. And the ancient, draped branches of the hundred-year-old tree only aid him in his assault.

Beaux laughs as he presses his body against mine. I throw my fists against his chest in an effort to fight him off. It's no use. Just as I fill my lungs with enough air to scream, he covers my mouth with his palm and presses me harder against the prickly bark. It scrapes my skin and tears jewels from my dress.

"I never hit you, Emma," he tells me, pulling my face toward him. "I never touched you in ways you didn't want to be touched," he says as he moves his free hand down my body. I wriggle underneath his touch, but he only squeezes my jaw tighter. I yelp in pain.

"I never made you do things against your will," he says, leaning into me. His breath is hot against my flesh as he brings his lips just inches from mine. "And if you *ever* get the slightest inkling that I did, well," he whispers into my ear. "I'm sure you can imagine how angry that would make me. And when I get angry, there's no telling what I'll do, *is there?*" I don't answer. "*Is there?*" he yells, pressing me harder against the tree.

"*No!*" I yelp. His jaw tightens. The veins in his neck throb.

His cold, blue eyes shine in the New Orleans night as he revels in my fear. "No," I say, again.

Every muscle in my body is on high-alert as I wait for Beaux's next move. I'm trapped, both physically and mentally, and he knows it. He enjoys it.

"That's a good girl," he says, with a nod. He removes his free hand from my chest only to move it to my neck. I wince and shrink back against the tree even more so. My heartbeat quickens. I remember the feeling of suffocating all too vividly. He rubs his finger up and down the center of my throat as if at any moment, he may press, obstructing my airway. My legs begin to shake. My palms sweat.

"Cancel your meeting with Clarissa James," he whispers. "Tell her nothing about me, you, or anything else." It's not a question or request. It's a demand, a warning. I nod in response. I'd be stupid not to.

Beaux smiles and, to my relief, takes a step back. I am left trembling and damp with sweat and tears.

"How *is* the new boyfriend, or should I say neighbor?" he asks. "You know, Mr. Turnip's sudden passing was a sure shame. I know how close you two were. Of course, he never did care for me much," Beaux says.

I wipe my eyes as my forehead wrinkles. What is he trying to say? Why is he bringing up Mr. Turnip? My head throbs and my stomach aches in his presence. I can barely see straight. Still, I manage to ask, "What are you trying to say, Beaux?" Though I'm almost certain I don't want the answer.

Beaux looks at me in an all-too-familiar way. And, like the Devil himself, he brings me to my knees. My palms crash into the cool dirt. The fabric of my dress pools around me as I collapse to the ground. "You didn't," I choke.

Beaux looks away from me, as if contemplating his next words. *He did.* He wouldn't be so careful if he hadn't.

"You never did find his checkerboard, *did you?*" he asks.

My blood runs cold. My stomach tightens in realization.

"*You* . . . you *murdered* him," I whisper.

Beaux approaches me, kneeling down to my level. I straighten my back in an attempt to distance myself.

"You know, I bet if you go to your boyfriend's house and look underneath the kitchen sink, you'll find it," he tells me.

My lips part and my breathing calms. For the first time in a long time, I see the *real* Beaux, the *human* Beaux. The Beaux who is so insecure and afraid of being second-best, he resorts to intimidation and false truths. He built a career on positioning himself as someone capable of anything. Perhaps we give him too much credit.

"You're lying," I tell him. "I was just there last night. We washed dishes. There was nothing underneath the sink but cleaning supplies," I say, speaking quickly. "You're . . . you're lying."

My lips draw into a small grin as the mighty monster loses an ounce of his power.

"*Hmm,*" Beaux moans. His isn't phased by my boldness. Rather, he finds it amusing. "Well, I guess that begs the question, how did it get there? More importantly, who put it there and when?" Beaux's lips draw into a smile, once more revealing his wickedly white teeth. At the sight of his, my smile falters.

Mr. Turnip's body was found just days after Beaux confronted me the second time. The coroner said there were no signs of forced entry, but . . . if Beaux knew where the spare key was, there wouldn't have been any signs. By the time the body was found, Mr. Turnip had been dead for days. The timing works out, but . . . *but why?* But that's the thing—there is no reason why, no reason for Beaux to react so violently, no reason for him to beat me and rape me, no reason for him to murder someone in cold blood. And yet, he did beat me. He did rape me. He has intimidated me and manipulated me. And what if, for once, he's telling the truth? What if he did kill Mr. Turnip? What if . . . what if Julian is next? Or Kat?

Beaux stands, replaces his masque, and leaves me to my thoughts. As the New Orleans night separates us, my mind begins to clear and my heart rate begins to calm. What if he is capable of anything? What if . . .? What if this is only the beginning? He's going to torture me for the rest of my life.

"Beaux," I call out, against my better judgement.

"Yes, my love?" he asks, turning to face me.

I shake my head at his remark. Even now, after everything he's done, he acts as if I'm his, as if I belong to him, as if I always will. Of course, I always was more of a possession to him than anything else.

"If you're so worried I'll say something, then why don't you just kill me too?" I ask.

My heartbeat quickens as I wait for his answer. It's not one I want, but I have to know. He's had a million opportunities to end my life. I always assumed my survival was due to his lack of gumption. Clearly, that was naïve of me.

Beaux purses his lips and takes two steps toward me. I dig my palms into the dirt as he moves closer to me.

Finally, he says, "Because I want you to live with what you did. Besides," he smiles, "there are other ways of keeping you quiet."

CHAPTER 18

"I want you to live with what you did," Beaux whispers against my neck. I feel his lips draw into a wicked smile against my flesh. He twists my t-shirt in his palm. His knuckles are rough against my exposed stomach. He moves his free hand to my chin, yanking my face toward him, but I refuse to look at him. He laughs then and balls his fist. I close my eyes and—

"Ah!" I wake screaming. My sleep shirt is soaked through with sweat. My eyes dart around my room in a panic. Once I'm sure I'm alone, I lie back against the comforter and allow my box fan to cool my damp skin.

"It was just a dream," I whisper. Yet, my words don't calm me. Because it wasn't just a dream, none of my nightmares are. My nightmares are memories and my monster is real.

* * *

I watch from behind the living room curtains as Julian leaves for work. Grey brushes up against my leg as if she can sense my unease.

After Beaux left me at the Gala, I found Julian and convinced him I was sick and needed to go home. It wasn't too much of a stretch. I spent the night vomiting my guts into the toilet while Kat held my hair. I didn't go into explicit detail or tell her what I assume to be true regarding Beaux and Mr. Turnip, but I couldn't deny the fact that Beaux was the reason I was so upset.

Kat told me that this was my second chance to speak out. I should go to the police right that instant and have them swab my neck for DNA. I told her it was no use. He was wearing gloves. In that moment, the thought occurred to me, he probably wore gloves when he . . . when he went after Mr. Turnip. And if the checkerboard really is under Julian's sink, there will be no evidence on it, nothing to connect back to him. Defeat washed over me.

How can I continue on under the shackles of Beaux's threats? How can I move forward with Julian if my being with him puts him in Beaux's crosshairs? The answer is, I can't. I can't live without knowing the truth. If Beaux killed Mr. Turnip, then he's one bad day away from killing someone else I care for—Julian, Kat. *Hell*, I wouldn't put it past him to go after my sister in Presley, even though we barely speak.

Julian. I can't . . . I can't risk his safety and I can't risk our future together by telling him the truth. And if I find the checkerboard in Julian's house, then Beaux is already too close for comfort. He said there are other ways of keeping me quiet, and he's right.

I bite my lip and shake my head.

But what do I lose in silence? I lose sleep. I lose progress. I lose a future where Beaux's threats no longer exist. I lose Julian. I lose . . . myself.

I reach down and pick Grey up. She's warm and soft as she purrs against my chest.

"How do I do it, Grey?" I ask. "How do I keep everyone safe while I take this bastard down?"

"Hey, Emma, I'm going to take a shower," Kat calls from her room. "How about ordering in and a *Gilmore* marathon when I'm done?"

That's our go-to wallow method that cures, well sort of, any issue of the heart. If I say no, I'll be met with a hundred and one questions that I simply can't answer. Though, perhaps Emily Gilmore will have a few lessons on how to destroy a threat.

"Okay," I yell back.

I place Grey in her favorite spot on the couch, nestled underneath Kat's fuzzy white blanket. She closes her eyes and drifts to sleep before I even get my flip-flops on.

I slip out of the house while Kat showers. I expect I have about twenty minutes before she notices I'm gone, and if I find what I think I will, I'll need time to hide it in my room before she sees.

If Beaux was just in Julian's house, that means he hasn't yet changed the locks. And since Beaux encouraged me to look for myself, the key must be . . .

"Right where it's always been," I say to myself.

I jog up Julian's porch steps and look under the planter to the left of the door. Mr. Turnip would change the flowers out with the season. When he died, it was home to a deep red poinsettia. What's left of it still rests, wilted, amongst dried dirt and potting soil.

I lift up the planter and find the key, using it to enter Julian's home. All is quiet and still. While the roses from the other night still sit on the dining room table, the candles are gone and so is the delicious aroma of Julian's baked, buttery chicken. I step onto the welcome mat and close the door behind me. I'm sure to take my shoes off so as not to leave any footprints. No doubt, Beaux did the same.

What replaces the ambiance of Friday night is the scent of Lemon Pledge, a faint hint of Julian's cologne, and retro masculine furniture that looks too new to hold any memories. Well, aside from the couch.

Allowing myself to be sidetracked, I cross the room to the blue velvet sofa and run my fingers over its soft texture. The cushions are still slightly disheveled from our almost-encounter. I smile a sad smile as I envision what could have occurred, the moment Julian and I could have shared. Instead, our night, much like the Creative Concepts Gala, was tainted by the pain-inflicting, stomach-turning Beauregard Thomas.

I stand straight and walk slowly towards the kitchen. Wooden boards creek beneath my bare feet as I move. I rest my hand against the exposed brick fireplace, unwilling to take another step toward the point of no return.

What am I going to do if Beaux is telling the truth? What am I going to do if I soon have reason to believe he murdered Mr.

Turnip in cold blood? There won't be proof, only speculation. And even if there was proof, there's no family to share it with. No one suspects foul play or is working to discover the cause of Mr. Turnip's untimely passing. There's only me and Kat. And that's exactly why Beaux wasn't afraid to boast about his recent conquest.

I shake my head in disgust and purse my lips.

He only wants to frighten me, and him sending me here is just another way in which he's able to control me, another way I *let* him control me.

"But what if it's true?" I ask. Unknowingly, I take two steps forward. That's it, the point of no return.

I move past the kitchen island to the sink. There's a small window above it that looks into Kat's and my dining room. My stomach turns as I imagine Beaux standing here, watching me as he planted the checkerboard.

With resolve, I squat down and take the cabinet handles in my hands. On three, I open both doors at the same time.

Outside the front door, I hear footsteps and a conversation taking place that I can't understand.

"*Oh no!*"

I close the cabinet doors quietly and half run half tiptoe to Julian's bedroom. I manage to make it inside and close the door behind me just as Julian enters through the front.

"I told you, Mason. I'm needed here. I can't just fly back on a moment's notice," Julian says, slamming the front door behind him.

"*My shoes*," I say aloud. I mentally curse myself and cover my mouth with my hand.

"No, being the boss does *not* mean you can do whatever you want," Julian says. I hear him move from the living room to the kitchen. He throws his keys on the island and a stack of papers. Maybe it's his mail?

Julian exhales loudly. I can sense his frustration from here. *Mason?* That name sounds familiar. Oh, right. His brother.

Julian moves closer to his bedroom door and I instantly step back. I scan the room for a way out or a place to hide—there's nothing. Even his bed is annoyingly fixed, or I could have managed to hide beneath his crumpled comforter. My cheeks flush and I search my mind for an excuse, anything that doesn't make me look crazy. I have nothing.

Julian's footsteps cease just before he reaches his bedroom door. Instead, he opens the fridge, then a kitchen cabinet, and pours himself a glass of water. I exhale.

"Look, Mason," he starts, but is drawn away by a knock at his door.

Who could it be? Not that I've been porch stalking Julian since he's moved in, but I don't think I've ever seen him have company. Well, aside from me.

Kat! How long has it been? Should I be weirded out that this is the first place she'd look? I pull my phone out of my back pocket and find no missed calls or texts. It's only been ten minutes. My heart rate calms as I imagine Kat still perfectly distracted as she showers to the tunes of Katy Perry.

"*Beaux,*" I say aloud.

My face turns pale. Small hairs on my arms rise in horror. *What if he was watching?* What if he planned to come after Julian all along, but wanted to make sure I was here to witness it?

I take two steps forward toward Julian's bedroom door. Just as my hand reaches the knob, Julian opens his front door.

"Mason?" Julian asks.

"*Mason?*" I repeat.

"Little brother," I hear an unfamiliar voice say. I hear sounds of an embrace, and Julian welcomes his older brother inside.

Once more, angels have saved me. But how am I supposed to make it back home before Kat notices *now?*

"What are you doing here?" Julian asks.

"Well, when you ignored my requests for your return and the private charter jet I offered, I realized my only other option for a family reunion was to make the trip myself," Mason explains.

I remember seeing photos of Mason when I did my deep dive on Julian. He's tall, like Julian, though a bit more muscular. He keeps his dark brown hair in a short, crew cut compared to Julian's tousled mop. And he doesn't have a tattoo on him, at least any visible ones, which is a stark contrast to his artsy younger brother. He's the more clean-cut of the two and from the tone of his voice, I'd say the more arrogant and narcissistic.

"Well, I'm not sure what kind of family reunion you expect based on how we left things," Julian says.

I feel uncomfortable listening in on Julian's conversation with his brother considering how hesitant he was to speak about Mason the other night.

"I never wanted it to come to this, Jules," Mason says. "I—I know I said some things that hurt you. I know I shouldn't have blamed you for what happened to . . ." Mason pauses. Clearly, both brothers are hesitant to fully express their feelings on why they are now estranged. "But I never wanted you to leave LA. I never wanted you to feel like I didn't want to be your brother anymore," Mason explains. "And now, you're here, over halfway across the country, and with articles like this . . ."

I hear a shuffling of papers and cringe as I imagine Mason holding up my Hub article.

"*New Orleans's adopted son*," Mason reads. "How the hell am I supposed to take this? Am I just supposed to let my little brother set up shop in the armpit of the South and say nothing?"

The hairs on my arms rise as Mason's temper flares. New Orleans is not an armpit and Julian doesn't need your permission to live his life.

"I don't know how you're supposed to take it, Mason," Julian says. "But you *are* supposed to take it."

I hear Julian exhale, and the sounds of footsteps let me know they are moving to the sofa. I inch closer to Julian's bedroom door to hear more clearly.

"Look," Julian says. "We're brothers and we always will be. But just because we're all each other has, doesn't mean our lives are meant to be parallel to one another. I . . . I like it here, in this armpit as you call it. And you are thriving in LA. You're great at what you do, as am I. But what we do is different. Who we surround ourselves with are different types of people. And the truth is, LA hasn't felt like home to me since we lost Mom and Dad," Julian admits.

I bite my lip and close my eyes. I wish I could run to Julian and hug him and hold him. I want to be there for him like he's been there for me so many times before. But, I can't.

"And what happened between us, the things you said," Julian begins. "It just made me realize more than ever that I needed—I *need* a break from it all. Maybe even a permanent one."

"What I said was stupid and wrong," Mason says.

"Maybe," Julian says. "But . . . it wasn't completely false. I do . . . I *do* feel guilt over what happened."

What? What guilt? What happened? What did Mason say?

"And it wasn't what you said that brought it on. I've . . . I've always felt it. You calling me out on it just made it something I could no longer avoid," Julian says.

There's a brief silence between the brothers, one in which I'm sure to hold my breath and steady my toes. These old wood floors are known to whine under weight.

Mason is the one to break the silence. "So, why don't you show me what this armpit is all about? I mean, *clearly* you've found something in this smelly, old, slightly dilapidated seaside town to keep you occupied and entertained."

Julian hesitates to respond.

"Look, Jules," Mason says. I hear him stand. "I'm not here to disrupt your perfect little world. I'd just like to understand what or who is to blame for my brother's newfound sense of being."

Julian smirks. I imagine his lips drawing up into a smile, much like mine are now.

"Let me show you Lucid," Julian says then. "I'm sure after a tour, you'll be just as excited about the possibilities of a New Orleans expansion as I am. And I'll even take you to lunch afterwards. I know this placed called Mimi's. They have the best chicken tacos."

"Great," Mason says. "And, then you'll introduce me to the real reason for your southern fascination, right?"

"Shut up."

I listen as Julian grabs his keys from the kitchen island and locks the front door behind him. I wait a few more moments, making sure neither one of them will return while I make my escape. Once I'm sure they aren't coming back, I slip out of Julian's bedroom and check the time on my phone. My time is almost up. Kat will be out of the shower soon.

I move to the kitchen sink and once more, open the cabinet beneath it. A lump forms in my throat as I pull out a rectangular shaped box wrapped in shiny, red wrapping paper. Small items rustle around inside as I lift it, small items like checkers. On the top of the box is a gold bow and a small envelope with an E written on it. It's Beaux's handwriting.

My skin turns to ice and my hands tremble as I open the envelope. Upon reading it, my head aches with the pressure of the truth. The note simply reads: *Now you know.*

My lip quivers. Tears fill my eyes, but I don't allow them to fall. I'm too angry to cry.

The note isn't signed, nor does it imply anything incriminating. I won't know for sure until I peel back the wrapping paper, but I'm almost certain. Beaux killed Mr. Turnip, and there's nothing I can do to prove it.

* * *

I spend most of the day mindlessly watching *Gilmore Girls*, trying to find a way of moving forward. I wrack my brain for every possibility.

Kat will be the last person Beaux goes after. If his goal is to keep what's transpired between us a secret, the last person he'll threaten will be the one who knows every creepy, sadistic thing he's done—well, *almost*. Eva is relatively safe because she's over five hours away. Not to mention, if he hurt her, he'd have the wrath of the entire Marshall clan on his ass. She's not as good at keeping secrets as I am. *But Julian?* Julian is the one he will go after next, and as much as I've tried, I can't think of a way to protect him. Nothing, except—I need to distance myself from him.

If Beaux is watching me, he needs to think I no longer care about Julian. Or else, he'll find a way to use him against me. Not to mention, I can't keep stringing Julian along like this. I can't keep telling him *yes* just to turn around and tell him *no*. It's not fair to him. I just . . . I hope he understands. If not today, then, one day in the future, one day when I can tell him everything.

"Hey, um. I'll be right back," I say, standing from my place on the couch.

"Okay," Kat says. She watches me curiously. "Where are you going?"

"To see Julian."

Kat smiles a mischievous smile and I play along. If this is going to work, she needs to think we're still together. In fact, she needs to think we're better than ever. I'll use Julian as an excuse for staying out late and any otherwise unexplainable absences I may have.

"Take your time," she says, shoving a handful of popcorn in her mouth. I nod and hold my smile until I make it outside.

The weight of what I'm about to do is unbearable. Julian excites me. He makes me laugh and smile. He's there for me when I'm upset. His kisses and touches feel like what I always imagined true love would feel like.

Wait. Did I just . . .?

I lift my fingers to my lips and turn away from his door.

"I . . . I love him," I say aloud.

The realization only makes this harder, and I pray he'll one day find it in him to forgive me. I pray I find it in me to forgive myself too.

Against my better judgement, I turn and knock on Julian's front door before I talk myself out of it. It's because I love him that I have to do this.

Julian swings the door open only to have surprise wash over him.

"*Emma?*" he asks.

"Hey," I say with a small wave.

"Hey," he says, looking behind him. *Oh, right.* His brother is here. "Come on in." Julian takes me by the hand and leads me inside.

"Uh, Emma, this is my brother, Mason. He just arrived from LA this morning, a total surprise," he tells me, eyebrows raised. I meet his look with a smile. "Mason, meet Emma."

Mason sits on the couch, lifting his eyes from the screen of his iPad to greet me.

"Now it makes sense," Mason grumbles. He stands and moves to shake my hand. "Emma is it? As in, Emma Marshall, the journalist who covered the piece on Lucid?"

"Yes," I say, shaking his firm hand. "It's nice to meet you."

"The pleasure is all mine." Mason smirks. He removes his glasses and bends to kiss my hand. His brown eyes seem to shift into slits as he watches my reaction. My cheeks turn a hot red, as do Julian's.

"Um," I stammer, pulling my hand back to my side. "Can we talk?" I ask Julian. "In private."

"Of course," Julian says, moving his hand to my back. I close my eyes and relish in his touch. After all, it may be the last time we share such a moment.

"Well, if you've got another article to write, you might consider hearing from the other brother this time," Mason says as I move toward the kitchen.

"It's not work related," I tell him.

"Of course it isn't," Mason says.

"Sit down and shut up," Julian tells him. Mason backs away, hands raised as if in surrender.

Inside Julian's room, I move toward the bed but decide it's best I stay away from there. Instead, I stand just inside as I wait for Julian to join me.

"Breathe, Emma. Just breathe," I whisper to myself. "It's going to be okay. You're doing this for him. He'll understand and if he doesn't, he'll forgive you, *eventually*," I tell myself. Though, I'm not sure I'm of much help.

Julian enters the room and apologizes for his brother's behavior as he closes the door behind him.

"He just came in today. I—I wasn't expecting him, and I know he can be . . ." Julian says, struggling to find the right adjective.

"No, no need to explain," I assure him. "It's nice that he's here, that you two are spending some time together. At least, I would assume so."

"Yeah, it is," Julian exhales. "We are working through some

things. I'm trying to make him fall in love with New Orleans the way I have so maybe he'll be a little more supportive of my decision to stay."

"*Stay?*" I ask. "Right. We talked about that," I stammer.

"Emma, are you . . .? Are you okay? I know you weren't feeling well last night," he says. "You look better, but also—"

"Another struggle to find the right adjective," I interject. I look down then and wrap my arms around myself. I couldn't have picked a worse time to do this. His brother is here and if getting dumped isn't bad enough, getting dumped in front of your family is worse. And just when I need to put distance between me and Julian, he's more certain than ever that he wants to stay in New Orleans. But what if my breaking up with him isn't enough? What if . . . what if Julian needs to go back to LA with his brother? What if that's the only way to keep him safe?

I'm suddenly aware that the room is quiet. I look up and find Julian's eyes on me. For the first time since meeting him, they are lightless. His cheeks are hollow. His lips part in anticipation of what I've come here to do, to say.

I sigh and drop my arms to my sides.

"There's no easy way to say this," I say. My voice is so low I can barely hear myself.

"Then, don't," Julian says. He's just as quiet and makes no moves to close the distance between us. He stands closest to his bedroom door. I stand closest to his bed.

My heart breaks for us, and what we're losing in this moment. We're losing a chance to be together, to be happy, to start over. We've both gone through so much and we only want a sense of home and a heart to embrace us. In each other, we both had found that. And now, right after he gets done telling me that I'm the reason New Orleans feels like home to him, I'm going to take it all away. I'm going to destroy us.

Without dropping his gaze, I take two steps back. Against my better judgement, I sit on the edge of his bed. I'm too weak to stand. I motion for Julian to sit next to me and he does. He watches me as I talk, but I don't face him. If I do, I'll break, even more than I already have.

CHAPTER 19

I was a client of Beaux's. I sought him out when I caught wind of the District Attorney's plans to charge me with corporate espionage. This was two years ago. Beaux said he'd be able to get me a plea deal with no jail time. There was just one thing I had to do for him. Beaux coerced me into having sex with him in exchange for my freedom. I'm not sure if you consider that rape. I suppose you could say it was a small price to pay in comparison to twenty years in prison. But . . . what I did, what I allowed him to blackmail me into doing, was worse than a prison sentence would have been. He destroyed me emotionally. I lost all respect for myself. I lost confidence in my abilities to run my company. I tried telling myself I was in control and that it was worth it. It wasn't. That's why I'm speaking up now, even though doing so will ruin whatever reputation I have left. —Marie Holt

Mr. Thomas and I met when I worked as a temporary assistant for another attorney at his law firm. I was twenty at the time, and I hoped to one day be a lawyer. I worked at Shaw Peterson for three months. During this time, I was able to sit in on meetings, use the company break room and gym. I had access to most areas, and it was there that Beaux made his advances. It started off as comments about my appearance. "You look nice today" progressed to things like, "I like that skirt on you" and "That shirt would look better if you just undid one more button." At first, I admit I liked the attention. He was

handsome, in my chosen profession, and respected by
his peers. When he offered to give me some career advice
over dinner, I thought, why not? But it wasn't long into
our date that I realized his career advice came at a price,
one I wasn't willing to pay. He rubbed my leg underneath the table. I told him to stop, but I guess I wasn't
firm enough. The higher his hand moved up my skirt, the
more uncomfortable I felt. I tried not to make a scene,
but I had to tell him to stop once more. His face got really
red and I could tell he was angry, which only made me
feel even more embarrassed. Beaux got the check, and we
left. We'd ridden in his car and even though I insisted on
getting myself a cab, he assured me it was okay and that
he would drive me home. In an effort to salvage a possible
work relationship, I accepted the ride. He raped me inside
his car, right outside my house. I . . . I never went back to
Shaw Peterson, and I never became a lawyer. He ruined
that for me. —**Samantha Carson**

I met Beaux when we were in college. My sorority had a
mixer with his fraternity. A girlfriend and I were playing
beer pong with these two guys. Beaux happened to be my
partner. He was kind. He didn't even make me drink the
beer. After we got done playing, he asked if I wanted to
go upstairs where it was quieter. He said we could talk
and get to know each other. I said yes. I learned soon
after that unless you want to screw, you don't go upstairs
in the fraternity house. You could hear the moans and
movement through the walls. They weren't very thick. As
soon as we sat down on Beaux's bed, we started kissing.
It was fine at first until he moved his hand up my shirt. I
told him, "I thought we were going to talk." He pushed
me back onto the bed and got on top of me. He said,
"Don't you want it? I know you do. You wouldn't have
come upstairs if you didn't." I was stunned. I . . . I tried
to say no, to move from underneath him. He pushed me
back down and said, "Don't be a tease." It wasn't what
he said that made me stay. It was the look in his eyes,

so cold, so unfeeling. And the way he pushed me; my chest ached from just the swift movement of his fingers. I was afraid of what he might do if I tried to leave again.
—Amy Hines

I wasn't raped by Beaux Thomas, but my best friend was. Apparently, she came home one day to an invitation taped to her dorm door. It was written on this old-style paper with gold calligraphy. I know because she showed it to me. The invitation requested her presence at the exclusive, secret club called Gent here in the city. We'd heard rumors about it around campus, but no one ever knew if it was real, which only made it that much more exciting when you received an invitation. Only the people who are invited know the truth and they swear you to secrecy before entry. How? They force the girls to strip down into their underwear and stand in front of a camera and reveal a part of themselves. If they speak of the club or what happens inside, the tape is released. I wish she would've left then. Maybe they didn't let her. She never said. If she did stay of her own free will, maybe she didn't mention it because she was ashamed. Maybe she felt her staying meant she deserved whatever happened to her inside, that she asked for it. Regardless of you or your reader's belief, what happened inside that club should in no way be accepted or defended in a modern society. No one knows where it is. No one knows how to find you once you're inside. They take your phone and your clothes. You have nowhere to turn. And they're there, waiting for you with a drink in their hands. They laugh and talk with you. They allow you to get comfortable, if that's even possible, and then they take you into their private room and . . . well, you can imagine. Ashley committed suicide two months after her assault. It was Beauregard Thomas. She told me herself. Now that she's gone, I know she'd want me to share her story with you. Just make sure you do everything you can to take these bastards down.
—Lauren Jameson on behalf of Ashley Roy

The day after ending things with Julian, I took a five-week sabbatical from work and started my deep dive into Beaux's past. I never could have imagined what I'd find. But with my hard-earned research skills and a few key details to start with—his name, workplace, university, and fraternity—I found myself on a path that never seemed to end.

Beaux's never been one for social media, but he is active in the New Orleans social scene. I checked guest registries for various corporate and charity events hosted in the city. I made a list of his dates, female coworkers, and tracked his notable female clients who have found new legal representation within the past five years. That's how I found Marie and Samantha. Then, I expanded my search criteria another five years. And that's when a single campus police report led me to Ashley Roy and the exclusive club no one speaks of called Gent.

I found fifteen women in total over a ten-year period that claim to have been sexually assaulted by Beauregard Thomas. Of the fifteen, only four agreed to speak to me. Their stories . . . I cry every time I read them, and I cling to them when my energy wanes and when I question the purpose of it all.

The women victimized by Beaux range in age, job, and social status. There is no pattern other than his incessant need to assert his dominance. He's a predator and has been his entire adult life. Through his fraternity he assaulted women in college and continues to do so in his workplace. *Extorting a client?* Even I wouldn't have thought him capable of that. Even now, his damaged soul surprises me.

I have enough against Beaux to turn over to the police. My fingers twitch over the keys of my laptop. With a few clicks of the keyboard, all of this could be over. I could email them everything I have and run to Julian, if he'll still have me. But . . . somewhere along the way, it became more than that. This isn't about taking down Beaux, not anymore. This is about taking down all of them.

* * *

Inside Club Gent, blood red and gold draperies cascade from the ceiling down the walls. They come together at eye level to enclose private rooms off the main space. Many of the rooms are open for viewing. Though I dare not walk too close. Aside from the private rooms, kitchen, and restrooms, Club Gent is a single room with cushions and couches cluttering the floor. In the middle of the space is a fountain adorned with flowers and candles. I'm sure to stay far away from it and the men entangled with women beneath it. Beaux is one of them.

I gained entry as a cocktail waitress. While my outfit, black underwear covered with a fishnet bodysuit, is barely more than the other women in attendance, I'm not supposed to be harmed. They handpick their victims. At least that's what the manager told me when she sensed my concern over working the floor. And from the looks of it, she was right. Each man here, all dressed in suits, has at least two, some three girls surrounding him. All the girls are half-naked in heels with a purple drink in hand. The men practically force-feed them until they beg for a place to lie down.

I move around the space, carrying my tray, hoping to gain enough footage to turn over to the police. I was able to borrow a body camera from The Hub's AV equipment and I've disguised myself with a short, brown wig, false lashes, deep burgundy lipstick and a hand drawn beauty mark.

It wasn't easy finding this place. I had to review city blueprints to find possible locations before narrowing it down. I—

I gasp as a male hand caresses my bottom. I turn sharply, nearly spilling my tray of purple drinks. Before me stands a man with dark hair and eyes. My fear excites him. I can tell by the way his lips curl and his eyes move into slits.

He grabs two purple drinks from my tray, making sure to assess my cleavage as he does. He smiles, pleased with what he sees. So as not to reveal my intentions, I smile back. With a few lingering looks, he moves past me and returns to his prey. I begin to sweat.

What if this was a mistake? What if I'm caught? No one knows I'm here, not even Kat. I could've just turned over the evidence I have on Beaux. With Lauren's mention of Club Gent, it would have been enough for the police to have a reason to investigate it. Why did it have to be me? Why did *I* feel the need to—?

Just as I've made up my mind to bail, I see Beaux drag a girl from the fountain to a private room in the back of the club, and I do mean *drag*.

"That's why," I whisper aloud.

I slowly walk the perimeter of the room until I find myself next to Beaux's room. The curtains are drawn, though there's a small sliver of open space between them. I see other waitresses walk into the rooms carrying their trays. Perhaps they're bringing more beverages to the pair. My stomach turns as I imagine how many people have had the opportunity to destroy this place but haven't.

"No," the girl breathes.

I can't. I can't just stand here and let her be raped. I slip through the curtain without drawing the attention of others. Inside, the girl lies on her back on a giant red velvet cushion. I catch Beaux attempting to undress her as he pins her down with his weight. I remember what that weight feels like. I feel it now. My throat begins to close as if he's choking me all over again. *What do I do now?*

"Come to join the party?" Beaux asks. He turns to me and pulls me toward him by my wrist.

I gasp, spilling my tray of drinks all over him and the girl beneath him.

"*What the hell!*" he yells.

Beaux stands, removing his jacket. From my time with him, I know how much he hates stains, messes, and all things sticky. The amount of sugar in those purple drinks is sure to drive him crazy.

"Clean her up," he tells me. "And be ready to make this up to me when I get back," he says. "That is, if you want your tip."

I nod, doing my best to avoid eye contact. Once I'm sure Beaux is gone, I tug the curtain tight behind him and attempt to wake the blonde girl before me.

"Hey," I say. The girl makes an incomprehensible sound. "I'm here to help you. But we have to move quick," I say, pulling her up to a sitting position.

The girl vomits all over me, the floor, and herself. Now, I have a reason to take her to the bathroom, which is plenty close enough to the kitchen for us to make our escape. I've never been so pleased to be thrown up on.

"Okay, do just as you are," I tell her. "Play the drunken girl with vomit all over her. I'll get you out of here." Most of what I say is only to calm *my* nerves. I doubt the poor girl has any idea where she is let alone what I'm saying.

I sling the girl's arm over my shoulder and allow her body to lean into mine as we walk through the curtain toward the bathroom. The bathroom is down the same corridor as the kitchen. If I can make it to the kitchen, I can make it out the same way I came in. Thankfully, I'm able to make it past all the possible threats without a problem. A sight like this must be common in this disgusting misogynistic rat hole.

Just up ahead, the bathroom is to the right. The kitchen is to the left. Just as I'm about to turn left, the door to the bathroom opens and out comes . . . *my father!*

I open my mouth to say *"Dad,"* but stop myself just in time. As the door to the bathroom swings behind him, I see a naked girl lying on the bathroom floor. *He's one of them.*

He looks me and my blonde companion, up and down like we're nothing more to him than dolls on a shelf. I nearly cry as every memory of my father becomes tainted. He was never perfect, distant even, but never did I see him as the monster standing before me.

"Come find me after you get her all cleaned up," he says.

His breath is alcohol laden and smoky. My body trembles. My lip quivers. He moves past us without touching the girl or me. Despite this, my body goes numb.

How? How is this possible? How could he do this? What else is he hiding? Beaux! Did he know him before we started dating? Did he know what he was capable of?

To my left is the door to freedom, yet I don't move toward it. I'm paralyzed, paralyzed by the reality that is now my own.

The girl, whose name I still don't know, begins to regain her consciousness just as I feel faint and dizzy.

"What? What are we doing? Where are we?" the girl mumbles, rubbing her raccoon eyes with the back of her hand.

"We're . . . we're leaving," I tell her, forcing through my panic long enough to escape.

We walk through the kitchen without being stopped. The cooks and other waitresses watch us with suspicious eyes, yet something about them tells me they understand and wish they had the courage to leave as well. I quicken my step as the exit door comes into reach. I reach for the handle and—

"Where do you think you're going?" a shrill, female voice asks. It's the manager or "the Mistress," as we were told to call her.

"I . . . um—"

"They're with me," a vaguely familiar voice says. I turn to find Mason, dressed in a black suit, standing just on the other side of the Mistress.

"*Excuse me,*" the Mistress says, turning to see Mason. "I don't believe I've seen you before."

"You haven't," Mason says. He compliments her beauty and says he would remember meeting a woman such as her. Mason goes on to explain he's a member of the Los Angeles chapter currently on vacation here in New Orleans. I'm not sure if that's true and I pray to God it isn't. Because if it is, then there are more of these heinous clubs, more women being victimized. And if Mason, someone so close to the man I care for, is involved, then their reach seems inescapable. My insides convulse at the thought.

"These two are coming with me. I have something special planned in my limo outside," Mason explains.

"I see," the Mistress says. "Well, as long as that one is back by 3:00 a.m. for clean-up, you can be on your way," she says, pointing to me.

"Yes, Mistress," Mason says. My blood runs cold as Mason refers to her as Mistress. He's telling the truth. He must be.

* * *

"That black car just up ahead," Mason tells me, pointing in front of me. "Here, let me."

Mason carries my blonde companion up the alleyway to the black town car he has waiting. I follow behind them, mentally searching for an explanation as to Mason's presence here tonight. Nothing I come up with eases the tension in my bones. Even more disturbing than his presence, I'm unsure of how he recognized me. My own father didn't. Has he been following me? The more I think, the more questions come to mind, and I don't expect any of their answers to give me comfort.

I consider running. But as Mason helps Marissa into the car, I know that isn't an option. In her drunken ramblings, she told us her name.

Mason turns and watches me as I take the final few steps up the alleyway to the car. If it's true, if he is a member then he is an animal, a monster. And yet, he doesn't seem to want to hurt me. With this single thought, I close the distance between us.

"Mason?" I ask, unsure of which question to pose first.

"Emma."

Suddenly aware of my lack of clothing, I attempt to cover myself with my arms. Mason smiles. "Here," he says, giving me his jacket. If I weren't so embarrassed, I wouldn't take it. I don't want a thing from anyone in any way associated with that club. Nevertheless, I slip it on over my shoulders.

Finally, I work up the courage to ask my questions. They come out like puzzles pieces scattered across a table, all at once and disorganized. "How did you know I was here? How did you recognize me? How did you even know about this place? Are you really a member?" I ask, praying my assumption is wrong.

"I was walking back to Julian's after grabbing some groceries when I saw you leave your house. I recognized the outfit and knew whatever you were getting yourself into wasn't good," he says. "So, I followed you. Sure enough, I found you here. And to answer your other question, yes, I'm a member. They have these clubs all over the place, especially in major cities. I...I used to be involved in the Los Angeles chapter, but I no longer partake in the pleasures, at least not in over two years," he explains.

I nod, surprised he's in any way related to Julian. Scum.

"Why did you follow me?" I ask. My nature is instantly more defensive.

"Like I said, I knew you'd find yourself in trouble, and trouble for you is trouble for my brother. He cares too much," he says.

Somehow his words feel like daggers.

"Well, for some, caring isn't a weakness. It's a privilege," I say.

"Or a curse," Mason offers up. "Especially when the girl you love dumps you for no good reason," he says.

I take a step back and wrap my arms around my body even tighter. Loves?

"He's not good, Emma," Mason says. "And I may be an asshole who has done things he'd rather not remember, but... Julian is my little brother, Emma. He's all I have, and you hurt him. Still, if something happened to you, it'd only kill him more," Mason says, taking a pause. "You need to talk to him, Emma. If you have any care for him at all, you need to give him closure. He deserves that much," Mason says, turning to leave.

"Mason, wait." He turns back to face me. I bite my lip and despite my better judgement, I tell the truth. "I love your brother, Mason," I tell him, throwing my arms to my sides. "It's because I love him that I have to stay away, at least for now."

I drop my head in defeat. Despite my good intentions, Julian doesn't deserve to hurt. He doesn't deserve to be strung along and played with. He shouldn't have to wait for me, even though I...I can't imagine him no longer being a part of my life. Still, that's the price I have to pay, not him.

My tear-filled eyes meet Mason's. "If you really want to help your brother, then you need to get him out of New Orleans," I choke. Tears stream down my face. "Do everything you can to get him on a plane back to LA. It's the only way I can be sure he's safe."

With that, I slip into the car and pull the door—

"Safe from what? From who?" Mason says, stopping the car door with his hand. I can barely make out his form through my blurry vision.

"Safe from Beauregard Thomas," I say. "Until he's either dead or behind bars, Julian isn't safe. None of us are."

CHAPTER 20

I sit on the stoop of my fireplace as Marissa tosses and turns on my mattress. Coffee is hot in my hand as the sun rises, creating slivers of sunlight on the walls of my bedroom. After we managed to escape Club Gent, I brought Marissa home with me. Kat spent the night with Demetri, so I didn't have to explain the drunken, half-naked girl's appearance. I do wonder what I would've said if she'd been home. My head hurts just at the thought.

I managed to clean her of the vomit, alcohol, and smeared makeup covering her skin. Back in Kat's more reckless days, I perfected the technique. She was conscious long enough to slip into some more comfortable clothes and ask me my name. I told her and she thanked me, and then fell promptly asleep. I, on the other hand, haven't slept a wink.

I was prepared for the unthinkable, for the drugs, alcohol, even for the occasional grope of a passing patron. I was prepared to witness the culture of rape so prevalent within the draped walls of Club Gent. What I wasn't prepared for is the unspeakable.

My father is a member of Club Gent. My father, though I didn't catch him in the act, raped a girl and left her naked and unconscious on the bathroom floor. And he . . . I shake my head and move my hand to my stomach as the nausea returns. He wanted me or, the girl I was disguised as, to come find him, to have sex with him. I can't imagine what I would've done if he'd touched me, his own daughter. Would he have recognized me? What would he have done if he had?

My throat aches as I realize I don't know the answers to my questions. I don't know what my father would have done. I don't know if he would've been angry or shocked. I don't know if he would've helped me leave. I don't know what he would've done to keep me quiet, to keep his secret from my mom and the town of Presley. He *is* the mayor after all.

My hand tightens around my coffee mug, so tight I could crush the glass with my palm with ease. I consider doing it and allowing the broken shards of glass to open me up and allow the pain to escape. I loosen my grip and exhale, knowing that that wouldn't solve the problem or ease what I feel inside.

How did he even find himself in this club? He must've been a member of the same fraternity as Beaux. And therein lies the most unspeakable truth of all. My father allowed me to date and almost marry a rapist, a cheater, a liar, an abuser of women. How is that even possible?

If it weren't for Marissa's presence along with the smudged eyeliner still present on my worn face, I'd think this is all a dream. There's no way this is real, but it is. Still, there's so much I don't know; and I need to know, now more than ever. Hopefully, Marissa will be willing to tell me more when she wakes.

I sip my coffee.

And then there's Julian *and* Mason.

Mason may have helped me escape for the sake of his brother, but he also admitted that he was a member of the club. Which, in so many words, means he's a rapist, an animal, just like the very men I'm working to put behind bars. Yet, he helped me. Yet, he loves his brother, his brother who I love, who I'm working to protect from predators just like his own flesh and blood.

How am I supposed to process this? How is Julian supposed to forgive me when I turn his brother in? And still, in the back of my mind, I wonder, does Julian know? Does Julian know about his brother's . . . *membership*? No, he couldn't. He . . .

I stand, short of breath as vomit rises into my throat.

"False alarm," I whisper after several deep breaths.

I look to Marissa. Her blonde hair is long, like mine. She is fair skinned and has thin lips. Her cheeks are naturally red, yet her skin is clear and fresh, without the hoards of makeup that is. She can't be older than twenty-one, though I'd barely give her that.

Is that what these men do? Prey on inexperienced, naïve girls? It's an invitation-only club and they handpick who they invite. *Sick*. Even with the threat of blackmail, they'd have to be smart enough to pick girls too afraid or too naïve to leave when asked to take off their clothes. These girls would need to be excited about the possibility of being asked to such an infamous, secret club, probably freshmen or sophomores far from home, looking for a way to be accepted in a new city. Despite all of this, they must have something to lose, whether it's their reputation, scholarship, internship, friends, or even the respect of their families.

I remember being their age. It wasn't that long ago, and I had the whole world in front of me. Despite the drama with my family, I had the courage to leave home and start anew. I was attending an incredible university where I received an excellent education. I met people who I truly connected with and I graduated with a job lined up doing what I loved to do. *My* life, the one that *I* deserved, was within my grasp.

These girls must feel the same way. And like me, they must believe if they speak up, all of that goes away. So many of the girls I spoke with talked of how their life changed for the worse after their assault. But . . . it doesn't have to be that way, at least not forever. Through Julian, I was able to learn that and now, I'm fighting for it. But the same can't be said for the old me. The same can't be said for so many other women before me. And it's because of men like Beaux, it's because of blackmail, it's because of shame, it's because of the rape culture and society's refusal to accept it that women, including myself, carry this belief with them. But not anymore, not if I can help it.

Marissa twitches as the sun illuminates her face. It won't be long now until she wakes.

* * *

Marissa sits across from me at the dining room table. After a cup of coffee and some eggs, she finally stops shaking. Though, she's barely spoken or looked at anything other than the floor.

"My name is Marissa. I'd prefer not to say my last name," she says quietly.

"That's fine," I tell her.

There's a tape recorder between us, which I notice she keeps looking at.

"I'd like to start by telling you that you're safe now. No one is going to hurt you here," I tell her.

She nods. "But what about out there?" she asks me. "What happens when the brothers find out I've spoken with you. They have footage of me . . ." she stops, wrapping her arms around herself.

"I know you're afraid," I say. "Believe me, I . . . I know exactly how you feel."

She looks at me then. "You do?" I nod.

"The same man who tried to assault you last night, Beauregard Thomas, he's my ex-fiancé," I tell her. "And the man who raped me."

My stomach is in knots as I speak. I don't think I'll ever get used to saying that word. It'll never be easy. But with this realization, Marissa seems to ease.

"I can't promise you that the footage of you won't be released," I tell her. "But . . . I can promise you that with your testimony, I will have compiled enough evidence to not only take down Beaux but to take down all of them, the entire brotherhood. They'll never be able to hurt you or anyone else again."

Marissa leans forward in her seat. Her brown eyes gloss over as she remembers back.

"But that's if they're arrested," she says. "If they . . . if they are bold enough to do this and clever enough to get away with it, then . . . they must have some sort of contingency plan if someone *did* speak out," she says. "They must . . ." she begins, but I stop her.

"Marissa," I say. She looks at me, doe eyed. "You're not wrong. But the thing is, they're arrogant and comfortable. Men like them are used to getting what they want. They're used to being powerful," I tell her. "But they only keep their power because no one has stood up to challenge it," I say. "We, the victims—no, *survivors*—we give them their power by staying silent. It's no different from anything else in our world. When a boss mistreats his employees and they stay silent, the boss stays in power. When there is an election and we don't vote, we forfeit our power. But you see, we *have* the power," I tell her. "We have power inside of us. We have power against our oppressors. We have the power to create change. But we have to speak up to harness it." I pause.

"I'll . . . I'll understand if you're not ready. Truly, I will. I've . . . I've sat on my own truth for nearly a year now. Many women will sit on theirs until the day they die, and that's okay," I say. "But our silence protects our predators," I tell her. "We cannot change the culture if we do not first acknowledge it."

Marissa listens to my plea and sits quietly for a while. I worry that I've pushed her too hard. In her situation, I would bolt and run as far as I could, away from the truth, and anyone who wanted me to speak out. This is why I'm thankful that Kat didn't push me, despite her knowing what Beaux had done. Still, she was right. Every day I didn't speak up, I allowed him to keep his power, over me, and over all the women he's harassed and assaulted since. Without Marissa, I will make my case. But with her, I am sure I—*we*—will win.

"Okay," Marissa finally says. "What do you want to know?" she asks.

My lips lift into a pained smile.

"Start where you're comfortable," I say. With Julian's words, I find my own sense of strength and sit quietly as Marissa tells her story.

"I first heard about Club Gent from my friend Stacy. We were both freshman at the time, and she and I had rushed the same sorority. The invitation she received made it clear that the club was secret, and she couldn't tell anyone anything about it. But we were really close, so she told me about receiving the invitation. She was so excited because she thought it was an exclusive mixer," Marissa tells me. "She thought it was a good thing, that she'd been noticed by the right people, perhaps was being invited to join some secret society," she explains, fidgeting in her seat. "She had no idea what she was getting herself into."

"So, she'd never heard of Club Gent before receiving the

invitation? She'd never heard any of the other girls talk about it?" I ask her.

"No," Marissa assures me. "But . . . I mean, every campus has some secret, exclusive activity and the less you know, the more exciting it is. The invitation was vague to say the least. Mine was as well. It was this old paper with beautiful, gold calligraphy, but . . . it had an address, a privacy notice, and . . . your name. That was it," she says, looking away.

"Stacy never told me what really happens when you accept the invitation," Marissa says. "She . . . she never spoke of that night and in fact, she hardly spoke to me for a good while after," Marissa says, remembering back. "Maybe she thought it best to keep her distance, for fear that I'd ask too many questions. But . . . I didn't press her, because I didn't want to jeopardize her membership to whatever amazing thing she'd just been invited to join," she explains. "I wish I would have, though."

"When I received my invitation, I recognized it immediately from the one Stacy had shown me. Like anyone, I thought it was cool," Marissa admits. "Because it had my name on it, I knew it wasn't some mass invite like the ones frats put on the windshield of your car or slide underneath your dorm door. This was . . . this was personal, and it was exclusive," she says with a nod.

"So, I went to the address it provided. There were about twenty, maybe thirty other girls between the age of eighteen and twenty waiting in a parking lot beneath some hotel in the city. I only recognized one or two of them. I . . . I don't know how they decide who to invite," she says. "Anyway, when I got there, I thought it was weird that the invite would send us to a parking lot. But then, two limos showed up, and a woman came out of one of them. She told us to call her Mistress and that she would take us to the club. But first, we had to give up our cellphones and purses and agree to be blindfolded," Marissa recalls.

She shakes her head and curses herself, wishing she would have recognized the scam then. I want to tell her it's okay and not to blame herself, but I know nothing I say will make this any easier.

"Anyway, I did it and at this point, I felt nervous, but not afraid. Nowhere in my mind did I think I'd be asked to . . . to take off my clothes and show myself in front of a camera," she chokes. Tears fall from her eyes.

"Can I ask," I begin, but stop myself.

"Why I didn't leave?" she offers up, wiping her eyes.

"Yeah," I say with a nod.

"I thought . . . I thought the worst was over, if I'm being honest," she says. "I . . . I didn't have my phone or wallet and I had no idea where we were. By the time I was asked to take off my clothes, I didn't know *how* to leave. And once I'd made it through the most traumatizing experience of my life, I . . . I couldn't imagine it getting any worse," she tells me. "I thought it was just some stupid, sadistic initiation and that we'd be given our clothes and things once we made it into the club. Obviously, I was wrong."

Marissa begins to cry, and I offer her a hug, which she declines. "No, I don't want—"

"It's okay. I get it," I tell her.

She takes a deep breath.

"I just . . . I wish I would've realized. I wish Stacy or someone would've warned me," she chokes.

My vision blurs as I think of all the women Beaux has assaulted because I didn't speak up. I think of how my life could've been different if the women before me would've said something. I shake my head, dislodging the ill thoughts from my mind. It's easy to get consumed in the avalanche of what-ifs, especially when your reality isn't one you would've chosen for yourself. But, in matters like this, it's best to stick to the facts. The fact is Stacy isn't the reason Marissa found herself in last night's predicament. Nor am I the reason Beaux has continued his assault against women in the months after our breakup.

"Now you're warning them. You're saving them," I tell her. And with my words, I hope she takes a little comfort.

CHAPTER 21

Marissa told me she was going home to Florida until my article is published in The Hub exposing Beaux and the brotherhood. I didn't tell her I didn't blame her, because the last thing I wanted to do was add to her fear. But she was right to leave. I just wish Mason would've taken my advice and gotten Julian out too, but it's been almost a week since he helped me escape from Club Gent and he and Julian are still living next door.

I shuffle through what passes as my closet, tossing things aside until I find my duffle bag. Tomorrow, I leave for Presley for Eva's wedding weekend. It seems like yesterday she was telling me of her engagement. Here we are, two months later, and what I thought would be my greatest source of anxiety is actually my saving grace. Don't get me wrong, I'm not thrilled to be going home, especially after what I've just learned about my father. But, under the given circumstances, I'll take him as my adversary over Beaux. Besides, there's one more thing I need for my article, and I have a feeling I'll only find it in Presley.

Kat's working this weekend, or I would've asked her to tag along. I suppose it's for the best. She'll stay with Demetri until I get back. I still haven't told her what I'm doing. But with each passing day, it becomes paramount that I do. Just as I worry for Julian's safety, I worry for hers. If Beaux caught even the slightest whiff that he might be exposed, there's no telling what he'd do.

Knock, knock, knock.

I gasp and turn, twisting my neck into a painful knot. There's someone at the door.

"I'm editing photos!" Kat yells from her room. "Can you see who's at the door?"

"Yeah!" I yell back.

My palms sweat and heartbeat quickens. We're not expecting anyone. Though, I imagine Beaux wouldn't extend the courtesy of knocking. With that as my comfort, I grab a knife from the kitchen on the way to the front door and hold it behind my back. Grey watches me with suspicious eyes.

"Who . . . who is it?" I ask. I move toward the door slowly, half expecting the person on the other side to knock it down at any second.

"It's Mason," Mason says from the porch.

"*What?*" I ask aloud. "Why the hell is he here?" I mumble to myself.

Remembering Kat still doesn't know about Julian and my breakup, I open the door, if only to get rid of him.

"What the hell are you doing here?" I whisper.

"Uh . . . okay," Mason says, raising his hands in surrender. "That's not necessary."

"What isn't necessary?" I ask. "You can't be here. My roommate might see you—or worse, Julian might," I tell him, glancing over my shoulder to make sure Kat isn't within earshot.

"Fine, but does that really warrant a stabbing?" He moves his eyes to my hip where the kitchen knife dangles.

"Oh," I say, moving it behind my back. "I, uh, I didn't know who it was and—"

"And you thought it might be your ex," he says, cutting me off. "And by ex I don't mean my brother."

I'm taken aback.

"*What?* What are you talking about?" I ask, playing dumb.

"I think we should talk," Mason says. He glances in the direction of Julian's house, as do I. My heart aches at the thought of him just a few feet away and so completely cut out of my life. "Preferably not where my brother might see. Unless, of course, you're ready to bring him in on this?"

"No," I say, crossing my arms over my chest. "It's bad enough you know." After another moment's thought, I cave. I can't very well leave him stranded on the front porch for one of the nosy neighbors to see. Beaux has many ways of gathering his information.

"Fine," I say. "But you have to stay quiet. My roommate, she . . . she doesn't know about all this or that Julian and I broke up," I explain.

Mason's eyebrows shoot up in curiosity, much like Julian's.

"As a mouse," he whispers, lifting his finger to his lips. I roll my eyes and drag him inside. Grey runs from the living room to the dining room at the sight of him. She always was a smart one.

Mason moves quietly through the house, and just as Kat opens her bedroom door, Mason makes it through mine.

"Who was it?" she asks.

"Uh . . . Jehovah's Witness," I tell her. "Anyway, I've got to pack, but do you want to do Chinese for supper?" I ask, moving into my room.

"Um, *of course*," Kat says, as if I need ask.

"Great! I'll place the order," I tell her, closing the door before she can respond.

"Thanks!"

I close my eyes and exhale as I lean against my bedroom door. I hear Kat pour herself a glass of wine in the kitchen and then retreat to her editing. If I'm lucky, then that and visions of Chinese food will occupy her for the next hour while I check myself into a mental hospital for allowing Mason, the rapist, into my bedroom.

Opening my eyes, Mason watches me from the edge of my bed. I'm instantly nauseous.

I ignore him and move to grab my phone from atop my dresser. I find my most recent playlist, click play, and turn the volume up. Regardless of my needing to tell Kat about my plan, it can't be like this. Once I'm sure she can't hear us, I turn back to Mason.

"Nope," I tell him. "*Up*. I don't allow rapists into my bed," I say, crossing my arms over my chest.

"*Wow*," he says, standing. "First you hold me at knifepoint, then you force me into your bedroom, and now I'm a rapist who's refused the right to sit?"

"Mason," I say, exhausted. "Whatever this is, I really don't have time for—"

"For the truth about your ex-fiancé's past?"

"What are you talking about?" I ask, less than impressed. It's then that I notice the yellow folder he holds in his hand. It's labeled *B. Thomas* with the name *Mathis* in parentheses. "What is that?" I ask, nodding toward the folder.

"Something I thought you should see. Something I think you're going to want to sit down for."

I bite my lip and reluctantly allow Mason to sit across from me as he shows me what he's found.

"Beauregard Thomas, then Beauregard Mathis, was ten years old when he was taken into Child Protective Custody on the grounds of abuse and neglect," Mason says.

Mason gives me the folder and what's inside breaks my heart. Beaux was abused by his father between the ages of eight and ten. There's court testimony in which his birth mother, Helena, admits that Beaux told her about the abuse and asked her to make it stop. Instead, she did nothing but drink. She didn't abuse her son, but she did nothing to stop the abuse he was already suffering.

There are photos of the house they lived in. It wasn't much bigger than my place now and just as old. There are beer bottles everywhere and rat traps on the kitchen floor. The furniture is covered with stains of God only knows what. Maybe this is why Beaux never liked coming over here. Our house is in no way in this condition, but it *is* small and old. He always complained about it and labeled it as such. Maybe it triggered something in him.

I shake my head, angry at the sympathy I feel for him.

Mason has photocopies of pictures Beaux drew in a therapist's office once he'd been adopted. He draws himself sleeping. He always colors himself in the color blue. A man drawn in red crayon watches him sleep. You don't need a degree in psychology to figure out what he was trying to say.

"I uh, I can't look at this anymore," I say, through tear-filled eyes. I hand the papers back to Mason.

"I—I didn't mean to upset you," Mason says.

"Then what *did* you mean?" I ask, turning to look at him.

"I just . . ." Mason exhales. He stands and walks toward the fireplace. Without facing me he says, "I wanted you to know *why*, why he hurts people, why he hurt you."

His words hit me like a ton of bricks. *He knows?* About . . . about *me*?

"*What?* What are you talking about?" I ask for what seems like the millionth time. I pray he's wrong. I pray he doesn't say—

"I needed to know why he was a threat to my brother," Mason says, turning to face me. "Obviously, Julian is at risk because of his connection to you. But what is your connection to Beauregard?" Mason asks. He drops his eyes to the floor and moves to sit beside me. "There's no record of it," Mason says. "No physical proof of any sort, not even a hospital admittance. But I know what he did," he assures me. "The same thing he did to all the others."

My cheeks turn red and I suddenly feel small in his presence. I haven't even told Julian about this. I can't have his brother know, his brother who . . .

"Well, if you know," I say, slowly. I refuse to look at him. "Then you know none of this information excuses what he's done."

"*I know*," Mason says, nodding. "But what if he could stop hurting people? What if he could be better? I mean, isn't that the point of everything you're doing?" he asks me. "Just because someone goes to jail, doesn't mean they won't go right back to their old ways once they're released."

"Well, maybe he won't be released."

"Oh, Emma," Mason says. "I barely know you and yet I know you're not *that* naïve."

He's not wrong. I know how difficult it is to prove a rape occurred, especially when there's no DNA evidence. And because of the time that's passed between the occurrence and now, there won't be. Of course, a good attorney could get Beaux on any number of other charges—extortion, bribery, sexual harassment, serving alcohol to a minor in the case of Marissa and I'm sure countless others. But the thing is Beaux *is* a good attorney with a stellar reputation among the New Orleans elite. Even with the video evidence from Club Gent, under the right circumstances, this case goes nowhere. I'll be dubbed an unreliable source due to my history with Beaux and the whole thing could be thrown out. But that doesn't mean I shouldn't try.

"So, what are you saying?" I ask Mason. "Are you saying I don't try? I sit on my evidence and the stomach-twisting testimonies of women who he's abused and wait for him to have some emotional epiphany?"

"No," Mason says. "In fact, I'm . . . I'm not telling you to do anything. But I just thought you should know, when given the chance to change, when shown true empathy, even the most vile and cruel can change for the better. I should know," he admits.

Mason fidgets in place as he considers what to say next. I grow tense beside him. The music plays loudly in the background. I begin to sweat at the thought of no one being able to hear my screams.

"Um," I start, standing.

"When I was eighteen and Julian was sixteen, our mom was diagnosed with breast cancer," he tells me then. He stares straight ahead as he speaks and I find myself sitting down, once more, next to him.

"She beat it, but she had to fight it for several years before reaching remission," Mason says. "During that time, my dad's worst qualities of impatience, dominance, and pride came to light. He started cheating on my mom, even going as far as to bring the women into their bedroom. My mom had her own hospital-grade room in a different wing of our home," he explains.

"Julian and I saw what he was doing, and it affected us both in two completely different ways," Mason says. "Julian was angry at my father, rightfully so. He threatened to tell my mom just to get my dad to stop," Mason pauses then, clearing his throat. "But, ultimately, he didn't because I begged him not to. It would've only hurt my mom, our mom, and who knows how it would've affected her recovery," Mason explains. I nod.

Mason's story of his father's infidelity brings me back to the night Julian cooked me dinner. We talked about his family, briefly, but enough to get an idea of Julian's relationship with his parents. He said he was sure his father went to Hell but didn't elaborate. It was clearly a sore subject for him, and I can see why. The weight he carried all those years must've been unbearable.

"Instead he pulled away from most people, especially girls, and he threw himself into his music. It was his way of escape, of dealing with the surrounding horror," Mason continues. "I took a different approach," he admits. His eyes shift in my direction as if considering whether he should continue.

"It's okay. You can continue," I say, though I'm afraid of what he may say.

"I started . . ." he begins. "I started viewing women as the problem. I—I blamed them instead of my dad for tearing my family apart. Even though my mom didn't know what was happening, Julian and I felt the divide forming between the four of us. And it was easier to blame them than my father, because, deep down, I—I wanted things to go back to normal. I wanted my mom to recover and my dad to be the doting husband he once was," Mason explains. "So, I . . ." he hesitates. "I hunted them down."

"The women?" I ask.

"Yeah." He nods. "I hunted them, and I made them never want to come back nor think the name John Cole ever again." His face turns red as he speaks. His fists clench.

"And . . . and how did you do that?" I ask, though I already know.

He's quiet at first. He closes his eyes as if to keep from crying. When he opens them again, they're bloodshot red.

"I raped them," he admits.

My blood runs cold, but I don't move. I knew this much. I just had to hear him say it.

"And it worked," he says. "They never came back. But, uh, turns out they weren't the problem," he tells me. "Even after my mom recovered, my dad never stopped cheating. By the time I realized I was punishing the wrong person, it was too late."

"What do you mean, *too late*?" My eyes move to the kitchen knife sitting just a few feet away. *Please God, don't let him say—*

"By the time I realized I was punishing the wrong person, I

couldn't stop. I was infected with this disease that fed on pain. The more pain *I* felt, the more I sought out a release—or revenge, rather. And through my involvement with the Gents, I only became an ever more dangerous predator," Mason admits.

"*Why?* Why are you telling me all this?" I ask. Blood rushes to my head as if to tell me to get the hell out, *now*. I don't listen.

"It's like I said before," Mason says, looking at me. "Trauma affects people in different ways, and even the most cruel and vile, when shown empathy, can work toward redemption," he says. "I haven't been involved with the Gents in well over two years now. I unofficially resigned the second my parents died. I say unofficially, because official resignation isn't allowed. And I—I haven't hurt nor thought about hurting another woman since," he tells me. "I *have* spent a small fortune on therapy and donating to charities that support survivors of sexual violence," he says. "I, uh, I realize what I've done can never be erased nor forgotten, especially not within the minds of the women I hurt, but . . . I'm trying, Emma. And at the end of the day, isn't that all we can do?"

I don't answer, because I'm honestly not sure how I feel. Instead, I ask, "And who showed you empathy?"

Mason looks at me then as if I should already know. "Julian," he says.

"What the hell is this?" Julian says, storming through my bedroom door.

"Julian," I say, jumping to a standing position. He moves past me and goes straight for Mason.

"What did you do? Did you touch her?" He yells.

Julian lifts Mason, despite his size, to a standing position and slams him against my bedroom wall.

"No," Mason says, but Julian isn't hearing it.

"I swear to God I'll kill you," Julian growls. He presses his brother harder against the wall. Mason squirms under his force.

Mason wasn't lying when he said Julian isn't doing well. His eyes look like he hasn't slept in days. His cheeks are hollow, and his hair is messier than ever.

"Julian!" I yell. "Nothing happened. We were just talking. I would never do that to you. Just, come here," I beg, tugging on his arm.

"*No*," Julian says, forcing me to take a step back.

"Was this your plan?" he asks Mason. "You read Emma's article and realized I'm actually doing good and decided to come mess everything up as payback for telling Mom the truth about Dad?" Julian asks. "You pretended you and I were good just so I'd invite you to stay and help me with the Lucid renovation. All the while, you were scoping Emma out, waiting for your moment to pounce," Julian growls.

"Julian, stop," Mason says. "This isn't revenge for you telling Mom the truth. I know I blamed you for what happened to her and Dad. The car crash and everything, but I was wrong. I told you that," Mason assures Julian through gritted teeth. He struggles under Julian's grasp.

"Yeah, right," Julian says. "You warned me. You warned me in LA that you'd make me pay for Mom and Dad's death. You blamed me. You blamed me for their car accident the second I admitted I told Mom the truth about Dad's lying, cheating ass. Never mind the fact that he was scum. *You* blamed *me*. After everything you've done, everything I've forgiven, *you* blamed *me*," Julian says. "And now, you expect me to believe that you and Emma were just *talking*, that you're some kind of fast friends. *Highly unlikely*. But you know what, shame on me. I should've known better than to expose the girl I *love* to you, for multiple reasons . . ."

Julian continues, but all I hear is the word *love* over and over again. *Love*. This is in no way how I wanted to first hear him say it, but it still feels exactly how I imagined it would. It fills me with hope and warmth and . . . a greater responsibility to protect him.

"Julian, I wouldn't . . ." Mason starts.

"Stop lying to him," I say.

"*What?*" Both Mason and Julian look to me at the same time. If I thought I broke Julian's heart before, what I'm about to say next will surely break the rest of him and me along with him. But I have no choice. My article will be published in three days and he'll be the first person Beaux comes after when it does.

"We can't keep hiding this connection, Mason," I say. The light leaves Julian's eyes as I speak. His grip loosens on Mason's shirt until he's barely standing himself. "After all, it's why I ended things with your brother in the first place."

"Emma," Julian says, taking a step back. "*What?* What are you trying to say? What's going on here?" he asks.

I drop my eyes to my bare feet and lift my hand to my chest as my heart aches beneath my skin.

"Julian, I'm with Mason now. I . . . I have been since he got to town," I lie.

"You're lying," Julian says. "I don't know why he's here, but I know it can't be that."

His face contorts as if begging for it not to be true. Unable to hold his gaze any longer, I look to Mason, who *clearly* isn't happy with me, but plays along despite this.

"It's true, Jules," Mason says. "You took everything from me when you told Mom the truth about Dad," he continues. "Any hope of us being a family again was gone the second she found out about the cheating. And you and I both know the driver didn't just lose control," Mason tells his brother. "Mom and Dad were fighting, fighting because you couldn't keep your mouth shut, and *they* distracted the driver," Mason says, taking a pause. "You're the reason they're dead and now, so is your chance at happiness," Mason says, moving to place his arm around me.

I do my best to conceal the tension in my bones and keep the truth from spilling out. The same can't be said for the tears that run down my face.

Julian stands tall in light of his brother's remarks. After a brief hesitation, he walks out without saying a word to either us. I wait until he slams the front door closed to move from underneath Mason's arm.

My legs grow numb, and I stumble to the edge of my mattress.

"What did I just do?" I choke.

Mason looks at me. Tears fill his dark brown eyes.

"Something I hope you can fix, *but* . . . something I doubt my brother will ever forgive."

CHAPTER 22

"Beaux, where are we going?" I ask.

Mosquitoes buzz around me as Beaux leads me, blindfolded, along the sidewalk. I've nearly tripped three times.

"We're almost there," he tells me.

Today marks our being together for two years. We had a fabulous dinner at Emeril's, where Beaux surprised me with a pair of diamond stud earrings. Afterwards, we took a romantic stroll through the French Quarter. I can't remember the last time we spent this much time together, having fun no less. Just as I thought the night was over, Beaux asked if he could blindfold me. Inspired by the mood of the evening, I said yes. But we've been walking for what seems like forever, and I'd give anything to take these heels off.

"Alright," Beaux says, positioning me. He pauses and breathes heavily.

"Still blindfolded here," I say. He doesn't respond. "Beaux?"

I sense Beaux move in front of me. His lips touch mine and we kiss. He tastes like the peppermint cheesecake we had for dessert. He pulls away and . . .

"What's going on?" I ask.

Beaux removes the blindfold and before me stands a gorgeous, tan and gray double-gallery home. Surrounded by a wrought-iron fence, green shrubs, and palm trees, the home is framed with a pair of French style lanterns and large floor-to-ceiling windows accented with brown shutters. Columns with ornate details line the porches on both the first floor and the second. The porches are lit with more lanterns that hang from the ceiling.

"Beaux, what? What are we doing here? Whose house is this?" I ask. I'm barely able to pull my eyes away from what might just be the most gorgeous home I've ever seen.

"It's yours," Beaux says then.

I look to him without saying a word. Beaux has been known for the dramatic party or ostentatious gift here and there, but this? There's no way he's bought me a house, though I do spot a "For Sale" sign on the front left edge of the property. Gosh, the grass is so green. And it's just far enough off the street for the perfect neighborhood views. The oak tree out front is the perfect touch.

"Beaux," I start.

"Emma," he says. His tone shifts to something serious. "It's yours," he tells me. His blue eyes bore into mine. "If . . . you marry me."

At that, Beaux drops to his knee and pops open a burgundy velvet ring box. Inside is the most gorgeous ring I've ever seen. A single diamond, emerald cut, sits atop a solid gold band. Classy, sophisticated, shiny, and expensive. I wouldn't be surprised if my finger ached under its pressure. My finger. My ring. My house. My . . . husband?

"I . . . um," I stammer.

Beaux stands and slips the ring onto my ring finger. It is heavy. And despite the darkness surrounding us, it nearly blinds me.

"Emma," Beaux breathes. "I know I don't say things like this, ever. But . . . you truly are the best part of my life."

"What?" I ask. I wouldn't have guessed that with the amount of time he spends at work and the little amount of time he spends with me.

"It's true," he says. "I know I put a lot of focus on work, but it's only because I want this," he says, turning to face the house. "I want the car, the house, the wife, the life. And I know you might be thinking, well, you already have everything, but I want to do it on my own, without my parent's money. And I want you," he says, turning back to me. "None of this is worth having if you're not a part of it too."

Wow, I . . . I've never heard Beaux speak like this, nor have we ever talked about marriage. I mean, I assumed we would get married. We've been together long enough. But . . . Beaux just isn't the romantic type. Spontaneous and outrageous? Yes! But down on one knee proposing to me in front of our dream home? It's too good to be true. I'm speechless, until I'm not.

"Yes," I say.

"Yes?" Beaux asks. His pink lips lift into a perfect smile.

"Yes," I say once more.

Beaux picks me up and spins me round and round. I grow dizzy, but I love every moment of it, just as I love the picture he's painted of our future. I can see us getting married, me walking down the aisle, us moving into this home. I can picture the life we would have, and I see myself happy, happier than I've ever been.

I wake up in bed covered in sweat and short of breath. My

head aches with a dizziness that is unwelcome and memories that I'd rather not remember. Ever since Julian left, I've felt ill. I spent the rest of the day in bed and didn't even talk to Kat. After a while, it became too painful to think of Julian. Instead, I thought of Mason and everything he shared with me regarding himself and Beaux.

It's strange to me to follow Mason's line of thinking. I mean, sure, people *can* change and grow, but for some reason, I don't know if I agree that the principle applies to rapists. It's one thing to hurt yourself, to overeat, to cut your wrists, to smoke and drink yourself into oblivion. But it's another thing to hurt someone else, and in Beaux's case, multiple someone's repeatedly. How does a person do that and then expect to be forgiven, expect to be treated like anyone else and given the same courtesy?

My heart aches for little Beaux. Despite this, I can't bring myself to extend the same sympathy to the Beaux I know. I can't view him as someone deserving of empathy, of forgiveness, someone capable of change, because I don't view him as human anymore. He's a monster.

I shake my head and force myself into a sitting position.

But what if he *could* be forgiven? What if he *could* change? What if this could all be over, and I could run to Julian and apologize for everything, and everything could be okay?

I find my phone amongst the covers and, using Star 67, dial Beaux's number from memory. He answers on the third ring.

"Hello?" he asks. At first, I don't say anything.

This was a mistake. What could a talk with Beaux possibly get me? Yet the look on Julian's face when he left me doesn't allow me to let Beaux hang up. I have to end this for Julian.

"Beaux," I say suddenly.

"*Emma?*" he asks. He's surprised to hear from me. The feeling is mutual. "Why are you calling me? It's 3:00 a.m., not that that's what's surprising me."

"I know," I say, rolling my eyes. "I'm as surprised as you are. I just . . . I want to try to understand," I blurt.

"*What?*" Beaux asks. "Understand what?"

I take a deep breath and say a small prayer. Whatever happens, God, please don't let me make things worse.

"I um . . ." I stutter. "I want to understand . . ."

Emotion swells inside me. I'm not sure if I can manage to say it. How will he react when I do? I feel like I could cry, but there are no more tears left inside me after this morning.

Finally, I say, "I want to understand why you raped me and all those other girls."

Beaux is quiet. The only noise between us is that of my heavy breathing.

"This isn't a trick," I say, breaking our silence. "I'm alone and I'm not recording you. I just—I need to know. I need to understand," I beg.

"Emma, I . . . I don't know what to say," he finally tells me. "I think you're confused, I didn't—"

"I found the sealed court records. I know about you, about what happened to you," I continue. "And I know about all the other girls. Well, going back the last ten years, at least."

Again, Beaux is silent.

"Like I said, this isn't a trick. I just . . . I need to know if you're sorry; if you have any regret at all," I say.

I think back to my dream, to the moment we got engaged. Beaux said I was the best thing in his life, even more so than his job. It was hard to believe then, and even harder to believe after everything that's happened. Was it ever real? Does it even matter? How could he hurt the person he loved so viciously and personally? Of course, how could his father abuse his own son? How could his mother sit back and let it happen?

I exhale and in a last-ditch effort to understand the man I almost married, the man who has henceforth ruined my life, I ask, "Did you ever love me?"

Beaux exhales and I hear a rustling noise. Perhaps he's walking. Glasses clank against each other. Liquid pours. He's at his bar cart in his home office. He must've been up late working. He drinks his scotch in one fell swoop and sets the glass to the side. Another two minutes pass.

I should've known better. He isn't going to admit to anything.

All I've done is expose my strengths and put myself and the ones I love in even more danger. I exhale and let my phone slip to my hip.

"This was a mistake," I mumble to myself.

Just as I lift my phone back up to my ear to tell Beaux to forget it, he breaks his silence.

"I didn't love you, Emma," he says then. "Not at first."

My ears perk up at the sound of his voice, and I wonder if I should lie and hunt for my recorder. Instead, I stay put.

"What constitutes *at first*?" I ask, pulling my knees into my chest.

"The first year," he admits.

"*What?* Then why did you stay with me?"

Oh, God. If only he would've dumped me, or if only I'd had the wisdom to leave him.

"I don't know," he admits. "Maybe because I knew it wasn't your fault I didn't love you. I just—I didn't know how to love you *or* anyone else, for that matter," he tells me. "So, I . . . I tried to make the best of the situation I was in."

My lips part. I drop my eyes to my covers. I didn't expect him to open up like this. He's always kept a wall up. Even before I knew it existed, it was always there, separating him from the world, from love.

"But . . . I don't know. Then things started to change," he says.

Glass clanks through the speaker of the phone as he pours himself another drink.

"How so?" I ask.

I watch myself in the mirror before me as moonlight streams through my bedroom window and pools around me. I look like a ghost in my white nightshirt. I feel like one too, empty yet filled with pain. If only he'd been honest with me, or at least himself, he could've saved us both so much hurt and time.

"I recognized a desire in you, a desire to create a life for yourself separate from your parents, from your childhood. And, you had an ambition that was admirable. You worked hard and loved what you did," Beaux says. "I guess, you still do. But . . ."

he pauses then. "Most of all, you—you had a heart filled with love and a respect for commitment. The more time I spent with you, the more I felt I could . . . I could count on you, count on you to stay with me, to love me. But, um . . . I wasn't fair to you," he says then.

"*What?*" I ask. His words take me by surprise.

Beaux clears his throat. "It wasn't fair of me to expect you to love me and stand by me in ways that I knew I never could for you," he tells me.

My chest tightens as Beaux's words race through me. I want to be angry, to curse him, and hang up. He has this revelation now? So perfectly he can discuss his feelings, but when we were together, nothing. He never would've admitted this. Even when I caught him cheating and even when he begged for my forgiveness, he never admitted any of this. And yet, for some strange reason, I feel one emotion more than anger—understanding.

"If . . . if you're aware of those records, then you must also be aware of why it was difficult for me to love, not just you, but anyone. But you were the only one," he says, clearing his throat. "You were the only one to truly love me and because of that, I never meant to hurt you, Emma."

I'm taken aback. My chest tightens and my throat closes. I feel his hands on me as they were the night of the first assault.

"But the second you caught me cheating, the second you saw the real me, the me that I . . . I work hard to hide every single day, I knew it was over," he continues. "When you left my apartment that night, I thought I'd never see you again. And—and I think I could've accepted that, I mean, eventually. But when you came back, when you said you wanted to talk, I clung to the hope that you would forgive me. I didn't . . . I didn't realize how desperately I wanted your forgiveness until I thought I might actually have it."

"*Why?*" I say, cutting him off.

"Why, what?" Beaux asks.

"Why did you cheat? If you loved me, if you thought of me as you claim to, then how could you cheat?" I ask. "It's . . . it's hard for me to believe anything you say, Beaux. It's hard for me to believe that you loved me and wanted to be with me, when your actions say otherwise. You . . . you cheated," I say. "If I would've forgiven you, would that have stopped? Would you have truly changed?" I ask.

Beaux exhales. I imagine him sitting at his desk at home, rubbing his temple with his thumb. If history is worth anything, he'll pour himself another glass of scotch in about two minutes.

"I don't know, Emma," he finally says. "I . . . I guess, I guess it kept me from being hurt. If I had sex with another woman and gave a piece of myself to her, then that was one less piece of me I gave to you. And *you*, Emma, I knew you were the only one who could hurt me if you ever did leave me. So, I—maybe I was scared," he says. "And when you did end things, I . . . I reacted in the way I do towards all disappointment. I reacted with violence and anger and that's because, in that moment, I knew I was losing more than just you and our future. I was also losing any chance I had left at a better life, the life I'd always wanted and worked for."

I exhale and close my eyes. Anger begins to cloud my understanding. He hurt me, knowing how it would affect me. He was a victim of abuse and he made me suffer the same fate, because I couldn't erase his pain for him. I couldn't undo the undoable.

"And I'd like to say yes, I would've changed if you would've forgiven me," he continues. "But somehow I never did," he admits. "I've . . . I've always thought if I could just have this or do that, it would be enough, enough to conceal the truth that I've tried so desperately to hide. My job, my clothes, *you,* the home I imagined for us, it was all meant to separate me from the truth of who I really am. And who's to say your forgiveness wouldn't have been the very thing to make it all go away, to flip the proverbial switch?" he asks. "But history shows otherwise, as you now know."

I process what he's said. I can accept what happened to him in his childhood screwed him up. I can accept that maybe he felt unsafe in relationships because his abuse was dealt by the people closest to him, the people charged with protecting him. I can *even* accept, sort of, the rationale of him being afraid to give all of himself to one person. But what I can't accept or understand in any form is that he thinks his interactions with the women he blackmailed and raped were acceptable because of the pain he suffered as a child. He speaks of his assaults, *my* assault, as if they are justified. He speaks of his infidelity as if it were an act of self-defense against a broken heart.

"Beaux, I—I realize that what happened between us is more complex than I originally thought," I say. "But you didn't just react with violence and anger, and you didn't just cheat on me." My chest rises as my breathing quickens. My cheeks flush and my forehead aches.

"You raped me, and so many others." My voice rises in anger, yet I hold my breath as emotion takes over me. "And Mr. Turnip," I choke. "Despite your horrific past, your actions are not justifiable or acceptable in any way. They are despicable," I spit.

I shake my head then and find my reflection in the mirror across from me once more. Despite the turmoil I feel inside, I sit straighter and look stronger. I hold in my tears and fight through the ache in my throat as I say, "You deserve to be punished, Beaux. You've done horrible things that you can't take back or begin to understand the effects of. You deserve to be punished," I say, nodding.

"You're right," Beaux responds. His admission takes me by surprise. "I *have* done horrible things. But, so have you."

My lips part. My hand moves to my stomach. The tears I've been holding inside become harder to hold in.

"I . . . I," I start, but can't manage to say much more. I know what he's talking about. It's why he attacked me the second time. It's why he went after Mr. Turnip. It's the thing I feared Julian would discover if I let him get too close to the Beaux situation, the thing I've been too afraid and ashamed to tell anyone, including Kat.

"I don't have to explain myself," I finally manage to say.

Beaux laughs.

"*You* don't, but *I* do," he says.

"You put me in an impossible situation," I blurt. How dare

he compare me to him? "I can't be blamed for how I reacted to the trauma you put me through."

Again, in the sarcastic nature I know all too well, he says, "*You* can't, but *I* can?" Again, he laughs and sure enough, I hear him pour himself another glass of scotch.

"Don't you see, Emma?" he asks. "We're all monsters. We all play a role in someone else's tragic story, and we all make choices we regret in response to fear, anger, abuse, loss. The list goes on and on," he says.

"So, you admit you regret what you've done?" I ask in an effort to change the subject. It's doesn't work.

"Don't you?"

"I am nothing like you," I say. Though, despite the certainty I convey to him, I know it's not true. I did something, something awful, something I do my best to blame on him, but I can't, not entirely.

Beaux guzzles down his scotch and sets the glass to the side. I know because of the loud clank that echoes through the phone. It makes the hairs on my arms rise as if he is only inches away.

"You hurt me, Emma. I hurt you back. You aborted our baby and I killed Mr. Turnip," Beaux admits. "A life for a life. Though one could argue, you took a life yet to be lived. While, Mr. Turnip, well . . . he only had a few years left."

His voice is dark as he speaks. I imagine his eyes share the same darkness. I imagine his fists clenched as his blood pulses with the high of his crimes.

"You're a monster!" I scream. I can't hold it in any longer. I break.

"*You* . . . you did this to me!" I scream as I writhe against the blankets. "You broke me when you raped me, and then I found out I was pregnant and I couldn't stomach the thought of raising *your* child—or worse, you demanding partial custody," I yell. "I . . . I couldn't do it! You left me with no choice."

Tears flood my face and snot pours from my nose. Even as I say it, I know it's not true. I had a choice. And as much as that baby was Beaux's child, it was mine too. Beaux may have broken me when he raped me, but I am the source of my greatest pain. I am the reason Mr. Turnip is dead. And that . . . that is my unspeakable truth.

"We all have a choice, Emma," Beaux says. "Your pain is of your own making."

He is calm when he speaks. It sickens me. I want so badly to reach through the phone and claw his face off. He deserves to feel every ounce of pain I do ten times over, but he never will. He isn't emotionally capable of love and so he isn't emotionally capable of knowing what it feels like to lose love, the love of a child, the love of a partner.

I force myself to an upright position and wipe my face with the back of my shirt. Through choked gasps I say, "I tried to offer you a chance at redemption. I tried to find it in me to forgive you, even though you don't deserve it. *But you?* You will never have my forgiveness and you will never find redemption, because you . . . you will never take responsibility for what you've done. You will never accept the fact that you've hurt people. You chose to hurt people, Beaux. Your parents may have been awful, but you didn't have to be. Now, it's too late."

With that, I hang up and fall back into the fetal position. My cries are silent, but they tug on every part of me. Beaux may be a hypocrite, but he's also right. We all have a choice. He chooses to be a monster. But in that moment of weakness, so did I. So did I, and I will regret my choice for the rest of my life.

CHAPTER 23

Kat takes the screaming kettle off the stovetop and brews us both a cup of hot tea. I sit at the dining room table, legs pulled into my chest. Turns out, my cries weren't so silent. After my talk with Beaux, I couldn't avoid talking to her anymore. She practically broke my bedroom door down to get inside.

My cheeks are red, as are my eyes. I intertwine my fingers just to keep my hands from trembling. I am raw, inside and out. Ever since Julian left me, something hasn't felt right inside. It's like a piece of me is just missing. And with the pieces Beaux stole and the pieces I gave away when I . . . I ended my pregnancy, I'm not sure how many more pieces I can lose until . . . there's nothing left of me at all.

"I've been lying to you, Kat," I say. My voice is scratchy.

"I know," she says.

She grabs our mugs and brings them both to the table to steep. *Honey Lavender.* It smells good. She sits mine down in front of me and I reach for it instantly to allow its warmth to warm my frozen bones. I close my eyes and inhale as Kat sits across from me.

We don't speak, though I can feel Kat's eyes on me, just like the tragic night I ended my engagement.

That night, the police arrived shortly after Beaux left. Kat opened my bedroom door, and the police found me sitting silently in the corner of my room. They watched me. She watched me. And after they left, she sat across from me for hours, just waiting for me to utter a single word. She was scared. I remember seeing in her the same wide-eyed anxiety as a new mother who watches her first-born child sleep.

She has the same look in her eyes now. I imagine she's asking herself, *"What did he do now? When will she ever speak up?"* Little does she know, Beaux isn't the reason for my tears, not this time.

"For the past six weeks, I've been gathering evidence against Beaux," I blurt. Her eyes grow in size, but she doesn't interrupt me. "I . . . I've reviewed his social media, college transcripts, even the list of plus-ones he's taken to work functions," I say. "It wasn't easy, but I found fifteen women who claim he assaulted them over the last ten years."

"*Wow,*" she breathes. "Fifteen," she whispers.

"Yeah," I say back. I pull my tea to my chest and sip. The hot herbal liquid runs across my tongue, down throughout my body. I feel it trickle down my esophagus, nourishing my insides. I can't remember the last time I've eaten.

"Of the fifteen, only four would speak to me," I reveal. "But these women, Kat," I say, shaking my head. "They range from polar opposite ends of the spectrum. They are brunettes and blondes, CEOs and interns. Some he assaulted in college, others he assaulted through his work, before, during, and after our relationship."

"One woman . . ." I pause. I place my tea on the table and clasp my hands together once more. "One woman committed suicide two months after the assault. Her friend testified on her behalf."

"*Jesus,*" Kat says.

I nod. My eyes glaze over as I remember their testimonies. It was selfish of me to call Beaux, to think that only *my* forgiveness and empathy mattered. This is bigger than me. I know that. But in that moment, I forgot. I wanted so desperately for this to be over, for Beaux to be out of my life, for Julian and I to try to start anew. I wanted the nightmares and panic attacks to stop. I wanted the memories to fade from my mind. But . . . it's not just *my* memories, *my* panic attacks, *my* nightmares, and *my* trauma that Beaux must answer for. I shake my head.

"How could I have been so selfish?" I ask aloud.

"*What?* How have *you* been selfish, Emma?" Kat asks. Her

face crinkles in confusion. It's time she knew about Mason *and* Julian.

"I've mentioned that Mason, Julian's brother, is in town," I say. Kat nods. I know she heard Julian storm in yesterday and subsequently, what occurred between the three of us.

"Um," I start, unsure of how to continue. "I . . ." I begin again.

"You're dating Mason," she says then.

"*What? No!* Disgusting," I embellish.

"Really?" Kat asks. She adjusts herself in her chair. "Then, why was he here yesterday? And why did the two of you let Julian believe you're together?"

I exhale and drop my head, burying it between my knees.

I can't think of Julian *or* Mason without seeing the disappointment and heartbreak written all over Julian's face. When I broke up with him the first time, I didn't feel the pain I do now, because I didn't say or do anything to deliberately hurt him. I told him I needed to work through some things, and I needed to do that alone. I knew that what I was doing was for the right reasons and that eventually, I'd be able to make it up to him. *But this?* I hurt him in a way that I don't know if he'll ever be able to forget or forgive. Even if he accepts *why* I did it, what if he can't accept my method? What if we try to work it out, but he's unable to trust me? What if he always questions his brother? His brother, who is the only family he has left, I tainted their relationship. *No,* I destroyed their relationship.

I lift my head and look Kat in the eyes. Her lips part as she waits for what I will say next.

"I really messed up," I say. The hoarseness from earlier returns and this time, I'm not sure the tea will be of much help.

"Julian and I ended things, or rather, I ended things with Julian over a month ago," I say. My heart pounds beneath my skin. My cheeks flush.

"What? Why?" Kat asks, shocked.

"The night of the Creative Concepts Gala, Beaux confronted me," I tell her. She nods. This much she knows. What she doesn't know is . . . "Somehow, he'd found out about my intent on seeing a lawyer. He . . .he threatened you and Julian if I didn't stay quiet and he wasn't bluffing," I say. "I know because . . .he told me the truth about Mr. Turnip's passing and he left evidence of it in Julian's house," I reveal.

"*What?* What truth? What evidence?" Kat asks, leaning forward in her chair. Her eyes squint in anger. Her lips part in anticipation.

I know I shouldn't tell her. It will only hurt her, but . . . I can't keep keeping these secrets.

"Beaux killed Mr. Turnip, Kat. He killed him in retaliation . . ." I say, stopping myself. "And he left the checkerboard in Julian's house for me to find. You and I never could find it. Even Julian looked for it. And there it was, beneath Julian's kitchen sink. And I'd just been there the night before. We'd washed dishes together. I saw underneath his sink and there was nothing there but cleaning products," I ramble.

Kat sits silently. Tears fill her dark blue eyes and trickle down her tanned cheeks.

"He found his way inside," I say. "At least twice, maybe more. Nothing but my silence would've stopped him from doing it again." I drop my eyes to my knees. "I'm . . . I'm sorry to tell you, like this, or at all. I just . . . I don't want to lie to you anymore."

"I . . . um," Kat chokes. She wipes her eyes and sips her tea. Her hand shakes as she lifts the glass to her mouth. "I just . . . I can't believe this," she finally says, covering her face with her free hand.

"I know," I say, moving to hold her. "I know."

I bury my head in her curly red hair and hold her tight as she cries. It takes a lot for Kat to break, and *this?* This is a lot.

After a while, Kat regains her composure and I take my seat. Her face is red and wet. The veins in her temples throb. The sight makes my own head ache.

"So, you . . . you broke up with Julian to protect him," Kat finally says.

"Yeah," I say. "But um . . . all I did was hurt him."

I tell Kat about Mason helping me out of Club Gent and why

he was here yesterday. I even tell her about Mason's past and why Julian was so upset when he caught us together.

"I used Julian's assumption as a way to push him further away, hopefully out of New Orleans altogether," I say.

"Is that really what you want?" She asks me.

"*No!*" I answer quickly. "I don't want to be apart from him. I don't want him to move. I don't want . . . I don't want any of this," I say. "But I don't have a choice. The second my article is published, and the police receive all the information I have on Beaux and Club Gent, it will be a rat's race to see who gets to who first," I tell her. "I couldn't put Julian in the middle of something so dangerous that he didn't ask for."

"You didn't ask for it either, Emma."

"No," I admit. "But . . ." I shake my head. "This is my fight, not his, not yours. After learning about Mr. Turnip, I . . . I couldn't risk anyone else I love getting hurt."

Kat nods. "Wait. *Love?*" she asks.

For the first time in what feels like forever, my lips lift into a smile.

"Yeah, *love*," I say. "I *love* Julian. I love him like I've never loved anyone else. I know we haven't known each other that long, but . . . ever since we first met, I've felt a connection to him, a pain, an energy that I can't ignore," I tell her. "Getting to know him, my feelings have only grown and I . . . I couldn't risk losing him to Beaux. But I . . . I also couldn't risk losing him to me."

"What do you mean?" she asks.

I take a deep breath and drink the rest of my tea. For this next part, I'll need all the strength I can get.

"Kat," I start. "Do you remember when I said I was going to speak to a lawyer and that before I did, I needed to tell you the whole story?"

"*Yes.*" Kat nods.

"Well, um . . . I didn't tell you the whole story," I admit.

"*What?* What else could there be?"

"The reason Beaux attacked me the second time; the reason he retaliated and killed Mr. Turnip; the reason I couldn't tell Julian the truth about Beaux, about any of this," I say. I take a deep breath, sit up straight, and . . . "Kat, I was pregnant," I admit. "And I . . ." I feel my throat tighten as I speak. Blood rushes to my head, making my arms and legs feel numb. I feel like I'm choking, like I'm suffocating. "I had an abortion," I blurt.

I struggle to breathe as Kat takes in my revelation. I won't blame her if she's angry, if she blames me for Mr. Turnip's death. I do, which only makes him being gone even harder. She'll probably never want to speak to me again. She'll ask me to move out or move out herself. It would be fitting. With everything that Beaux has taken from me, Kat, the most precious friendship I have, will be the last.

"Emma," Kat says. She reaches her hand out across the table for me to take.

"What? What are you doing?" I ask. My face crinkles in confusion.

"Take my hand," she says. I do with hesitation.

"Emma, you have nothing to be ashamed of," she tells me. "Nothing you've done warrants the abuse Beaux has put you through, the abuse he's still putting you through by making you think, in any way, that you deserve to be hit, raped, threatened, and blamed for the despicable murder of Mr. Turnip," she says. "And if Julian is the one for you, if he loves you the way you deserve to be loved, then he won't let your past derail the future the two of you could have together," she assures me. "And if he does, then he isn't the one. As difficult as that may be to process, it's true."

"You're, um, you're not mad at me?" I ask. "You don't blame me for—?"

"Emma," Kat says, squeezing my hand tighter. "You are not to blame for how you react to the pain that asshole has put you through. He killed Mr. Turnip," she says through gritted teeth. "He made the decision to do that, just like he made the decision to rape you and countless other women. This is not your fault, Emma," Kat says. "It's his."

Her acceptance allows me to breathe again. She's right. Beaux made the choice to kill Mr. Turnip. I shouldn't blame myself for his death. As heartbreaking as it is and as responsible as I do feel,

I shouldn't. But... I made a choice too. I lean back in my chair and listen as Beaux's words replay in my head.

> *We're all monsters. We all play a role in someone else's tragic story, and we all make choices we regret in response to fear, anger, abuse, loss.*

"But they are our choices," I say aloud.

"Hmm?" Kat asks as she sips her tea.

"They are *our* choices," I tell her.

She still doesn't get it.

"Beaux made the choice to rape me. He made the choice to kill Mr. Turnip. He made the choice to threaten me and you and Julian into silence. Regardless of the reasons he uses to justify his choices, those are the choices he has to live with," I say. "But I made the choice to get an abortion, to rid myself of the child I saw only as his, but that was really mine too. I chose to lie about it and hurt Julian, destroying his relationship with his brother, just to keep my own selfish secret." I lean forward in my chair. "Beaux is a murderer, and he hurts people to keep his secrets. How am I any different?"

"Emma, stop," Kat tells me. "You can't do this. You can't compare yourself to Beaux."

"The similarities are there, Kat. And I . . . I think I've known it since I came back from having the procedure," I admit.

Kat shakes her head as if I'm being unreasonable, but I don't think I am.

"Beaux is worthy of blame for many things," I say. "Don't get me wrong, he is, but . . . all this time, I never stopped to acknowledge the choice I made. I buried it inside me along with the realization of what he'd done to me the night our engagement ended. I never spoke about it. I tried my best not to think about it. But inside, I was broken and in pain, and filled with anger and unending grief," I say.

"In the moments I couldn't ignore my pain, I blamed Beaux. I told myself, just as you have, that I couldn't blame myself for the choices I made in response to the trauma I suffered at his hands.

I . . . I had to believe he was to blame, because if I didn't, I'd be forced to accept the inconceivable," I tell her.

"I killed our baby, *my* baby," I choke. "I . . . I did that." My chest aches with the weight of my reality. "I did it, Kat," I cry.

"Emma," Kat says. She tries to console me, but I'm inconsolable. All the pent-up emotion, all the secrets I've kept bottled for the past year come flooding out. I told Beaux he couldn't use his past trauma as an excuse for his present-day behavior. I told him to take responsibility. But, if I blame him for the choice I made, refusing to take responsibility, then how am I any more worthy of forgiveness than he is?

When I finally catch my breath, I say, "I called him."

"You did what?"

"That's why I was crying," I tell her. "I called him to confront him, to try to understand . . . to try to understand why he hurts people."

"I wanted it to be over and I thought, if I could forgive him or at least show him some empathy, then, maybe this hole inside me would start to fill, maybe I wouldn't have to continue this crusade of gathering evidence and I could just be done," I say. "I think I was trying to find a way to justify his actions so that, maybe, I could justify my own," I admit. "But . . .there is no justifying what he's done, and I can't find it in myself to forgive him, especially when he refuses to take responsibility for what he's done. And I don't want to be like him, Kat. I want . . .I *need* to take responsibility for what *I've* done. And I need to find a way to forgive myself," I say. "It's the only way I can escape this pain, this pain which is far greater than anything Beaux has put me through."

I take a deep breath and so does Kat. I can tell she doesn't agree with me. She doesn't blame me for my choices. And, if the roles were reversed, I wouldn't blame her either. It wouldn't be my place to blame or hold her responsible. We are all free to make our own choices, just as we are all free to stand by our choices, regret them, or learn from them. I regret my choice to have an abortion. My regret is my right just as much as my free will is. And now, I must answer to myself. And Beaux, he must answer to those he has wronged.

"I can't wait for justice, Kat," I tell her then. "I can't wait for Beaux to have an emotional epiphany and suddenly become human." I shake my head. "I have to take back control for myself, not wait for someone else to give it to me. I . . .I've been working on an article. With each sentence I type, I try to find an excuse not to finish it," I say then. "Calling Beaux tonight was just another excuse, but—I'm done making them. I have to do this, Kat, for myself, for the women before me, and the women who will come after me." She nods and squeezes my hand.

In speaking with Marie, Samantha, Amy, and Lauren, one thing became painstakingly clear. Beaux broke them just like he broke me. Marie lost confidence in her ability to run her company. Samantha never became the attorney she always dreamed of being. Amy lost her ability to trust. And Lauren, well, she lost her best friend. Ashely Roy paid the ultimate price after she was assaulted by Beaux. And I'd be lying if I said I never thought about doing just the same.

I run my fingers over my wrists. Thin scars are bumpy underneath my touch. Yet another choice I must take responsibility for.

Beaux may have broken me, but just as I have the power to expose him, to destroy him, I have the power to rebuild myself and rebuild my life. No more tragic stories. We don't have to stay broken. We don't have to live in the shadow of our predator forever. We just have to choose something different, and that's exactly what I'm going to do.

"If it's the last thing I do, I will expose the truth, my truth, Beaux's truth, even the truth that is the most unspeakable," I say.

Kat scrunches her nose.

"What's that?" she asks.

I bite the inside of my jaw, knowing that once these words come out, they can never be unspoken.

"My father is a member of Club Gent," I reveal. "He's a rapist, a liar, a cheater. He's just as bad, if not worse than Beaux," I say. "I can't expose the brotherhood without exposing him."

I will keep my promise to my mother. I won't ruin my sister's wedding. But once the happy couple is on their way, all bets are off.

CHAPTER 24

Stately Oaks welcome me home as I turn off Roberts Road onto the long drive toward Marshall House. Gravel crunches beneath the wheels of my rental car as the white, antebellum home becomes more visible. In the city, I've never needed a car. And, I'll be honest, my not having one has always been a decent go-to excuse for not making the six-hour trek north to Presley more often. Nevertheless, here I am. *Late,* but here.

Pink azaleas and red roses are in full bloom as I approach the house. The sun sets, creating a glow of yellow and orange against their rich, green leaves. I used to play amongst them when I was younger. I'd pretend I was a fairy princess, and each blossom was my subject. It's a shame we don't realize how beautiful those simple, sweet moments of childhood are until we've lost them. But if as children we realized our lives wouldn't always be so sweet and simple, then the simplicity of childhood would be lost altogether. My, how I crave that simplicity, that innocence. But before there was Beaux, there was Carrington and Anne Marshall. And under their care, the azaleas and roses are about the only thing that's flourished.

I adjust my white denim and pick the lint off my black tank top as I step out of the car. White jeans are work to wear, but I learned long ago anything less was not acceptable for Marshall House, especially on the eve of Eva's wedding. God only knows who she and my mother invited, and I'll never hear the end of it if I embarrass my mother in front of her friends. Hints why she picked out and purchased all my formal attire for this weekend. For once, my less-than-ladylike style has come in handy.

I grab my duffel bag from the backseat and sling it over my shoulder. Yet another point of contention for my mother.

Ladies don't use duffle bags, Emma. We use satchels or suit-cases and nothing else.

"*Jesus,*" I mumble to myself. All I have to do is hold it together for a day and a half. I made a promise and I'm going to keep it. Though the closer I get to the house, the more my stomach twists.

How am I supposed to see my dad? How am I supposed to hug him, and act like everything is fine, normal? What *is* normal?

I feel like I could vomit, but in this heat, I'm scared of what insects it would attract.

I reach the grand steps that lead to the second-floor entrance. The white paint is chipped, and they creak beneath my feet as I climb them. Just up ahead is the front porch, which wraps around the entire exterior of the home. As I reach the top of the steps, I stop to take it all in—the grass, the trees, the flowers, the pond that glitters as it absorbs the setting sun. This is the setting of my childhood, and it is beautiful. Despite this, I count the hours until I'm able to leave again.

"Emma! You're here!" Eva squeals.

My sister, dressed in a tea-length ivory dress, runs out of the house to embrace me. I let my duffle bag fall to the ground and return her hug.

"Happy wedding weekend," I say. "You look beautiful." And she does. The bodice of her dress is all ivory lace and has an off-the-shoulder neckline. The skirt is plain with a scalloped hem but is packed with enough tulle to fill out her slender frame in all the right ways.

"Thank you," Eva says. She looks behind me as if she's expecting someone else and seems confused when she finds I've come alone. "No Julian?" She asks.

"No," I say, forcing a pained smile.

"Aw, Emma."

"No, don't . . . don't worry about me," I say, waving her off. "I'm fine and this is *your* weekend. Now show me inside before I have to re-curl my hair. This humidity is a killer."

"Emma!" my mom says, standing from her seat in the sitting room.

"Mom," I say.

I drop my duffle bag by the door and move to give her a hug. She practically winces at the sight of it. Some things never change, including the inside of Marshall House.

The floors are still a deep mahogany wood. The walls are shades of gray and cream. The furniture, wood-trimmed floral upholstery, must be within reach of its hundredth birthday. Everything looks the same. Everything smells the same—like pot-pourri and the ancient air of the inside of a museum, or a casket.

My mom pulls me in for a tighter hug than normal, which takes me by surprise. She's dressed in a cream and pink floral print dress with cap sleeves that nearly blends in with the furniture.

"You look nice," I tell her.

"Thank you, dear," she says. "And your dress is hanging up in your room," she tells me.

"Gotcha," I say, giving her an awkward thumbs up.

I turn from my mom and find my dad across the room, leaned up against the bar cart. His brown hair is slicked back, and his stubble is freshly shaven. He's dressed in a navy-blue day suit with black loafers and holds a crystal glass filled with the rich, warm liquid of expensive scotch.

"Emma, dear, come give your daddy a hug," he says, extending his arm out to me. So as not to tip him off, I oblige his request, moving past the settee and glass coffee table with care. "The drive was okay?" he asks.

"Um, yeah. Just long," I say.

He pulls me in and kisses me on the cheek. Thankfully, no one is standing behind him to see me cringe. He smells like the perfect mixture of cologne, alcohol, and cigar smoke. I imagine he'll indulge a bit more than usual this evening in celebration of Eva and Bill's nuptials. That'll be when I make my move. Speaking of Bill . . .

"And the groom-to-be," I say, pulling away from my dad.

Bill is tall, lanky, and classically handsome. He has blonde hair and hazel eyes, wears a crisp gray suit with a white button-down, no tie, and looks rather perfect next to my perky and polite sister. Which, I'm sure, is about all anyone is concerned with. Oh, and he's an investment banker, which is a plus, according to my mother.

"Hi, Bill," I say, standing on my tiptoes to embrace him.

"Hi, Emma," he says, kneeling to give me a respectful hug.

"So, what's next?" I ask, successfully completing all my pleasantries.

"*What's next?* You act as if this weekend is a piece of furniture from Ikea. *What's next?*" My father says, finishing off his glass of his scotch.

My cheeks flush and my skin feels hot, and not because of the hundred-degree, mosquito infested sauna that waits for us outside

"Now, now, Carrington," my mom says, giving my father the side-eye. "I'm sure Emma is just tired after her long drive," she says to my father.

Wow. I don't think she's ever defended me once in my entire life, let alone to my father. Maybe she took a Valium or Xanax, or both.

"No Julian?" she asks me then. Her blonde brows raise.

"Uh . . ." I stammer. I shove my hands in my pockets to keep from fidgeting.

"Julian? Who's Julian?" my dad asks after downing what could only be his third glass.

Who's Julian? I would've thought my mother couldn't wait to run home and tell my dad about the mop-headed, tattooed boy she found at my house. *Hmm.* I wonder why she didn't.

My mom looks to me as if I'll explain, but I just say, "No. He wasn't able to come."

My mother nods and says, "Well, that's too bad." She then goes on to explain Julian to my father as a kind, interesting young man she and Eva met when they went dress shopping in New Orleans. No digs or condescending word choice. Okay, maybe three Valium. My father grunts in reply, as is his norm.

"Alright," my mom says in a change of subject. "Why don't you go upstairs, darling, and get changed. We'll need to make our way outside for the rehearsal in about forty minutes," she tells me.

"Okay," I say.

Bill offers to help me with my luggage. I decline. Eva gives me one last hug before heading out to the rehearsal area early. And my mom fixes me a plate from the kitchen to hold me over until dinner. My dad retreats to reviewing stocks on his iPad. I leave him with a parting smile before making my way up the curved staircase to the third floor.

* * *

My room is just as I left it at eighteen, except cleaner. The floral print sheets on my bed have been freshly washed. The down duvet has been fluffed. All the wood furniture has been dusted, and the fluffy cream rug has been vacuumed.

I close my bedroom door behind me and revel in the cool air. The beige linen drapes have been kept closed all this time and therefore, my room might be the only place in the entire four-story home that is a reasonable temperature. The house is old, to say the least, and has been in my family for more generations than I can count, going back to when opening the windows, front porch sitting, and manual fans were your only hope to not sweat through your dress.

Moving further into the room, I toss my duffle bag on the foot of my bed and make my way, immediately, to my three-mir-rored vanity. I sit on the gold upholstered stool and review the mementoes stuck in the crevices of my mirrors. Pictures of my friends and me clutter the edges of the frames, so much so I can barely see my reflection. I run my fingers over them and reminisce on a time filled with hope. These were taken before I met Ezra, before I realized how truly cruel this little town is. I attended bonfires and parties down at the lake. I competed in pageants and came out at cotillions. Of course, the last two were not my choices. Nevertheless, they are a part of me. Or at least, were.

I move my fingers to the glass perfume decanters and dainty jewelry that still sit just where I left them. I grab one, an old favorite. I pop the cap off and inhale. *Mmm*—it's strong and sweet. It's the perfect blend of cinnamon, vanilla, and bourbon. It makes you feel warm, in a good way. Ezra used to like this one. I open my eyes then.

"*Wait*. I wonder . . ." I say aloud.

I return the perfume to its place and lift my rug to expose the wood floors. I tap the wooden planks until I hear the familiar hollow sound.

"Gotcha," I say.

I pry back a wooden plank and find an old, green box with doodles of hearts and flowers and the names Emma and Ezra written on top. I pull it from its place and begin shuffling through.

When Ezra and I started dating, I knew I needed to be careful and keep our connection a secret from my parents. So, I found a way of hiding anything that tied me to him—love letters, dried flowers, photos, even the doodles from my school notebook. I smile as I see, written on a crumpled piece of lined paper, Emma and Ezra Forever.

You know, I take back what I said earlier. I'm glad I didn't know then how things would pan out for the two of us, how things would pan out for me. Kids deserve to be happy and to love in their childish way before life comes in and takes it all away. I just pray that life was kinder to him than it was to me.

"Knock, knock," my mom says, entering my room.

Oh, no! In all these years, she never knew where my secret spot was. I'm here less than twenty minutes and I'm caught red-handed.

My mom's eyes scan over the scene before her. I sit on the floor in the midst of a misplaced rug, a hole in the mahogany, rifling through a box of things that she would've discarded long ago if she knew they were here. This moment is teenage Emma's worst nightmare, before she learned what it means to be truly scared.

"Chicken salad sandwich with sweet potato fries?" she asks me, holding the plate up.

"*Yum*," I say.

My mom places the plate of food on my vanity along with a glass of sweet tea. I quickly replace the floorboard, adjust the rug to its previous position, and hide the box of Ezra and me underneath my duffle bag.

I sit at my vanity to eat and my mom, surprisingly, sits on the edge of the bed and visits with me until I finish.

She asks me about the drive, work, Kat, and when the basic topics of conversation run out, she asks me about Julian.

"I don't mean to pry but was Julian not able to come or did you not ask him?" she asks.

I pop my last fry into my mouth and contemplate my response, or rather, why she feels the need to ask such a question.

"I'm not sure why that matters," I respond.

"Well, I suppose it doesn't," my mom says. She moves her eyes to her shoes as if thinking about her next words. "I just . . . I realize that what I said about Julian, after first meeting him, was a bit harsh. And I'm hoping you didn't not invite him because of me."

I'm taken aback. Never in my life has my mom apologized for something, let alone on behalf of my love life. *Is she dying?*

I wipe my mouth and turn to face her. "Mom, what's going on? You're being really nice and it's kind of confusing me," I admit.

"Well, gee, thanks," she says with a smile. We both laugh.

I bite my lip and tell her the truth, not about why or how we broke up, but just that we did.

"Well, I'm sorry to hear that," she says.

"Thanks," I say. I want to say *me too*, but don't. That would only force me to have to give a deeper explanation of what happened between us, and it's impossible to discuss without discussing Beaux. She still doesn't know the truth about what happened.

My mom stands from her seat and brushes out the wrinkles in her dress.

"Well, we should be heading down for Eva's rehearsal," she says. "Your dress is hanging in the armoire as is your gown for this evening."

"*Gown?*" I ask.

"Yes, your sister has opted for black-tie formal," she says. "I did my best to pick out the shortest heels I could find that were still tall enough to be considered heels. I know how much you hate them."

"I do. Thanks, Mom," I say.

I hand her my plate and empty glass. She takes them and heads for the door.

What the hell was that? Either my mom had a personality transplant or . . . "Emma," my mom says. She turns to face me, and her eyes are sad.

"Yeah, Mom," I ask. I straighten my back to look alert.

"I'm sorry about everything with Ezra," she tells me.

Woah.

"I . . . I don't know what to say," I tell her. My face crinkles in confusion. Where did this come from? Why is she telling me this now?

"You don't need to say anything, just listen," she says. My mother places the plate and empty glass on the floor and once more sits on the bed. "Come here," she says. I do.

My mother takes my hands in hers and what comes next changes everything.

"When your father and I first met, I was nearly out of college," she says. "And my mother, she . . ." She pauses then. "Let's just say, coming home without a husband wasn't an option."

"What? What do you mean?" I ask.

"It just . . . it was a different time," my mother reveals. "And my mother was very old-fashioned. And that's not to say I married your father for the wrong reasons. No. I . . . I loved him," she says. I raise my brow at her use of past tense. "I love him," she corrects herself. "But . . . there was a certain pressure, even more than normal, to make the marriage work," she says. "And so, that's what I've done all these years. I've made the marriage work. And, in doing so, I . . . I've done some horrible things," she admits.

"Mom?"

"The greatest of which is tearing you and Ezra apart," she reveals.

I exhale and relax into the pillows on my bed.

"Your father has always had this vision of what your life would be like, yours and Eva's," she tells me. "But with you being the firstborn, there was just a level of pride your father took in you that he didn't with Eva or anyone else, for that matter," she explains. "He . . . he had visions of what job you'd have, the house you'd live in, and who'd you marry. And those visions didn't involve Ezra St. Germain, or the damaged reputation that being with him would undoubtedly cause," she says, exhaling.

"To preserve your father's pride, I had Ezra arrested. I had his name removed from the graduation program," she admits. "And I know it sounds crazy. I'm a grown woman and I had a choice, of course. But, Emma, it didn't feel that way. If I would've let things between you and Ezra progress, your father would have viewed me as a failure. This whole town would have. And then, where would I be?" she asks me. "He's a powerful man, Emma. If he chose to leave me, then . . . I'd have nothing," she reveals. "But, perhaps, even greater than my desire to please your father was the resentment towards you that grew because of it," she says.

"What?" I ask. My mom resented me? Why? *How?*

My mom exhales. Her rosy cheeks burn even brighter as she reveals her great shame.

"You were always his favorite," she reveals. "And, I guess, somewhere deep down, I always knew, I was—*am* replaceable. *But you?* You are irreplaceable to your father," she tells me. "You are the one he's always loved. I'm just the one who paints the pretty picture he can sell to the people of Presley."

"Mom, no," I say, shaking my head. "You are more than that. And, Dad, he . . ."

How am I supposed to tell her the truth about Dad? How is she supposed to accept it? I can't tell her, not yet, not until . . .

That's when I notice, the wrinkles around her eyes seem to deepen in sadness. Her hands feel frail as they hold mine. Her cheeks are hollow. For it to be the weekend of her daughter's wedding, you'd think she would've gone overboard on the Botox and self-care, but no.

"Mom, what's going on? Why are you telling me all this now?" I ask.

My mom hesitates and lets my hands go. She takes a deep breath and, "Your father and I are getting a divorce."

"*What?*" It's not that I don't support it, especially after recent events, but . . . "I'm—I'm confused," I say.

My mom nods. "That's exactly what I said when your father served me with papers," she says.

"*Wait,*" I say, shaking my head. "He served *you* with papers?"

She nods and fights back tears. She's not one to ruin her makeup.

"On what grounds?" I ask.

My mother takes a deep breath, clasping her hands together to stop the shaking.

"The papers say *Irreconcilable Differences*," she tells me. "But none of it makes sense to me. We haven't been fighting. Nothing has seemed unusual. It literally came out of nowhere," she says. "And Emma, I . . . I don't know what I'm going to do."

She breathes heavily as she holds in her emotion.

"I met your father while I was still in college, so I've never had to work. This house has been in his family for generations. Everything I own, he's paid for," she explains. "And with his legal connections, I'm going to be left with nothing, and I don't even know why we're getting divorced."

I pull my mom in for a hug and she lets her tears fall, drenching my shirt through to my skin. What is my dad up to? If anyone should be filing for divorce here, it's my mom. The evidence I have from Club Gent alone would guarantee her whatever she wants, but there's something else going on here, something else he's hiding.

My dad wouldn't just up and abandon his family. He's spent his entire life building his reputation in the community. He's the mayor, after all, and in a small, gossip-filled, God-fearing town. Divorce is not something you want hanging around your neck unless you have a damn good reason for it. And as awful as my mother may have been to me, she's right. She's always been the doting and dutiful wife. None of this makes any sense.

"Emma, I'm," my mom says, pulling away. "I'm only telling you this because I know you'll understand, and I know you'll keep it a secret. Eva doesn't know. No one else does. I made your father promise we wouldn't announce it until after Eva and Bill return from their honeymoon. I don't want to ruin anything for her," she says.

My mother stands and makes her way to my vanity to blot her tears and freshen her makeup.

"It *is* ironic after all," she says. "I'm getting divorced, and she's getting married. Even more so, I asked *you* not to ruin your sister's wedding and here I am trying to do just the same."

"Mom, I . . . I'm sorry," I tell her. And it's the truth. I'm not sorry she and my father are splitting. In light of my father's extra-curricular activities, it's for the best. But I am sorry my mother is having to go through this. I know what it feels like to be blindsided by the man you love. But, for my mother, she's been with my dad for over half her life. This isn't just him blindsiding her. This is him betraying her on the most intimate level.

"Don't be, darling," she says to me. She turns to me then.

"Just . . . just know I'm sorry for all the things I've done, all the pain I've caused you. I know I've always spoken poorly of your independent nature and the choices you've made as far as your education, career, and relationships are concerned," she admits. "But it turns out, even when you think you've got it all figured out, you can be left dumbstruck on the side of the street without a pot to piss in," she says. "Pardon my language," she blushes. I can't help but smile. "And when that moment happens, you wish you were more like you, more self-sufficient, more in control," she tells me.

If only she knew. Me in control is the furthest thing from the truth.

"I admire you, Emma. I admire you for knowing what you want and don't want and standing strong in the face of disappointment. Now, maybe, you'll share a little of your strength with me?" she asks.

Her words take me aback. Never did I imagine having this conversation or anything similar to it with my mother. She's getting divorced. She admires me. She's apologized. All the horrible memories of my childhood were because of my father, not her. Well, that last part is sort of believable after recent events.

I'd be lying if I said I wasn't confused or considered this entire encounter to be another ploy on my father's behalf. All that talk about me being irreplaceable and the one he loves most. *Hogwash.* My father, much like the other members of Club Gent, know nothing of love. Perhaps he's caught wind of what I'm doing in New Orleans and is trying to use my mother to gather information from me. *Yes*, I realize I'm paranoid. But rather than dismiss this strange and unexpected opportunity for a renewed relationship with my mother, I hug her and tell her I love her. She does the same.

CHAPTER 25

The rehearsal went as well as you can expect. We walked in a straight line. I pretended to adjust my sister's imaginary train. And we all smiled. Now, back in the main house, we greet the guests for a pre-wedding reception. I'm not sure if this was Eva's idea or my mother's, but whoever thought of a pre-wedding reception sure knows how to stretch a wedding out.

All my friends are married with at least one kid and another on the way. All except for Shaylee who is ahead of the curve with two kids, an ex-husband, *and* a fiancé. I think I might actually die if one more person asks me why I'm not married yet, what happened with that fiancé of mine, or when do I plan on having kids?

I grab a glass of champagne off the tray of a passing waiter and slip through the hordes of guests out the side entrance. Warm, summer air welcomes me as does the soft sway of a rocking chair overlooking the pond. If it weren't for Eva's wedding, it'd be impossible to see at this time of night. Due to the special occasion, my mother had the entire grounds doused in string lights. The whole yard seems to glow.

I make my way to the rocking chair and manage to sit despite the amount of tulle filling out the skirt of my blush floor-length gown. It's quite beautiful, with floral patterns made out of lace scattered all over the bodice down to the hips. It's an A-line cut with a deep sweetheart neckline and fitted waist, held up by spaghetti straps adorned with tuffets of lace. I never would've picked it for myself, but I suppose it wouldn't be a wedding if the maid of honor wasn't dressed in something she otherwise wouldn't wear.

I exhale and sip my champagne as I rock back and forth on

the wrap-around porch. Inside, the chatter was so loud I could barely understand the people next to me, which I used as an excuse to leave the attempted conversation altogether.

I imagine my parents' divorce will come as a shock to all of them. They certainly know how to play the parts of the much-in-love husband and wife. They walk, hand-in-hand, around the party greeting guests. They talk highly of each other and laugh as loud as anyone here. Of course, I, nor anyone else, should be surprised. The more people pretend to be perfect, the less perfect they actually are. And my parents have been pretending to be perfect my entire life. And Eva has followed in their footsteps.

Don't get me wrong, she and Bill make a lovely couple, and I have no reason to think they are anything but. But . . . I see in her so much of my mother. She smiles and laughs and rubs her husband, or soon-to-be-husband's, back. She sits back and lets him take charge of the conversation and probably everything else. With everything my mother is going through now, you'd think she would say something to her. But, as adults allow children their naïve happiness, so do the divorced allow the married to think it will never happen to them.

Of course, I've been told I project my own insecurities and trauma onto my sister's relationship. And for that, I pray. Because in no way do I want to be right about this. And in a weird way, I don't even want it to be true about my mom and dad. I hate the concept of divorce. I've always thought of it as this easy way out for when people stop trying. And the ripple effect is selfish. Divorce never affects only the couple. It affects the children, the parents, the friends. But recent events have shown that's a naïve perspective. Whether my mom knows it or not, it is for the betterment of us all that my parents part ways. Still, I don't want it to be true, just like I don't want it to be true that my father is a member of Club Gent and all that entails. Nevertheless, this is my life, my family. I just hope my sister's way out is more effective than mine ever was. Whether she realizes it or not, the only chance her marriage has at making it is if she stays far away from this family and Presley, Louisiana.

"Emma?"

The hairs on my arms rise in response to his voice. I glance down at my champagne glass and question if I've had one too many. Surely it can't be . . .

I turn and before me stands Ezra St. Germain, more handsome than ever, dressed in an all-black suit.

"Ezra!" I say.

I stand, a bit too quickly, and trip over my dress as I move toward him. I fall, scraping my palms as I catch myself.

"*Ow*," I yelp. My hands are chapped and bleeding.

"I see not much has changed," Ezra says, kneeling to help me up. He has a goatee now and his hair is buzzed short. Still, his eyes . . . they're just as I remember, dark and mysterious.

"If you only knew," I say. He smirks and takes my hands in his to examine them. "Ah," I gasp. "It stings."

Ezra smiles. "Not too bad. If you have some peroxide and bandage wrap, I could clean this up for you," he says.

"I, um, I . . . sure," I say.

Ezra helps me to my feet, and we sneak past the party guests to my bathroom upstairs. My mother, despite her newfound fondness for me, would have a coronary if she sees me with a white bandage wrapped around my palms. For one, because it's white and I am *not* the bride, and two, because it would completely ruin the fairytale inspired Pepto Bismol look she so carefully picked out for me.

Ezra tells me to sit on the bed while he searches for the supplies in my bathroom. I watch him as he does. Life has been kind to him. Well, at least, it appears to. He's tall, much taller than he was when we were together. And his muscles . . . even in a suit jacket, I can see the indentions. Still, it's not his appearance that attracts me to him, or did. It's his nature. He's so calm and protective. He sees past all the bullshit and just sees me. Much like someone else I've come to love.

"Found it," he calls from the bathroom.

"Yay," I say.

Okay, so I'm a bit awkward. He was my first love and the way things ended . . . I haven't seen or spoken to him in almost ten years. And the last place I'd expect to run into him would be my parents' home. To say I'm surprised to see him would be an understatement.

"*Yay?*" Ezra comments. He sits next to me on the bed and places my hands on his lap. "Spill it," he says.

I smile and just like that, I feel sixteen again and all the pain of the last nine years falls away.

Turns out, Ezra went on to become a doctor, which explains how he knew to wrap my hands up so well. He works in the cardiology department in a hospital about an hour north of here. He's never been married, though he did come close. He's single now. Knowing this and in an effort to make up for her past sins, my mother called him and invited him to tonight's reception.

"So, what about you, Ms. Journalist?" he asks me.

"How do you know I'm a journalist?"

"Well, I may stumble across your Hub articles from time to time," he says.

"Which means you basically stalk me."

"Basically," he agrees. We both laugh.

Ezra stands and moves to the window overlooking the garden, leaving me on the bed.

"Do you remember when you snuck out to meet me in the pool house?" he asks me.

"All too vividly," I say. I brush my hands over the skirt of my dress. "My dad came in with his work friends and almost caught us making out on the pool table," I say, remembering back.

"Yeah," Ezra laughs. He turns to me then with a twinkle in his eye. "We had a lot of good times."

"We did," I agree. Though they don't bring me much joy. Instead, thoughts of Ezra and I only bring me sadness, sadness for the way my family treated him. Even more so, I mourn the life we could've had together.

"Yet, you don't seem too happy to see me," Ezra says, returning to his place next to me on the bed. He removes his jacket.

My lips part as I contemplate what to say. I mean, what *can* I say? I was heartbroken when you left. I hated my family for what they did to you. All this time, when I think of myself as happy,

I think of myself with you. None of those things matter now. Perhaps in another life, we end up together. But not this one, and certainly not after all that's happened.

He is familiar. He is kind and strong and protective and intelligent. He is the Ezra St. Germaine that I fell in love with. But I am not the Emma Louise Marshall he once knew.

"Talk to me," he says.

He moves his hand to my shoulder and massages it. His touch brings me back—to the pool house, to the lake, to the backseat of his truck, to all the times I wish I would've given in to him, to us.

"It's not that I'm not happy to see you," I finally say. I close my eyes, reveling in his touch. "I'm—I'm just surprised. I—I never thought we'd see each other again, especially when you didn't even say goodbye."

At that, Ezra exhales and pulls his hand back into his lap. I open my eyes and realize how selfish I must sound. After what my parents did, of course he didn't want to say goodbye.

"Ezra, I . . ." I start, but he cuts me off.

"How could I?" he asks me. Though, something tells me I'm not meant to answer. "Not only was I embarrassed and shunned, but my family was also. My mother cried for weeks after what your parents did," Ezra says. "And when I left for college, I couldn't bring myself to face you, knowing the pain your family had caused mine."

I nod. "I understand."

Ezra regains his composure.

"Look, I'm sorry, Emma," he says. "It's been almost ten years. I'm past it. And clearly, I didn't let it keep me down," he says with pause. "But I've never stopped thinking about you," he tells me then. "I think if you would have been eighteen, I would've asked you to run away with me."

My lips part in surprise. He moves closer to me, bringing his hand to my thigh.

"I never wanted to let you go, Emma. And now, maybe I don't have too," he whispers.

Ezra leans in closer. I feel his breath on my neck and then his lips. They are soft and gentle. Yet my insides don't burn for him like they used to. My body doesn't crave his touch. My heart doesn't long for his company.

All these years, I've fantasized about what my life would be like with Ezra, and I think it would've been amazing. But that's not the path we took and now . . . my body, mind, and spirit longs for another.

Ezra's lips move from my neck to my jaw, and just as he leans in to kiss my lips, I pull away.

"I . . . I can't do this," I say, moving from the bed to the opposite side of the room. "I . . . I'm sorry. It's just . . ."

"Emma," Ezra breathes. "You don't have to explain yourself. I get it," he says, standing. He drops his eyes to the floor and shoves his hands in his pockets.

"I just hope that whoever has stolen your heart is worthy of it," he tells me then. His eyes meet mine.

"He is," I say.

My heart fills with warmth at the thought of Julian. Despite the fact that he may never speak to me again.

"I'm happy for you," Ezra says, slipping into his jacket. "And it was nice to see you, to say goodbye, if you will."

His lips draw into a sad smile, as do mine. I may not be in love with him anymore, but I will never be prepared for goodbye. I close the distance between us, and he pulls me in for a hug.

"You will always be my first love, Emma Louise Marshall," he whispers into my ear. My heart aches at his words.

"And you will always be mine," I whisper back.

Our eyes meet one last time and Ezra kneels to kiss me on the forehead.

"Goodbye, Emma."

My throat burns with concealed emotion.

"Goodbye, Ezra."

* * *

By the time I compose myself and rejoin the party downstairs, most of the guests have gone and my mother is rounding up the stragglers.

"Now, now, the bride must get her beauty sleep. We'll see you all tomorrow," she says.

I find Eva and Bill swaying back and forth in the sitting room as the record player plays something I imagine Julian playing. It's a violin tune accompanied by the best keys of the piano. It's painful and filled with longing. They are beautiful as they dance to it. And for the first time, I am jealous of my sister and her fiancé. And that makes me truly happy.

My mom moves next to me and places her arms over my shoulders. I give her a pained smile and just as I go to look away, she pulls me back to her and wraps her arms around me.

"One day, Emma," she whispers to me. "One day."

Tears fill my eyes, but I don't allow them to fall.

"One day," I whisper.

My mother rubs my back and pulls away. "I'll be in the kitchen preparing for tomorrow, if you need me."

"Okay, Mom," I say with a nod.

"Hey Bill! Why don't you join me and a few of the guys in the pool house for a night cap?" my dad asks.

"Yeah, sure thing, Mr. C," Bill calls back. "Let me just say goodnight to Eva first."

"See you out there," my dad says with a nod.

I slide into the foyer before my dad notices me and wait for him to make his way through the dining room and out the back through the family room. This is it—my moment.

CHAPTER 26

I sit on my bed in the dark and plug the jump drive I stole from my dad's office into my laptop. It took a while to find, but I knew it would be here. Someone as arrogant as my father would never dream of someone slipping in and stealing it, especially when they don't know what they're looking for. But the second I saw the letter G, I snatched it and ran. It's just after midnight and he'll be in from his nightcap soon. I download all the files to my computer without looking at them, just in case I run out of time. Once the downloads finish, I take a deep breath and click on a few to make sure the files transferred properly.

What I find is not only disturbing, it's disgusting. There's a registry of members spanning multiple U.S. states and it holds thousands of names. One in particular stands out—*Mason Cole: Member ID, 576891, Status, Active, Location, New Orleans, LA.* I pray that's only true because of the night he followed me there.

I scroll through the list and find members in all the major U.S. cities. This list, along with the video I have from the other night, is grounds enough for the police to investigate them. But wait, what's this?

I click on a folder labeled *BM 1*, and it is filled with video after video of men confessing their darkest, most perverted secrets. It's the elite's form of hazing—*blackmail*. They keep the girls in line with videos of them stripping naked. They keep the members in line with video evidence of the worst things they've ever done.

A pit forms in my stomach as I realize my father is on one of these tapes. Until now, I thought the most horrible thing he'd done was accept membership to this sadistic club. And if that isn't horrible enough, I imagine they only accept members who they can ensure will stay quiet about goings-on. That assurance only comes with leverage.

"He was a monster even before he joined," I whisper. "They all were."

Despite everything in me telling me not to, I search for my father's video. If I'm going to do this, I need to know the full story.

The videos are dated and appear in descending order. I have to scroll back thirty years before I find him. The video is dated 9/10/1990. He's a junior in college and is barely recognizable from the man I know today.

"State your full name and age," a voice says from behind the camera.

My dad sits on a stool located underneath a spotlight. He wears khaki shorts and a sweatshirt with a fraternity logo. I write the logo down.

"Carrington Lee Marshall, age twenty-one," he says.

"And what do you have to confess on this day of 10 September 1990?" the voice asks.

My dad bites the inside of his jaw, like I've done so many times before.

"I'm here to confess to a murder," he says.

What?

My dad goes on to tell the story of how he participated in a hit-and-run a few years back. He was eighteen at the time and was worried his college acceptance and scholarships would be jeopardized if he came forward.

And that's when it started. It all went downhill from there. I consider watching Mason's video but decide against it. If Julian can find it in him to forgive his brother, then I don't want to jeopardize that any more than I already have. Instead, I find Beaux's and hold my breath. Of all the horrible things he's done, what was his original crime? His moment of no return?

"State your full name and age," the voice says.

"Beauregard Ashton Thomas, age nineteen," Beaux says.

"And what do you have to confess on this day of 9 August 2010?" the voice asks.

"I killed my mother," he says. He is unwavering as he speaks. He doesn't flinch or show signs of remorse. He doesn't shy away from the truth.

"And *why* did you kill her?" the voice asks.

Beaux looks away from the camera. *There it is.* He isn't ashamed of what he's done. He's ashamed of what happened to him.

"Because she didn't stop it," Beaux finally says. He begins to shake back and forth in his chair.

"Didn't stop what?" the voice asks.

Beaux's face turns red. He's getting angry.

"My father," Beaux chokes.

"And what did your father do to you?" the voice asks.

A single tear rolls down my cheek, and I fast forward through Beaux's recount of his abuse. I can't stand to hear it.

"Last question," the voice asks. Beaux is red-faced, in tears. He said he works every day to hide the real him. Is this the real him? A scared little boy one hair-trigger away from completely losing it.

"How did you kill your mother?" the voice asks.

I lean forward to listen carefully. Beaux's demeanor shifts once more to cold and unfeeling. He wipes the snot from his face and sits up straight.

"I made her suffer the way I suffered for so many years, and then I choked her," he says. "I choked her so hard, I broke her neck."

I hit pause. Just as I do, Beaux's lips lift into a grin. He stares back at me and I wonder, if Kat hadn't called the cops, would he have killed me too? Choked me to death?

I lift my hand to my throat and work hard to keep the memories from taking over. I haven't got much time left, and there's still so much I need to know.

I click out of the video file back to the main folder. I find a list of membership dues, expenses, even club locations, but no photo evidence of any wrongdoings. Of course, an organization that operates with the use of blackmail would ensure none was available to be used against them.

Just as I think I've found all I'm going to find, a folder catches my eye. It's separate from the Club Gent files. It's a personal file of my father's saved on the same jump drive, and it's labeled B.T.

A lump forms in my throat at the sight. *Please don't tell me . . .*

Inside the folder are years' worth of communication logs between Beaux and my dad, starting before Beaux and I even met. Apparently, they first met when my dad got into some legal trouble back in 2016. Beaux had only been practicing for a couple years at this time and . . .

"*What?*" I ask aloud.

Beaux bribed a girl to drop a sexual assault suit against my father and his company. In addition to being the Mayor of Presley, my father is also the co-owner of a rather large drilling company. Since the oil and gas industry has brought millions to the pockets of rural Louisiana citizens, it makes sense why he hired Beaux's firm to make the case disappear. They're known for being the corporate elite's go-to. Not to mention, my father had to have been aware of Beaux's connection to the brotherhood. I bet it was in their best interest just as much as my father's that this case never saw the light of day. But Beaux didn't just make the case disappear. When the bribe didn't work, he made the girl disappear.

My father has a copy of the police report. Her mother reported her missing when she didn't show up to Sunday lunch that weekend. A news article written several weeks later details the findings, in so many words, of a young, brunette girl found at the docks in New Orleans. The article claims she drowned, which may or may not be true. Regardless of the cause of death, Beaux committed the act.

The records don't indicate that my father requested this of his attorneys, but indicate Beaux acted alone. It was one of his first big cases, and it put his name on the map among his firm's sleazy clientele. He's made a career off that one case, one murder, probably his payment for completing the heinous crime.

At that, I close out of the files and shut down my computer. Darkness surrounds me, both physically and figuratively.

My father knew of Beaux's involvement with Club Gent and the sex crimes he committed when we started dating. He knew about the abuse Beaux suffered as a child. He knew about him torturing and murdering his mother. He knew about the murder he committed with no provocation at all, just to save a stranger's hide. And he did nothing but encourage us and celebrate us when we got engaged. He gave me no warning. He had no concern for my safety. All the while I had no clue who I was dating, sleeping with, planning to spend the rest of my life with.

None of this makes sense. What kind of father allows his daughter to marry a murderer, a rapist? He didn't need the insurance. He already had enough blackmail on Beaux to keep him quiet about anything he may have known about him. Not to mention, attorney-client privilege and the fact that Beaux had more to lose than him.

Why would my father let me walk right into the arms of the man destined to ruin my life?

There's a knock at my door. I hide the jump drive beneath the skirt of my dress.

"Who is it?" I call.

"It's Eva. Can I come in?" my sister asks.

"Oh, yeah," I say. I thought she'd already gone to bed.

Eva opens the door and flips on the light switch. My eyes take a second to adjust to the bright lights.

"Why are you sitting in the dark? You still haven't showered?" she asks.

"Ugh, no, not yet. I just—I love this dress and I was um . . . Face Timing Kat," I lie.

"Oh, okay," Eva says. She's wearing pajama shorts and an old high-school t-shirt.

"Is everything okay?" I ask.

"Yeah," she says with a nod. Her smile soon falters. "I'm not sure."

"Cookies or cake?"

"Huh?" she asks.

"Cookies or cake?"

* * *

After showering, I meet Eva downstairs in the family room, where she has cookies and milk set up for both of us.

"I couldn't sleep," she tells me.

"Why is that?" I ask, taking a bite of my cookie.

"If I knew that, I wouldn't need you," she barks. My eyebrows rise in response. "Sorry," she says. "I just . . . I think I'm getting cold feet, for lack of a better phrase."

I nod and set my snack to the side. This deserves my full attention.

"Okay," I say. "Well, why do you think that may be? Are you nervous about the ceremony? Or is it something deeper, like nervous to be someone's wife?" I ask.

"I'm not nervous about the ceremony," she tells me. "It'll be beautiful, and I love my dress. It's just . . . I think about you and Beaux and you two were together nearly three years before deciding to part ways," she says. "I don't know, sometimes I think maybe we're moving too fast. I worry that two years from now, Bill will get sick of me and want a divorce."

I can't lie to her. It's a possibility. Bill seems like a nice guy and they make a beautiful couple, but you don't know someone until, well, until you do. And to get to know someone, you have to experience life with them, see them at their best and worst. And even more so, you have to be willing to *see* the bad. Don't have blinders to the truth like I did.

"You never did tell me why you and Beaux broke up," Eva says then. "I guess, I thought of all people, you might have some advice on this matter."

I nod and am glad my despair can be of some good to someone. Though, I'm not sure I'm willing to tell her the whole story, at least not yet.

"Eva," I start. "I can't lie to you. Two years from now, ten, twenty, hell, even thirty years from now, one of you may want a divorce."

"Oh, I'll never—"

"You don't know that. You can't," I say. "But do you have

any reason to believe right now that Bill would leave you or that you may grow unhappy with him?"

"No," she says.

"Good. Do you think he'll be a good husband? Take care of you when you're sick? Listen to you when you speak? Respect your mind and your body?" I ask.

"Wow, that's a lot to ask for," she says.

"No, it's the minimum requirements," I say.

"But do you think . . . do you think that's why you and Beaux didn't work out? You expected too much of him?" she asks me.

"No," I tell her, shaking my head. "I expected too little, and I accepted even less." I bite my lip and contemplate my next words. "Eva, when I left Presley, it was because I no longer wanted to live in this world of southern expectation, of watchful eyes, and under the rule of our overbearing mother. But . . . after a few years of being away, I started to feel this void inside me," I tell her. "I didn't miss Presley or even the way things were. I just . . . I missed what they could have been. I mean, what daughter doesn't want her parents to be proud of her, her mother to support her career choices, her father to welcome the man she loves into the family with open arms?" I ask.

I look away from her then and take a deep breath. This next part isn't easy for me to say or admit to myself.

"When I met Beaux, I think I gravitated towards him because he reminded me of home. He was everything I knew Mom and Dad would love and approve of, and they did. And it felt good to feel a part of the family again, to feel Mom and Dad's pride," I tell her.

I find myself angry, angry at my parents for making me work so hard for their affection. I nearly killed myself just to make them proud.

"Emma," Eva says. It's then that I notice I'm crying.

"No, it's okay," I tell her, wiping my cheeks. "*I'm* okay." I take a deep breath and . . .

"The relationship Beaux allowed me to have with Mom and Dad allowed me to stomach the relationship he and I actually had. I just . . . I didn't realize it at the time," I tell her.

"But what does that mean?" she asks, leaning forward.

"It means, there is no perfect man and there's no guarantee you won't get hurt," I say, trying to change the subject. "But you should never accept less than you deserve, and that doesn't mean you have to be treated like a princess. It means you require him to treat you as an equal, as a partner," I tell her. "And with being a partner, there is responsibility and hard decisions and arguments and disagreements. But if you trust the person standing next to you and you feel in your heart that you love him and he loves you, then it's worth it, no matter how it ends. Because life is hard either way. And take it from someone who knows. Being alone is no way to go through life."

Eva nods and thinks to herself while I eat a few more cookies and finish off my glass of milk.

"When did you realize that Beaux wasn't treating you as an equal?" Eva asks me.

I pause and contemplate her question. In truth, I can't peg the exact moment that I knew he was no good for me. I think it started long before I realized he was cheating. The cheating was just the final straw.

"Eva, I'm not sure I can give you an honest answer," I tell her. "But . . . I can say this. I don't think Beaux changed. I don't think he started off as this great guy and over time morphed into what he was when we broke up. I used to," I admit. "But not anymore. I think . . . I think it was me who changed. I'm the one who suddenly became aware of the type of man he was and who realized that he was not only not treating me as an equal, he was treating me like an object," I tell her.

"I was his doll that he played with on the weekends, that he brought out for corporate functions. What I used to think was special became something meaningless," I say.

"But," Eva cuts me off. "But do you think he treated you that way because of how you treated him?"

"*What?* What do you mean?" I ask. My brows furrow in confusion. My cheeks radiate in defense of her remark.

"Well, you said that what drew you to Beaux was that you knew Mom and Dad would approve of him. And you said that you stayed with him perhaps longer than you should have, because you liked your newfound relationship with Mom and Dad," Eva says.

"Yeah, I guess," I say, crossing my arms over my chest.

"So, it sounds like you never really liked him for him. And you certainly didn't stay with him for so long because you loved him. You stayed because you liked what the relationship gave you," Eva tells me.

"No, that's not . . . that's not what happened," I assure her.

"Are you sure?" she asks me.

No, I admit to myself.

I asked Beaux if he ever loved me, but I never thought to ask myself the same question. I mean, I thought I loved him. Beaux told me himself I was the only one to ever love him. But I suppose he isn't the best judge of what love looks like and feels like. *Did I? Love him?* Perhaps, after everything that's happened between us, it wouldn't be fair of me to answer that question now. Regardless of my feelings, past or present, I know I can't be blamed for Beaux's infidelity or violence against me. Maybe I *can* be blamed for the emotional distance between us when we were dating. Maybe I *did* go into the relationship for the wrong reasons. Or, *at least*, maybe I stayed for the wrong reasons. *But* . . . that isn't why our relationship ended. That wasn't the unsurpassable truth that resulted in where we are now.

There were things I liked about Beaux that attracted me to him. His smile, his style, his confidence, his determination and drive. I loved the fact that he was driven, not just in his career, but in his effort to live the most fulfilling life possible. It was something we connected on. Even when I thought the Thomases were his biological parents, I admired him for wanting to step beyond their shadow and create a life that was his own. My decision to leave Presley was for similar reasons. Now that I know what his childhood entailed, I have even more admiration for that part of him. But none of that changes what he did, what he's continued to do to me and to other women. Mason may have found a path toward redemption. But I'm not sure Beaux ever will. And I'm not sorry that I won't be by his side to watch him destroy himself and me along with him.

"Eva, there are things you don't know about what happened between me and Beaux," I tell her. "Things that I can't explain right now. And, maybe you're right. Maybe I did go into the relationship for the wrong reasons. Maybe if I would've been more willing to see Beaux for who he was rather than what he gave me, then I would have known long before that he wasn't the man for me," I admit. "So, take a look at Bill," I say, leaning forward in my seat. "Examine his best and worst moments. Consider how he makes you feel. Take away the excitement of getting married, changing your name, and having your own home. Think beyond that and consider yourself in five years. Without children or other distractions, who is Bill and how does he make you feel?" I ask her. "And if you don't have the answers you feel you need, talk to him. Talk to him tonight all the way through the second before you walk down the aisle. Tradition be damned," I say. "If he loves you, he'll understand, and he won't judge you for asking. If he *does* judge you or get angry with you for having these questions or concerns, get out now, because marriage doesn't solve problems. It amplifies them," I tell her.

She nods and contemplates my words.

"But, Eva," I say, interrupting her thoughts. "You can't know someone until you do. You can't plan out your life at twenty-two. You can't know if you'll be married forever or if the relationship will end in divorce. But . . . if you love him and he's proven to you that he loves you, then . . . it's worth figuring out together."

CHAPTER 27

My family and the remaining wedding guests make a tunnel lit with sparklers for Eva and Bill to walk through. They did it. They got married. And after last night, I can honestly say I'm happy for my sister. And I think she knows what she's doing, as best as any young bride can.

Bill's best man pulls around a pink Lamborghini as Eva and Bill appear at the top of the Marshall House steps.

She made a gorgeous bride in a sleeveless dress with a deep V-neck and a bodice completely covered in ivory lace. Her tulle skirt was much simpler than I expected of her, yet the way it cascaded behind her as she walked down the aisle couldn't have been more perfect.

I hold my sparkler high and draw a heart in the air as Eva and Bill make it to the end of their farewell march. The photographer's camera flashes brightly against the dark night. Bill spins Eva around and kisses her in a dramatic fashion. Everyone cheers.

Eva gives me one last glance before getting in the car. Her smile is as big as I've ever seen it. Little lines branch out from her blue eyes. I mouth the words *"I love you"* and she mouths the words *"You too."* And with that, the happy couple speeds down a gravel drive lit with string lights, completely unaware of the chaos they've just escaped.

* * *

Inside, my mother marches around, giving orders to the cleaning staff, and my father retreats to his study. I'm left alone in the foyer to watch as men and women dressed in all-black outfits zoom around my childhood home, removing any signs of Eva and Bill's nuptials. They blow out candles and pick-up flowers. They clear plates and glasses from random tables. The more they clean, the more I'm reminded of what truly lies beneath the pomp and circumstance of my sister's wedding—a house of secrets and spilled blood.

I make my way upstairs, admiring every photo, every scrape in the wood, every inch of memory that comes rushing back. After tonight, I don't plan on returning to Presley. Even if I wanted to, I doubt I'll be welcome.

I undress, removing the glittering, one-shoulder dress my sister insisted on, and replace it with blue jean shorts and a plain white t-shirt.

My bed is fixed. My bag is packed. In a final act, I make my way to my vanity and sit once more on the gold upholstered stool. It's there that I find my heavily painted reflection. So many times before, I've sat in this spot. Each time I've seen something different. From curly Q curls to inflamed, teenage skin, to the utter panic I felt when I left home for college, to now . . . I'm a grown woman, and for the first time in my life, I think I know what that means.

I remove my fake lashes and unpin my tightly wound hair. I wipe the lipstick from my lips and the base from my face.

"Let go of what once was and embrace what is," I say aloud.

Tonight, I say goodbye to my father. I say goodbye to the man who raised me, who watched me perform in the Christmas musicals, who sat in the high-school gym as I cheered. I wish I could believe he wasn't always this monster, this animal. I wish I could hang onto the moments that were good. But after everything that's happened, everything I've learned, I can't. He was always a monster. Like Beaux, he was just really good at hiding it.

I take a single bottle of perfume, a few pieces of my favorite jewelry, and the green box filled with memories of Ezra and me and I shove them in my duffle bag.

This room was many things for me, a haven at the center of a tragic world. Now, it is the coffin of the girl who once was.

I turn out the light and close the door behind me.

* * *

I walk into my father's office and drop my duffle bag at his door before taking a seat. He's on the phone. It sounds important. I stare at him, lips pursed, until he excuses himself from the call.

"Emma, you look like you have something on your mind," he says, clasping his hands together.

I nod, though I can't bring myself to form the words. My dad nods his head and stands, pouring himself a drink from his bar cart. "I think I know what this is about," he says, moving closer to me. He leans up against his desk. I readjust myself so that my body is further away from him. "You're upset that your sister made it down the aisle before you. But I've got to tell you, Emma, marriage isn't all it's cracked out to be," he says, sipping his scotch.

I'm suddenly reminded of my parents' impending divorce.

"I mean, no offense to your mother," my father goes on to say. "But marriage is hard and—"

"Is marriage hard or is being faithful hard?" I ask, cutting him off.

My father is shocked at my statement. Our eyes lock. His fist tightens around his glass.

"What do you know?" he asks me. His cheeks are blazing hot.

"I know that Mom is beside herself trying to figure out what *Irreconcilable Differences* means," I tell him. "I know that you wouldn't just abandon your family unless you had a good reason too, even if your only reason for staying was for perception," I say. "So, tell me Dad, who did you get pregnant?"

I'm bluffing, of course, but it wouldn't surprise me if he did. The more I press him on the divorce, the more I work up my courage to confront him about Club Gent.

My dad sets his glass down on his desk and moves past me to close the door to his office. As a child, I always wondered what those closed-door conversations were about. Looks like I'm about to find out.

My father doesn't speak as he makes his way back across the room. He moves around his desk and takes his seat across from me, clearly in an attempt to regain dominance. I'm just thankful for some distance between us.

"Emma, I don't know what you think you know," he begins. "But your mother and mine's relationship is a private matter."

"You didn't deny it, Daddy," I say. I uncross my legs and lean forward in my seat. "So, who is it? Someone you met on a business trip? Or one of the women you drugged and raped at Club Gent?"

There it is—the unspeakable truth that can't be unspoken.

The veins in my father's neck throb. He loosens his tie, popping his knuckles as he clasps his hands together.

"It's okay. You don't have to say anything," I tell him, leaning back in my chair. "I just wanted you to know that I know. I know about the club and what happens there. I know that you not only cheat on Mom, you do it with inebriated, unconscious and at times, underage girls."

Emotion wells inside me as I confront my father, *my father.* Don't think it hasn't dawned on me how truly messed up this is.

"Emma, I think you're confused," my father starts. *That phrase!* That condescending, egotistical phrase that Beaux has used on me a thousand times. Is that where he got it from? My own father?

"I saw you last Friday night," I say. "Only I didn't look like myself. I was wearing a waitress' outfit and a short, brown wig. You ran into me and the blonde girl I was helping escape as you came out of the restroom."

All the blood drains from my father's face.

"I also saw that you weren't alone when you were in there. You left that girl lying there like a piece of trash," I scold him.

"What are you talking about? How could you . . .? Those girls are . . ." he starts, but I cut him off.

"Those girls are young, naïve, inexperienced, young women with everything in front of them and everything to lose, and you and your brethren of sick sadists manipulate and use them," I tell him. "I know, because I've met them. I've interviewed them. Hell, I practically was one of them."

"No," he gasps. "No, that's impossible," my father says,

standing. "You were supposed to be protected. You were never supposed to know about any of this!" He yells.

"Don't act concerned for me now," I tell him. "You knew who Beaux was, what he was capable of, and you did nothing to protect me from him. You were going to let me marry him!" I scream.

My father slams his fist on his desk so hard his scotch tips over, wetting his papers. I jump.

"I couldn't stop him," my father blurts.

"*What?*" I ask. "What do you mean you couldn't—?"

"I knew who Beaux was, Emma. You're right about that, but as much as I may have said otherwise, I never wanted you two together," he reveals.

My father exhales and grabs his glass from his desk, pouring himself another glass of scotch.

"I didn't have a choice," he mumbles into his glass.

"*What?*" I ask. "*You* didn't have a choice? *I* didn't have a choice!" I yell.

I stand from my seat and shove my chair to the ground.

"Do you know what I went through just to make the relationship with him work? I only stayed with him for so long because I thought that's what you and Mom wanted," I say. "And when I finally did have the sense to leave, do you know what he did to me?" I ask.

My father refuses to look at me. I bite the inside of my jaw and pounce across the room, forcing him to face me.

"Do *you* know what he did to me?"

His dark eyes peer into mine. As I look up to him, I feel like a child again, helpless and scared. He was supposed to protect me. He was supposed to scare the monster away. Instead, he became one.

Tears blur my vision and I pull away from him, retreating to the opposite side of the room.

"I—I don't know what you mean by I was supposed to be protected," I tell him. "I don't know what crazy deal you had worked out with Beaux. I don't—I don't know why you didn't step in and make your opinion known, *but Beaux . . .*" I stop.

"He raped me, Dad, and beat me. And I got pregnant and I . . . I made a decision that haunts me, a decision that I don't know if I will ever overcome."

My dad throws his glass at the floor. It splinters into a hundred pieces.

"*That*," I say, pointing at the broken shards. "That's what happened to me the second he put his hands on me."

Tears slip down my cheeks and I quickly wipe them away. He doesn't deserve to see them, not anymore.

"And now, every time I try to put the pieces back together again, Beaux is there, threatening me and everyone I love into silence," I tell him. "But not anymore."

I close the distance between us and look him in the eye. What I see is unrecognizable. The man who raised me is now a stranger.

"I'm taking back control, Dad. I have everything I need to destroy him, the brotherhood, *and* you," I say. "I can't do one without the other and I wouldn't even tell you. I know there's a risk in doing so, but . . . I won't live without closure, not anymore." I nod and take two steps back. "This is goodbye, Carrington," I say. "You are no longer my father."

"Emma, wait," he says, pulling me back to him.

"No!" I yell, shrugging out of his grasp.

"Emma, you don't know these people," he yells. "You may think you do, but you don't." He exhales then. His cheeks flush. "It's why I couldn't stop Beaux from being with you."

"What are you talking about?" I ask, crossing my arms over my chest.

My dad drops his eyes to the glass-covered floor and . . .

"When you first introduced us to Beaux, I . . . I was shocked, but I couldn't let you or anyone else know that. So, I . . . I played it off until I could speak to him in private," he reveals.

My head throbs as my dad tells his story.

"I forbid Beaux from seeing you. I told him to break it off and never see you again. I didn't want you in any way exposed to the brotherhood. But he wouldn't listen. He said, this was payback for . . ." My dad stops then.

"For the girl," I say.

The girl Beaux had to murder to keep my father's secret and the heat off the brotherhood— he wanted revenge for her, for the moment that shackled him to his past forever. I was his revenge. All that talk about him not knowing how to love me and it wasn't my fault, that was the truth, but only half the truth. He came into our relationship with ill intentions in mind, until . . . until he fell in love with me. And, by then, he couldn't have let me go even if he wanted to. I was the only one for him, in the most messed up way possible.

My father looks away from me in shame, but he doesn't deny it.

"Beaux assured me that this was between me and him," my dad says then. "He said he would never expose you to the brotherhood. You were supposed to be protected from them."

"Yeah," I say. "I was protected from the brotherhood. But not from Beaux," I say. "You didn't protect me, Dad. You knew what kind of man he was and you . . . you were going to let me marry him."

Disbelief floods my features. The more I think about it, the more shocked and angrier I become.

"Look, I don't know what you're planning, but they have eyes and ears everywhere, especially in New Orleans," he says. "Because of your connection to Beaux, they'll send him to make the problem go away," my father tells me. "And Emma, *you're* the problem."

My father exhales and shakes his head.

"I understand that you no longer consider me your father, but Emma, you will always be my daughter," he says, taking a step toward me.

I take two steps back.

"It's not worth it, Emma," my father says, shaking my head. "If you do this, you'll be giving up everything and for what? A few assholes beyond bars?" My father asks. "More are born every day."

I nod. His words only make me even more determined to follow through on my plan.

"Well, then, I guess I better get started. You know, to keep up with the number of assholes being born," I tell him.

At that, I back away, grab my duffle bag and . . .

"Oh, and Carrington," I say. "I'm not the problem. *You are.*"

* * *

"Emma? You're leaving so soon?" my mother asks. "It's almost midnight. You can't drive all the way to New Orleans in the dark. Why don't you just stay one more night?" she begs.

I feel bad for leaving her, I do. But I can't stay one more night in this house. And to be honest, I wish she wouldn't either.

"I can't, Mom. I—I wish we could talk more. I really enjoyed spending time with you this weekend, *but* . . ." I exhale.

"Emma, what's wrong?" she asks.

I glance behind me. There's no one there. Still, I don't want my father to think for one second that my mother knows the truth. It would only put her in even more danger. And while he may not be willing to kill me, I can't say the same for her.

"Come here, Mom," I say, pulling her in for a hug. As she embraces me, I slip a copy of the jump drive into her pocket. "You need to pack a bag and get out," I whisper. "You're not safe here."

As I pull away from her, I make sure she's aware of the insurance I'm leaving her with. She moves her hand to her pocket and confusion washes over her.

"Take care, Mom. Come visit me soon."

CHAPTER 28

My fingers twitch over the keys of my laptop. It's done. With the last bit of evidence I gathered in Presley, I made it home and finished my article. Now, all I have to do is hit send and come 9:00 a.m. tomorrow morning, it will be published across the digital pages of The Hub's website. So why can't I hit submit?

My dad tried calling me five times between the time I left Presley and made it back to New Orleans. I didn't answer. I *did* listen to his voicemails, though. He left four begging me to stay quiet. He assured me that one person would not punish the crimes of the many. What he doesn't understand is that I don't represent my own selfish interests in this matter. Sure, I used to. But that's before I realized how truly widespread this issue and the predatory actions of a select group of men is. This organization exists in *my* city and in many more cities across the country. But it is not the only one of its kind. It can't be. My father doesn't understand how one voice can so quickly become many.

When he finally accepted that I wasn't entertaining his pleas, he left a final voicemail, apologizing. He apologized for what he's done, for what happened to me, and for not protecting me from Beaux. Apparently, he was more afraid of what Beaux would do if he forced him to stop dating me than what he would do if we continued dating. Still, I'm not sure if he was referring to what Beaux would do to me or him.

Despite all of this, I'd be lying if I said my father didn't cause some hesitation in me. As much as I hate him for what he's done and the fact that he never said he planned on stopping, or offered to help me in my efforts, he's still my father. He's the man who

I've looked up to my entire life, despite my jaded childhood and sudden departure after high school.

And then there's Mason. I didn't watch his video, not that it would've changed my opinion of him in any positive way. But I do give him credit for trying to be better. I thank him for helping me out of Club Gent and for caring about Julian the way he does. And, I know, the fact that his name will be turned in along with my father's and Beaux's probably won't help my efforts to make things up to Julian. But none of that excuses his past mistakes. And as much as I would like to spare him for the sake of mine and Julian's future, it's not *my* forgiveness that Mason needs.

I exhale and with resolve, click submit. Now the whole world will know about me, Beaux, and the brotherhood. I thought it would feel more cathartic, more freeing. Instead, I feel nauseous.

"It's done?" Kat asks, popping her head through my bedroom door.

"Yeah. It's done," I breathe. I shut my laptop down and set it on my nightstand. Kat nods and comes to sit beside me on the bed.

"Do you think Fran will be mad you used The Hub for a personal story?" Kat asks.

"Kat," I say. "Fran is the least of my worries *and* yours. Are you all set to stay with Demetri?"

"Yeah," Kat nods, falling back against the sheets. "I have things for about a week. If I need to stay away for longer, I'll just use a laundromat or buy something new."

"Good," I say pulling my knees into my chest.

We both sit in silence.

I don't know when I'll next see Kat. My father may be wrong about many things, but one thing is for sure. Beaux will come for me. And when he does, Kat can't be anywhere within his reach. She's leaving the city with Demetri tonight. I don't know where they're going. I think it's better that way.

"Emma," Kat says.

"Don't say it," I tell her.

"Don't say what?" she asks, sitting up straight.

I bite my lip, refusing to look at her. "Don't say goodbye," I finally say.

"Oh, Emma," Kat says. She pulls me into her arms, and I rest my head against her shoulder.

In truth, I don't know what's going to happen. I don't know if Julian will forgive me. I don't know if I'll be able to convince him to leave the city with me. I don't know if I'll make it through this alive. I just know I'm proud of myself and I will fight for my truth, the truth of the spoken survivors, and the truth of the unspoken until the fight is done.

"I wasn't going to say goodbye," Kat finally says. "Goodbye is beyond the realm of our bond." I smile. "I was just going to say . . ." She stops herself, pulling away from me.

"I want you to look at me when I say this to you," she says.

"*Okay*," I say, moving to face her.

"Emma Louise Marshall," Kat says. "I'm proud of you. I am *beyond* proud of you. And whatever happens," she says, shaking her head. "Your voice will not be silenced, and your voice will speak for those who can't."

I'm reminded of Ashley Roy and wish that she could be here to see Beaux go down. I wish she wouldn't have felt alone, and that there was no way out. Still, I understand how she could feel that. My hope is that no girl or woman ever has to feel that again.

"Thank you, Kat," I say, squeezing her hand.

"Now," she says, slapping her thighs. "You need an outfit that is both revenge-worthy and apology-worthy."

Kat moves to my closet and starts yanking out dress after dress. I now see why this room is so hard to keep clean.

"I get the apology," I say. "But what's the revenge for?" I ask.

"For Beaux," Kat says. She turns to me then, holding a burgundy, velvet tuxedo dress with a practically non-existent neckline. "If he really does come after you, best to leave him with an image of what he'll be missing while he's locked away in some dungeon with nothing but his thoughts."

I'm not sure I want to leave a lasting impression on Beaux, but if Julian is to forgive me, I'll need all the help I can get.

"Fine," I moan. "But if we're doing this, we're doing this. Get me some stripper heels too."

"Hell yes," Kat says. She tosses the dress on the bed and rifles for the most uncomfortable black, strappy heels she can find. *Damn.* I meant to throw those out.

"By the way, I've never seen you wear this," Kat says. "When did you get it?"

Kat's features shift from excited to disgusted as she sifts through my jewelry collection. I can't help but laugh.

"In college," I tell her. "Pair it with some angel wings and voila, sexy cupid," I say.

"Well, honey, you're going to have to trade in those angel wings for something a little more devilish, if you want your man back," she says. "How about these?"

Kat holds up a pair of sheer, black stockings with small diamonds scattered across them. Yet another memento from my college days. I must have blocked more of that time out than I thought.

"Well, you only crash your ex-boyfriend's record shop reopening party and apologize for completely breaking his heart and destroying his relationship with his brother once, so yeah, stockings it is," I tell her.

* * *

Double-sided tape and a prayer are the only things keeping me in this scrap that passes as a dress as I make it down the steep steps into the speakeasy. The renovation of Lucid Records turned out beautifully. It's clean and crisp, and with the recessed lighting and added windows, the space looks much larger than it did before. But that's not what everyone is raving about. What's beneath the surface has caught the attention of almost everyone with a pulse here in New Orleans. If I didn't know about the secret entrance from the record shop, I'd be sweating my skin off in line with the rest of the soon-to-be patrons.

Unlike before, when I was met with darkness, bowling-ball-sized rats, and the stench of mildew, the bottom of the staircase has been expanded into a large, formal landing. Chatter fills the air along with the sweet smell of fresh wood and vanilla. From my elevated vantage point, I am able to take in the entire space. The large, underground speakeasy is adorned with hardwood floors, dark painted walls, and up-lighting to create a cozy effect. There are highboy tables on either side of the space with a large dance floor in the middle. Straight ahead is a bar with solid wood stools. Mirrors back the glass liquor shelves, reflecting the performance stage for those dabbling in the drinks and eats.

And the stage . . . I move from the stairs to the bar area to get a better view. It's lifted high above the dance floor and is framed with dangling crystal chandeliers, black velvet curtains, and spotlights that shine red.

"It's quite something, isn't it?"

I turn at the familiar voice and find Mason standing behind the bar. He's dressed in a red suit with a black button-down shirt and lapel. It looks odd on him, but I suppose it matches the decor.

"It is," I say, taking a seat across from him. "I knew Julian would do justice to it."

Mason nods. He grabs a martini glass and mixes up a bright plum concoction in an attempt to match my dress.

"For you," he says, placing the drink in front of me.

"I've sworn off purple drinks, but thank you," I tell him.

Mason's face shifts from playful to serious. He removes the drink from my presence and pours it down the drain without a word. I realize then he isn't privy to my Purple Death story and probably thought I was referring to the purple drinks they serve the women at Club Gent. Despite my social slip, I don't apologize.

"So, um, how is he? *Where* is he?" I ask, scanning the room for his impeccable hair. Nothing.

"He's backstage," Mason says to me. "What's your drink of choice?"

"White wine—Moscato, if you have it." Mason relays my order to the bartender. "So, backstage, is he performing?" I ask.

"Yeah," Mason says. "He, um, he didn't take the hint," he says, handing me my drink.

"*What?*" I lean forward, unable to hear him.

Mason eyes the men and women crowding the bar. I find the exit and see more and more people flooding in. It won't be long until every inch of the space is filled.

"Can we? Can we talk in private?" Mason asks.

I hesitate. He may be Julian's brother and my subsequent neighbor, for the time being, but that doesn't mean I can trust him, especially after learning of his membership to the most exclusive club you never want to join.

Mason rolls his eyes.

"I'm not going to hurt you, Emma. After all, you *are* my fake girlfriend," he jokes.

"Well, in that case . . . fine," I tell him, though I'm sure to keep several feet between us.

Mason leads me from the bar area through a black door you'd hardly know existed if you weren't looking for it. I watch as the door closes behind me and all the chatter fades away. It's soundproofed. Suddenly, I second-guess my decision to follow Mason into the unknown. His name *is* on the list I plan to turn over to the police.

What if . . . what if the brothers sent *him* instead of Beaux?

"Are . . . you okay?" Mason asks, leaning up against a sound deck.

"Oh, it's um, it's a recording studio," I say. I twirl around, taking in the space. There's a couch, a few stools, a sound deck, and one large recording studio enclosed in glass.

"Where did you think I was taking you? The back alley?" Mason smiles.

"Uh, maybe," I admit.

Mason shakes his head and offers me a seat on the couch. He, respectfully, sits on a stool across the room from me.

"So, like I was saying, he didn't take the hint," Mason says.

"What hint? That we're together?" I ask.

"Oh, no, he got that." Mason assures me. "That is permanently burned into his brain." I cringe and swallow half my allotment of wine in preparation for where this conversation is going. "What he didn't get is the hint to get the hell out of this city," Mason reveals.

"*What?*" I ask. "How could he want to stay? I thought for sure that would be enough to—"

"To drive him away," Mason says, cutting me off.

"*Yeah*," I admit, slouching into the plush cushions of the couch.

"Well, it wasn't," Mason reveals. "I don't know why he's intent on staying, but he is. He turned this space into a recording studio, signed two local artists to our label and is planning to produce their albums *right here*," Mason says, pointing at the studio. "That's how intent he is on staying."

"It doesn't make sense," I say.

"Well, it makes sense that he would want to be away from me," Mason comments. "I'm based in LA, so, of course, he wouldn't want to be there."

"But it doesn't make sense for him to want to stay in New Orleans and live next door to the girl who broke his heart," I say. "Unless he . . ."

"Unless he what?" Mason asks, clasping his hands together.

My chest tightens. My throat burns. I inhale the rest of my Moscato.

"Unless he's found someone else," I say, setting my glass to the side.

Mason is quiet.

"I mean, it would be fair," I admit. "I lied to him and I broke his heart, his trust," I say, shaking my head. "I even ruined his relationship with you, his brother, the only family he has left."

Mason drops his head and closes his eyes.

"I'm sorry for that," I tell him. "I—I'm going to tell him everything. That's why I'm here. It's why I'm dressed like . . . like a freaking sexy cupid meets devilish enchantress," I say, picking at the hem of my dress. "I just—I just hope he can find it in him to understand. Even if he can't stomach the sight of me, I . . ." Tears fill my eyes. My insides burn as I hold them inside. "I just hope he can forgive you," I tell him.

Mason nods, but he doesn't say anything. I take it he doesn't have much faith in my optimism. In truth, I don't either, but it's the only thing keeping me sane right now.

"So, what's the plan?" Mason asks. "Even if he believes you and forgives you and the two of you live happily ever after, there's still the very real reality that New Orleans isn't safe for you or anyone close to you. And, Emma, I know firsthand how far and wide the brotherhood's connections run," he says, shaking his head.

"If you do this, you'll be running for the rest of your life," Mason says.

I stand from my seat and brush the wrinkles out of my dress. It's not that his words don't scare me. It's just . . . there's no going back.

"It's already done," I say. And with that, I leave him to himself.

Our last look is one of deep understanding. Even without him knowing what I gathered in Presley, he knows I have enough to take down the brotherhood, at least the New Orleans operation. And when one falls, so will the rest—so will he. It'll just take time.

CHAPTER 29

I close the door to the sound studio behind me, and immediately my strength leaves me. *You'll be running for the rest of your life. They'll send him to make the problem go away and, Emma, you're the problem.* The words of both my father and Mason race through my mind, and my resolve begins to wane.

I did this to take back control of my life and overcome my fear of Beaux, of men, of being hurt, of being cheated on and lied to. But what if it was all for nothing? What if my old fears are only replaced by new ones of being hunted, not just by Beaux but by all the brothers? *What if* . . . what if Julian can't find it in him to forgive me and I'm left alone, alone after I worked so hard just to be able to move forward with him? *And what if* . . . what if he does forgive me, and my dad and Mason are right? What if we can't outrun the brotherhood? How is it fair to ask Julian to give up his life, a life he clearly treasures here in New Orleans, just to run with me toward unknown enemies? The answer is simple. It isn't.

With resolve, I make a B-Line for the staircase. That is, until the MC welcomes Julian to the stage along with two of his protégés. Everything in me tells me to leave, to spare him and myself of another goodbye. But I can't. Like there is an invisible chord tying us together, I am pulled to the stage.

I work my way through the cheering patrons until I find myself front and center. The chandeliers that hang above cast a warm glow over the stage. There's a stool in the middle and a microphone adjusted for a guitar or . . . a violin. To the right is a piano, and to the left is a cello.

My heart aches as I remember the first time I saw Julian play.

It was the same night we met. I'd just found out my sister was engaged, and Kat and Demetri hadn't yet mastered their sexual volume. I found myself at Mimi's. He took the stage. And the second he moved his bow against the strings, I knew. I knew he was special, intellectual, deep, the kind of man who isn't afraid to feel. And he made others feel too. He made me feel something other than pain for the first time since I couldn't remember when. I suppose it's only fitting I attend one last performance.

Julian walks out on stage. He's wearing a white button-down shirt and black trousers. Underneath the lights, the tattoos on his skin seem to peek through. His icy eyes seem to glow.

He doesn't see me, not yet at least. He takes a seat on the stool while a young girl sits at the cello and a young man at the piano.

"On the violin we have Julian Cole, musician, Co-Owner and Director of A and R for Cole Creative, and the man responsible for the fabulous renovation of the New Orleans landmark, Lucid Records. Accompanying him tonight are two diamonds Julian discovered while performing at Mimi's here in the city. We have Lee Holiday on the piano and Ursula Prescott on the cello," the MC announces.

Everyone cheers. I can't bring myself to speak. Instead, I clap.

"Tonight, they will be performing an original song that is sure to tug at the hearts of us all. Here is *Goodbye*," the MC reveals.

At that, the lights dim. The bodies of the people surrounding me start to sway. My lips part. And almost as if he can hear my unsteady heart beating, Julian's eyes meet mine.

His pupils dilate. The vein in his neck throbs all the way to his temple. I can't bring myself to smile. I can't bring myself to move. I am entranced by him and he is . . .? Surprise washes over him and I am unable to tell if he wants me to stay or leave.

The piano opens the song. It is the most painful, slow melody I think I've ever heard. Julian nestles his violin between his shoulder and his neck. Suddenly, the tempo increases, and Julian brings his bow to his instrument. Without removing his eyes from me, he plays. The song feels like the dance of us, a constant battle of love and loss, of coming together and pulling apart. My skin ignites under his gaze. My heart pulls toward him as if it might jump out of my chest. Yet my legs want to crumble beneath me, to protect him from all the pain and uncertainty I bring with me. The cello joins in. Julian's movements become sharper and the piano becomes deeper. The music builds and builds and then it—it just stops. Just like we stopped, right when things started getting real.

I suppose I'd somehow hoped I'd have the answers I needed, the resolve I needed by the time he finished. And while I can't bring myself to accept that Julian is no longer a part of my life, if the song means what I think it means, the choice is no longer mine. I said goodbye to him and now he's saying goodbye to me.

Julian finally pulls away. His eyes are red and watery as they drift from me to the floor. He composes himself and takes a bow, congratulating Ursula and Lee.

I find myself drifting, drifting further into the crowd as clapping and cheering fans rush the stage. Emotion pulses through me, begging to escape. I don't let it. Instead, I put my heels to good use and run toward the exit.

* * *

"Emma, wait!" Julian calls after me.

I round the corner, moving from the secret stairwell to the store area. I pass the register and the rows of records and . . .

"Emma," Julian breathes. I feel him closing in. His shadow meshes with mine. "*Wait*," he says once more.

He moves his hand to my shoulder and pulls me back to him just as I reach the exit. Our bodies are inches apart. Sweat glistens across his chest as he towers over me. I feel his eyes on me, though I can't bring myself to look at him. If I do, I'll either cry or pounce on him. And given what he must think of me, I'm not sure which would be worse.

"What are you doing?" I whisper. I feel small in his presence. My chest rises and falls as I try to control my breathing.

Julian looks away from me, though our proximity remains the same.

"You once told me," he breathes. "I take it you've never

had your heart broken." There's a tiny crackle in his throat as he speaks. I close my eyes to hold in my tears. "Well, you were right," he tells me. "I . . . I hadn't had my heart broken, not in the way it breaks when you lose the person you love."

My lip quivers and I'm forced to open my eyes. He looks down at me then. My cheeks feel hot as he watches me. He lifts his hand to my chin and forces me to look at him.

"You taught me what it is to be broken by the person you love, Emma Marshall," he says then.

I gasp at the weight of his words. Just like Beaux broke me, I broke him. Tears fall from my eyes, cascading down my face. Despite the pain I've caused him, Julian only treats me gently. He wipes away my falling tears with his thumb. I want to lean into his touch, into his gentility, but I don't. I don't deserve to.

"But you also taught me what it means to love and . . ." He pauses. "How scary it is to think of putting yourself out there again."

My brows furrow. What is he trying to say?

"I thank you for teaching me, Emma. And I understand why we couldn't work, why Mason was the better choice for you," he says then. "Because he can never hurt you the way I can, because what you feel for him will never be as real as what we have . . . *had*," Julian corrects himself.

He looks away from me then and takes two steps back. With his movement, the imaginary chord that once connected us pulls taunt and then breaks.

Julian nods and shoves his hands in his pockets.

"I just wanted you to know I get it. It hurts, but I get it," he says.

He takes me in, looking me up and down. Clearly, sexy cupid doesn't impress him.

"Anyway, I'm glad we had this chance to say goodbye. I didn't think I needed it. I thought the song would be enough, but seeing you . . ." he says, shaking his head. "Seeing you made me realize I needed more. And now," Julian breathes. "Now, I need to inform my brother of his 6:00 a.m. flight back to LA. It's one-way," he says.

Julian turns and . . .

"It was all a lie," I blurt.

Julian stops.

I close my eyes and when I open them, his back is still toward me. Yet his head is turned so he can listen. I exhale and . . .

"I was never with Mason," I say. "I only said that because . . ." I hesitate.

I said no more secrets, so no more secrets. Here goes nothing.

"I only said that because I needed you to hate me. I needed you to want to leave New Orleans," I reveal. "I thought . . . I thought when your brother came to visit you, with me out of the way, he could convince you to leave. He never wanted you to come to New Orleans anyway," I ramble.

"But why?" he whispers. "Why did you need me to leave the city?" Still, he refuses to face me.

I bite my lip. My heartbeat quickens. As much as I've anticipated this moment, I am in no way prepared for it.

"Because I was scared." I take a step toward him. "I was scared our relationship might jeopardize your safety, and I couldn't let that happen. I've been hurt too many times. I've lost so much, my innocence, my safe place, my trust in humanity, my family, Mr. Turnip, myself," I reveal. "So much of me has been destroyed by a single man. I couldn't lose you too, but . . . in trying not to lose you, in trying to protect you and shield you from whatever hell was lurking, I pushed you away. I . . . I ruined us."

I look away from him then, remembering the moment he found me crying in the corner after I'd snuck into Lucid after hours. He held me until my tears dried and then we danced. He asked me how my day was. And, in that moment, I could've told him everything. I could've told him everything and none of this would have happened. If I'd just been honest . . . I shake my head.

But how can I say that? One different step and I would never have found out about Club Gent. One different step and so many women's stories would've never been told. If my future with Julian is the price I must pay to bring Beaux and the members of

Club Gent to justice, then . . . I suppose I have to accept it and all that comes with it.

I take a deep breath and . . . "And now I have to live with that," I say with a nod. "But just know, Julian, I . . . I love you," I reveal, closing the distance between us. "I'm in love with you like I've never been in love before. And everything I did, in my own twisted way, was so that we could be together, that I could be with you without the fear of moving forward, without having panic attacks, without having the memories of another man's hands on me every time you touch me," I choke.

I want to reach out to him, to caress his back and shoulders, but I don't.

"And Mason never betrayed you," I tell him. "All he did was try to help me, because he knew that's what you would want him to do."

Julian is quiet. He looks straight ahead, as if contemplating if he'll stay or not. Finally, he turns to face me. His cheeks are bright red. His eyes brim with tears. They scan my face as if searching for any evidence of a lie.

"I love you, Julian Cole," I say once more.

Julian's lips lift into a half smile and he almost seems taken aback. He closes the distance between us and pulls me into his arms. Our lips collide. I wrap my arms around him and pull him tight against me. Julian's hands glide down my body to my thighs. He lifts me up and I straddle him, moaning as he kisses my neck and chest.

I run my fingers through his hair as he twirls me around, pressing me up against the wall. He stops then.

"I can't do this," he says.

"*What?*"

"Not until you tell me everything. If we're going to do this, if we're going to work, there can't be anymore secrets, Emma," he tells me. Julian lowers me to the ground. The heat of our moment is lost. Yet, it is replaced with something greater. "Because, Emma, I . . . I love you too. I'm *in* love with you."

And with his words come a promise for the future, a future I once thought I'd never have.

* * *

We slip past the guests inside the speakeasy and make our way into the soundproof sound booth. My hands feel clammy as Julian leads me to the couch. I want to tell him the truth, and I am, but there's still a part of me that worries about how it will affect our relationship. Of course, we won't have a relationship if I don't open up. It's just . . . I'm ashamed, ashamed to tell him the truth about what I did, the choice I made. He may forgive me for lying, but can he forgive this?

Julian offers me a seat on the sofa while he pours us both a glass of wine from his secret stash. I exhale and before I chicken out, I begin.

"Do you remember our lunch at Mimi's, after I interviewed you for The Hub?" I ask.

"Of course," Julian nods, handing me my glass. "You introduced me to the chicken tacos, and we shared our first kiss."

"Right," I say, sipping my Moscato.

"Come here," he says, sensing my nerves. I exhale and toss my legs over his lap. He removes my heels and massages my feet.

"Ah," I moan. "You have no idea how many brownie points you just earned," I tell him. He smiles.

"I know this isn't easy," he says. "It's the least I can do."

I nod. And he's right, this isn't easy. I wrote an entire article about what Beaux did to me and all those other girls, yet I can't bring myself to tell him. I suppose it's easier to speak to strangers. They don't know you and you don't know them. You don't have to watch their face change from understanding to horrified as you relive the worst moments of your life.

"Breathe," he tells me.

"Okay." I nod. I take a deep breath and I let it all out.

"There was a reason why you kissed me that day," I say. "A reason you felt the need to. You—you saw I was upset, and you put two and two together. The guy who walked in, whose presence triggered me, he . . . he's my ex-fiancé," I reveal. "His name is Beauregard—Beaux Thomas, and we were together for three years. We dated for two and were engaged for one."

Julian watches me intently, yet his face doesn't change.

"I . . . I ended our engagement. I ended it because I . . . I walked in on him with another woman," I say.

Unlike before, this truth doesn't hurt me anymore. This truth is only the precursor to the real pain. Still, my mention of Beaux's infidelity strikes a chord in Julian. He breathes heavily. His eyes flash with anger. It's then I remember what Mason shared with me, about his and Julian's parents. His dad cheated on his mom, repeatedly, while she battled cancer. This affected Julian greatly.

"But, um," I drop my eyes to my fidgeting fingers. "What he was doing, the pain he caused to me and so many others, it was more than the pain of infidelity."

"What do you mean?" he asks.

Julian's eyes search mine. My chest rises and falls under his gaze. My palms begin to sweat. He knows. He can see it all over my face and in the way my body tenses beneath him. His eyes beg for it not to be true. I look away from him then.

"When I ended the engagement, it was because of the cheating. But what triggered me that day at Mimi's, was what happened after, after I broke things off with him," I say.

Julian's face comes in and out of focus as tears fill my eyes. I wipe them before they can fall and speak the unspeakable before I can no longer speak at all.

"He beat me and raped me," I say quickly. "I didn't press charges, because I didn't want anyone to know," I say, picking at the hem of my dress. Despite the lump in my throat, I continue. "About a month or so later, I found out I was pregnant and I . . .I had an abortion," I reveal. I wince as the word crosses my lips.

My conversation with Kat gave me the strength I need to have this conversation with Julian. Still, I don't know how he'll respond to the truth or what his response will mean for our future.

"He found out about the procedure, and he beat me again," I continue. "That's um . . .that's the night," I say, running my fingers over my wrist. "I hated him before then, but that's the night I started hating myself."

Julian closes his eyes and leans his head back against the sofa.

His lips press into a flat line. He stops massaging my feet. I wait for him to say something, but he never does. My chest tightens.

I've dreaded this moment since I first realized in order to move forward with Julian, I'd have to face my past. My past is tragic and stained with blood. I've never wanted to be seen as a victim. It's why I've been so adamant about keeping my past a secret. But, perhaps more than being seen as a victim, I feared I would be seen as the monster I thought myself to be. I hated myself and I thought others would hate me too because of my choice to have an abortion. I thought Julian would hate me. And I couldn't risk losing him and the hope he brings into my life. But Kat was right—It isn't Julian's place to judge me or condemn me. And it isn't his forgiveness I need. It's mine.

"Julian," I say, breaking our silence.

"I'm going to kill him," he says then. He opens his eyes and brings his hand to my cheek. With the same sincerity that made me fall in love with him, he repeats, "I'm going to kill him."

I lean into his touch. A small smile briefly lifts my lips. "If he doesn't kill you first," I whisper.

"*What?* What are you talking about?" Julian asks.

I exhale and move to a standing position as my legs begin to fall asleep. My throat is dry and hoarse with the truth, but my mind is light as my secrets leave me. I cross the room and chug down the rest of my wine.

CHAPTER 30

"The night of the Creative Concepts Gala," I start, leaning up against the sound bar. "I told you I needed to go home because I was sick. And, I guess, that was true, but it wasn't because of the heat or something I ate," I admit. "Beaux was there. He found me and confronted me while you went to find us some drinks."

"*What!*" Julian says. "How? How the hell could that have even happened?" His face flashes red.

"Well, because I never pressed charges, there wasn't—*isn't* a restraining order. There's nothing stopping him from coming near me, talking to me, harassing me, or . . . threatening me," I say.

"What do you mean? What happened the night of the Gala, Emma?" Julian asks. He leans forward in his seat and clasps his hands together, perhaps to keep him from punching something.

"He um, he had found out I was planning to see an attorney, that I was planning to press charges," I reveal. "And um, long story short, he threatened you and, in so many words, Kat, if I didn't keep my mouth shut. He said, if I didn't believe him and what he was capable of, I should check underneath your kitchen sink."

Confusion washes over Julian. "*My* kitchen sink?" he asks, pointing to himself. I nod. "How would he even know how to get in?"

I bite my lip and drop to the stool to my left.

"Because" I say. "Your house used to belong to Mr. Turnip and . . . you never changed the locks. I know, because I—I kind of, sort of broke into your house after you went to work one day. Or, rather, I thought you'd gone to work. You almost caught me when you came back in on the phone with Mason." Julian's jaw drops. "Anyway, I did it, because I wanted to know if he was telling the truth, about what he'd left underneath the sink, about what he's capable of," I say.

"And what did you find underneath the sink?" Julian asks.

I can't tell if he's pissed or proud of my sneaky abilities. I twirl my empty wine glass back and forth between my palms. This part still gives me chills.

"I found the checkerboard. Mr. Turnip's missing checkerboard," I reveal.

Julian leans back on the couch and crosses his legs. His eyes squint as he runs through the possibilities in his head.

"But the only way he could've had it would be . . ." Julian starts.

"If he was there the night Mr. Turnip died," I finish.

Realization washes over Julian and once more, he closes his eyes, lifting his fingers to the bridge of his nose.

"Mr. Turnip's body was found days after the coroner suspected he died. And . . . it would make sense," I say. "The night Beaux found out about my . . . about the pregnancy, the night he came over, was also the night they believe Mr. Turnip fell."

Julian opens his eyes and moves to pour himself a glass of whiskey. I've never seen him drink hard liquor before.

"Kat and I searched the house top to bottom for that checkerboard. It was the only thing either one of us wanted to remember him by," I say.

My cheeks ache. With everything that's been going on, I haven't had a chance to truly process Beaux's crime against Mr. Turnip, the fact that he killed him, the fact that he was so cruel to take the one thing he knew I'd be looking for. Maybe he had hoped I'd discover the truth, just so I could feel the pain of Mr. Turnip's loss all over again. Well, it worked.

"There's only one explanation for why he'd have it," I whisper.

"He killed him," Julian says then. His back is toward me.

"Yeah," I say. "*And* . . ." I compose myself. "And he all but threatened to do the same to you, so I knew I needed to distance myself. That's why I broke things off. That's why I let you believe Mason and I were together. That's why I needed you to get out of New Orleans, so that he couldn't find you and hurt you," I tell him.

I stand, moving to his side. He stares blankly ahead, sipping his drink.

"Julian, I—I realize this isn't fair of me to ask, but . . ."

He turns to me then.

"I still need you to leave the city. Only, this time, I hope we can do it together," I say.

I tell Julian about the past six weeks, about the other girls Beaux assaulted, about Club Gent, even about my father and Mason's involvement. Despite him knowing about Mason's crimes against the women his father cheated with, he was surprised to hear this about his brother. I quickly change the subject to my article before we get sidetracked. It will be published at 9:00 a.m. tomorrow morning, and I hope to be far away from Beaux and this city by then.

Julian presses his back against the countertop and finishes off his stiff drink while he considers all that I've said. That's it. He knows everything. And for the first time since falling in love with him, I can breathe. For the first time, there are no secrets between us. At least, I hope there isn't.

"Emma," Julian breathes. "I can't leave the city with you," he says then.

He doesn't look at me when he speaks. My shoulders droop. I feel weak. I barely find it in me to nod and excuse myself to the sofa. Julian stops me as I move past him. I turn to face him. He wraps his arm around me and pulls me back to him. I bite my lip.

"Does this mean . . .does this mean we're over?" I ask. I try to stay strong. Despite this, my throat cracks as I speak. "I . . .I know I kept a lot from you, but . . .I was scared," I tell him. "I was scared for your safety, scared of losing you. And I didn't want you to view me differently because of my past and the choice I made, the choice I regret. I just . . .I know I took it too far by using Mason," I ramble. Tears flood my face.

"Hey, hey, Emma," Julian says. "I'm not breaking up with you."

"You're not," I choke.

"No," Julian says, taking my face in his hands. He wipes the falling tears from my cheeks. "I don't blame you for keeping the truth about your past a secret, not for one second. And I certainly don't judge you for your choice in a matter that I am in no way a part of. It was your choice to make, Emma. And if you regret it, then that feeling of regret is also yours to feel. It's not my place to condemn you or tell you how to feel." Julian drops my gaze then.

"Mason," I whisper. Julian nods.

"I, um . . .I said some hurtful things to my brother. And it breaks my heart that my mind immediately went to the thought of him going after you. It just shows how broken we are. And, in light of what you've told me, I don't . . .I don't know what kind of future we'll have, what kind of future we'll be able to have, what kind of future I'll even want," Julian says then.

"I'm sorry," I say. "I only made things worse."

"No. Don't blame yourself. The cracks in my brother and mine's relationship predate you, and his behavior predates New Orleans." I nod, though I find myself confused. If he doesn't hold my choices against me, then why can't he runaway with me?

"Julian . . ." I start.

"I can't leave the city with you, not because I don't want to be with you, Emma," Julian says then. "I can't leave the city because I'm going to face this bastard head-on."

My brows furrow and my arms tingle. "But *why*?" I ask. "Why would you risk it? Why would you put yourself in danger for someone else's fight?"

"It's not someone else's fight, Emma," Julian says. "It's yours *and* it's mine."

He looks away from me then. His jaw clenches. He clasps his hands together behind my back, pulling me closer to him.

"What aren't you telling me?" I ask then.

My eyes scan his for the truth. He's hiding something. I know he is. He looks down then and bites the inside of his jaw. He exhales and his eyes fill with tears. I move my hand to his hair to comfort him. What could it possibly be?

"Do you remember when I told you that my mother never knew her father, that he was some one-night stand my grandma had with a man from New Orleans?" Julian asks, his voice cracking.

"Yes," I say. It's hard not to blush when he speaks of his grandmother having a one-night stand. I bet she was a lively woman.

"Well," he composes himself. "After I'd had some time to process my mom's death, I started trying to track him down."

My chest tightens. *No. Please, don't tell me . . .*

"When Mason and I had our falling out and the opportunity to visit New Orleans arose, I knew it was my chance to find him, to get to know him, to have a family again," he tells me.

"No," I whisper.

Realization washes over me. And in the dim light of the recording studio, I start to see the resemblance. Julian's pale green eyes, his dark hair, his tall, lanky physique, his humor, his intuition, his love of music. How did I not see it before?

"Mr. Turnip was my grandfather, Emma," Julian reveals. His pale eyes fill with tears as he speaks.

I drop my head in sadness and rest my forehead against his chest. Mr. Turnip was his grandfather, and I just told him he was murdered by my psychotic ex.

"So, it's like I said. This is my fight too," he tells me.

Julian's heart beats slowly within his chest. I close my eyes and listen to its rhythm. It's the most beautiful sound in a room otherwise silent. I imagine what Mr. Turnip would've thought of Julian, his long-lost grandson. I imagine he'd be quite surprised considering he never even knew he had children. But he would've loved him. They would've talked about music and books and played checkers till midnight. I smile then at the strange twist of fate that brought Julian and me together.

When I moved to New Orleans and found myself living next door to Mr. Turnip, I could never have imagined how important he would become to me. He was there for me when I needed a handyman and a friend. He cooked meals when I couldn't afford to. He helped me get a job when I'd run out of money. He was never without an interesting comment or caramel candy piece. He was my support system before I even knew what one looked like. And now, Julian has become all of those things and more for me. I don't deserve him, but I'm thankful for him.

After a time of silence, I lift my eyes to his, moving my hands up his stomach to his neck.

"So, now what?" I ask.

Julian leans down and kisses my hair. I close my eyes in response. He pulls me tighter against him and I inhale his intoxicating scent.

"We enjoy our last night of simplicity," he tells me then. "Tomorrow, you'll leave and—"

"I'm not leaving," I say then, bringing my eyes to his. "We've been apart for too long. I'm staying with you."

He smiles and brushes my hair from my face. "I would insist against it, but something tells me you wouldn't listen," he says then.

"I wouldn't," I admit. We both laugh.

"Still, tomorrow things will become complicated, even more so with Mason, and we don't know how long this fight will last," he tells me.

"So, what you're saying is," I say, moving my hands to the buttons on his shirt. "We should pick up where we left off, like *right* where we left off."

I unbutton his shirt, exposing his chest and abs. Just as I imagined, his body is chiseled in the most perfect way. I slip his shirt down his arms, revealing his tattoos. One, in particular, draws my attention. From his left arm, sprouting from a cross are vines with thorns and roses that cascade across his chest and down his arm. The further the roses drift from the center, the more withered and dead they appear. Entangled in the vines are broken parts of a key. It's almost as if a piece of him was broken, and he's unsure of how to put himself back together again. My, how I know the feeling.

I trace his tattoos with my finger and kiss each piece of broken key. He cups my face in his palms and forces me to look at him. I blush, parting my lips.

"Precisely," Julian whispers.

He kisses me then, lifting me by my bottom to straddle him. I moan as he kisses my neck and chest. He walks me to the sofa and lays me down. He runs his fingers through my hair and caresses my body with his eyes.

"Are you sure?" he asks me.

"Yes," I gasp.

Julian undoes the buttons of my dress, exposing the black lace Kat insisted I wear. He positions himself on top of me, but I push him back.

"Let me," I whisper.

Julian sits back against the sofa and I straddle his lap.

"I want to see you," I tell him.

And with that, we make love for the first time. And all I see, all I feel, is him.

* * *

I wake to a snoring Julian knocked out on the sofa. It's pitch-black in the sound booth. I wipe my eyes and feel around for my phone and clothes. I find Julian's white button-down first and cover myself with it.

"What time is it?" I ask aloud. "*Oh, crap!* The article!" I say. Julian grunts and turns on his side.

I drop to my knees and cover the floor of the room in search of my bag. *Finally,* I find it. The bright light of my cellphone scorches my eyes as it shines into the darkness.

It's 10:00 a.m. My article should have been published an hour ago. I go to my app for The Hub and check my recently published articles. *It's not there!* I double-check, triple-check. It was never published. My heart sinks. I try calling Fran to ask what happened. She doesn't answer.

"*What the hell?*" I ask into the darkness.

My phone dings and it all becomes clear.

I'm sorry, Emma. I can't put my family in jeopardy over this. Beaux paid me $10,000 not to publish the *article. That was him being nice. After reading your article, I don't want to see the other side of him. If I were you, I'd get out of town. He knows, Emma. And he's coming for you.*

"He knows," I say aloud. My heart sinks and my blood runs cold. "Beaux knows."

I stand and stumble through the room to wake Julian. Just as I reach the sofa, I remember . . .

"We didn't turn off the lights last night," I whisper.

I turn around and—

"*Ah!*" I squeal, but Beaux's hand conceals my cries before I have a chance to wake Julian.

It's dark. I can't see him, but I can feel him. He covers my mouth with his hand and wraps his arm around my waist, pulling me backwards.

"*Shh.* If you wake him up, it'll only be worse for him," Beaux whispers into my ear.

He nibbles at my neck. I try to fight him off and use my body-weight to throw him off balance. He only squeezes me tighter. I gasp. With just a little more pressure, he'd break my ribs.

Beaux pushes the door to the speakeasy open. Bright light shines into the dark recording studio. I pray it wakes Julian. It doesn't. The black door closes behind us as Beaux drags me out of the room. Any hope of Julian hearing my cries is lost.

It's then that I see Mason. He's knocked unconscious on the floor of the speakeasy. Blood covers the back of his head and neck. I can't tell if he's breathing.

"*No!*" I yell. Still, Beaux's hand muffles my screams.

My head begins to ache as fumes invade my nostrils. It's then that I notice the puddles of pale liquid scattered across the hardwood floor and the red plastic can that sits in the middle of the stage. It's gas. He's going to burn the place down and leave Mason and Julian to die in the flames.

Beaux forces me up the stairs to the record shop. The fumes grow stronger the higher we climb. I feel faint. As we reach the top of the stairwell, I fall limp in Beaux's arms. He catches me and I use the moment to snatch his lighter from his pocket. I throw it down the stairs, pushing him away just long enough to close the door to the speakeasy. Beaux doesn't know how to open it from this side and now, burning the place down is no longer an option. So, what's next? What's his Plan B?

"It's over, Beaux," I tell him, wrapping my arms across my chest. In only Julian's button-down and my black underwear, I feel naked as I stand before him.

"It's not over until I say it is," Beaux grunts. "And I have far more plans for you." My eyes grow wide at his remarks.

He steps toward me and slaps me. I fall hard against the floor. My head rings as I wipe the blood from my mouth onto my sleeve.

"I used to think you deserved to live with what you did," he says, walking toward me. I scurry back using my hands and feet. "Now, I know," he breathes. "You don't deserve to live at all."

CHAPTER 31

Beaux's lips lift into a sadistic smile. His fists clench. His eyes grow dark. My chest tightens and before he can come any closer, I push myself up and run as fast as I can for the door. He laughs. And just as the door comes into reach, he pulls me back to him by my hair. I yelp. No longer concerned with concealing my cries, he pulls harder and pushes me into a row of records.

"Ah!" I scream as the sharp corner of the table jams into my stomach. The records fall, sliding all over the floor. Beaux crushes them beneath his feet as he walks toward me. Once more, I try to run, but he pulls me back to him, shoving me face down against the table.

I scream. He pulls my hands behind my back. My entire body shakes as I imagine what will happen next.

"You know, I thought I knew you better than this, Emma," he says as he presses his pelvis against me. "I thought you were smart enough to know the consequences of crossing a man like me. Clearly, you need another lesson in obedience."

He pulls my hands tighter behind my back and begins to unbutton his pants.

"It's you who needs a lesson," I say.

"What's that?" Beaux asks.

He spins me around to face him. My arms are still restrained behind my back. Blonde hair sticks to my bloody mouth and . . . I spit the pooling blood from my mouth onto his face. He gasps and is forced to let me go.

I use this distraction to put distance between us. I run behind the register and grab the baseball bat Mr. Edgar gave me for when I worked nights.

"*You* need a lesson on how to treat women, Beauregard Thomas," I say, hitting the bat against the floor. "And in forgiveness and progress and common decency and, *oh yeah*, how to love," I say. "Just because your parents fucked you up, doesn't mean you have to be this . . . this animal."

I move to the opposite side of the room, keeping distance between us.

"It's a vicious cycle, Emma," he says then. "People hurt people and those people hurt people and those people hurt people. Sometimes, we don't even realize we're doing it. Other times, we do. One thing is certain, though. The pain never ends."

Beaux moves closer to me, but I swing the bat to keep him away. We can't do this forever. I have to get through to him.

"You forced me to own up to the pain I caused you," I tell him. "You forced me to take responsibility for ending my pregnancy, so why can't *you* own up to what *you've* done?" I ask. "You say you do what you do because you were hurt, but we all hurt Beaux. Life isn't fair for anyone, so why do *you* get a pass? Why do you get to spend the rest of your life making other people pay for your pain, while the rest of us stomach through and try to forgive?"

"*Forgive?*" Beaux laughs. "How can you forgive someone who's hurt you in so many ways? How can you forgive the person who stole your innocence, who scarred you for life, who . . .?" He trails off.

It's then that I realize he isn't talking about me forgiving him or even him forgiving me. He's talking about him forgiving his parents.

"I don't know, Beaux," I say then. "I'm not an expert, but I *am* trying."

He looks at me then. His eyes grow dark once more.

"You call that article of yours forgiveness?" he asks me. "You outlined every horrible thing I've done for the last ten years, that you know of. You exposed me, my . . . my parents."

As he speaks, his anger grows.

"If that article would've been published, you would have ruined my reputation, made damn sure I'll never practice another day of law, and even still, you put my life at risk. Because the second the brotherhood finds out about what I *almost* let you get away with, *and they will,* they'll kill me, Emma," he tells me. "So, is that forgiveness? Is that even justice?"

"Forgiveness doesn't mean you're excused from the pain you've caused," I tell him. "Forgiveness is in spite of the pain, in spite of your crimes. You still have to take responsibility for what you've done, not just to me, but to all the other women. And so do the members of your brotherhood."

Beaux laughs. "Yeah, I'd like to see you say that to them."

"*I will.*"

"You do that, and you'll be signing your death warrant," Beaux tells me.

I drop the bat to my side, shaking my head. *When will he realize?*

"Haven't you figured it out yet?" I ask him. "Haven't you felt it for yourself, this numbness inside? I haven't exactly been living this past year, Beaux. I've been . . . surviving, barely. You know, you say my days are numbered, but I think they're just starting," I tell him. "I get a second chance at life because I have overcome my fear. I have overcome my pain. I . . . I forgive myself."

I pause then, thinking back on his words. He doesn't see a way out. He never has. Ever since he was a little boy, he hasn't been able to escape the pain his parents caused him. Adoption wasn't enough. Becoming Beaux Thomas, hotshot New Orleans attorney, wasn't enough. *I* wasn't enough. Nothing has ever been enough to allow him to move past his tragic childhood.

I know I don't have all the answers, but . . . there *is* something to be said for hope. I have hope that I can have a better life. I have hope that I can trust again, that I can love again. I have hope that there is more to life than surviving. I have hope that I can live, truly live, free from the shackles of pain, of regret, of my past.

"You said that this life is a vicious cycle of unending pain," I say then. "Hurt people hurt people and it happens over and over again. Well, not anymore. Not for me. I'm breaking my cycle. And with each person who does, the world becomes a little better and a little safer," I tell him. "You can break yours too. You just have to forgive, let go of the pain your parents caused you. Own up to the things you've done wrong. And *try,* with every fiber of your being, to start over."

Beaux's smile falters as if he's considering my words. His eyes seem to lose their snake-like glare. His body shifts from its intimidating stance. I hold my breath and pray that something I said will stick with him. There is a wall of silence between us as Beaux thinks to himself, broken only by the single ding of his cellphone. It's a sharp chime in the space between us, and the color leaves his face instantly.

Beaux closes his eyes and slowly pulls his phone from his front pocket. My chest tightens as he reads the words on his screen. For the first time since knowing him, Beaux Thomas is afraid. This reality only makes my fate even more uncertain. I feel as if I should run, as if I should take the opportunity to escape. But I don't. I can't. Because if Beaux is afraid, it can only mean one thing. The brothers know.

Beaux places his phone back in his pocket. With his other hand, he pulls a gun from the inside of his suit jacket. My heart stops within my body. I should've run when I had the chance.

"Unfortunately, you won't be getting that second chance at life," he tells me. His voice is cold. His eyes are unfeeling. Any ounce of humanity, of hope that remained in Beaux has left him.

"*What?*" I gasp. "I didn't . . . I didn't . . ." I repeat, backing away from him.

"I know," Beaux says. "Your father did."

Beaux walks toward me, forcing me further down the hallway.

"I can only imagine it was to take the attention off you. But still, the damage has been done. The media has already reported the developing story of the small-town mayor who cut a deal to serve as a witness against an organized sex crime ring based in New Orleans. Intel suggests he's turned over everything he had on the brotherhood to the police—names, locations of the meeting grounds, and . . ." Beaux pauses. The gun dangles at his hip.

"*The tapes,*" I say. Beaux winces.

"Yes," he whispers, stopping in his place.

I turn and look behind me. Even with his brief moment of distraction, he's got me trapped within the confines of the hallway.
There's no way out except through the speakeasy and I'll never be
able to get the door open before he . . . before he pulls the trigger.
Not to mention Julian and Mason. One gunshot amongst all that
gasoline and this whole place will go up in flames.

This is *my* problem, *my* fight. I must face him alone.

"And now the whole world will know what happened to
me," he says, moving his eyes to me. They shine brighter than
normal as tears fill them. If I weren't so afraid of him, I would cry
for him. No child should suffer the abuse inflicted upon Beaux. It
hurts me to have sympathy for him, to care for him in any way.
But . . . I'd be lying if I said I don't.

"But . . . maybe it's a good thing," I tell him. "Maybe, now,
you can stop hiding. You can stop pretending to be perfect to
conceal how truly imperfect you are."

I gasp as I reach the end of the hallway. The cool cinderblock
is hard against my back. I imagine bright red chunks covering its
pale paint. If I can't reason with Beaux, I won't make it out of
here alive.

"But don't you get it?" Beaux asks me. "Beaux Thomas, *this
facade*, it's been the only thing keeping the real me at bay. It's the
only thing keeping the monster in his cage, away from the public
eye. It's the only thing allowing me to pretend to be *normal*."
Tears fall from his eyes as he speaks. "Now, the curtain has been
pulled. Everyone knows the truth, the unspeakable truth. And
now, I can never be normal again," he whispers.

My lips quiver. My vision blurs with tears. I know all too
well the need to be normal, the fear associated with telling the
unspeakable truth. It's why I struggled to tell Julian the truth,
why I didn't press charges, why I kept my family in the dark. You
can never be normal once you've been exposed. At least, that's
what I told myself.

"Now," Beaux says. "I can only ever be the monster," he
whispers.

My chest rises and falls as I watch him. As if embracing his true identity, he stands tall. The veins in his neck throb and his face turns bright red.

My body shakes in response and emotion swells inside of me. I've run out of time, out of words. He's going to kill me. And I'll never see Julian again. We'll never live a life together. We'll never have another conversation. We'll never share another kiss. *And Kat?* She's been my best friend, my family for years, and I'll never see her again. She'll never help me get dressed in something way too slutty and uncomfortable. She'll never annoy the hell out of me with her and Demetri's lovemaking. We'll never spend another Sunday afternoon watching *Gilmore Girls* reruns. *And my mom?* We'll never find out what our relationship could have been without my father's influence.

"It's over, Emma," Beaux says then. His eyes are cold as he speaks.

Beaux points the gun at me. I say a silent prayer for my soul and close my eyes. As the gun fires, I scream, dropping to the floor. I cover my ringing ears with my hands. I hold my breath, waiting to feel the pain of the entry point. It never comes.

I open my eyes and find a bullet hole in the ceiling above me and Julian and Beaux wrestling on the floor amongst hundreds of broken records. The gun is loose.

I feel weak, paralyzed. Yet I force myself to my feet and down the hallway in search of a phone.

"Emma! *Run!*" Julian yells. He slings his fist into Beaux's face. Blood splatters.

I shake my head. I make my way behind the register and find the landline. My fingers tremble as I dial 911.

"911—what is your emergency?" the woman asks.

"Lucid Records. 1941 St. Clair Avenue," I say. I can barely hear myself as I speak. My ears ring and my throat feels as if it's closing in. "There's a man here trying to kill me. He's armed. His name is—"

I drop the phone to the ground as another gunshot rings through the brick walls of Lucid Records. The phone shatters into pieces, as do the glass windows, as does my heart.

Julian lies beneath Beaux. Blood covers the glossy record

envelopes surrounding him. He's been shot in the stomach. Blood gushes from him quicker than my eyes can process.

"No," I whisper. "*No!*" I scream.

I charge Beaux and throw my entire body at him. I scratch and slap him. I push him, though he barely moves. With each blow I deal him, he laughs more. I reach for his gun. He holds it up high beyond my reach, as if this is some child's game.

"Why are you doing this?" I scream. "It's over, just like you said."

I turn away from him and take off my shirt to wrap Julian's wound. I am exposed, but I don't care. I have to stop the bleeding.

Julian looks at me. He is fading. The cops will never get here in time. He tries to lift his hand to hold mine, but he can't. His white button-down is soaked with blood within seconds.

"I warned you what would happen if your boyfriend interfered," Beaux says.

"I'm sorry," I say to Julian. "I love you," I choke.

My face floods with tears. I feel Beaux looming over me. But I don't move. I hold the pressure against Julian's wound until—

Beaux falls to the ground, bloody and unconscious. I turn and find Mason standing behind me. He's holding the bat, which is now smeared with Beaux's blood and bits of hair.

"Here," Mason says, handing me his coat.

"No. Julian . . ."

"Can have everything else. Now put it on," he tells me. I do.

Mason kicks the gun away from Beaux and drops to his knees. I notice the back of his head is still bleeding. He tightens the wrap around Julian's wound using his shirt and pants. Finally, I hear the police sirens in the distance. Julian is still conscious, though with the amount of blood he's lost, I'm not sure for how much longer.

"It's okay," I say to Julian. "We're going to be okay. The police are coming. An ambulance is coming. We're going to take care of you."

Julian is unable to respond. I try to hold in my tears, to stay strong for him, but I can't.

"This is all my fault," I say.

"No," Mason says. "It's his," he says, looking at Beaux.

He nudges him to make sure he won't be waking up anytime soon. Beaux doesn't even grunt.

"But it'll all be over soon. We've just . . . got to get Julian to the hospital," Mason says with resolve. Despite this, worry consumes him. I know he received the same text as Beaux. If word of the brotherhood has made it to mainstream media, when the police get here and discover who he is, they won't just arrest Beaux. They'll arrest him too.

"Mason, go," I say.

"*What?*" he asks, looking at me. "*No!* I'm not leaving my brother *or* you," he says.

"If you stay, this will be the last time you see your brother. I mean, *really* see him. So go," I tell him. "I'll find a way to reach out when Julian is in the clear. You guys deserve to have a last goodbye, or whatever you want to call it."

The sirens get louder as the police get closer. Mason clenches his jaw and pulls Julian's bandage tighter as it soaks with more blood.

"Okay," he says then. Tears fill his eyes. He nearly breaks at the sight of his brother. "Take care of him."

"I will," I say. He nods and kisses Julian on the forehead.

"I love you, little brother," he says. Julian doesn't say anything. But like so many times before, Julian doesn't have to speak to tell you how he feels.

"And take care of yourself," Mason says to me then. With that, he leans toward me and kisses me on the forehead as well. I close my eyes.

"I will," I whisper.

The police cars and ambulance screech to a stop outside Lucid's front entrance as Mason makes his way down to the speakeasy and out the side entrance.

"It's okay," I whisper to Julian. "I love you. I love you so much. It's all going to be okay."

I take Julian's hand in mine just as he closes his eyes. His hand is bloody and cold. The police rush in, followed shortly by the EMTs.

* * *

The doctors marked his time of death as 11:15 a.m., but he was dead long before that. It wasn't the skull-crushing blow dealt by Mason that cast Beaux's soul from this world. It was the first time his father touched him in ways he never should've been touched at only eight-years-old. Beaux was a victim before he became a predator. He was abused and neglected, and he never found it in himself to forgive—to forgive his parents, to forgive others who may have disappointed and hurt him. And ultimately, he never found it in him to forgive himself.

You see, the truth about unspeakable things is that it demands to be spoken. If not, it eats away at you. It instills anger, and it feeds off pain, your pain and the pain you cause others. Hurt people hurt people. Beaux was the perfect example of this, the perfect victim. Victims allow their pain to destroy them. They succumb to it. Survivors use their pain as inspiration to affect positive change. And the issue of sexual assault and the rape culture so prevalent around our world is not one person's issue, one person's truth, or one person's fight. It is an issue that affects us all, an unspeakable truth we must all accept.

In this, Beaux was right. This life is a vicious cycle of pain, but that's where his thought process ended. Here is where mine begins. We all feel pain. We all hurt. We're all dealt unfair cards. But it's how we respond to that pain, *that trauma* that determines who we are. I'm not proud of all the choices I've made in response to trauma I've experienced. But I can accept responsibility for the choices I'm not proud of. I can forgive myself. And I can choose differently in the future. In doing this, I take back control of my life. I shed the shackles of the victim and embrace the armor of the survivor. My armor is welded with truth.

I sit with my head in my hands, waiting for Julian to wake. Thankfully, the bullet went straight through him. Still, he had to have emergency surgery to repair the internal damage. He lost a lot of blood, but he's expected to recover.

My phone vibrates in my pocket. Thankfully, a nurse allowed me to have one of her extra pairs of scrubs. I pull it out, half expecting it to be Mason calling from somewhere over the Atlantic. Instead, it's—

"*Dad?*" I ask aloud. I hesitate, but nevertheless, I answer. "Hello."

"Emma," he says. "It's good to hear your voice. I—I was worried."

I don't respond.

"I'm sure you know by now that I've turned myself in and . . . I'll be informing on the brotherhood," he says.

"Yes."

"I just want you to know, I did it for you," he tells me. "I did it so you don't have to. I know I haven't been much of a father to you, especially with the whole Beaux situation. And this doesn't make up for that, but I hope . . . I hope it's a start, a small show of my love for you," he says. "Because I *do* love you, Emma. And I want you to have the life you deserve, and you don't need this controversy jeopardizing it."

"Dad."

"Yes, sweetie?"

"I'm glad you turned yourself in and I'm glad your testimony will corroborate mine."

"*Emma,*" he starts.

"*No,*" I say. "No, I need you to listen. You once told me that I was the problem. But the thing is, *you* are. You're my dad and I hate that this is our reality, but . . . it is, Dad. And I can't change it any more than you can," I tell him. "Now, I believe—I believe people can grow and change, and I believe in forgiveness. But before any of that happens, you have to accept responsibility."

"But, Emma, how else do you want me to do that? I've literally given up everything to make this right for you," he tells me.

"I need you to stop calling it a controversy. A controversy is, by definition, a disagreement. Sexual assault is not something to debate or disagree on. *It's wrong.* In any way, shape, or form, *it's wrong,*" I tell him. "And I don't need you to try to give me an easy way out or take the fall for me."

I drop my phone to my hip and lean against the cool glass separating me from Julian. The steady beat of his heart monitor is the only thing keeping me sane at this point. Finally, I lift the phone back up to my ear.

"I *will* live a life filled with love and happiness and acceptance and whatever else I choose, Dad," I say. "And it's because I won't live in pain, that I will be able to live in love. So, while you spend the next however many years alone, with nothing but your thoughts, remember this—there is no greater prison than your own mind. And those walls and bars may keep you from hurting us, but they won't keep the pain of your actions from eating away at you. Your silence feeds the pain. It gives it power over you," I say. "So, don't do this for me. Do it because you're ready to accept responsibility. Do it because you truly want to change. It's the only way, Dad. It's the only way."

With that, I end the call. I don't tell my father I love him. Part of me wishes I would have. I put my phone in my pocket and return to Julian's bedside. As I sit, his heart monitor begins to beat louder and quicker.

"Julian," I say.

His eyelashes flutter and his fingers twitch.

"*Julian?* Nurse!" I yell, running to the door.

The heart monitor slows and steadies.

"*Nurse!*" I yell once more.

"How was your day?" Julian asks then. His voice is hoarse and barely audible.

I turn and his pale lips draw into a smile. The color starts to return to his cheeks.

"It's better now," I say.

CHAPTER 32

One Year Later

My mom preheats the oven as I unpack the last of the boxes. It's been a year since I've seen her, a year since Julian and I have been in one place.

When my dad turned himself and his information on the brotherhood over to the police, the brothers scattered. Most were never seen of or heard from again. I assume they changed their names and fled on private jets to places without extradition. The few that were caught, based on my father's testimony and the video footage I secured from the New Orleans Club Gent location, lawyered-up and waited.

Marissa was certain they would have a plan, a failsafe in case of exposure. And she was right. We just didn't realize how right she was until it was too late.

When my dad turned himself in, he handed over his computer. When the police went in to access the files he had on the brotherhood, they were gone. Apparently, the folder wasn't a permanent folder on my dad's hard drive. It was a folder housing an access portal to a digital drive controlled by the nameless President of the brotherhood. All digital records each member possessed with blackmail on other members and the girls they abused were all wiped from the digital drive and the computers that were previously allowed access to them.

Even the jump drive that I gave my mother and the copies I made for myself were of no use after the brotherhood caught wind of the breach. The second the jump drives were plugged in, a virus attacked the files and destroyed everything else on the computer with it.

It looks like Beaux's secrets will stay with him even in death, as well as the blackmail footage of the girls who were manipulated and used by the members of the brotherhood.

To make matters more complicated, when the media first broke the story, the members' names were not disclosed, only the names of the cities with Club Gent locations. After the digital drive was destroyed, this was all the police had to work with. U.S. Officials were in a frenzy looking at city blueprints to try to find the secret club locations. They still haven't found all of them. The ones they have discovered, including the New Orleans location, provided no DNA evidence.

News articles published in the days following the initial break described the stench of bleach and impeccably clean surfaces. It appears cleaning crews were immediately sent to the brotherhood's Club Gent locations.

With each day that passed, the brotherhood's plan to conceal their actions unfolded, limiting the evidence that could be used against them as an organization.

Julian and I left New Orleans the day he was cleared from the hospital, but not before providing the police with the New Orleans Club Gent location, my article, the video evidence I gathered at Club Gent, and the testimony I gathered in my efforts against Beaux.

The video footage helped the police make some arrests via facial recognition here in the city. But without video evidence of their crimes against women and without the testimony of the women they undoubtedly raped, the men were released.

Through the girls I initially spoke with while gathering evidence against Beaux, the FBI was able to find more girls claiming they were assaulted by men of the brotherhood. Most of them were able to name and physically describe their attackers, much like Lauren Jameson identified Beaux on behalf of her friend, Ashley Roy.

To this date, fifty arrests have been made based on the testimony of survivors. Of these arrests, ten cases were referred to prosecutors. Half of the cases have been dismissed due to a lack of evidence. Half are still being fought. This is the reality of survivors of sex crimes. Regardless of the brotherhood and its extensive efforts to cover its tracks, we live in a world of he said/she said. A world where two percent of sexual assaults that are reported to police end in a felony conviction.

Because of this, it shouldn't come as a surprise that the brotherhood was not prosecuted as an organized sex crime ring. Despite more than fifty women confirming its existence *and* the video footage of underage drinking and the exploitation of women at the New Orleans Club Gent location backing them up, the brotherhood turned into a modern myth. We all know it existed, but without the monsters to stand trial for their actions, the tale of the brotherhood is just a story, a nightmare that has forever changed the lives of countless survivors.

My father was the only member to speak up and validate the testimony of the women who came forward. He told the truth about the brotherhood. He was murdered in prison shortly thereafter, before serving as an official witness. I did not attend his funeral.

The remaining members in custody were released, because no one testified against them. Now, any justice that will be served rests solely in the hands of the women now speaking up and the law system meant to protect them.

Julian and I have been on the run for a year, though we didn't let ourselves think of it that way. We traveled to beautiful places and made beautiful memories. We stayed on the move, never knowing if the brothers were searching for us to exact revenge.

My father exposed them. Julian's brother was a member. And I contributed evidence to the FBI. It wasn't out of the realm of possibility that the brothers would want to keep us quiet. Even my mother, Bill, and Eva went into hiding.

There were times I wondered if we'd be running the rest of our lives, much like the brothers are now. There were times I considered leaving Julian, not because I didn't love him, but because I knew he'd be better off without me. But I never could. Of all the things he's sacrificed for our relationship, I couldn't abandon him, even if it was for his own good.

Mason fled New Orleans the day Julian was shot. In the days and weeks after the initial break, Julian resisted the urge to reach out to his brother. Not that he would have even known where to begin to look. Then weeks turned into months. And we began to question if we would ever see Mason again. Was he alive? Was he in jail? Where did he go?

A small comfort came to us while visiting Paris. We figured if the brothers were planning anything, Mason would know. If they planned to come after us, Mason would find us and warn us. This comfort gave Julian and I the strength we needed to return home.

My mother moves around the kitchen preparing her famous pork chops, mashed potatoes, roasted carrots, peas, and rolls. I sit at the kitchen island, watching the flames of the gas stove flicker back and forth before being concealed by a pot filled with water.

Julian sold Cole Creative the second we returned to New Orleans. In learning of his brother's role in the brotherhood, paired with his father's infidelity, he felt it best to cut ties and start over.

Starting over, that's what we're doing.

He bought us a home—*us*, because we're together and in love. It's a two-story galley style home in the Garden District, much like the one I once envisioned myself living in with Beaux. You would think it would bother me to live the life I planned to live with Beaux with Julian. But it doesn't. I realize now, the life I envisioned with Beaux was never his and mine. It was *mine*, mine to live with the man I love. Julian is that man, and despite everything, I'm happy.

I'm happy to have left The Hub. I'm happy to be re-renovating Lucid Records with Julian. We're going to run it together while Julian scopes out local talent to sign to his new record label, one that is free from the sins of our past. And I'm happy, happy to be in the city that embraced me when no one else did, happy to have Kat blab my ear off about everything I've missed the past year. And I'm happy to see my mom, the *new* Anne Marshall.

She moves around the kitchen, dressed in a billowy linen dress and flip-flops. Her hair is down and wavy without the confines of the hot iron and hairspray. Her face is fresh and free of most makeup. She hums as she cooks.

When my father turned himself in, he admitted to all of his crimes, as well as the affair he was having with a woman in Dallas. My mother had no resistance in divorcing him and securing all the marital assets, which she then sold. She split the money between my sister and me, even giving a lump sum to my father's mistress for their unborn child.

As I watch her now, I see her with new eyes. She was a kept woman, plagued with the responsibility of perfection. Much like Beaux, she worked her entire life to create an image so pristine no one would ever see the truth. Unlike Beaux, she embraced the pulling back of the curtain. She allowed herself to grieve her marriage to my father and most of all, the years she spent being a shell of the woman she was always meant to be. But now, she is not a shell. She is not perfect. She is real and free. And she is my mother.

She accepts me for my choices and who I am, not because of who I'm dating. She accepts Julian despite him not being what she considered the ideal companion. She admits she was wrong to put so much pressure on me to date a man who she truly did not know.

Learning of Beaux's crimes against me was the hardest truth of all for her to accept. She blames herself for what happened to me, for not noticing the pain her daughter was feeling, and for continuing to bring up Beaux even after I told her not to. But I don't blame her for this. I don't think I ever did. I knew I was keeping the truth from her, and I knew it wasn't fair to her.

Still, I don't regret keeping my assault to myself, and only speaking when I was ready to. Nor do I blame the women who continue to keep their truth to themselves. There is no handbook for surviving this most intimate assault. But I am thankful to have survived, thankful for God, for Kat, for Mr. Turnip, for Julian, and even Mason. Mason, who has done terrible things, but has also shown me that growth and change are possible.

"So, where did you say Julian is?" my mom asks then.

My cheeks flush red and my lips draw into an awkward smile. My mom and I are trying to build a new relationship on honesty and respect. Still, she doesn't know Mason was a member of the brotherhood or that he contacted Julian shortly after we moved back to New Orleans. Julian has gone to see him now, to bring him money from the sale of Cole Creative, and to . . . to say goodbye. It won't be safe for them to have a relationship, nor would it be safe for Mason to turn himself in. We have evidence of that in my father's untimely passing.

"He's um," I start. "He went back to LA to get the last of his things. His move to New Orleans was never meant to be permanent."

She gives me a knowing look. *Oh God!* Bad choice of words. Bad choice of words. My mom smiles.

"I guess there's something about this city," she says. "You know, I'm in need of a new place and I noticed there's a house for sale just down the street."

"*Okay . . .*" I scoff, moving to the fridge. "Anne Marshall in New Orleans, my how things have changed."

"Ha," she laughs. "Hey, are we doing wine or sweet tea?"

"I think Kat is . . ." I start but am stopped by a loud noise coming from the front door.

My mom and I share a look of concern at the sudden interruption. I suppose one year without visitors will do that to you.

I close the fridge and grab a knife from the butcher's block. I motion for my mom to grab the skillet from the cabinet. She does, and we both move slowly to the front door.

"Come on, bitches!" Kat yells. "This stuff is heavy, and I miss my best friend!"

"*Ah!*" I squeal.

I drop the knife and yank the front door open, sending both mine and Kat's hair flying.

"*Kat!*" I say, pulling her in for an embrace. Kat leans into me awkwardly as she holds onto the giant pitcher of margarita.

"*Emma,*" she says.

"Here, let me take that," my mom says, grabbing the pitcher from Kat.

"Thanks, Mama Marshall," Kat says.

My mom retreats to the kitchen while Kat and I catch up on the porch swing.

"God, *a year*," Kat says. "It doesn't seem real."

"I *know*," I tell her. "I never would've imagined how things would turn out, how the brotherhood covered their tracks, Julian and I being on the run, my dad and everything related to that to now being back in New Orleans, having this house, running Lucid, and rebuilding things with my mom. And get this," I tell her. "Eva is pregnant!"

"*What?* Well, they sure didn't waste any time," she says.

"They never did."

"That's true," she agrees.

We swing back and forth, enjoying each other's presence. The wind chime dances in the warm, summer breeze. A hummingbird swirls around the feeder, drinking his daily allotment of nectar. The Garden District trolley moves up and down the street as tourists snap photos of all the beautiful homes.

"It's weird, isn't it?" I ask. "We look around and it's as if the past year, really the past two years if you think about it, it's like it never happened. The sun rises. The wind blows. The hummingbird drinks. People walk up and down the street each day without realizing what really happened here, what I'm dealing with, what so many people are dealing with."

"Time doesn't stop for anyone," she says.

I nod.

"And yet, for some, their lives stop even when the sun rises, even when the days keep passing," I tell her. "For two years now, I haven't lived. I survived in fear of Beaux and his wrath. I survived on the run from an invisible predator. But now, now I wake up with flushed cheeks and a smile on my face. I don't dread the morning light or the new day. I don't cringe at the thought of commitment, at the thought of giving my heart to someone," I reveal. "I'm not the girl I was before, but I'm happy, Kat."

Her sun-kissed cheeks blush. Her strawberry curls blow in the breeze.

"He didn't break you," she says then.

My lips draw into a smile. I hold my head high, allowing the afternoon glow to warm my skin.

"He didn't," I tell her. "He really didn't."

ACKNOWLEDGEMENTS

I was 17 when I wrote my first novel. In truth, it was a 55,000-word skeleton with an uninspired title. The summer I spent writing that novel was the summer I realized my dream of being a published author. Even more so, I realized my ability to accomplish my dream. And yet, at 17, I never imagined the journey that has led me to *The Truth About Unspeakable Things*.

I'd like to thank Marissa Corvisiero, a literary agent who read my rough work at a conference in Boston. Your feedback, Marissa, gave me a sense of confidence in my writing I never before had.

I'd like to thank Alexa Bigwarfe and the speakers of her Women in Publishing Summit for opening my eyes and mind to the vast possibilities self-publishing offers. Furthermore, I'd like to thank Alexa and her team at Write Publish Sell for helping bring this book to life. Alexa, you are a knowledgeable, inspiring woman and when I first stumbled across your Summit in 2019, I couldn't have imagined the role you'd grow to play in my professional journey. Thank you for everything.

I'd also like to thank Chanticleer Book Reviews, my wonderful beta readers, copyeditor, and proofreaders for providing key feedback in my revision process. Special thanks to Aubrey Knorr who served as a beta reader and a proofreader.

You all have played incredible roles in my journey toward publication, but before I could run, I first had to walk.

Thank you to my mom for always believing in my writing abilities. Without your encouragement, I would not have had the confidence to pursue my dream. Thank you to my foundation-layer, Ashley Haire, who taught me English 7th–12th grade. Your teachings gave me the tools I needed to succeed. Thank you, Darrian Pierite, who when faced with the opportunity to let me run or hold me back, chose to let me run. Darrian, I thank you from the bottom of my heart. And thank you, God, for granting me the gift of words. Though I do not write Christian fiction, I pray my work brings You glory.

ABOUT THE AUTHOR

Emily A. Myers is a Women's Fiction author based in Louisiana. Her debut novel, *The Truth About Unspeakable Things*, sets the tone for Emily's future works as it follows a young woman's journey through the dangerous pitfalls of adult relationships and the complexities of growing up. In addition to writing fiction, Emily also dedicates time to her blog, *Self Publish Source*.

Connect with Emily on
Facebook and Instagram at @emilymyersauthor.

Continue the Discussion

To access Emily's exclusive Book Club
Discussion Guide, subscribe to
her email list via her website.

emilyamyers.com

CPSIA information can be obtained
at www.ICGtesting.com
Printed in the USA
LVHW052035220321
682109LV00024B/1622